MASTER OF THE FIELD

AN HISTORICAL NOVEL

by

NORMAN TUCKER

"Sir William Brereton is master of the field
in Cheshire."—
LORD CAPEL TO PRINCE RUPERT

BRIAN BEVERIDGE LIMITED

20 NICHOLAS STREET . CHESTER

Brian Beveridge Limited
20 Nicholas Street, Chester

First published in Great Britain by
John Long Limited, 1949
Copyright © Mildred Tucker 1971
Made and printed in Great Britain by
C. Nicholls & Company Ltd, Manchester, England

ISBN   0   903638   00   2

NOTE

Much of the historical information for this book has been obtained from the Journal of the Chester and North Wales Archæological and Historic Society's Volume 25 (New Series) prepared from manuscripts of the late Canon R. H. Morris, D.D., F.S.A., and edited by Alderman P. H. Lawson, F.R.I.B.A., F.S.A. Other books consulted were Ormerod's *Cheshire*, James Hall's *History of the Town and Parish of Nantwich*, H. Parry's *Royal Visits and Progresses to Wales*, Roland Phillips's *Civil War in Wales and the Marches*, Henry Taylor's *Historic Notices of Flint*, Firth's *Cromwell's Army*, Charles Ffoulkes's *Arms and Armour*, Pennant's *Tours in Wales*.

I should like to express my appreciation of the ready help given me by the Public Librarians at Chester, Nantwich, and Crewe. In particular I am grateful to Mr. E. H. Edleston, of Nantwich, for his generous advice.

N. T.

CHAPTER ONE

THEY say that Sir William Brereton never was buried.

His coffin, so the story goes, was swept away by a flood as it was borne home from Croydon, where he dwelt sumptuously in the archbishop's palace until the Restoration. But Sir William's death was in April 1661, and it marks the end and not the beginning of the story.

And what a sorry if stirring story it is! A story of divided loyalties, of enmity and heroism, of strife among neighbours. It is the story of a struggle which turned the fair land of Cheshire into a debatable ground where there were raids and skirmishes and sieges and battles almost too numerous to be recorded. Chester, the loyal city, Chester with its quiet dignity, became a beleaguered fortress. Houses flamed, mines exploded, and the spectre of starvation stalked its streets. Chester possessed strategic importance. It was the door through which a steady stream of men and munitions flowed to strengthen the royal cause. Families of quality whose homes graced the parklands of the County Palatine had their city houses in Chester. It was, by the nature of things, the rendezvous of these parts. Thus it became the prize for which men strove.

Now, it may be that the legend of the manner of Sir William Brereton's end is true. The registers of Handforth Chapel in Cheadle Church contain a record of his death, but not of his burial. Those who were his opponents in the field may have derived satisfaction from this, attaching sinister significance to it. This matters little, for it is a sure thing that the commander who exposed himself so dauntlessly on many a field would have recked little what became of his body so long as the cause he had espoused was secure.

Sir William would not have troubled what happened to his coffin, for he died a disillusioned man He saw ideals crumble. He saw the leaders with whom he had consorted dragged with contumely and calumny from their graves. He saw honest men mocked and profligacy exalted. Long had he striven to overthrow a dynasty he despised, yet he lived long

enough to see another Stuart installed in Whitehall. So he
who, at Stow-on-the-Wold, received the surrender of the
last Royalist army in the field, might well turn his face to the
wall and rejoice to let his soul return to its Maker, for there
seemed little to tempt a man to live. He was fifty-five years
old at the time of his death; a good age, so men held in those
days, yet Sir William might well have seen his three score
years and ten had not his heart been broken.

Had Sir William, staunch Puritan as he was, been possessed of a spirit of divination, had he been able to foresee
what lay ahead, of a surety he might have deliberated
whether the issue was worthy of the sacrifice, but such
events were mercifully withheld from his eyes.

There was, in consequence, no man more eager to serve
the Parliament than this Member for Cheshire, this newly
appointed Deputy Lieutenant. He made his contribution to
the cause—four horses and £100.

And now, this hot August of 1642, he rode north, at the
request of the House, to take up his duties as Commander-
in-Chief in Cheshire and the counties round about. As a
nucleus on which the local militia could build there went
with him a troop of London horse and a regiment of dragoons.

The tiring march across England was not without its
value. It was a testing-time for these soldiers in the making.
It was a breaking-in. By the time a week had passed that
ardent and earnest young officer Cornet Ryder Yale
considered himself almost a veteran.

Sir William rode at the head of the dusty column, his
handsome face shaded by a broad-brimmed hat. Cornet Yale,
who was in attendance, could not resist glancing back, taking
martial pride in the sight. Flies swarmed about the tossing
heads of the sweating horses. The troopers, riding three
abreast, receded down the curving road as far as the eye
could see. The horse came first, with dour Captain Gideon
Aiken at their head, followed by one of the two trumpeters.
The troop was a hundred strong—soon to be increased to
one hundred and twenty when recruiting could be attended
to. On the flank rode Yale's comrade, Lieutenant Mark
Trueman. Like Ryder, he was the eldest son of a prosperous

yeoman farmer on Sir William's Handforth estate. Behind the horse followed the dragooners: men armed with muskets who fought on foot and who merely used their nags as a means of transportation.

"Is anything amiss?" Sir William had noticed the young man's intent gaze.

Ryder flushed under his tan. "No, sir." He was addicted to telling the truth. "I could not refrain from looking. It is a goodly sight, the moving column with the sun gleaming on the men's head-pieces and breast-and-back."

Sir William looked grim. "A little less glitter and a little more comfort would be more acceptable. This sun tells on man and beast. It is my intention to halt in the shade of yonder wood which flanks the road. There is a dingle there. Ride on and see whether any water remains in the brook."

Ryder Yale, eager to undertake any task, trotted forward. He looked about him keenly as though the discovery of water in a stream was a matter of paramount importance to a soldier—as, indeed, it might well be.

A fine picture of brave young manhood he made. Though the wearing of uniform was, as yet, not strictly enforced, and though the colour thereof was largely a matter of the colonel's private taste, Ryder had been to some pains and no little expense to equip himself in what he considered the correct apparel—jack-boots, buff-coat, broadsword, barred head-piece and cuirass. The armour almost stifled him, but he endured it with a stoicism worthy of a better cause. The time had not yet come when soldiers preferred the risk of being shot to the discomfort the encumbrance entailed. So Ryder endured his breast-and-back though the sweat trickled down his body.

Once under the shade of the trees he removed his head-piece and wiped his brow. A frank, open countenance was revealed, steady-eyed, almost handsome. It was the face of one who took life seriously, one who knew that he would have to give an account of his stewardship, the face of one who smiled, but rarely laughed. For Cornet Ryder Yale was entering upon this internecine war with all the zeal of a crusader. It was, for him, a holy war. He fought for the freedom which Englishmen held dear, for liberty of conscience.

He was prepared to suffer, to die if need be, that men might worship as they thought seemly and not be moulded by force into an ecclesiastical pattern. Bred of yeoman stock, he had in his veins a sturdy independence. He reverenced his betters, but he would tolerate patronage from no man.

Across the white dust of the road spread the dark trickle of a woodland stream. Mossy stones on either side showed how low the water had sunk by reason of the drought, but there was a sufficiency for the horses. Ryder cantered back to report.

"Tell Corporal Garnett to post eight men as sentinels. We remain here until the sun goes down."

The weary men unsaddled their jaded horses and took their ease on the grass, all save the horse-holders. Sir William drew apart, seated himself on a fallen tree and removed his cuirass. He was bare of head and Ryder had fresh opportunity to marvel on the serenity of the noble forehead from which the long hair curled to his collar. With his slight, pointed beard Sir William looked more like a Cavalier than a Parliamentarian. Breeding will show, and the Breretons traced their ancestry back to the Conqueror's day.

Ryder Yale was still at the age for hero-worship, and Sir William was his hero. He had known him from childhood, known him as scholar, traveller and sportsman, a man who studied the conditions of the poor, one who had visited the United Provinces and there learnt the art of warfare.

"No further orders, Ryder."

Sir William could be stern and formal when on duty; he knew how to relax upon occasion. The baronet glanced not without admiration at the stalwart frame and comely face of the young man.

"May I ask, sir, when we shall reach our destination?"

"What is our destination, Ryder?" Sir William's smile was enigmatical.

"I understood your worship intended to make Nantwich your headquarters."

"Nantwich, yes. It is unprotected, but it is so placed that it is the perfect pivot from which we can swing north or south or west. It must serve for the time being. But our destination, Ryder, is Chester."

"Chester, sir! It is alive with malignants. Folk term it 'the loyal city'."

"There is a small but active party who are well affected to the Parliament. Prebendary John Ley is a thorn in the side of Bishop Bridgeman. There is Calvin Bruen, my good friend Alderman William Edwards, and Peter Ince. The general distemper has been kindled to a fine flame in Chester. It might not be beyond the powers of man to raise the city for the Parliament. The Commission of Array for the King have oppressed many honest people. Are you acquainted with Chester?"

"As a boy I was taken there, sir."

"Do you know my city house—that which was once St. Mary's Nunnery?"

"I knew your worship had a house in the city; I have not seen it."

"It lies near the castle within the city wall. I have no doubt you will visit it some day."

The baronet stared abstractedly before him. "You are well equipped, Ryder; better than most in these makeshift days."

The young man flushed with pride. "I have bought these things piece by piece, sir, in anticipation of this day of deliverance."

"Lieutenant Trueman is less fortunate. Let him wear your buff-coat, and take his russet jacket in exchange. You might also leave with him your steel-pot, your breast-and-back and your sword."

"Sir?"

"Exchange your jack-boots for the spare shoes you carry in your snapsack.[1] When you have done so, return hither."

The cornet's eyes grew wide in amazement. The blood rushed to his face. He bit back the words which surged to his lips.

"Cornet Yale!" His commander regarded him sternly. "A soldier does not question the orders of his superiors."

"Sir! I uttered no word."

"Your expression spoke louder. Remember, he who

[1] Knapsack 'Snapsack' is used in contemporary accounts.

subdues his own passions is mightier than he who vanquishes a foe in the field. It is the unknown, unseen fights with self which make or mar a character."

The young man returned in a plain russet coat. His face was composed. If Sir William's eyes regarded him with approval he allowed no trace to be manifested in his voice.

"You desire an explanation?"

"Not unless you wish to give it, sir."

"You carry out orders without question?"

"Yes, sir."

"There are hard times before us, Ryder. You will be called upon to make greater sacrifices than doffing your buff-coat. The days which lie ahead will test men's souls. Men who are free will not bow the neck to a tyrant, but freedom requires its price. There will be no place for the faint of heart. We must try to gain Chester now before the strife actively begins. We may fail. But soon or late Chester must fall."

"They say it is full of malignants, sir."

"Though the city were packed to the walls with King's men it is my resolve to enter those proud gates. I must have intelligence of what goes on there. It is in my mind to venture there myself to recruit for the militia. But first I would have you spy out the land."

"You would have me go to Chester, sir?"

"At once. You are not known in the city and may mingle freely with the throng."

Something within Ryder Yale cried out at the injustice of it. He had enlisted so that he might serve honourably in the field, and now he, who would have drawn his sword against aggression, must adopt a role of ignominy—to his thinking, infamy. There was turmoil in his tortured brain. He felt a spy. A spy! Sir William's eyes, penetrating eyes, were upon him.

"What have you to say?"

"Nothing, sir."

"There is a cottage in Nuns Lane, kept by an old retainer. You may stay there. A secret door leads to my garden, so you may enter when you choose without exciting attention. Your harness will be kept for you at Nantwich until you return. Stay—you do not go alone."

Ryder's eyes brightened. "Does Mark Trueman accompany me?"

"Lieutenant Trueman remains with the troop. Walk across yonder field. When you come to the lane you will find your companion awaiting you. The horse you will ride will attract less attention than your charger."

Ryder felt puzzled. It seemed unreal. The hot August afternoon was sultry and still. There was no sound but the drone of insects, the crunching of the grazing horses, the occasional tinkle of a bit-ring. Troopers and dragoons sprawled at their ease. He could see Lieutenant Trueman trying on his borrowed head-piece.

"And my companion, sir—may I inquire his name?"

"Verity Hill."

"A—a woman, sir?"

"One wholly devoted to my interests and to the cause. Follow the footpath, Ryder, to the stile. God keep you and give you success. I shall expect news whenever a messenger can get through the malignants' lines."

CHAPTER TWO

THE way across the meadow was erratic, as is the fashion of footpaths. It seemed indicative of the road of life. Ryder Yale had believed he was a traveller on a broad highway and now, unexpectedly, he found himself a wayfarer bound he knew not whither. His existence had hitherto been a matter of routine, methodical, as he had been brought up to believe a well-ordered life should be. Now it had become unreal, mysterious, uncertain, unpredictable; in fact, more true to life. He was thrown, for the first time, on his own resources.

Perhaps this was how Sir William intended it should be. Ryder gazed towards the distant stile. Would the unknown woman be awaiting him there? If so, how was Sir William aware of it? He was annoyed that a woman had been selected for his companion. It embarrassed him. His mother and his sister represented the womanhood he knew. He revered their sex for their sake. To encounter a wholly unknown woman was a novelty he had not experienced. If Sir William had so arranged the meeting it must be correct; well he knew Sir William's irreproachable principles. Still, it was all strange; very strange!

He could see a tall hedgerow ahead. There had not been many hedges along the route, which lay, for the most part, across open heath and common. Now they neared more cultivated country. He liked the sight of hedgerows, in summer their honeysuckle and wild roses, in autumn the hazel nuts, or the hips and haws bright as red seals.

The path led remorselessly to the stile. Soon he must embark on this new way of life. Balancing on the top step, he looked into the roadway. There was no sign of a horse. This afforded him a feeling of relief until he noticed a track in the dust, not the hoofmarks of a charger, but the broad shoes of a workaday farm animal. Round a bend came a woman.

He could not discern her features for her face was hidden by a sunbonnet, but her figure was slim and trim and she wore a neat grey dress with a small apron. He found himself looking into steady grey eyes and a calm face, the face of a maid not quite his age. She appeared older because she was serious.

"You are Mistress Verity Hill?" he inquired in his direct fashion.

For a second she looked blank. An unexpected smile wrinkled her eyes and made her attractive. "Why, of course. I had forgotten my name. This will never do. A bad start. Pray call me Verity, for that name is my own, the other is borrowed. It would be seemly for you to call me Verity, for we are cousins."

"Cousins?"

"So Sir William has decided. You can thus accompany me to Chester with perfect propriety. I know you are Cornet Yale, but I must learn to call you Ryder. That is your real name?"

"It was my mother's maiden name. I like it, for a rider I have ever been since I clung to the mane of my first moor pony. Where is your horse?"

"Our horse. He is under the trees, out of the heat."

"What puzzles me," remarked Ryder as they fell in step, "is how Sir William knew that you would await me here."

"There is no mystery. Sir William is a distant kinsman of mine. I have importuned him to allow me to serve the cause, for I am an orphan, and oh! it is intolerable to sit idle while great issues are at stake. I prevailed upon him to allow me to go to stay in his house in Chester so that I could send him intelligence of all that transpired within the city. Last night, at your bivouac, I visited him for the final instructions and found him reluctant to let me incur what he considered risk. Somebody, he asserted, must accompany me as a protector. He chose you." She glanced up quickly. "I am glad he did."

"I agree with Sir William; it is not a task for a woman of gentle birth."

"And why not, pray? Is not a woman's heart as loyal as a man's? Are not a woman's wits as astute? A woman may attract less suspicion than a man. They say that in Chester my Lady Cholmondeley recruits more for the King than any man, and that my Lady Strange is like to prove every whit as good a soldier as her husband. Surely it is the will of God that we women should strive, and suffer if need be, for the freedom we desire! I pray daily for the triumph of our cause."

Ryder Yale's brow was more thoughtful than usual. "And you believe God's ears are open to such prayers?"

"Can you doubt it?"

"I am perplexed. Last week, in London, a man on guard in the Tower told me that Laud, he who was archbishop, prays continually for the success of the King's cause. How, then, can God grant both petitions?"

"Our duty is to pray. The manner in which God will answer is not for you or me to understand. It is, as you say, Cousin, a matter of much perplexity—yet one truth stands clear. Much will depend on our own zeal and the strength of our arms. That is why you and I must perform our allotted tasks, leaving the issue in higher hands."

They came to the horse, a sturdy, stolid grey which cropped the roadside grass. It had a bridle, but in place of saddle a sack was strapped to its broad back.

"How far is it to Chester?" inquired Ryder as he slipped the bit between the reluctant animal's teeth.

"Ten or twelve miles."

"Then you shall ride and I walk. Twelve miles is nothing."

After a shy glance at the girl he stooped in a business-like manner and quickly hoisted her on to the back of the horse.

"You are strong," said Verity admiringly.

Ryder smiled. He was remarkably free from vanity, but he was proud of his strength.

"I trust my character will prove as strong in the day of adversity," he said as the horse moved forward along the road, the road which led to Chester, the road which led to a future all unknown.

Throughout the hot afternoon the two adventurers made steady if slow progress. Ryder adapted his pace to the patient plodding of the horse. The girl began to converse with him, so that the way did not seem long. Thought followed thought. They had this in common—an implicit belief in Sir William Brereton and a desire to render him service. It was a tie which bound. Verity had a way of addressing Ryder as 'cousin' which was so acceptable that he had well-nigh accepted the relationship as genuine, when, on cresting a slight rise, they saw in the distance the spires and towers of Chester and caught the silvery gleam of the Dee.

At Ryder's suggestion they watered the horse at a way-side brook; at Verity's suggestion they rested. It was nearly evening and a hush was settling on the world.

"What is it that you have in mind?" inquired the man as he relaxed.

"I shall make my way quietly to Sir William's house. An old retainer of Sir William's, one Amos Bowman, dwells in a cottage in Nuns Lane nearby. He will attend me and he knows how to find his way out of the city. The Nunnery Gardens are conveniently situated. It will not be difficult to climb the walls after dark. The country folk are well disposed to Sir William, whom they regard as a benefactor.

"What rôle do I play?"

"You must stay in Amos's cottage. Pretend to be a gardener."

"I shall be acting a lie. Verity, this is hateful to me. I planned to encounter the enemy in battle; never did I think I should be called upon to serve thus. I am little better than a spy."

"Joshua hesitated not to send forth two of his young men to spy out the land. If you are a spy, I am too. If we are slaves we row in the same galley."

"Then let us start without delay," cried he, leaping up. "The city gates are sure to close at dusk."

That was typical of Ryder. If there was anything unpleasant to be undertaken he was all impatience to finish with it.

"Do you take the horse now, Cousin Ryder. The short walk will do me good. When we come to the fork of the roads we had best separate and enter the city by different ways."

"I do not like to forsake you; was I not sent to be your protector?"

"It is better thus. I shall incur greater risks before this strife is ended."

And so they parted, Verity with that calm assurance which characterized everything she did, Ryder with regret. The young man stood watching her slender form recede; saw her pass Boughton Chapel, and then the gallows at the roadside. Once she had reached the turnpike which led to The Bars which marked the city boundary, he turned away satisfied. The sleepy horse mended its pace once Ryder was on its back. He rode across a broad field until he came to a road, the Warrington Road he learned it was, and on the far side he saw the gables and chimneys of a spacious dwelling set in its own park.

The house did not interest him, but the park did, for a great and colourful crowd congregated there amid banners and flags. The sound of music came pleasingly down the evening air, not martial music but the rhythmic, melodious strains of a country dance. Curiosity bore him nearer. A fire gleamed brightly. Above it was suspended an entire ox. Though stripped of its hide, the horns remained to add a ferocious aspect to the sizzling carcass. There were barrels of ale and long tables spread with cakes and junkets.

The centre of all was a great high-backed chair set upon a dais over which was a canopy of roses. On this floral throne sat a girl with a chaplet of roses set on hair so dark and glossy that Ryder had never seen the like before. Her conspicuous position caused her no embarrassment. She appeared to accept homage as her due. Her dark eyes sparkled with merriment, especially when she bent forward to address an elegant Cavalier who stood at her side and returned her glances with looks as unwavering as her own.

"Gay and Godless," was Ryder's muttered comment, yet he dismounted, and fastening his horse to a rail mingled with the throng. As a sop to his conscience he told himself he had been sent to learn all he could about the King's party. Though his eyes roved they returned again and again to the girl on the floral throne. He had never seen eyes so expressive, never seen colouring so rich and yet so delicate. She wore a light cloak of velvet, red as the roses in her hair.

"What is it all about?" he inquired of a man at his side.

"Mistress Rosea comes of age today."

Voices were clamouring for a song. A man in tattered finery thrust his way through the onlookers and with needless authority cleared the way. Then he carried forward a great gilt Welsh harp, and a slip of a girl in a red cloak seated herself and began to run her fingers with amazing dexterity over the responsive strings. Ryder imagined that the harpist was to sing, but he was mistaken. It was the girl on the dais. She stood up and smiled as a burst of clapping drowned the notes of the harp.

Her cloak was thrown back and he could see she was gowned in velvet the colour of a kingfisher's wing.

She began to sing, not a gay song such as he would have expected, but the plaintive melody 'Greensleeves'. Long, long, Ryder remembered that moment—the low, rich voice, the expressive eyes, the listening crowd, the hush of eve, the setting sun. In years to come his ears retained an echo of the song—

> "And O Greensleeves was my delight,
>   And O Greensleeves was my heart of gold,
>   And who but my lady Greensleeves."

Most men cherish in their hearts a concept of their ideal woman. Many never have the fortune to encounter her. Ryder felt that he had found his.

He had not sought her. He had just come upon her by chance—or so it seemed. Was life fashioned by chance or design? He wished he knew. How little men were aware of what lay ahead! But for Sir William's unwelcome orders he might have gone riding to Nantwich with his troop of horse; he might never have seen this radiant personage. Mistress Rosea! He would remember her name even though he never encountered her again. To think he might never have seen her! The contemplation of such a possibility turned him cold. The crowd clamoured for another song. "No, you grow greedy!" she protested. "No more songs. Let us have a toast instead."

There was a scramble about the barrels. "Friends!" her voice rang out loud and clear. "Here's a health to his Majesty. Confusion to all rebels and traitors!"

They drank and they cheered. This done, the lady became practical.

"Royle, is it not time for the bull-baiting?"

"My dear Ro, this is scarce the place for it."

The man spoke with affected indifference. His whole demeanour seemed to indicate that he found life either boring or amusing, but certainly not serious.

"Absurd, Royle. It will be safe enough if the servants erect the ropes. I want some giddy-paced excitement. Never before have I known you cautious.

"In honour of your birthday, my dear. Well, have it your own way. The brute lacks spirit, and I have no doubt the dogs will keep it in its place."

At a signal from him a number of serving-men ran forward with stakes and mauls and quickly formed a ring. The man in the tattered finery carried the great harp away, followed by the girl in the red cloak.

The crowd parted with some confusion. A bull with a ring through its nose was led by a man into the arena, several bulldogs held in leash growling at its heels. The animal, a Welsh black, though not massive, had great breadth of shoulder. Its vicious eyes showed how its proud spirit resented the indignity accorded it. The man at the nose-ring leaped back. The bulldogs were released. They knew their work. Cries of encouragement from the crowd almost drowned the panting and the snarling as the animals contended for mastery.

Ryder turned away in disgust. Something within him revolted at the sight of human pleasure derived from suffering. It was sport of the devil's devising, he thought. Suddenly the shouts changed to a cry of apprehension.

The bull, having gored one of the dogs, caught sight of the canopied throne rising above the heads of the spectators.

He lowered his head and charged. The crowd scattered. The man in tattered finery was knocked off his feet. The elegant Cavalier lost his lassitude and whipped out his rapier. The slim blade only gashed the thick neck. The bull rushed on. Women screamed. Men scrambled. The throne tottered and fell.

Mistress Rosea lay stretched on the trampled sward, her chaplet of roses fallen. Ryder acted without premeditation. His instinct was to interpose his body between the angry bull and the prostrate girl. He had no weapon, but he had his strength. He hurled himself against the shoulders of the brute and grasped the short, thick horns. His heels slithered as he endeavoured to hold back the bull. He was in time to divert it before it reached the girl. The brute tossed its head angrily, but its opponent was not to be shaken off. Ryder was panting with exertion as he strained every muscle. His whole frame felt the jar of the bull's angry wrenching. He would not let go.

"Run!" he yelled to the girl, and he was conscious of her scrambling to her feet. The velvet was stained and rent, the roses scattered, but she was unhurt. With a snarl a bulldog buried its teeth in the bull's nose. It was flung off, carrying with it a portion of flesh as a trophy. Another dog dashed between Ryder's legs, tripping him. With a mighty heave the bull broke free and tossed the struggling man from his horns. Ryder struck the ground with a thud. He saw the bull's broad head and bloodshot eyes turned upon him. He saw, too, a debonair figure with drawn sword leap forward and bury the blade in the animal's neck. The snorting bull fell, pinning Ryder to the bloodstained earth.

CHAPTER THREE

THEY carried Ryder Yale across the park to the house, carried him in the broad scarf which Royle Wilding, as an officer, wore for this very purpose. When Ryder came to himself he lay on a canopied bed stripped to the waist as Royle Wilding with expert fingers explored rib and muscle.

"Not a bone fractured, my gallant bull-baiter," he said cheerfully. "A pulled muscle, bruises by the score, but never a break. A day's rest will set you on your feet again."

"No! I must depart," said Ryder stubbornly. He endeavoured to rise, but an excruciating pain made him drop back.

"That argument is more convincing than mine. Your shoulder is well-nigh dislocated. Lie still. We owe you a debt, and, by gad, it shall be paid."

"Indeed, yes," agreed a pleasant voice. "But for you my features might have been irretrievably ruined. And Royle will tell you my face is my fortune."

Ryder was unaware of any other person in the room. He hastily dragged a shirt towards him as he saw the girl Rosea walking from behind the bed-curtains. She had changed her torn robe for a gown of flowered silk, cut low at the shoulders. It was edged with a collar of deep lace. Her hair hung in glossy ringlets, framing her face and accentuating the rich colouring of her cheeks and the darkness of her eyes.

"I asked for excitement," said she, laughing. "Faith, I have been accorded it, full measure."

"You are unharmed?" Ryder spoke awkwardly as he struggled with his shirt.

"Unharmed, thanks to you. Nothing suffered but my dignity. Lud, Royle, do help the poor man with his shirt. He is as bashful as a boy, though why he should be ashamed of such magnificent shoulders passeth my understanding. Royle, if you had such muscles you could break a man's back——"

"With the ease you could break his heart, my dear! I bear testimony to his strength. Gad, you have added novelty to bull-baiting. You must teach me the knack of it. I'll vow it will brighten the sport immeasurably."

Ryder closed his eyes. Flippancy was something he could not comprehend. To his serious mind the hearts of both ought to have been filled with thankfulness for a merciful deliverance. He felt a small, cool hand laid gently upon his brow.

"Royle, we fatigue our guest with our chatter. He had best sleep."

"It will do him more good than a blood-letting!" agreed the man.

With a touch of femininity which sat quaintly upon her graceful shoulders, Rosea shook the pillows and straightened the coverlet. With a friendly smile she followed her companion from the bedchamber.

The shutters were closed. Two candles pierced the gloom with their flickering points. Ryder ached so fiercely that he required no exhortation to sleep. He was well content to lie within the warm caress of the feather bed, but though his body was at ease his mind was not.

Slumber was not to be easily enticed. So he remained very still and allowed his thoughts loose rein. Life had become confused. Hitherto the path stretched clear and plain before him. He had chosen to turn his back on the broad road which led to destruction. His way, though narrow, was clearly defined. And now, without warning, the familiar landmarks disappeared. The path twisted and turned bewilderingly. Because he was confused he began to think. Never before had he found occasion to think—it had all been done for him. He imbibed what he was told.

His smooth brow held an unfamiliar pucker as he stared at the candle-flame as though seeking inspiration from its feeble light. What ought he to do? He was befriended by those he ought to regard as enemies. This man Royle Wilding, with his immaculate clothes and his frivolous speech, was a Cavalier, a supporter of the monarch who abused the liberties of his subjects. All Cavaliers, so Ryder had been taught, were arrogant, profligate, sinful, yet here were two who accorded him courteous treatment, who showed him a friendliness which disarmed him. They had not so much as asked his name or whither he was bound. They took him on trust, conscious only of a debt which they would repay.

He hated himself for his dissembling. He wanted to shout aloud: "I am Cornet Ryder Yale of Sir William Brereton's own troop of horse. You take a snake to your bosom. I am an enemy. I am worse. I am a spy!"

Yet he was a soldier under orders and he must carry out Sir William's instructions. He must be true to his principles. Vaguely he seemed to discern diverging principles. Cornet Yale of the Parliamentary horse pulled one way; Ryder Yale, the lover of truth, pulled another. He grew weary of the mental struggle and his thoughts turned to happier things. Finally he fell asleep musing upon the girl Rosea—Rosea, lovely as a rose.

Ryder was up betimes. His body still ached, his head still pained him, but he was sustained by a stubborn pride which would not let him accept the hospitality of these people a moment longer than was necessary. His clothes, brushed and mended by a valet during the hours of darkness, lay folded on a chair. Ryder flung back the shutters and let the light of an August morning transform the room.

He stood looking across the parkland. Through a gap in the trees he could see the turreted tower of Chester Cathedral. The light of the morning sun gave the walls a rosier tint. It looked a place of peace. Was it soon to become a scene of strife?

As he gazed he ruminated. A mental picture of the girl Rosea kept intruding. He had not thought anyone could be so beautiful. The women he had encountered before had been demure and restrained. Rosea was their antithesis. She was so animated, so vital, so heedless of convention. Was such beauty a snare of the Devil about which he had been warned? It was impossible to think so; she had been so gracious, so friendly, so sincere, so appreciative, and yet— Ryder was always candid with himself—she was not of his class. She was an aristocrat. He could tell a thoroughbred at a glance. And she was a follower of Charles Stuart.

No, he would have none of their hospitality. He would

escape from the atmosphere. Lovely though Mistress Rosea was, she was not for him. It was idle for him to hold her image in his thoughts.

The slight groan which escaped his lips as he turned quickly towards the door was not wrung from him wholly by his wrenched muscles. Ryder descended the broad staircase cautiously, one hand steadying his steps. He moved quietly, but not quietly enough. A step sounded in the hall. Royle Wilding, faultlessly attired, walked towards the stairs.

The two men regarded each other steadfastly before speaking. Wilding was thinking, "Quite a presentable fellow—a pity he is such a sloven." Ryder thought, "How effeminate a man looks bedecked in lace and silk." But neither voiced his thoughts. It was Wilding who spoke first, and his tone was courteous and pleasant.

"You are early astir," he said. "It would have done you good to rest."

Ryder shook his head. "The early morning calls me. I was never one to lie abed."

"Breakfast is not yet ready, but I will see what the servants can produce."

"There is no need. I must not tarry."

"I would not detain you against your inclinations, but accept my assurance that there is no occasion for you to hasten your departure."

"I had an appointment last night. My absence is unaccounted for."

Royle Wilding's eyes grew merry. "Lud, man, it pays to keep the ladies in suspense. I assume it was a wench you were to meet? Ah, but I embarrass you! Forgive me. I fear I have long outgrown the stage where anything discomposes me."

"Allow me to thank you for taking me into your home."

"Not our home—we are guests. I have rooms next to the Pied Bull Inn should you care to call."

"I would beg of you to present my farewell to Mistress Rosea—I fear I do not know her full name."

"Mistress Rosea Cressage. She will regret your departure. We are both prodigiously beholden to you."

He held out his hand spontaneously. Ryder shook it with reserve.

"Had you a horse?" inquired Wilding. "My man said he thought you had one, but I fear it has vanished. Allow me to offer you the pick of the stables."

"There is no need." Ryder spoke hastily and moved towards the open door.

"Adieu." Wilding's voice was courteous. "The service you have rendered will not be forgotten."

Ryder was anxious to escape. He did not want thanks. Perhaps he was ungracious, but there was that stubborn independence about him which would not tolerate the acceptance of favours. He had acted because he chose to, not to receive recognition. As he walked along the road which led to the city he told himself that he was unreasonable, that no one could have acted with greater kindness and consideration than Royle Wilding and Rosea Cressage.

Deliberately he turned his mind to Verity. What would life in a Royalist city be like? The place was getting more populated now. Carts laden with produce rumbled towards The Bars, the high-built gate which marked the city boundary. A few soldiers lounged against the walls, basking in the morning sunlight. They did not appear to take their guard duties seriously—men of the city train-bands, not yet accustomed to the rigour of military discipline.

A pack-horse train was crossing a field. Ryder walked through the open gateway without being challenged. Men seemed to come and go as they pleased. He was in Foregate Street now. Scattered houses stretched to where the city's Eastgate rose, dignified and formidable. He entered and found himself within the walls of Chester. He did not consider it wise to inquire for Sir William Brereton's house; instead he asked a man to direct him to Nuns Lane.

Ryder remembered how, as a boy, he had walked along the Rows thinking that he had never seen anything quite so unusual. In memory of those early days he ascended some steps and leaned over a worn balustrade. He became absorbed in the spectacle. There were among the passers-by men and women who, by their sober mien and sad-coloured raiment, appeared to be of puritanical persuasion. For the most part the city was given over to Royalists. There were soldiers, there were grooms who led horses which aroused envy in Ryder's heart, there were retainers who wore the livery of the noblemen who had houses in Chester—the Stanleys, Grosvenors, Cholmondeleys, Savages, names known to all who dwelt in Cheshire or the country round about.

He heard snatches of gossip. The old Earl of Derby was sinking fast. His son, Lord Strange, had designs to seize Manchester—that London of the north—from Parliamentary hands. Leisurely he made his way down Watergate Street and turned into Black Friars Lane. Frequently he turned to gaze about him, memorizing landmarks he had passed, the names of taverns, taking his bearings by the sun. He was moving south towards the Castle. Nuns Lane lay ahead. That must be Sir William Brereton's house standing in its grounds between the Lane and the city wall. He entered the drive and made his way towards the front door. At his vigorous pull a bell clanged. A chain rattled and the great door was opened a few inches. The weather-beaten features of a serving-man looked forth.

"Be pleased to go to the side door." The order was curt.

Ryder flushed and obeyed. This time the door was opened wide.

"Step inside, sir. You are welcome. You must pardon my directing you hither, but the house may be watched. Sir Thomas Smith's place lies yonder just beyond the garden wall. Mistress Verity expects you."

"You must be Amos Bowman?"

"The same, sir. I served Sir William in the United Provinces and trust I may serve him again once the fighting breaks out."

Verity walked to meet him as he entered the hall. Though she had spent but a night under the roof of the house she appeared as much at home as if she had been born there —or so it seemed to Ryder. The walls were adorned with weapons and armour, heads and horns. Verity led him into a front room.

"I have been concerned about you," she said, "fearing that some mishap might have befallen you. Ah! I was right.

There are stains of blood and dust on your clothes. Have you been assaulted?"

"By nothing more dreadful than a bull at a baiting." Ryder spoke with feigned indifference. "I was knocked down. As I was somewhat shaken some good folk kindly allowed me to rest for the night."

For some reason he could not comprehend Ryder could not bring himself to mention Rosea's name.

Verity was not curious.

"You were hurt more sorely than you admit," she accused him. "You are still pale and your shoulder is stiff and sore."

"You are far too observant, Verity," he said.

"For the remainder of the day you are to rest."

"What a tyrant you are!"

"I can be. Sit down. Amos has been searching for you. You are to stay at his cottage in Nuns Lane. Later he will show you how you can cross this garden to the door in the wall so that you can come here practically unobserved."

Though Verity insisted that Ryder should rest, she herself was busy. It seemed contrary to her disposition to be idle. She bustled about the house, intent on her duties. Presently she called: "Come to the kitchen, Ryder. You may keep me company while I cook a meal. All the serving-wenches vanished while the house was shut up and we must care for ourselves."

"Good practice for campaigning," he said, moving stiffly to a rocking-chair which was set beside the hearth. "Have you no other servant than Amos?"

"There is another man, but he is absent, having gone with a message to Sir William."

"You must show me how the messages are sent."

"At present it is easy," asserted Verity, sprinkling some flour on a pastry-board. "There are guards, but no one knows why they are set. They stop nobody and search nobody. I think it is because no person quite knows what step to take. Both sides are waiting for something to happen."

"They will not have to wait long."

"That is what I think. Let us eat well while we can, Cousin Ryder. When you feel recovered I will show you what arrangements we have made for getting over the walls and crossing to the other bank of the Dee, where a well-disposed man dwells in a cottage. Once the gates are closed and a watch strictly set we shall have to get messages out of Chester as best we can. I have had Amos embed a hook on our side of the wall so that we can let down a rope ladder. There are no dwellings on the other side of the wall—just the Roodee, which stretches to the river's bank. If you feel well enough to walk I will show you.''

Ryder rose to his feet. Verity, instead of moving, paused with her head on one side in a listening attitude. Ryder was about to speak, but she held up her finger to quiet him.

As he listened his ears caught the clangour of a bell.

"It is the Common Bell," said Verity with an anxious look. "The bell which is rung only at the command of the Mayor. It signifies that a matter of great urgency has arisen. All citizens are expected to hasten to The Crossing with their arms."

Verity dusted the flour from her hands and walked towards the door with brisk step. "We must get our hats, Ryder, and see for ourselves what it signifies.''

They left Amos in charge of the house and hurried down a walk edged with clipped yew until they came to a postern gate which opened on to Nuns Lane.

CHAPTER FOUR

It was on Monday the eighth day of August that the great tumult occurred.

That day was long remembered in Chester—an eventful day, an amazing day, a fateful day, the day on which Sir William Brereton had the temerity to walk into the heart of the loyal city and cause a drum to be beaten as he called for volunteers for the Parliamentary militia. Though many of the people who had leanings towards the Parliament had gathered together what goods they could carry and left the city for places of greater safety, there still remained a number who were disaffected. What prompted Sir William Brereton thus to walk into the lion's den? Was he foolhardy? Had he overestimated the Parliamentary sympathizers in

Chester? Was he still indignant at having been assessed for ship-money on his property, St. Mary's Nunnery, which lay within Chester's walls?

No man knew his motive—all they knew was that Sir William was there, walking down the main streets, Alderman William Edwards at his side, surrounded by Parliamentary halberdiers. It savoured of unreality.

Verity turned a bewildered face to Ryder as they caught snatches of conversation from the moving throng. Men came out of houses and shops, wrestling with bandoliers and headpieces and corselets, as they hurried to obey the clamorous summons of the Common Bell. Many disbelieved their neighbours when told what the commotion was about. Yet there, unquestionably, was the drum, rapping out its message of defiance. And above the babel of voices sounded the bell of St. Peter's, bidding all good burgesses arm themselves and hasten to The Crossing.

Ryder could see the principal actors distinctly. Verity, on tip-toes, clung to his arm and strove in vain until he found a place for her to stand on steps which led to the Rows.

The intruders had paused now. The Parliamentarian halberdiers formed a ring. The drummer still drummed. Men in the crowd were beginning to shout. They hurled not merely abuse but missiles.

Sir William raised his voice, but it was lost amid the uproar. Then came a fresh commotion. The dense throng parted. Bright as blood showed the robes of the Mayor. Mr. Thomas Cooper was approaching, having tarried to array himself in his robes of office for so momentous an occasion. With him walked his mace-bearer, his sword-bearer, aldermen in their mulberry gowns, and constables.

The Mayor's face was flushed with indignation. An ardent loyalist was Mr. Cooper. He caught one of the Parliamentary halberdiers who obstructed his passage and flung him towards the constables. The man's halberd clattered to the roadway.

"Cease your din!" he bellowed, pointing to the drummer, but the man still plied his drumsticks, awaiting orders from his master. The Mayor followed his peremptory order by still more peremptory action. His hand grasped the hilt of a halberdier's sword, and before the owner could stay him Mr. Cooper whipped out the blade and drove it through the offending drum. The noise came to an end abruptly, but the irate Mayor was not content. He slashed the parchment to shreds.

"Now, sir," he cried, turning to Sir William Brereton, "how come you here disturbing the peace of his Majesty's city?"

"I am here by right as Knight of the Shire and as a Deputy Lieutenant." Sir William looked haughty.

"You come without advice and you enter without my consent."

"I appear on behalf of the honourable Houses of Parliament to summon loyal men to attend the Militia muster."

"Loyal men have already responded to the appeal of the Commissioners of Array. You cannot dissuade honest men from their duty to their King. Faithful and loyal citizens will not harken to your treasonable talk. In the name of his Majesty I bid you disperse."

There was an ominous pause. Sir William endeavoured to address the crowd, but the Mayor interposed. Those of the town guard who had appeared with arms in their hands were crowding in upon the halberdiers. "Sir William, I have spoken you fair. I am loth to exercise my office, yet I must say to you that unless you disperse this band of impudent rebels instantly I will call upon the Recorder to hand you all over to the constables."

"You cannot prevent my exercising my right except by raising a tumult," observed Sir William contemptuously.

The Mayor turned with a gesture of exasperation. At his signal a rush was made for the halberdiers. The crowd surged forward.

Ryder caught Verity as she was swept off her feet. His bruised shoulder caused him pain, but he kept a protective arm about her.

"Ryder, Ryder, what will they do to him? Will they imprison him?" she whispered. "Oh, why was he so foolish as to appear?"

"Hush. We must let things take their course. We are powerless." He edged the girl to the comparative security of the wall of a house and, staring over the bobbing heads, kept her informed of all that took place.

"The constables have led off the halberdiers. They are all under arrest, and the drummer. Only Sir William and Alderman Edwards remain. Listen, the Mayor is speaking."

"You are suffered to depart to Alderman Edwards's house," the Mayor said curtly. "Disturb the peace of the city again at your peril!"

There were those who held that Sir William ought never to have been suffered to go free. People considered that many of the misfortunes which befell Chester were due to the vindictiveness of Sir William for the treatment accorded him. And yet it was no light matter for a Mayor to place under arrest a Deputy Lieutenant and a Knight of the Shire, especially one of Sir William's ancient lineage. So he was suffered to depart, though much threatened by the hostile crowds as he walked through the streets. The Mayor sent an armed guard to protect him.

As Sir William passed under their arch of crossed halberds he carried his hat in his hand and bowed as though he thanked the citizens for so unaccustomed a favour. The Chronicler records:

"But this levity the people much lamented after (when it was too late) because he was the princpall agent of all the miseries that befell the city and county in succeeding years."

With Verity it was otherwise. Her heart was filled with thankfulness. To her it savoured of a miracle that Sir William should thus be permitted to escape from the hands of his enemies. She said as much to Ryder as she accompanied him back to Black Friars Lane. Few observed them. Curiosity had led the populace where the noise was greatest.

As she turned to the gate of Sir William's house she glanced at Ryder, who moved awkwardly. "Is your shoulder worse?" she inquired quickly. "You look pale."

There was something almost maternal in her solicitude. She gave him the impression of being a young woman whose first consideration was the welfare of others.

"It pains," he confessed. "I shall have to endure far worse before this war is ended."

"I shall make you rest for the remainder of the day. It was through protecting me from the mob that it has become worse."

Once they were inside the house she led him to a chair. "I will fetch Amos to examine your shoulder. He is an old soldier."

"You make much of a trifle," protested Ryder, but he submitted to Bowman's adept manipulation. The injured arm was rested in a sling. It felt easier, but Ryder was not averse to remaining in the comfortable chair while Verity resumed her interrupted cooking.

Idly he watched her neat movements as she crossed between the table and the fireplace. Her fingers were deft and businesslike. Health had given her a complexion like a wild rose, but otherwise she had few claims to beauty. Her eyes were grey and kindly, her mouth somewhat large, but there was a tender touch about it which Ryder found appealing. Her hair was drawn back with deliberate severity as though its owner scorned the vanities of life. Ryder found himself comparing her with the rich beauty of Rosea. How lustrous was Rosea's hair, how dark and flashing her eyes with their long lashes and arched brows! It seemed an unfair comparison.

"Of what are you thinking?" Verity, conscious of his gaze, glanced up quickly from her pastry. The blood surged to Ryder's face. He, who prided himself on his truth-telling, found no words with which to answer. Verity spared him.

"That is not a fair question to put to you," she said with composure. "Perhaps you were thinking that I am plain-featured and it would distress you to confess it. Indeed, my looks do not trouble me. It is not the face of a man or a woman which matters save only as it serves as a mirror to reflect what is in the mind and the heart."

"Then it is no wonder that your face is kind," said Ryder with conviction. "Already I have discovered the gentleness of your heart."

She walked from the room and Ryder wondered whether he had given offence. She returned with Amos.

"We will go to the attic," she observed calmly, "and Amos will show you how we propose to signal by lanterns from the dormer windows."

From this high vantage-point Ryder looked across the neat garden and over the high red sandstone wall which encircled the city. Beyond it stretched the broad Roodee, on which many cattle were grazing. Several mounted men idly watched over their safety. Beyond the Roodee the river curled, its surface dotted with the sails of several small boats. Then the left bank rose abruptly, crested with bushes. There were several cottages on the top.

"It will not be difficult to lower a rope ladder from the walls after dark, nor will it be difficult to cross the Roodee," said Verity.

"But surely the river presents an obstacle?"

"Amos has bought a coracle from a Welsh fisherman. He can carry that on his back. That is the cottage where our sympathizer dwells. If he is to expect a messenger we set a light in this window."

As they were descending the stairs Verity paused suddenly and held up a warning finger. "I heard a sound!" she whispered. "Someone is in the house."

"Remain here," said Ryder quickly. Quietly he took a sword from the trophies on the wall. Amos selected a battle-axe. At the door of the dining-room they both paused and peered through the hinge crack. A man was bending over a bookcase, the lower portion of which served as a desk. There were papers strewn beneath his fingers.

"Hold!" Ryder's voice rang out sharply as, blade poised, he stepped into the room. The intruder wheeled quickly.

"Sir William!" The amazement in Ryder's tone brought a grim smile to the baronet's face.

"So you will not allow me to ransack my own house?"

At the sound of his voice Verity hurried into the room. "You are safe—quite safe? I thank God. How have you managed to escape from your enemies?"

"I have not fully escaped, as you perceive, Verity. I must get outside the walls tonight or the Parliament will be deprived of my services. An order is to be made that houses are to be searched—mine among them. They have designs on Alderman Edwards's and Alderman Aldersey's, and the Red Lion and the Golden Lion are also to be searched for

C

arms. I came to secure my papers, and found, so I imagined, the house deserted."

"We were in the attic. I have explained to Ryder how we are to signal to the Welsh bank of the river."

"You may experiment at once. Bid Amos intimate that I shall cross as soon as it grows dark."

The day dragged until eventide, Ryder, because of his injured shoulder, was set to watch from the front windows lest any of the King's party should attempt to enter; Amos guarded the rear. Verity aided Sir William in his search. The great hearth in the kitchen grew black with ashes as documents were burned. Other papers were packed in valises and with them silver plate. Verity served a meal and then they stood in the garden waiting as the sky grew darker and the stars came out.

"Is there not a guard on the walls?" inquired Sir William.

"They make the rounds, but not frequently," replied Verity. "Now that they have passed, Amos has let down the rope ladder."

A slight scraping sound caused them to listen intently. Sir William and Ryder crept towards the wall. They saw in silhouette a figure cross the coping. A man came down the steps which had been set against the battlements and followed them silently indoors. When the door was shut the newcomer saluted Sir William.

The next instant Ryder was gripping the hand of Mark Trueman. "Be seated," ordered Sir William. "You are not on duty now. Verity, fetch me the miniature of my late wife; it hangs on the wall above my desk."

Sir William passed a hand over his brow. His face, kindly in repose, looked sterner now. Though not yet forty, his countenance had assumed a melancholy cast since the death of his first wife, she who was daughter of Sir John Booth of Dunham Massey. His was a handsome face, a resolute face, the face of one who had forsworn the pride of life.

"Sir William, was it wise of you to enter Chester?" Verity could not conceal her anxiety.

"Not wise, my dear, but necessary. We must show the malignants that the power of the Parliament is not to be despised. I must take with me what things I value most, for

I doubt whether I shall see my goods again. If I am any judge, this place will be pillaged as soon as hostilities break out.''

He looked about him regretfully as though loth to part from a familiar home. "The day will come when the proud folk of Chester will regret their treatment of me," he said, a trifle bitterly. He turned to the girl.

"I do not like to leave you here alone," he said with concern in his voice. "Get your cloak, girl, and escape with me while the way lies open. Yale shall remain to send me what news he can gather. Only God knows what lies ahead of us. Chester will not be a pleasant place for a woman."

"I shall be in infinitely less danger than Ryder Yale," she said calmly. "I have not yet commenced my duties. Our opponents are chivalrous to women. Have no fears for me, Sir William. I have none for myself."

"You are a brave girl," he replied. "I accept your sacrifice, not for myself but for the Parliament." He turned to Ryder Yale. "I intended ordering you back to your troop, but it is clear that you must remain here. Mistress Verity must be protected. You shall account to me if harm befall her while she is in the city of Chester."

He turned quickly away as one who would not face the formalities of farewell. Lieutenant Trueman picked up the bulging valises and followed Sir William Brereton out into the night.

CHAPTER FIVE

IT was a unique experience for Ryder Yale and Verity Hill to be within a walled city in the midst of enemies. The knowledge that a false step would cause disaster at first disturbed and then stimulated them. Verity was the more calm. She was, at the start, the more venturesome. The cause might have been physical, for Ryder's shoulder still caused him pain and the feeling of incapacity sapped his self-assurance. For several days after Sir William's visit the young man remained indoors or walked in the garden. Verity, armed with nothing more formidable than a shopping basket, made her way along streets which daily grew more crowded as soldiers and volunteers flocked to the loyal city.

Packhorse trains were beginning to come in bearing arms and accoutrements purchased by Lord Strange. It was obviously the intention to turn Chester into a magazine for the Royalist forces in the district.

When candles were lighted and shutters closed Verity and Ryder would survey each day's events, sifting the essential news for transmission to Sir William Brereton at his headquarters in Nantwich. He was now officially appointed Commander-in-Chief for Cheshire and the surrounding counties by the Parliament. When the letter was penned Amos would be lowered over the wall to go, crab-like with his coracle on his back, to where the river rippled in the darkness. So far there seemed little matter of military moment. Ryder felt that he wasted his time. Verity's companionship made the inactivity endurable. Yet there were occasional matters of importance. An Assembly held early in the month moved that an assessment of a hundred marks be levied on the inhabitants for the repair of the gates and the fortification of the wall. A committee was formed for the oversight of this work. Money was voted for the purchasing of powder and shot. A dozen great guns with ammunition were obtained for the Castle. Now that the King had raised his standard at Nottingham war was inevitable.

Ryder, as soon as his arm permitted, went into the city. The streets were abustle. More troops were arriving, mostly from Lancashire. Ammunition trains and waggons loaded with equipment rolled through the Eastgate. Chester was becoming an armed camp. Muskets and bandoliers were brought by packhorses to Lord Strange's house. It was rumoured that five thousand men were coming from Lancashire; no one knew where they would be housed or how they would be fed.

The town grew more noisy, more rowdy. Mingling with the dialects of Cheshire and Lancashire sounded the voluble voices of men from North Wales. They were, for the most part, Flintshire miners, portion of the fifteen hundred men raised by young Roger Mostyn, heir of Mostyn Hall, who astounded everybody by creating a regiment in the space of twelve hours. It was rumoured that the King was to commission him as its colonel.

The men of the new regiment were crowding into the taverns eager to drink his health. Perhaps it was only natural that they should get out of hand. The old order of city life had changed. A new element had crept in. There was indignation still at the action of Sir William in drumming for volunteers in the loyal city. Men of Chester were chagrined that their enemy should have been allowed to obtain his freedom easily. Brereton had escaped, but his house remained.

Ryder caught rumbles of the gathering storm. He felt particularly impotent in the midst of so many armed men and longed for the comforting touch of his good broadsword slapping against his leg. His thoughts turned to Verity. The conviction came to him that he had done wrong to leave her unprotected. The impression was so strong that instinctively he forsook the crowded thoroughfares and walked briskly towards St. Mary's Nunnery. He hoped the intrepid girl was safe indoors.

The shouting and the chattering rose and fell like waves of sound. At first it was low, like a distant rumble. As Ryder walked away the noise, instead of decreasing, grew more distinct. There were angry voices, clamorous voices. He could hear the words now. They sounded ominous in the gathering dusk.

"Wreck his house! Burn the canting rogue's house!"

Intuition told Ryder to what house the raucous voices referred. He broke into a run. Swinging the iron gates with a clash, he bolted them—they might cause momentary delay. The mob came streaming down Black Friars Lane. He could see men running along the walls, men leaping down to the lawns.

Ryder hurried towards the front door, wondering whether he would be able to gain admittance. Before he could touch the great knocker the door opened as if by an invisible force. As it closed behind him with a clang he saw Verity slip the chain into its socket and turn the great key.

"I was watching and saw you," she explained. "Can you thrust in the top bolt? It is too high for me."

He looked down on her, marvelling at her calm. A flush showed on her cheeks; that was all.

"Escape by the side door," he ordered. "There is time. I will guard the house."

Verity shook her head. "I do not desert my charge," she said. "Sir William prophesied that they would loot his house. Do you recollect? I wonder what it will be like."

"We shall know shortly." Ryder's voice was grim. His eye scanned the walls with their decorative weapons.

"Our best swords have gone to arm the troops." Verity gave a forced laugh. "You have a choice of battle-axes and maces."

Ryder took down a hanger and tested the blade; it was sadly inferior to his own good sword, but it might serve. Verity was peering through the dining-room window. "They have forced the gates and are trooping up the drive."

"What valuables are there?"

"None. Sir William took all the plate for melting. Ah!"

"What is it?"

"Some jewels. He overlooked them in his haste."

"Where are they?"

"In a leather bag about my neck."

"Madness! You invite trouble. Give them to me." Ryder looked about him for a safer place of concealment. A powder-horn made from an ox-horn hung among the trophies. It had been pleasingly carved with crests and monograms. He reached for it, drew the stopper and wedged the tiny bag inside. Then he hung the horn high on the wall. He was just in time. A heavy thud sounded on the great door. It was a stout door of double thickness, heavily studded. Cudgels were battering it. The shouting increased.

"Open the door! Down with it, then! Has anyone a crow?"

The wood was rent and splintered, but the door held firm. A shutter was wrenched from a window. A brickbat crashed through the pane, sprinkling Ryder and Verity with glass. It was an ornate window on which the Brereton escutcheon was displayed in tinctures.

"Hurt?" inquired Ryder anxiously. His cheek was cut.

"It is nothing; a scratch," replied Verity, putting her

kerchief to her neck. "There's worse to follow. Here they come."

Dusk had turned to night. The driveway was lit by the ruddy glare of torches. The dancing light showed the up-turned angry faces, drink-reddened faces. Men were hurrying forward with sledge-hammers. The viciousness of their blows was frightening. The door went down. The crowd surged in. Ryder thrust the girl into a corner where the gloom hung thickest and stood before her, ready to fight to the death.

The excited men who rushed into the room did not see or did not heed him. It was loot they wanted. The first man snatched the candlesticks and fought his way through clutching, covetous hands. Drawers were emptied and their contents scattered. It was an ordeal to stand motionless, watching, wondering what would happen next. Ryder was conscious of a small, warm hand slipped into his. It afforded him comfort, and fired him with a fierce resolve to die if need be in protection of this trusting girl. He felt drawn very close to her during those tense moments. The shouting grew louder.

"They have found the winecellar!" The whisper came from Verity. The room was stripped of everything save a refectory table too ponderous to be moved. Verity ventured cautiously forth.

A man was coming along the hall. Ryder recognized him. It was the fellow in tattered finery whom he had seen at the merrymaking. He walked with an arrogant swagger, a bottle in one hand and in the other—a carved powder-horn. Discretion forsook Verity at the sight.

"Give that to me!" She clutched the trophy.

"Hi! You pilfering jade! Give that back!" The man endeavoured to wrench it from her hands. The horn fell to the floor. He grabbed Verity roughly. Ryder knocked him down and the man lay dazed and still. An angry roar sounded from the crowd who witnessed the blow. There was an instantaneous uproar. Ryder swung Verity on to the stairs and turned, hanger in hand, to prevent any attempt to follow. The girl climbed to the landing; Ryder backed, cautiously, stair by stair, his eyes never leaving the angry faces in the hallway below him. Few of the men had swords.

Many carried sticks. Ryder broke the forearm of one man who struck at him. The remainder hesitated.

There was something about the stalwart, stern-featured young man with the poised blade which made them pause. The courage of one possessed a greater spiritual quality than the bravado of a crowd.

The pause was of short duration. The man in the tattered finery rose slowly to his feet and stood frowning at Ryder. "Have at him, Milo!" yelled the crowd. "Use your sword, Milo!" The bravo was not loth. With the deliberation of one accustomed to a task, he drew his blade. It was an ornate rapier which he carried, a weapon which hinted at better times. The man Milo took up his position near the newel-post with a certain swaggering assurance which showed that he was no novice at the duello.

His blade touched that of Ryder, cautiously as though he would feel his way. Then they began to fence, slowly at first. The silence was unbroken save for the rasp of steel. Suddenly Milo leaped up the stairs and thrust. Ryder turned the rapier ceilingwards and the two paused, weapons uplifted, breast to breast. As they stood on the precarious stairs the drunken rioters saw in their posture the chance they desired. They stamped up the stairs, upsetting both fighters, friend and foe alike, spurning their struggling bodies beneath their trampling feet. Up they rushed to where Verity, pale of face, leant over the banisters.

Rough hands caught her. She cried aloud. Her cry did not go unanswered.

A Cavalier was standing in the doorway. One neatly booted foot was on the splintered wood of the door. The light of torches showed his tall, elegant figure, clad in plum-coloured velvet. A lace collar served to accentuate the dark arrogance of his haughty face. He looked the picture of indolence. At the girl's cry his languor forsook him. Lithe as an animal he bounded up the stairs, heedless of whom he trod underfoot. He was among the men on the landing. His fists struck right and left. "Loose her, damn you! Take your filthy hands away!" It was Royle Wilding—Royle in a fighting mood, Royle with fiery temper in his eyes and curses on his lips. Out came his sword.

He struck at the struggling horde. As though disdaining to stain his steel, he used the flat of his rapier and whipped them down the stairs. He followed close behind, cursing and kicking, so that more than one rioter pitched headforemost down the stairway. The landing was clear save for a prostrate form or two. Wilding gave a reckless laugh as he took up a position at the top.

"Come on—all of you. Force a passage. I'll hold these stairs against all comers."

There was something almost theatrical about him. His teeth gleamed in a smile. He seemed, thought Verity as she gazed in amaze, to be enjoying himself.

She had regarded fighting as a stern duty; this new-comer, with his handsome face and fine raiment, appeared to look upon it as a pastime. Verity had never seen his like before. The men hung back. Royle Wilding turned to Verity and bowed low.

"Your servant, madam."

"A very active servant, sir," said Verity, who found herself blushing as she spoke, "and, may I add, a most welcome one."

"I ought to whip these curs for annoying you," he protested, and stared at the mass of angry faces in the hallway as though he regretted that he had not completed his task. There came a commotion. Lanterns glowed in the night. The light fell on a red robe. The Mayor walked into the disordered hall. The men of the night watch were at his back, halberds ready. They were not needed. Law and order was restored by the mayoral presence. The raiders slunk away, by back door or window. Soon the building was quiet and almost deserted. Verity moved with calm dignity down the stairs.

"I do not think these rascals will molest you any more, madam," said the Mayor formally. "I regret that this should have happened to your home."

"Not my home, sir. You must surely know that the house belongs to Sir William Brereton."

"Pray convey to Sir William Brereton my regret for this outrage. Such goods of his as I can recover shall be restored to him. I deplore Sir William's political views, but when I fight him it shall be in open warfare and not by such intolerable methods as these."

"I am grateful, sir, for your courtesy."

The Mayor bowed stiffly. Followed by the guard, he walked into the darkness. Verity waited until the last man had departed and then she finished descending. She looked about her, pained and bewildered by the confusion. Gone were the rioters. Gone was the bully called Milo. Gone was Ryder Yale. Verity became conscious of Royle Wilding standing close beside her. "My gratitude to you, sir, for your kindly aid, and your courage."

"Courage?" Royle looked up from sheathing his rapier. "It calls for no courage to scatter curs of that breed. I am concerned that their plebeian claws should have touched a lady. Otherwise I have not enjoyed myself so prodigiously for many a day."

He bent over her hand. Verity offered no protest as he kissed her fingers. It was a courtesy she had not known before. As Royle Wilding stepped back his foot touched an object on the boards. It was a powder-horn. He picked it up and examined the carving. "Ah, a pretty example of craftsmanship. By these shields it has been in many hands. Great heavens!"

"What is it?" Verity was curious.

"I see my own crest among them. May I have this as a souvenir? A reminder of our encounter? A memento of this merry night?"

Verity tried to speak, but no words came. The bold eyes were smiling at her. How could she refuse his request? It was not her voice which gave the answer.

"No!" It came abruptly, so abruptly that Royle Wilding turned quickly.

Ryder Yale was standing in the doorway, dishevelled, the hilt of a broken hanger in his hand.

"Ah, my bold bull-baiter, so we meet again?" Wilding smiled.

There was no answering smile in Yale's eyes. It was Verity who spoke.

"You may keep the powder-horn, sir, if you wish."

CHAPTER SIX

FOR several days after the looting of Sir William's house Ryder was conscious of a change in Verity.

It was subtle and defied analysis. Both he and Verity went about their tasks in silence. There was much to do. Carpenters and glaziers were repairing doors and windows. The Mayor was as good as his word. Restitution was attempted. Many of the baronet's goods were gone for ever. The loss included some valuable horses. Such goods as were recoverable were returned. The messengers performed their task formally. It was obvious that it was integrity and not goodwill which prompted the Mayor's punctiliousness. Ryder worked hard; so did Verity. They never spoke unless the occasion called for words. It might be attributable to reaction which followed a trying experience. Ryder was irritated because he had not been able to defend Verity unaided. Why had it been necessary for a stranger to come to the rescue? His pride was wounded and he brooded.

One morning he voiced the thought which simmered in his mind.

"Why did you give him the trophy?" he demanded.

"To whom do you refer?" Verity played for time. Ryder had not known her in a mood like this before.

"You know perfectly well to whom you presented the powder-horn."

"But I do not know his name, Ryder!"

"His name, if you must know, is Wilding—Captain Royle Wilding—and he is an arch-malignant."

"He is a brave and courteous gentleman."

"He is an enemy. Yet you bestow on him a gift which was not yours to bestow."

"I know. It troubles me."

"Did you forget about the jewels?"

"No."

"Then it was flagrantly dishonest. I am at a loss to understand you. Why did you do such a thing?"

"Indeed, Ryder, I wish I could explain. It has been much on my mind. He—he looked at me so that I had not the heart to refuse after the great service he had rendered. It was done on the impulse of the moment.''

"This is not like you, Verity—you who are so calm and wise.''

"Human nature is unpredictable, Ryder. I do not understand myself. He rescued me from those unclean beasts. When he smiled at me I could not say him nay.''

"It is the loss of so many jewels that troubles me.''

"And me likewise.''

"Do you think that he suspected——''

"Ryder, how could he? How could he possibly suspect?''

"I shall seek him out and ask for it back.''

"No, no. It might provoke a quarrel. I could not bear that. Pray allow me to seek him.''

Verity made herself ready and went into the city. She was gone so long that Ryder grew first impatient and then concerned. When she returned he gave vent to his relief in a petulance he could not have explained.

"Have you recovered the jewels?''

"No, Ryder.''

"Why not? You went with that intent: or so I understood.''

"I could not find Captain Wilding.''

She fell silent, sitting with her hands idly clasped in her lap, staring through a window at a chaffinch active on a bough in the September sunlight.

"And is that all you have to say for yourself?'' Ryder was impatient.

"I have so much to say that I do not know where to begin. I have heard something which drives all thought of lost jewels out of my head, so surprising is it.''

"Are you going to tell me?''

"Ryder, the King is to come to Chester.''

"The King!'' Ryder was incredulous. He uttered the word as if unable to grasp its significance. The King had been a name, a visionary figure. The idea of the King, a man of flesh and blood, riding into the city as Earl Rivers or Lord Strange might do seemed incomprehensible. "The King coming to Chester! What are we to do?''

"We must send a messenger to Sir William tonight.''

"What can he do to prevent its happening?"

"I cannot tell, but Sir William must know without delay."

Verity placed quill, paper, ink and sand upon the writing-table and together they worded the message. Engrossed in the task, Ryder forgot about the jewels, forgot about Royle Wilding. They were interrupted at their work by Amos Bowman. There had been a signal from the Welsh bank to say a messenger was to arrive. They had often sent messages from the city; this was the first occasion to receive a message. They waited, wondering, until the night was dark. Amos lowered the rope ladder.

It was Mark Trueman who made his way into the room. Ryder greeted him warmly, but Mark did not respond. He looked worried. He looked weary.

"I am glad to see you," said Verity. "We have news for Sir William. You must take it to him without delay."

"I do not know where Sir William is." Mark Trueman spoke in a dull tone.

"He is in Nantwich, is he not?"

"Nantwich," said Trueman heavily, "is taken by my Lord Grandison's army and the town disarmed."

Neither Verity nor Ryder spoke. The surprise was too great for words.

"We are all plundered and undone," went on Mark. "The houses of all who stood for the Parliament and the militia are ransacked and the owners forced to run for safety. The malignants have disarmed all the great houses, first Sir Thomas Delves's, then my Lord Crewe's, then Sir Richard Wilbraham's, and all the other gentlemen round about us. They are forced to leave their houses.

"Men and women are at the mercy of these villains, who will have what they list or else they set a pistol to our heads and swear, damn me, that they will make us swallow a bullet. They take what arms they find, and, not content with that, must have money and clothes, plate and meat. They steal our horses and drive our women and children to run to the wilds or lie in the woods and ditches. Those who stay at home are made slaves or forced to enlist for the King. We shall be utterly undone and ruined. It is pitiful to hear the

shrieking and howling of the women and children. God grant
that I nevermore hear the like."

"What would you have me do?" inquired Ryder.

"Why, there is naught you can do. I do but bid you send
no more letter-carriers lest the messages get into wrong hands
and the bearer is hanged for his pains."

"You must seek Sir William, wherever he may be, and
say that the King comes to Chester." Verity spoke calmly.

Mark Trueman remained only long enough to have a
meal. He was too agitated to relax. The Parliamentary cause
in Cheshire had received a grievous blow at the outset. He
must help to gather together again the forces scattered by
Lord Grandison's surprise raid. Ryder went as far as the wall
and watched his colleague vanish into the mysterious night.

"Tomorrow you must seek a tailor and get yourself a
new suit," remarked Verity when Ryder returned. He
protested at the extravagance. Verity was adamant. "If the
King is in the city there is no knowing whom you may meet.
People will put on their best raiment. You must not attract
attention by not following the fashion."

The following day, with a docility which was foreign
to his nature, Ryder purchased a new suit, quiet in colour but
of good texture. He found the city agog with excitement.
Banners and flags were draped from windows. On the
Roodee the train-bands were drilling. There was but one
topic of conversation—the coming of the King from Shrewsbury. Carpenters were erecting a dais in front of the Honey
Steps near the Eastgate. It was here that the Mayor was to
receive the King.

Friday the twenty-third of September was the day on
which King Charles came to his loyal city of Chester. Though
his Majesty left Shrewsbury with only an escort of cavalry
he was joined along the route by forces raised by loyalists,
so that by the time Chester was reached the King had a considerable following at his back. At Milton Green, King Charles
was met by Mr. Richard Egerton of Ridley with six hundred
musketeers. When the royal party came to Hatton Heath
and Rowton Heath they were joined by troops of horse
raised by Earl Rivers, Viscount Cholmondeley and Sir
Thomas Aston.

So the long line of horsemen, gay with colour and bright with steel, came to Spital Boughton, where the liberties of the city began. It was nearly five o'clock. Bareheaded in the September sunshine the two sheriffs, Mr. Thomas Mottershead and Mr. Hugh Leigh, waited at the boundary to welcome their sovereign. With them were the sheriffs-peers and leave-lookers, all gowned in scarlet and mounted on horseback.

Bells of the cathedral, bells of the churches, broke into jubilation. Trumpets sounded. Drums added their stirring welcome. Along the sides of the road, musketeers of the train-bands raised their ponderous weapons and fired a salute into the air.

King Charles had come to Chester.

The train-bands and the volunteers with their banners and their muskets lined both sides of Foregate Street. They took up the firing as the King passed by. Inside the Eastgate the street was lined by the city companies with their colours.

Ryder Yale, standing in front of the crowd, was conscious of the thrill of expectancy in the very air. It needed not the cheers and the bells, the trumpets and the musket-shots, to proclaim a great and momentous event. The glad tumult stirred him, but its effect was to make him withdraw more into himself. The walls were crowded, the streets were crowded, the Rows were crowded, yet Ryder felt he was not part of this curious throng. In half-timbered houses which bent forward as if they, too, wished to have a better view, casements were open and persons leant out precariously to witness the amazing spectacle. Two riders were making their way up the road. It was the horses which held Ryder's gaze. He feasted his eyes on the easy action, delicate forelegs, and coats, glossy as satin. The leading Cavalier, resplendent in royal blue silk, passed by. The second horse was reined in. A woman bent from the saddle and smiled upon Ryder. So richly dressed was she that he did not recognize Rosea until his eyes met hers.

"How good to see you! You have quite recovered?" Her tone was friendly, gracious, solicitous.

"I thank you—yes."

The first rider, Royle Wilding, had reined in and was glancing back. Rosea shook her reins and left Ryder with a smile. The Parliamentarian looked after them with mixed emotions. He wished he had not seen Rosea. Her beauty disturbed him. Rosea and Wilding blended so admirably with the proceedings, they seemed so much in harmony with the spirit of the occasion, that more than ever he felt his isolation —apart not merely in mind but in spirit.

He had no further time to meditate, to brood. The captains of companies were shouting orders. The pikemen stood stiffly alert, their weapons bristling like a fence of silvery spikes. The shouting and the firing grew nearer. With it mingled the sound which was music to Ryder's ears—the clatter of hoofs. The King was coming. The King was at hand

The life-guard came first, drawn swords pointing upwards. They were fine horsemen, well mounted. Ryder Yale, cornet of horse, appraised them. There were men of quality there, proud to serve in the ranks of those who guarded their monarch. Their sashes and breast-plates, their velvet doublets and lace collars, gave them a gay and gallant aspect, but it was the horses, always the horses, which held Ryder's eye.

The last rank passed on its way. There was a space in the procession. It enabled Ryder to look across the roadway to the dais draped in green and gay with flags. He saw the Mayor in his red robe, the aldermen in their mulberry robes, the Recorder, the mace-bearer and the sword-bearer, all motionless, for the King was at hand.

He saw a solitary figure on a white horse, a horse with the grace and delicacy of an Arab. There could be no mistaking the noble face of the rider, slender, almost foreign-looking, with pointed beard and melancholy eyes. It needed not the blue riband of the Garter with its pendant George to proclaim that here, in truth, was Charles the First, King of England. A few paces behind rode a youth in his early teens, dark eyed, dark haired, swarthy as one from southern climes —his Royal Highness Charles, Prince of Wales and Earl of Chester.

The Mayor and those about him dropped on their knees. The Recorder, Mr. Robert Brerewood, serjeant-at-law, stepped forward with the scroll of his loyal address in his hands.

"Most Gracious Sovereign, we, your Majesty's most humble and obedient subjects, do in all humility crave leave to take the boldness to bid your Majesty and our most noble Prince, our hopeful Earl of Chester, welcome to this place. . . ."

The rest of the Recorder's eloquence was drowned by the shouts of the humble and obedient subjects.

The Mayor descended and on bended knees delivered the city's sword for the King to touch. The King returned the weapon and the Mayor, mounting his horse, carried the civic blade uplifted before the King as he led the procession to the Pentice, where, under the civic roof, a banquet was prepared.

Two hundred pounds in gold was presented to the King and a hundred to the Prince.

Ryder Yale, with many others, was shut out from these high matters. He still stood in the streets watching the parties of Royalist horse clatter through the city's Eastgate when he felt a pluck on his sleeve. He glanced down and saw that Verity was at his side.

"I have much to say." Her voice was low. "While you watched this pageantry I have heard—many things. Let us return to the house with all speed."

In the quiet seclusion of St. Mary's Nunnery, Verity tossed her hat on a nearby table and seated herself. "Eighty horseloads of muskets and bandoliers have just arrived from Lord Strange, who has sent in two troops of horse. That is of little consequence, however. I have heard where the King means to have his headquarters, and Sir William must learn of it without delay."

"Some say Shrewsbury and some say Oxford."

"Neither, Ryder. The King wishes to establish himself here, in Chester."

The man stared incredulously.

"It is a walled city," explained the girl, "and, moreover, it is the port for Ireland, and it is to Ireland that the malignants look for support and reinforcement."

"It is resolved that the King stays here?"

"Not finally resolved. His Majesty is to hold his Court in the Bishops' Palace. The issue will be discussed tomorrow. You must get out of the city and find Sir William without delay."

D

"You are sure of this?"

"I know that the Mayor has been asked—nay, commanded—to deliver up the keys of the city gates. His Majesty is resolved to make this his chief place of residence. The Mayor, loyal though he is, has been taken aback."

"Will he comply?"

"The city has not yet consented. They fear that if they consent to these demands Chester may be left exposed to all the hazards of these troublous times."

"It is not certain, then?"

"When I came from the city the debate was still in progress. All the same, it is of the utmost urgency that Sir William learns without delay. Say to him, too, that it would be wise if you did not return to Chester, for all the train-bands are to be reviewed by his Majesty on Hoole Heath, and every man between sixteen and sixty will be enlisted."

"If I do not return you must escape also."

"Oh no. It will be safe for me to stay."

"I will not leave you alone in such dire peril."

"You will carry out what Sir William instructs—neither more nor less."

It was one thing for Ryder to resolve to seek Sir William, it was another matter to put that resolution into execution. With the appearance of the King came extreme vigilance. Sentries were posted at intervals along the walls. Parties of horse patrolled the neighbourhood. Some were encamped upon the Roodee. To cross the river by coracle was out of the question. Ryder resolved that he would attempt to walk boldly from one of the gates.

He found the city in a fever of excitement. Every tavern was crowded almost to suffocation. Colonel Mostyn's Welsh levies mingled with reckless adventurers from Ireland; French volunteers drank with troopers from Lord Cholmondeley's cavalry. The populace rubbed shoulders with soldiers of fortune.

Each gate was guarded. Soldiers were billeted in the suburbs. Every road and lane was picketed. There were soldiers, soldiers everywhere.

Ryder lingered in the streets gathering the latest gossip. It was said that the Earl of Derby was sinking fast, that he was not likely to last the night. There had been skirmishes in the Midlands, bickerings at Puritan Manchester. The King's German nephew, Prince Rupert, was proving a dashing cavalry leader despite his youth. Stolid Parliamentarians could not withstand his furious onslaughts. The military were growing elated and optimistic. The civil section was less enthusiastic. Practical-minded burgesses were grumbling about the drain on the financial resources of the city. They were aggrieved because the King was so little satisfied with the gift of two hundred pounds which his loyal subjects had made him. Then, too, the position of Chester would be hazardous if the train-bands were marched off to form the royal army. Who would defend the city if Sir William Brereton delivered an attack? So the talk went on.

Ryder attempted to leave by the Northgate. He was turned back. He tried the Eastgate. Again he was stopped. No man might leave the city without a pass signed by Earl Rivers or Sir Thomas Aston. He stood moodily watching the moving throng, uncertain what step to take. Like a light upon his darkness came a gorgeously clad Cavalier, leisurely forcing his steed through the thronged thoroughfare. It was Royle Wilding.

Hope, born of desperation, stirred Ryder to attempt something he had never before done in his life. He would ask a favour! Perhaps Royle Wilding would procure for him a pass. He thrust himself past some weary pack-horses and touched Wilding as he passed by. The Cavalier's haughty stare changed to a smile as he recognized Ryder.

"A word with you," pleaded Yale hastily.

"A thousand, my dear sir, and a drink, too, but demme, not here. Let us first get free of this rabble. Lord, the stench of the unwashed! One is more in need of a scent-bottle than a sword."

Wilding made his horse plunge, sitting complacently until the curvetting animal had cleared a passageway.

"Follow," he called over his shoulder.

"Yes, pray follow," repeated a woman's voice. For the first time Ryder realized that Rosea was close behind. There was a smile of invitation in her dark eyes.

CHAPTER SEVEN

OUTSIDE the Pied Bull Inn they halted. Royle assisted Rosea to dismount and a groom led away the horses. Wilding flung open the door of an adjoining house. "My humble lodging," he apologized. "A man is thankful for small mercies these crowded days. Enter. Nay, Mr. Bull-Baiter, I shall take no refusal."

"You must join us," added Rosea. "You owe me an explanation, you know."

"An explanation?" Ryder glanced quickly at the girl and met a smile which set his heart beating faster.

"I seem to remember a guest stealing away in the early morn while I still slumbered."

"Oh, I am sorry. I offer my apologies."

"I shall only accept them in the room above." Rosea mounted the dark stairway.

"I merely wished to ask a favour," said Ryder hurriedly, as he turned to Wilding.

"Granted. Ask anything but a loan. I beg you absolve me of parsimony, but my purse is as impoverished as a Puritan's soul." He pulled a golden coin from his pocket and regarded it ruefully. "My last!"

"You are serious?" began Ryder.

"I am never serious. It is the one fault I never commit. Yes, this is my last. I must not part with it. It is symbolical."

"Symbolical?"

"My sovereign is my all! Demmed witty that, don't you agree? I must tell Ro. She considers I have no brains."

"Would you care to borrow . . ." began Ryder awkwardly.

"Your horse, yes, or your mistress, but money—no. I have so few principles that I needs must make the most of those which survive."

Wilding led the way upstairs. A fire burned cosily in a spacious room with a wide, lozenge-paned casement which looked down upon the street. Lighted candelabra illumined a table set for two. Cut glass and silver gave to it a lavishness which seemed almost iniquitous to Ryder's frugal eye.

"They emptied my pockets at cards last night," said

Wilding easily, as he dropped into a chair. "I shall have my revenge tonight. All or nothing. Play for high stakes, Mr. Bull-Baiter. It adds piquancy to life's insipid repast. If it is not money you require, what is it?"

"A permit to leave the city."

"The devil! When?"

"Tonight."

"Ask me for the crown of England. Hell's flames, man, I myself have just been turned back when I essayed to escort Rosea to her rooms in Love Lane. As it is, Rosea must spend the night in my rooms, while I, for propriety's sake, must suffer privation. No, my bold toreador, you must stay within the gates tonight, even as I. Why the impatience? Has it ought to do with a wench?"

Ryder thought of Verity and spoke the truth. "Yes." He coloured when he said it. Wilding accepted his answer with easy nonchalance.

"Women are like wine, Yale, the longer you keep 'em the better the taste. You must dine with us. No, demme, you shall take my place."

"I would not hear of such a thing."

"A word in your ear. You would do me a favour. I have danced attendance on Rosea all day and have earned a night's freedom. Lud, Yale, I could, if I tried, stay true to a dozen women, but to be faithful to one is more than my nature can endure."

He stood up and affected a yawn. Ryder felt ill at ease. The Cavalier's easy flippancy filled him with resentment, a resentment which had to be smothered for hospitality's sake. Rosea walked into the room. She had removed her hat and tidied her hair. Even in her riding habit she made so alluring a picture with the candlelight giving sparkle to her eyes that Ryder stared at her anew. Suddenly he felt grateful to Verity for persuading him to buy a new suit. It was sober indeed when compared with Wilding's splendour, yet its very simplicity served to reveal his splendid proportions and to show in strong relief his healthy colouring and clear-cut features.

"Our friend will dine," observed Wilding.

"Of course, Royle. Let me ring for another place to be set."

Royle's hand restrained her. "As you entertain a guest I will deprive myself of the pleasure of your company."

"How transparent you are, Royle! You persuade Mr. Yale to stay so that you may escape. I have a mind to keep you out of pure caprice. But I will be merciful. Off with you. I will be tactful and will not inquire whither you are going. You would only vow you were on guard before the King's quarters——"

"Ro, you shameless baggage! I have a mind to remain ——"

"Not you. I know you too well."

Royle rested a hand on each of the girl's shoulders and kissed her lightly. "Because I never lay hands on a woman——"

"Indeed, Royle?" Her brows were arched provocatively.

"Violent hands," corrected Wilding. "Because of my innate chivalry I will not administer the chastisement you merit. During the cold night watches as I stand on guard I shall recall your heartless words. Adieu."

"Is he truly on guard tonight?" Ryder was puzzled.

"Not he. It will be cards which lure him—or a wench. He prates of sacrifice, but he welcomes your presence as a means of his release. But fall to. I am ravenous."

Now that the excitement of the day had ended both realized how hungry they were. It was a silent meal. When the servants had cleared the table and they were left with their wine, Rosea leaned back with a sigh of content. "Lord, I have only now discovered how weary I am."

Ryder, with a boldness which astonished him, pushed the candelabra aside.

"Why do you do that?" Rosea was watching him indolently.

"I could not see you properly," he informed her.

"Better that you should see me properly than improperly." She saw the colour flood to his cheeks. "Lud, did that shock you? Blame my association with that rascal Royle. Push this table aside. It might be a bastion separating enemies. No, don't sit down. Stand there where I can see you."

Her tone was peremptory. Ryder complied. He stood

motionless, erect as·a soldier on parade, and as expression-less.

"You are strong." She spoke softly as if in soliloquy. "Amazingly strong. I keep recalling how you clung to that furious beast. I admire strength. You may sit down now. Among life's qualities I place strength and courage para-mount."

"There are other virtues."

"Truly. Which do you place first?"

"Readiness to sacrifice for what is right."

"But how foolish!" Her tone·was shocked.

Ryder grew argumentative.

"Foolish! How could it be foolish?"

"Who is to say what is right and·what is wrong?"

"Your conscience tells you."

"My conscience is most amenable and always approves of what I desire to do."

"You know right from wrong," said Ryder stubbornly.

"But you might sacrifice for something believing it to be right only to find later that it was not right. Then your sacrifice would be in vain."

"Sacrifice for a principle can never be in vain. It is simple to tell right from wrong."

"Nothing is less simple. What is right to me may be wrong to you. No two people are ever wholly agreed. And if they did agree for a while they would soon disagree."

"No. Right is right and wrong is wrong."

She laughed. "How delightfully straightforward your life must be! Free of all complications. Tell me, have you ever kissed a woman?"

"No." Ryder's answer was curt. He felt awkward.

"You think it wrong?"

"Unless a man wants to marry the woman."

"How do you know whether you want to marry her until you have kissed her?"

"I cannot see how that has anything to do with the matter."

"Suppose you kissed the woman, intending to marry her, and then changed your mind?"

"I should still marry her. It would be a point of honour."

"Poor woman. Condemn her to a life of disillusionment and misery—and call it right."

He looked so perplexed, so distressed, that Rosea burst out laughing. Ryder rose with dignity.

"No," she cried, sobering suddenly. "You are not to go. Have I hurt you with my folly? I am sorry. Truly, I am sorry. You see, I have never met anyone like you before, and I do not know how to conduct myself. Royle and I consider life at its best is but a mockery, so we mock that which makes mock of us. Oh, believe me, I would never hurt your feelings of intent. I beg of you believe that. I owe my life to you. I do not forget that you saved me. I shall never forget. Never."

She looked so earnest that Ryder paused, astonished. It was an aspect which was new.

Slowly he sat down again, leaned back, and regarded the girl pensively. Was she acting? Was she sincere? Her eyes were upon him, serious now. He thought them lovelier than ever. How utterly dissimilar was their mode of thought! What was the subtle magnetism which attracted? Why did she desire him, a yeoman's son, a plain homespun man, when she was accustomed to consort with silken gentlefolk? Had he something to learn from Rosea? Had she something to learn from him? Then doubts assailed him. Suppose this beauty of hers was but a snare of the Devil meant for man's downfall!

Rosea was thinking: "How virile and wholesome he is, yet how simple. His body is magnificent, but he has the mind of a child."

"Right can often be wrong," she said slowly, thoughtfully.

"Impossible."

"No. It is merely a point of view. You speak the truth?"

"Always." He paused. "As far as it is possible so to do."

"How naive you are! In your endeavour to speak the truth you confess to not wholly speaking the truth. Tell me, if a party of those accursed rebels raided this house intent to slay me, and inquired of you whether I were here, would you lie?"

"I—I would defend you with my life."

"You are evasive. Would you lie?"

Ryder put his face in his hands. "God grant I am never in so terrible a predicament."

Rosea smiled. "You see, Ryder—there is no point in our being formal when we are going to be friends—it all depends on your own point of view. You believe in loyalty?"

"Yes. Emphatically yes."

"I am loyal to the King. Are you?"

Ryder's face set in stern lines. "I am loyal to the King and the Parliament," he averred, for such was the profession of all Parliamentarians. "His Majesty is head of the State, but he is ill advised."

"How innocent you are! So you are a Roundhead?"

The blood drummed in Ryder's ears. Why had he been lured into talking? What a fool he had been! Why had Sir William chosen him for this hateful task? Straightforward cut and thrust in the field was what Ryder expected, not this battle of words, this dissembling. He loathed the whole business. Why should he lie? Rosea's dark eyes were watching him intently.

"Yes," he said. "I serve the Parliament. I draw five shillings a day as a cornet in Sir William Brereton's own troop of horse. You see what manner of man you are entertaining!" He spoke wildly, bitterly.

"That was why you wished to get out of the city tonight?"

"Yes." He sat silent, staring at the beamed ceiling.

Rosea's eyes were fixed on a candle's flame.

"I believe in loyalty," she said softly, as though repeating a creed. "I believe in loyalty to my King. Also, I believe in loyalty to my friends. You see, Ryder, in life it is not always a choice between right and wrong, as you seem to believe. How easy would be a decision if it were! Often it is a choice between two rights—which is the greater and which the less. Or two wrongs. I must decide which loyalty is the greater— loyalty to my King or to the man who risked his life to save me from a horrible death."

"No thoughts of me must divert you from your duty. I am a soldier. I know the risks I run and I am prepared to abide by what befalls."

Rosea stood up quickly as though she had made up her

mind. "Get your hat. I believe I know a way whereby you can leave the city unnoticed."

"You would help me to escape?" Ryder was dubious.

"Do you doubt my sincerity, man to whom I owe so much?" Rosea came close to him and stared up into his face. "Look into my eyes, Ryder, and see if there is treachery there."

He shook his head.

"I do not know what that means," she persisted. "Say aloud, 'I trust you.' Say it! Say, 'Rosea, I trust you!'"

Ryder stared, hypnotized. "I trust you." The words were muttered. He hardly knew his own voice.

"Ryder, could I betray you? I am your debtor for life. I would repay, not betray."

"You shall not forsake your principles, not even to repay a debt. I am your enemy."

"Not my enemy, Ryder. You fight against the King. I shall fight against the rebels. But you are my friend. Harken. What is the life of one man in the general sacrifice? A mere cipher in the total. Yet the life of one man means much to you—and to me."

"Does Royle Wilding know I am for the Parliament?"

"Royle? That scatterbrain! Royle is gallant, Royle is daring, but his mind aspires to nothing more subtle than dice and damsels. He considered himself astute in inveigling you here so that he might have the evening for his own devices, yet for days I have wondered how I could have a minute alone with you so that I might try to express the gratitude I feel. Now my chance has come."

Rosea regarded him intently. Ryder thought that he had never seen eyes so eloquent, so tender. "Fetch my cloak. I am sure I can smuggle you through the cordon. It is imperative you go tonight?"

"It is."

"You shall go."

"Impossible. The gates are guarded and the walls surrounded."

"I know an unfrequented way. The Truant's Hole they call it. I will wager it is not watched; it is worth attempting.

It leads to the Roodee; once there you must trust to your wits."

"Bless you." He spoke so fervently that Rosea smiled.

The streets were still gay despite the darkness. Every window was alight. Many citizens could recall King James visiting Chester. It was a proud occasion to have a King again within the walls. Cressets flared. Link-boys with torches thrust their way through the throng. Rosea led the way past the Cathedral, which loomed with ponderous majesty against the night sky. Parsons Lane was deserted—dim as the main thoroughfares were bright. They came to a garden wall, the wall which once enclosed the garden of the Grey Friars. At a wicket-gate they paused.

"Now you had best go back," whispered Ryder, solicitous of her safety.

"You are safer while I am with you." She laughed at his surprise. "How innocent you are! A man by himself is instantly suspect. A lover and his lass may lurk in dark corners without arousing anything but envy."

A moving light attracted Ryder's notice. "Surely you had better retire while you may; here comes the night guard."

"It would be fatal," whispered Rosea, watching the bobbing lantern. The tramp of men sounded. "Pull your hat low. Put your arms around me. Don't be shy, man. Your safety depends on it."

Reluctantly Ryder complied. A slim, warm form pressed against him in the darkness. The watch drew nearer. Ryder from beneath his hat brim could recognize the leader. It was the man Milo, with whom he had already crossed swords.

Milo's eyes lit on them. He raised the lantern and flung an innuendo over his shoulder. It set the men laughing and brought a flush to Ryder's cheek.

He did not move until the men were out of sight. "Never before," observed Rosea with a laugh, "have I had to ask a man to put his arms about me. Was it a novel experience, Master Puritan? Well, now the ice is broken you had best kiss me farewell."

Ryder shook his head vigorously.

"Don't you wish to, Ryder? Not once?"

"No. Yes, I do want to, only—God help me to resist this sore temptation. I must stand true to my principles."

She drew back and looked up with surprise in her eyes. "I did not mean to cause you such concern. Does it mean so much to you?"

"Yes. You torture me, Rosea."

"Call me Ro. It is the pet name I like best."

"I will kiss you if you wish, Ro." He spoke almost savagely.

"No, Ryder—not if *I* wish. Only if *you* wish."

"You have made me wish to do so. For the first time in my life! If only I were sure it is not a wile of the Devil! If only I were certain this is true love! How can one tell, Ro?"

"There is nothing so elusive as love. It is like the wind——it bloweth where it listeth. This may be but the stirring of the emotions. That can only be known by testing. Time proves all things. The hour has come, Ryder, for you to go your way and I mine. But believe this—there's a corner of my heart which is always yours, man to whom I owe so much."

"My heart is yours, Ro. Not a corner. All of it."

"When this war is ended will you come back and tell me so? I wonder. But no. It is all hopeless. So hopeless. Better part and forget."

A rush of feeling swept over him at the tenderness of her tone. He bent his lips towards hers, but she slipped unexpectedly from his grasp.

"No, Ryder. You—you might regret it. I want you to have only happy memories. God keep you!"

She gripped his hand and ran down the lane, head bent. Inclination prompted him to follow, but some instinct held him back. He stood listening until the tapping of her tiny heels faded into the night. The hand she had touched still tingled.

Ryder leant against the wall. To him it was a new experience; an awakening. It left him disturbed, almost dazed. Slowly he passed through the wicket-gate, crossed a garden path, soft with weeds, and came to a low door in the city wall. The bolt was stiff, but his powerful fingers eased it. The hinges creaked. He closed the door softly behind him. He was outside the ramparts. Beyond him stretched the dark Roodee. A lighted tent of the piquet glowed in the distance like a luminous cone. He stepped cautiously on to the grass. A hoarse whisper sounded from the crest of the wall. It made him pause. He turned apprehensively.

"There he is, Milo!" The husky whisper came down to him. "Shoot, man, shoot!"

Ryder flung himself to the ground. A carbine crashed. The spurt of flame was followed by another. Lanterns twinkled. There were shouts of alarm.

"Your shot hit him, Milo!"

He was only vaguely conscious of the voices, for his leg was throbbing fiercely. He saw dim forms running towards him as he writhed on the damp grass of the Roodee.

CHAPTER EIGHT

IT had been a cruel night—March in its fiercest mood. Ryder slept badly. Draughts or driving rain penetrated every crevice. He sat huddled in a cloak and waited for the dawn. And now a feeble sun afforded consolation and warmth. Somewhere near the river a thrush was singing to welcome the coming spring. Sunlight streaming through the barred window of his cell traced a cheery pattern on the wall. It enheartened Ryder; it also filled him with a wild longing.

He had endured the cheerless, bitter winter with stoicism, but this hint of spring stirred something primitive in his blood. He wanted to be out, he wanted to be free. What a blessed thing was freedom!

The wound in his leg had healed. It left a scar the more pronounced because of the probing of a surgeon who wasted little tenderness on a Roundhead prisoner.

Fragments of news had filtered in from the outside. They began in November with a change of gaoler. The new custodian was the man Milo, he of the tattered finery, the bravo with the long sword and longer tongue.

A blustering man was Milo Preen—*Captain* Milo Preen he required to be called. No one knew how he came by the title, but few chose to dispute it, for at the slightest questioning the swashbuckler would give his moustache a bellicose twist, drop a hand upon his hilt and glare about him as though challenging any man to deny his assertion. He had been to Edgehill, where he had ridden with Sir John Byron's brigade. He had a tale of plundering to tell. It was of more consequence than the battle.

Milo came in bearing a bowl of soup and a hunk of bread. Ryder accepted the food thankfully. The soup was hot and he was cold. Milo seated himself on the pallet. His plum-coloured doublet was stained with food and wine. Threads hung from the points of his crumpled lace collar. Boots, devoid of polish, had a rent in one seam. His taste aimed at fashion rather than fastidiousness and fell lamentably short of both. Milo loved to talk, and here was a victim for whom there was no escape. He could swear in French, in Spanish, in Dutch when English failed him.

"You will not be exchanged," Milo remarked with relish. Ryder went on eating.

"*Madre de Dios*, do you heed what I say?" he demanded.

"No." Ryder prided himself on speaking the truth.

"I tell you that the truce has fallen to pieces. Your damned Parliament will not recognize the conditions drawn up by commissioners selected by both parties in Cheshire. The war is resumed. Here you remain."

"I trust you will feed me more adequately."

"*Mon Dieu!* Do I not give you enough already?"

"Not nearly enough. You had better stuff my unfilled crevices with news as you are niggardly with bread."

"The Welsh soldiers under Colonel Mostyn got out of hand. They have wrecked Bully Brereton's house. A proper job they made of it this time, my lad. No spoil-sports to say us nay."

Ryder laid down his horn spoon and glanced anxiously at the speaker.

"What happened to the lady of the house?"

"Ah! Roused you at last, my bully! As to the wench, she ran away."

"Where to?"

"To the Devil, her master, I have no doubt."

Milo fell to whistling in a manner which irritated Ryder beyond endurance. What could have happened to Verity? He could have caught the wretch by the throat and forced the truth out of him. As he sat glaring at Milo the rich, pleasing notes of a harp floated through the barred window, pleasant as the spring song of a bird. Milo frowned, rose, went out of the cell, shutting the door with a clash which seemed to indicate annoyance. The rasp of the key jarred upon the melody.

Ryder jumped for the bars of his window and drew himself up until he could look into the courtyard outside. A cluster of soldiers lounged against the sunny wall. Conspicuous even amongst their bright-hued doublets was the red cloak of a girl—the harpist he had seen at the bull-baiting. The girl, whose slender wrists and tapering fingers seemed to possess subtle strength, was plucking music from the strings with an ease which seemed magical.

She was bareheaded. Her fair hair drawn back from a smooth brow gave to her features an almost ethereal expression. Her eyes, which she raised expressively to the heavens as she played, seemed the embodiment of innocence. The tune was a Welsh lament. Every vibrant chord plucked at the heartstrings. She closed her eyes, as though in prayer, and Ryder noticed how long were the dark lashes which fringed the pale cheeks.

"Well done, lass!" shouted a burly pikeman as he lurched forward to pat her on the shoulder. His foot touched the harp.

"You great clumsy *ceffyl*,[1] keep your huge hoofs off my harp." Her small hand caught his cheek a resounding smack which set his comrades roaring with delight. She turned on them in a fury. "Cease! It is uncouth you are. You have the minds of swine—and the manners. Am I to waste my talent upon the likes of you? Be silent!"

She stood with both hands upraised until a hush descended on the sheepish soldiery. When stillness reigned she swept a hand through the air as though obliterating the unseemly disturbance. Once again her white fingers wove patterns as they moved. Her face was the face of an angel

[1] Welsh for 'horse'.

as she played "Dafydd y Garreg Wen". When the applause died away she drove the men off as if they had been children.

"Now go. I shall play to you no more. It is heathen you are. I play to please myself, not to please you. Music is wasted on you English *moch*[1]. I will cast no more pearls. Count yourselves fortunate that you have listened to Telynores Elwy."

When the last man had gone the girl walked slowly across the deserted courtyard and looked dreamily at her harp. She began to draw a covering over the instrument. Her deft fingers were gentle, as gentle as those of a mother caressing her child.

Ryder was not aware that he had made a sound. It must have been intuition which made the girl wheel and stare straight at the barred window through which he peered. Her eyes, large and serious, encountered those of Ryder. She continued to stare with an unblinking intensity which he found disconcerting. There was neither surprise nor curiosity in the glance. She seemed to be pondering; weighing him in the balance of her mind.

"It is a prisoner you are?" she asked softly. There was a pleasing lilt about her words. "Pity, too!"

"Who are you?" Ryder was curious despite himself.

She drooped her eyelids modestly. "In Wales there is no greater player on the harp than Telynores Elwy."

"Your name is Telynores?"

"*Diawl*, no. That is my bardic name. Telynores means minstrel. You have heard of my fame?" The question came sharply.

"I fear I have not."

"It is ignorant you are. Would you insult me?"

"You should pity me."

"Because you are a prisoner?"

"Because I have lived until today without hearing you play."

"You said that nice. I will come again tomorrow. For those boors I would not waste my time. They have no souls. Music is the greatest of all the arts and the harp is the queen

[1] Welsh for 'pigs'.

of all instruments. And in all Wales there is no greater harpist than Telynores——" She broke off abruptly. "You may call me Myra," she said with the naivety of a child. "To others I am Telynores Elwy; to you I am Myra Pughe. You look a very proper man. Are you tall?"

She walked nearer. Her gaze grew more intense. "I have seen your face before. Something told me we had encountered before. Now where? Where?" She put a small white fist to her brows.

"Do you recall the merrymaking on the birthday of Mistress——"

"I remember! I remember! It was you who wrestled with the Welsh Black. *Diawl,* what strength! I looked back as I fled." She raised her eyes with an affectation of demureness. "I am glad that you were not slain."

"I escaped with a bruise or two."

"Good! I like a tall, proper man. A woman should be good and clever, like me. A man should be strong and tall and courageous. Tell me, do I not play lovely?"

Ryder began to comprehend that the lady did not weary of praise.

"I have never heard a harp played so beautifully before."

"Maybe you have not heard a harp before?"

"Never," replied the teller of truth.

"Fool!" The girl stamped her foot. "How can you judge? But there, it is not your fault, poor man. I do wrong to be angry, and you a captive, too. I will play again tomorrow. It is comfort you need."

"It is freedom I need." Ryder spoke grimly.

"Freedom!" The girl's eyes followed the flight of a wild duck. "Free as a bird on the wing. Poor man. My heart aches. How can I help?"

"Tell me what happens in Chester. Is the King making it his headquarters?"

"No. He has changed his mind. Since the battle of Edgehill they say he will have Oxford for his abode."

"What else? Have there been any battles fought in Cheshire?"

"Battles! Why do men bother over battles when they could harken to music? It is sinful to fight."

E

"I saw you strike a soldier."

"The fool kicked my harp."

"The King threatens the people's freedom. That is why I strike back."

"Well, if you want news of battles! Sir Thomas Aston led an attack against Sir William Brereton and was worsted. Captain Bridgeman of this place was captured."

"Good news."

"In February the King's men had the better of a skirmish at Tilston Heath."

"And I linger here."

"Patience, big man. Your Brereton's men were victorious at Middlewich. They took Colonel Ellis."

"He who planned the defences of Chester?"

"So I've heard tell. It is little I know about such matters save that a trench is cut from Deeside without The Bars to Deeside by the New Tower. There are drawbridges and gun-mounts, and pitfalls to snare the enemy. So I've heard Milo tell."

"What of Sir William Brereton's house? It was pillaged?"

"Ay! My countrymen despoiled the mouldy rogue. Feather beds sold at twenty shillings apiece. I wish I had purchased one. It would be good to lie warm, wouldn't it, big man?"

"It is more than I have done this winter. Tell me, what happened to the lady who was at the house?"

"What is that to you? It is in love with her you are!"

"Is it needful that you should talk such arrant nonsense?"

She twisted the corner of her red cloak with restless fingers. "I will say nothing about her. Maybe I am jealous. I do not know. You are a proper man."

Ryder's exclamation of exasperation was interrupted by swaggering footsteps. Milo Preen strode into the court-yard.

"Ha, you baggage, you have talked long enough! Waste no sighs on yonder knave."

He picked up her harp.

"Fool! Have a care!" The girl ran after him, anxiety in her face. Ryder slid down to the floor of his cell. He rubbed his cramped fingers. A strange episode, he mused. At least it had broken the day's monotony.

CHAPTER NINE

SOMETHING untoward had happened. Ryder could tell that from the sounds which came down the air—sounds of firing, of trumpets, of drums, of cheers. He was racked with curiosity. Did this indicate a victory for the Royalist forces? Had Sir William Brereton met with defeat? The Parliamentary baronet was confronted by a hard task. The Earl of Derby (no longer Lord Strange) was in Chester, and forces from Lancashire, from Wales and from Shropshire were thronging to serve under him.

Ryder fretted. Every man was needed to swell the ranks of those who fought for freedom. He raised himself to the window and pressed his hot cheeks against the iron bars in an endeavour to look into the tantalizing world outside. It took the voluble Captain Milo to satisfy his curiosity.

King Charles had been pleased to appoint Sir Nicholas Byron as Governor of Chester. The knight, so Milo assured him, had just arrived to take over his new office. With him rode several of his nephews, fighting men all. The Byrons were ardent loyalists. The news made Ryder more restless than ever. He must break out. He must get away from this durance.

"Can you not arrange an exchange?" he demanded.

Milo's smile was sardonic. "For a man of quality, yes."

"How much will you take for allowing me to escape?"

"I am a man of honour," said Milo with dignity. "You have nothing in your pockets, my young spark."

"I have friends who would pay you once I was free."

"No doubt, if they did not forget. How comes it you grow dissatisfied? Is not the company vastly entertaining?"

"You have never been a prisoner of war!" Ryder's tone was bitter.

"'Zounds, you know nothing about the matter. There have been times when the fortune of war was such that not even the sword of Milo Preen could make amends. I remember once, in the United Provinces, I lay nigh twelve months in a cell half the size of this with only rats to bear me company. My wits got me out. Let your wits extract you."

Another day dragged wearily by. Then another. Ryder tested the window bars, tried to scrape away the mortar, but achieved nothing to compensate for the worn skin of his fingers. A pebble struck his cheek. He looked up from his task. Myra Pughe stood in the courtyard. The shadows were beginning to lengthen. Her back was to the fading day. Her cheeks appeared more pallid, her eyes deeper, more innocent.

"I come back to look at you," said the girl in her lilting voice.

"A sorry sight for a woman's eyes."

"I must think otherwise. You would soon get good colour in your cheeks were you out of that rat-hole."

"I know it."

"I could have you out in less than no time."

"Tell me how."

"Ah! That would be saying, now, wouldn't it?"

"I pray you tell me. Imprisonment is driving me mad."

"Secrets have their price."

"Help me attain my freedom and I will pay your price."

The girl lowered her eyes and began to sing to herself. The tune was "Greensleeves".

"Not that tune," he protested, as a vision of Rosea came to his mind.

"It is a pretty tune. Sad, maybe, but I like sad tunes. They are like life. Life is sad."

"A captive knows it. But pray sing on. I have no right to choose your melody. Imprisonment makes me petty, I fear. As you say, it is a pretty tune."

The girl fell silent. "I do not want to sing now you say I may."

"You are capricious."

"I am a woman. You have not found that out, maybe?" Her eyes were upon him. There was something fascinating about the innocent face with the compelling eyes. "I could set you free—if I wished."

"So you say. But will you?"

"At a price."

"I have told you I will pay any price."

"It is not money I desire, it is a husband."

Ryder looked incredulous. "You do not suggest——!"

"If I free you, will you marry me?"

"And exchange one captivity for another! You are mad. You do not know me."

"Mad? I wonder. Maybe. You have stirred me."

"I? I have done nothing."

"You do not need to. It just happens. Love is like that."

A sudden revulsion took hold of Ryder Yale. Who was this creature with the face of an angel who talked glibly of marriage? He turned from the thought of anything so sacred being bartered like a chapman's wares.

"I will stay in prison for ever rather than harbour such a thought."

In his indignation he moved impulsively. His foot slipped and he crashed to the floor. He rose smarting physically as well as spiritually. When next he looked from the window the courtyard was empty.

    *   *   *   *   *

What effect has moonlight on the minds of men? Can moonbeams streaming into a room at night, casting long shadows, stir the emotions? The cell of Ryder Yale was as light as day, or nearly so. It left him wakeful and restless. He lay listening to the beating of his heart, pondering many problems.

A tiny sound, unrecognizable, was sufficient to set his nerves alert. He held his breath as he listened. There was a soft shuffling sound in the corridor outside his door. Slowly, very slowly, a key was inserted in the great lock. There came a click. The metallic sound echoed with astounding clarity. It was sharp; ominous. Surely all the building would hear it? But nothing broke the silence until a hinge creaked as the heavy door began slowly to open. From half-closed eyes Ryder watched the moving shadow. What did it signify? Assassination? Or release? He would soon know.

The door was open now. The visitor was not Milo. It was a small figure which stole stealthily towards his pallet. The moonlight lit up a cloak, a red cloak. The little harpist crept towards him on soundless feet. It was uncanny. Ryder felt like a mouse before a stalking cat. The girl was beside him now, looking down with her wide, intent eyes. From beneath his lowered lids he was conscious of her penetrating stare. His breathing almost stopped, so tense did he feel. She dropped on her knees beside his bed.

"*Cariad*, are you awake?" The whisper held a caress. "Did you know I would come to you, sweetheart?"

Ryder did not move. Her fingers, those slender, expressive fingers which wove magic patterns on the harp-strings, touched his face. They strayed, delicate as the antenna of a butterfly. Though it thrilled him he shrank from the contact.

"Why have you come here?" he demanded, and his voice, though low, was harsh. "How did you get here?"

"Love can always find a way, *cariad*."

"Have done with that word. I command you."

"That fool Milo sleeps like a hog. I put something in the wine. It was not difficult to get the key. I know their ways. Ay, a woman can use her wits when it comes to serving the man she loves."

"It is folly to talk thus. You do not know me."

"Know you? I knew you before you were born, boy *bach*. In another age we were lovers and now we meet again. As soon as I looked into your eyes I knew you were the one for whom I waited. You make me want to compose music. That is the effect you have on me. Your soul speaks to mine. Tell me your name."

"If you knew me in another age how came you to forget it?" His tone was cutting.

"*Cariad*, it is cruel you are—heartless. I have told you I am Myra. You will not tell me your name. It is discourteous you are."

That stabbed deep.

"I am Ryder Yale." His voice was reluctant, sullen.

"Ryder, master of steeds! I hear the notes of your war-song. I shall play it to you some day."

Her fingers cupped themselves about his face. "Marry me, *cariad*, and you shall go free this night."

He could not have acted in the strong light of day, but

moonlight has a witchery of its own. Subtle influences were at work. The burning eyes in the pale face filled him with a fierce resentment; he forgot her womanhood and thought of her only as a temptress. He caught her by her slender throat. He saw her moist lips gasp, but she uttered no cry. He dragged the blanket over her head and knotted it clumsily about her waist. She did not struggle. After flinging her unresisting form across the disordered cot he strode to the door. He paused to gather his boots and coat. Standing in the flagged passage, he could hear stertorous breathing. The night watch snored in drugged slumber. He paused, gazing grimly down on the tattered splendour of the somnolent Milo. There hung the keys. Ryder picked them up. There, too, was Milo's rapier, a fine weapon with a richly chased hilt. Milo lay across the scabbard as though he would protect his treasure even in his drunken sleep. Ryder slid the blade carefully out of the sheath.

With the keys of freedom in one hand and a drawn sword in the other Ryder made his way across the moonlit courtyard. His heart beat fast either with excitement or exultation, or both. Was Myra Pughe suffocated to death in the blanket's folds? He neither knew nor cared. All he knew was that he had a sword in his hand again; that liberty lay beyond one locked door, and of that door he had the key.

CHAPTER TEN

THE woods were tender with the fresh green of spring. When Ryder drew near to Nantwich he paused. From the top of a gentle slope he could see, through a gap in the trees, the curve of the meandering Weaver and beyond it the thatched roofs and chimneys of the town. And towering over all the pinnacles and octagonal tower of the Church of St. Mary—a cathedral in miniature. He had forsaken the roads and took his way across country, for patrols of Royalist horse made highways unsafe.

The twenty miles had tired him, for his muscles were soft from six months' incarceration. He had clambered on to a hayrick to sleep. A few eggs stolen from a hen-coop formed his only sustenance. A strange figure he must have presented, with crumpled clothes and hair and beard shaggy from six months' growth. The only brightness came from the naked rapier he carried—and this was not his.

As' he reached the edge of the wood he sat deliberately upon a log. Now that he was so close to Nantwich he paused. Lord Grandison's raid had been of short duration and the Parliamentarian stronghold speedily returned to Brereton's hands. It was not a matter of safety which caused Ryder to hesitate. At first he could not account for his reluctance. He had pictured himself hurrying breathlessly in his eagerness to rejoin his companions. It was borne upon him, as he sat meditating, that he had been solitary for· so long that a sudden encounter with crowds of people would prove an ordeal.

It occurred to him, too, that he was a different person from the young cornet who had ridden Londonwards as one of Sir William's escort. In a few months he had learned many things, less from soldiering than from life. He knew what it was like to be wounded, to· be captured, to be imprisoned. He had seen the King. He had tasted jealousy and found the draught bitter to the palate. He had learned how kind a woman could be. He had learned how disturbing a lovely woman can be. He wondered what had happened to Verity. He wondered whether he would ever see Rosea again. He wondered whether he was responsible for the death of the little harpist, that strange elf-like girl who hungered for music—and men.

It was all bewildering and complicated. Perhaps, after all, it would be comforting to resume the orderly existence of a cornet in a troop of horse where one had hard work and routine and risk, but not problems such as these.

He stood up, stretching himself leisurely. He could see on his left the stately chimneys of Dorfold Hall and behind it, above the elms, the crenellated tower of Acton Church. Before him lay the town, with its bridge and its mill. Why, he wondered, had Sir William selected this unprotected market town as his headquarters? The river was neither wide nor deep, an impediment rather than an obstacle in the event of an assault.

Yet the site was well selected. It must have been, for the

town had been there in Roman times, a convenient stopping-place on the route from Chester to London. In a direct line to the west, some sixteen miles away, was the famous bridge at Holt which led to the land of Wales. The road which dipped before him bore the old, old name of Welsh Row, reminder of the days when Welshmen drove their ponies along it for sale in the Nantwich fairs and returned home with panniers laden with salt. He left the meadow and tramped the road. He passed by the high red-brick wall which surrounded Townsend House, the tall and stately mansion of a Cavalier Wilbraham. Few persons glanced at him as he passed by. In peaceful times he would have attracted attention, but already men and women, and children, too, were becoming accustomed to untoward events. Their chief concern was personal safety. Appearance or convention had ceased to count greatly. Nantwich itself bore testimony to the changing times. There was bustle, there was activity. Trees had been felled, meadows robbed of their turf.

As Ryder neared the Welsh Bridge he realized that Nantwich was a town at war. There was a barricade at the bridge. A sentinel with a carbine paced the roadway in front. Several musketeers with matches burning sauntered from the gateway and paused to watch the approach of the bareheaded, unkempt man with a drawn sword. Ryder halted at the challenge and awaited recognition.

Once across the bridge he found fresh evidence of Nantwich's resolution. A chain was drawn across the road and behind this a rampart of tumbrels and waggons.

A glow of warm sentiment surged through Ryder as he looked about him. It was like a home-coming. There was a friendliness about the streets. Most houses were Elizabethan, with carved gables and half-timbered fronts which gave that pied effect so pleasing to the eye. Old Nantwich had been practically wiped out by fire in December 1583. Some of the oak beams testified that Queen Elizabeth had assisted in the restoration by a gift of timber from the great forest of Delamere.

The sight of the Crown Inn made Ryder ravenous for food. He had no money, but they fed him first and trusted that payment would follow.

Sir William Brereton, with an escort of horse under the direction of Lieutenant Mark Trueman, had ridden to Middlewich and would not return until evening. Ryder went out into the streets again. Passing down the Swine Market, he came upon a scene of activity.

A great mud wall, starting from the bridge, was being built to protect the town. Men, women, and boys laboured between the town and the river. Almost before he realized it Ryder had stripped off his coat. Picking up a maul, he began to drive stakes. His presence attracted no attention. Everyone was expected to work; the safety of all depended on the speedy completion of the fortifications. The earth was churned to mud and the men who plied mattocks and spades were mired to the waist. They had dug a trench four feet deep and six feet wide. Two double rows of stakes were driven with a two-foot space between them. Within this were packed clods of earth. Ryder could see great areas of turf being stripped from the adjoining fields. These sods were carried to the wall-builders, sometimes in barrows, more often on wooden stretchers. The space between the sod ramparts was filled with clay in which mortar was sprinkled. Water from the river was flung on to this, a task in which the town boys gloried. Never before had youth been allowed to get so dirty without admonition.

The walls, when completed, were ten feet thick. It was intended to make them twelve or fourteen feet high.

When the workmen paused for their mid-day meal Ryder made a detour of the ramparts. They stretched in a formidable line. Ruins of brickwork showed where house or cottage had been demolished to make this possible. Only when a main road was reached was there a gap in the wall, and here stout barricades were built. There was one across Hospital Street, which took its name from the medieval hospital of St. Nicholas. Another was at Pillory Lane. He paused to gaze at the pied façade of the Church Mansion and then walked slowly up Hospital Street.

The afternoon he spent at a barber's and emerged with greater self-respect. Mark Trueman, having learnt of his arrival, came seeking him, rejoicing at his escape.

"Our time has been spent profitably," Mark assured him,

"and though I have had less varied experiences, the troop has been so actively employed that there is not a man of us who does not consider himself a veteran campaigner by this time."

"I heard, while I was a prisoner, that Sir William had beaten off Sir Thomas Aston's attack."

"Sir William was coming towards Nantwich to relieve the town, when Aston with some five hundred horse lay in wait and met us near the end of Hospital Street. We joined battle at four o'clock and fought doubtfully until it was too dark to see. Sir William had brought with him a case of drakes, which he discharged and so affrighted the King's party that they scattered and were routed completely. We took Captain Cholmondeley and Captain Bridgeman with about a hundred soldiers and plenty of arms, cloakbags and pillage. We entered the town at eight o'clock amid great rejoicings and have held it ever since."

The narration filled Ryder with unrest. He felt that he had fallen behind his comrades. One of his first requests was that Mark Trueman would seek out his buff-coat and his head-piece and the rest of his harness, and arrange for him to have his horses again. There were patrols each day, said Mark, and raids whenever an opportunity presented itself.

Sir William Brereton had taken up his headquarters at the Lamb Inn, which lay close alongside the yard of the church. Ryder went in search of the Commander-in-Chief. He found Sir William looking leaner and older after a winter's campaigning. He had, in defeating Sir Thomas Aston at Nantwich, and by defeating him yet a second time at Middlewich, not merely discredited the luckless Sir Thomas, but won for himself a reputation of being one of the rising commanders on the Parliamentary side.

Ryder reported to the General, who listened to his story without comment.

"I received no word of you and feared you were slain," said Sir William. "Your presence here is welcome as there is a dearth of officers. Have you eaten? There is no shortage of food yet; eat while you may."

"I have taken food with Lieutenant Trueman, sir. I fear

there is little I can tell you about affairs in Chester save that Sir Nicholas Byron has recently been appointed governor by the King. I regret, sir, that I have been of such slight service. I trust you will find me of greater use in the saddle."

"You shall labour for the cause soon enough, Yale. The men are overworked, the horses more so. The malignants grow more daring. We are continually repulsing raids by parties of their horse who come down the Tarporley Road or up from Whitchurch. So far they have not made an assault in force. I shall rest easier when the outworks are completed."

"After Chester's massive stone wall, sir, Nantwich appears but ill provided for."

"That is where you err, Yale. I learnt in the Low Countries how effective a mud wall can prove. Your stone walls crumble before bombardment. There will be more wounds caused by flying splinters than by roundshot. Balls fired into our mud walls will be embedded without causing harm. They will neither shatter nor penetrate the defences. It is not safe to judge by appearance."

Sir William leaned back. He was in a genial mood, pleased to relax after a heavy day in the saddle. "You may not have heard I have had the honour of being proclaimed a traitor by the King. So now I fight with a price on my head. To amend this the Lords and Commons assembled have issued a declaration for my protection. I trust that the blessing of God and the height of our mud wall will render the first void and the second needless."

"I am impatient to rejoin my troop, sir. But first, might I ask whether Mistress Verity is safe?"

"You knew St. Mary's Nunnery was pillaged?"

"I was present on the first occasion, sir, and my gaoler told me of the second raid. He may have lied."

"He could not make matters worse by lying. The rogues have carried off my two best horses with saddles and pistols, and have taken six hundred sheep and all my remaining horses. All my goods are gone. The malignants have matters to their liking at present, Yale, but the tide will turn. If God be for us, who can be against us?"

"But Mistress Verity, sir, is she safe?"

"It is not for you to question me, but rather for me to question you."

"I ask your pardon, sir, that my natural anxiety for her safety should have caused me to forget."

"To set your mind at ease I will say she is alive and well. Report to Lieutenant Trueman."

Ryder found Mark awaiting him at the inn door. The lieutenant had a buff-coat of his own now, and looked a seasoned soldier. Ryder's first request was to be allowed to see his horse. It was good to be in the stables again, to smell the warm blending of horseflesh, leather and hay. He next got into buff-coat and boots.

"I trust I shall never doff these until peace comes to our unhappy land, Mark," he observed, "for of a truth I am little cut out for such missions as that on which I was sent."

"I envied you not. Were you occasioned much uneasiness?"

"I was, though not from the enemy. But let us climb the tower of the church. I would see the lie of the land."

As they crossed from the stable-yard Ryder paused to glance up at the towering red sandstone church, which dominated the town like an ecclesiastical fortress. He never wearied of admiring the mullioned windows, the beautifully carved faces at the bases of the hood moulds, or the ornate pinnacles. The skill of the masons filled him with awe. How did they manage to merge a square tower into an octagonal top?

There was little breath left for talking as the two climbed the steep stair to the leads. From the battlemented summit they looked down upon the gabled roofs, the twisting thoroughfares; the mud walls on which the townsmen toiled, the river, the bridge and the fields. Beyond the broad woods which sometimes sloped to the river's edge Ryder could discern the dignified outline of Acton Parish Church on a rise a mile or so away.

"They say," observed Mark, "that the base of Acton Church is on a level with the top of this tower."

Ryder took deep breaths. It was good to breathe free air after imprisonment.

"No," he said abstractedly, as though resuming an interrupted conversation, "it was not the enemy which occasioned me uneasiness, Mark. It was women."

"Women!" Trueman's tone indicated his amazement. "You talk like a Cavalier. What had you to do with women?"

"Too much for my liking; yet it was not of my seeking. First Sir William himself sets me off with Mistress Verity, as you know. I found her a good comrade, demure but courageous, zealous, yet seemly in her conduct. Then I was the means whereby a girl was saved from being gored by a bull at a baiting. She was of gentle birth and was strong for the King, yet she and her companion showed me much kindness. Though her manner of speech and of living was strange to me I believe she was sincere of heart. It was she who pointed out a way of escape, but during the attempt I was shot in the leg from the walls and flung into prison."

"A strange encounter."

"She was so beautiful, Mark, that almost I feared lest she should be a menace to my soul."

"Then think not of her, friend. The very doubt in your mind should be of itself a warning."

"As if I had not enough to harass me, a young Welsh girl came playing the harp beneath my window. Truly she played with such ease and dexterity that I still marvel at the wonder of it. She played like an angel and had a face like an angel, yet for some reason she took a fancy to my luckless self. It was she who drugged the guards so that I could escape, claiming as her price—guess?"

"How can I guess?"

"That I should marry her."

"The Lord protect us! And your answer?"

"Was to bind a blanket over her head. She may be dead for aught I know."

"It is well you escaped. You will find life simpler here in Nantwich. We provide no such diversions in this godly place."

"One other thing troubles me. This." Ryder held up the unsheathed rapier he carried.

"I have noticed it. A true Cavalier blade."

"I took it from my gaoler while he slept. I feel like a thief and a robber."

"Regard it as the lawful spoils of war. Is it not meet that we should smite the Philistines?"

"Had I beaten him in open combat I should have kept it with pride. To filch it while he slept is a scurvy trick. I beg of you ask Sir William to return it to the man—Milo Preen is his name—when next a flag of truce goes to Chester. My broadsword is good enough for me."

"Why not ask Sir William yourself?"

"I have offended the General with my importunity. I inquired what had happened to Mistress Verity, and when he did not reply I asked him again."

"She came out from Chester after the Nunnery was pillaged and is working for Sir William elsewhere." Mark paused in his explanation, and peered earnestly towards Acton Church. "See! Did you catch a flash of steel? There, by the gap in the hedge."

"You are right, Mark! There are horsemen coming this way. A score or more Cavaliers!"

Trueman did not pause, but went thundering down the stairs at breakneck pace. He grabbed the bell-rope and sent forth a warning clanging.

Men were assembling along the Churchyard Side when Ryder came from the tower door. Troopers were leading their horses from the stables and tightening girths. He ran towards the Lamb yard; a groom had already saddled his charger. All about him he could hear soldiers assembling. It was new to him: to them it represented a daily occurrence. Mark Trueman at the head of a half-troop was trotting towards the Welsh Bridge barrier. The guard there were alert, watching the road with muskets poised and matches burning. Two by two the horsemen passed over the bridge. Ryder had not waited to put on his breast-and-back. He overtook the rear files as they crossed the bridge.

"The malignants have taken Dorfold Hall!" yelled a man who came running down Welsh Row towards them.

The trumpeter raised his instrument to his lips. At its brazen notes the half-troop broke into a canter, drawing their pistols as they rode. And behind them, with Milo Preen's rapier in his hand, rode Ryder Yale, glad to have finished with spying, eager to come to blows in the open field.

CHAPTER ELEVEN

WHAT impressed Ryder most was the businesslike manner in which the troopers went into action. They seemed neither excited nor apprehensive. It was borne upon him that while he lay in prison these men had become accustomed to the trade of war. They had grown used to daily sorties. The troopers with whom he rode were not men of the London train-bands, but local militiamen with homes in Nantwich. They had a stake in the community, a personal interest in driving back enemies who threatened their homes. The struggle went deeper than an issue between the King and the Parliament; it was a fight for self-preservation. There was a rough uniformity about their garb. Though head-pieces and swords differed in pattern, all men wore buff-coats and each was distinguished by a band of orange-tawny—the colour adopted by the Parliament.

As they neared a curve of the road Ryder could discern the figures of sentinels posted on the tower of Acton Church. They fired their muskets and shouted as the advance of the Parliamentarians was observed. From the gates of Dorfold Hall a Cavalier on a graceful grey mount rode into the roadway. He turned in his saddle and signalled towards the house, whereupon a number of horsemen walked their horses into the roadway and took up position. Each man drew his holster pistols and, at a signal from the leader, opened an irregular fire on the men of Nantwich.

Ryder saw a horse stumble, heard a cry or two from men wounded as they rode, but the fusillade had singularly little effect. The leader flung his pistols into the roadway, drew his rapier and spurred recklessly towards the Parliamentarians. The men of the King's party followed suit, dividing into two lines as they rode. They swept forward, gay of doublet, a gallant wave of tossing mane and feather.

Their furious gallop was in keeping with their gay and reckless appearance. The double lines of grim, silent Roundheads drew apart to make way for the charging Cavaliers. Rapier and broadsword rasped and clashed as with thrust and slash the opposing columns swept past each other. Though the Cavaliers had the advantage of a slight incline and a swifter pace, the broadswords of the Parliamentarians took a heavier toll than the slender rapiers, which were frequently turned by the thick buff-coats they encountered. It was fast and furious work.

To Ryder, watching from the rear, it seemed that each side would be exterminated. Yet there was surprisingly little serious damage done. Most of the swords turned slightly in the fury of the cut so that a glancing and not a direct blow was sustained. It was the rapier points which caused the most serious hurt. When these got under a guard more than one rider reeled in his saddle. Ryder, clear of the press, found the issue less confused than those who bore the heat and burden of it all. The Cavaliers were somewhat spent by the time they reached him and he fought coolly and with deliberation, taking heavy toll. His position was to his advantage, but to counteract this he was alone, and so was liable to be attacked from both sides at once.

The last Cavalier to break through was sagging in his saddle. Blood streamed from his uncovered head and stained the blue silk of his doublet. Ryder, blade poised, experienced a pang of pity. He stayed his hand, he knew not why. Then he thanked God he had done so. The pale face of the man who clung to his horse's mane was familiar. It was Royle Wilding! Ryder experienced the reaction of a man who has narrowly escaped committing a murder. The last horseman passed by. The charge was over. The Parliamentary horse were reining in. Mark Trueman's voice was raised, calling upon his men to rally. They formed ranks and sat their panting horses. A few who were wounded began to bandage their cuts. Ryder had time to look about him. There were several figures stretched in the roadway, some writhing, some still. Riderless horses strayed along the verge, or trotted away from the scene of the combat. Shouts of encouragement sounded from Welsh Row. Pikemen were hurrying from the town, advancing at a clumsy run, their sixteen-foot pikes advanced.

F

The leader of the Cavaliers put his grey to the roadside hedge and cantered across the meadow. His men streamed after him. Mark Trueman watched them anxiously, wondering whether they would return, but they had had enough.

Trueman sent a corporal to watch the retreat of the raiders while he inspected the men who had fought. He totalled the result of the clash as methodically as a banker would add up his accounts. One Nantwich man was slain, seven wounded—three seriously. Two horses were missing. The King's party had lost three killed, five wounded. Four horses were captured. When the pikemen came up he passed the wounded over to their care and led his half-troop on to Acton Church. They paused at the road junction. Trueman summoned Ryder to his side.

"Ride and see whether Corporal Garnett has determined what the malignants intend to do. If there is any sign of their rallying send him back to me with word of their movements. I do not think they will return. They are few and the alarm is given. I must search the church and the Star Tavern."

As Ryder trotted along the Tarporley Road he was aware that he trembled. Excitement, he presumed. He was unhurt, though his right palm still smarted from the fierceness of his grip. He glanced at Milo's rapier. It was ironical that the first blow he had struck at the King's party should be with a Cavalier's weapon. He would be glad when he could return it to its owner. Ryder was not given to borrowing—he asked for nothing that was not his own.

As he mused, his eyes roved the countryside. There was no sign of Corporal Garnett. Ryder rose in his stirrups to obtain a clearer view. In a distant field he saw a horse move. It was not Garnett's mount. The corporal, he recollected, rode a black, and this was a light chestnut with a white foreleg. It seemed familiar. It must be one of the riderless steeds which had strayed after the charge. He could not resist the impulse to secure so valuable a mount.

The chestnut pricked up its ears at his approach, stared, then walked towards him with trailing reins and swinging stirrups. A glance told Ryder that this was a Cavalier's horse, a lovely animal, sleek from grooming. It had an expensive saddle. Ryder dismounted and coaxed the stray until he secured the reins. As he patted the smooth neck his mind caught the image of a rider clinging to the mane. It was Royle Wilding's mount. He rode a light chestnut.

Somewhere between that spot and Dorfold Hall the chestnut's owner must be lying wounded—or dead. Ryder tethered both animals and followed the track of the riderless horse across the trampled grass until, near a hawthorn hedge, he saw a patch of colour, a huddled heap of blue. He quickened his pace. Royle Wilding lay with eyes closed, still as a sleeping child. His dark face was no longer reckless. His immaculate attire was stained with his blood.

Ryder was moved to compassion. Across the shapely head was a wound, half bruise, half cut, where a broadsword's edge had turned, stunning where it meant to slay. Ryder looked about him. At the margin of the wood was a cottage, a one-storey structure with an outhouse or two. He dropped on to one knee and hoisted the unconscious man across one of his shoulders. Wilding was heavy. Ryder was conscious of his muscles having been weakened by inactivity; but he staggered towards the shelter. An elderly woman opened the door reluctantly. At Ryder's request for succour she shook her head. She did not want a dying man in her house. A soldier had been brought to her the week before and he had died.

"This man," said Ryder, "will not die. He is rich. He will pay you well."

The woman mumbled, but stood aside. The cottage was dim. Ryder had to bend his head as he groped towards a cupboard-bed built into the thick wall. He loosened Wilding's clothing, made him comfortable, found water in an earthenware jar and sponged his face. Prompted by an impulse for which he could not account, Ryder thrust Milo's rapier into the empty scabbard which was suspended from Wilding's baldrick. Here was a way of returning the weapon to its owner.

"You have a stable?" he demanded of the woman.

"A lean-to, of sorts."

"I will put this gentleman's horse there."

As Ryder walked to fetch the chestnut he felt uncertain about his plans. All he knew was that he did not mean that

Royle Wilding should be taken prisoner if he could help it. Was it, he asked himself, for Rosea's sake? Certainly her words were ringing in his ears, the words she had uttered when she helped him to escape—one man more or less would have little effect on the total.

When he returned to the house he found the woman at the door. "'E's woke up."

As Ryder's eyes became accustomed to the gloom he saw that the man on the bed had moved, that his eyes were open, eyes which looked vacant, bewildered.

"Do not be alarmed. I am Ryder Yale. You remember me?"

The mouth twitched in an attempted smile. "The bull-baiter. How came you here? Where in Satan's name am I? It's as gloomy as the grave."

"In a cottage near Acton Church. Do you remember the charge?"

"Ah, the charge! I was enjoying it prodigiously when some inconsiderate fool gave me the devil of a crack. Lord, four bottles could never produce such a head!"

"The blade turned—or you would not be here."

"Blades usually do. Use the point, Mr. Bull-Baiter. It is neater and more effective. So I am your prisoner! A demmed unlucky start along the road to glory."

"I do not see why you should become a prisoner!"

"I see every reason. I played for a stake and lost. I must pay. I shall not whine."

"You believe in paying debts?"

"When I can afford to."

"I have a debt to pay. When I wanted to get out of Chester, Mistress Rosea showed me a way——"

"The devil she did!"

"Did she not tell you?"

"Not a word. The minx! Well . . ."

"Perhaps I ought not to have mentioned it."

"Lord, man, I'll not betray you! What happened?"

"I was shot in the leg and taken."

"You mean—you've been held a prisoner in Chester?"

"Until two days ago. Did you not know?"

"Damn me if I did. Had I heard a whisper I should at

MASTER OF THE FIELD

least have brought you a pack of cards. Ro remarked more than once that she wondered what had become of you."

"I would not have you endure what I was called upon to suffer. I have put your horse in the shed. By tomorrow you may be well enough to sit in the saddle. Or perhaps the next day."

"You are a stout fellow, Yale. I'll not forget."

"Then do me a favour."

"A thousand."

"There's a rapier in your scabbard. It belongs to my late custodian—Milo Preen by name. I borrowed it while he slumbered. Pray return it to him and say I hope to take it from him by honest methods some day."

"You must try to overcome this honesty of yours, Yale. It's the devil's own handicap to success in life. So—I've lost my good blade, eh? Damn my luck. Yale—do *me* a favour. Return me my sword if it comes your way. I'll pay handsomely to get it back. It has our crest—a wyvern—on the pommel."

Ryder rose to his feet. "I must go. I am on duty. Pray give my felicitations to Mistress Rosea. I trust you find your way back to Chester."

At the barricade at Welsh Bridge Mark Trueman was awaiting him.

"What happened to you? I began to wonder if you were captured."

"I could not find Garnett."

"He returned by another way The malignants have ridden off. You've lost your sword?"

"It was not mine."

"Better collect your own. And your breast-and-back. There may be another alarm soon."

Ryder armed himself, visited the paymaster, arranged for a bedchamber at the Lamb, and went in search of Mark Trueman. He did not find the lieutenant, but he encountered Corporal Garnett, who was making a list of weapons picked up at the scene of the encounter.

"What happens to these, Corporal?"

"They go into the common store, sir, to be drawn upon if needed."

Ryder was examining the rapiers. He found one which bore a wyvern. Unobtrusively he placed a sovereign on the table. "A handsome weapon this, Garnett. Do you think I might retain it as a memento?"

"Well, sir, it is not strictly in order, but better it should go to one who prizes it than to one who don't. And you have no sword, sir, as I see. I should say you have earned it after today's piece of work."

Ryder took his souvenir back to the Lamb. He felt singularly pleased that he had secured it. That was the best of acting promptly. It would be pleasurable to restore Wilding his sword—a gesture which Rosea would be bound to appreciate.

A servant-maid came to him as he entered the inn to say that a lady waited for him in the parlour.

He found Verity seated there—Verity better dressed but still garbed in grey simplicity. For a moment he could not speak. Slowly he placed the rapier on the table. Verity's face was flushed. He took her hand in his.

"I wondered whether we should meet again," he said.

"I hoped that it would be so. You just vanished! Your friends could find no trace of you."

"I was taken."

"Sir William has just informed me. I waited to welcome you back."

"Have I kept you waiting? I have been active to-day."

"So I understand. Mark told me you were in this morning's skirmish and carried yourself well. Is that a weapon you captured?"

"Hardly captured. I had it after all was over. It is strange you should notice it."

"Why strange?"

"It belongs to a certain malignant who is not wholly unknown to you—Royle Wilding by name."

"He was not slain?" The colour ebbed from her cheeks.

"Only wounded. Can you keep a secret, Verity?"

"Would Sir William trust me if I could not?"

"I came across Wilding and carried him to a cottage."

"Where?"

"It lies at the edge of a wood, half a league beyond the church."

"Was there anyone to attend to him?"

"An old crone."

"Oh, Ryder, he should be properly nursed. He may die of neglect or fever."

"It is a risk he must run. He is a soldier—and an enemy."

"Yet you befriended him. You are not as hard of heart as you pretend, Ryder. I am glad. We ought not to make this warfare more terrible than it need be. And—this is his sword."

She took it daintily in both hands and examined the slender blade and richly chased hilt. "How strange that so much skill and beauty should go into making something which is intended to destroy life. It's very elegance is a mockery. All the same, it fascinates. Ryder, I do not ask a favour often. May I have this, please?"

"It is not mine to give. I have promised to return it to its owner some day. He values it."

"Let me take care of it until that day."

"A strange souvenir, Verity!"

"There is something human about it, something which makes it more than a mere trophy of your prowess in action. It may fall into heedless hands and get lost. It will be safer in my keeping. You will grant my request?"

"I don't think I should be justified." Ryder hesitated.

"Please, Ryder!"

She looked at him so appealingly that he could not resist.

"Well—have it if you wish," he said. "Why should I refuse you, though the request seems strange? Only—you must return it to him some day. I gave him my word."

"He shall have it, Ryder. I solemnly promise."

She stood there, balancing the dainty blade across her fingers. Her eyes gazed at the rich chasing, but her thoughts seemed far away. Ryder decided that she looked prettier than he had ever noticed before. Such is the subtle magic of a sword.

CHAPTER TWELVE

RYDER YALE was constantly in the saddle.

He was allowed two horses and he had need of both. He was worked until he was weary, but not too weary to think about Verity. As he rode back after a heavy day's scouting he looked forward to seeing her friendly face again. But she was not to be found. The following day he headed a dozen troopers who acted as escort to a convoy of food, for it was Sir William's policy to husband foodstuffs for man and beast. Again he went in search of Verity. No one knew where she was.

Ryder felt mildly irritated. He could not tell why. It might have been that his long imprisonment had awakened in him a hunger for company. It might have been that she appeared more attractive now. Never had he seen her so comely as the time when she gazed at Wilding's rapier; her eyes held a look he had never before beheld. Of course she could not compare with Rosea, but already Rosea's picture was growing dim in his mind. Rosea seemed like a dream; a beautiful dream, but none the less a dream; whereas Verity was flesh and blood; a good comrade; a woman he could trust; a woman he could respect; a woman he could understand! Or could he understand her? At first he thought he understood her perfectly, but of late he was not quite so sure. All the same it would have pleased him to talk to her when the day's work was ended.

They were busy days! By the end of April Sir William was master of the field in Cheshire. So Prince Rupert was informed by Lord Capel, who was appointed the King's Lieutenant-General for the district in the hope that he might repair the harm occasioned by the luckless Sir Thomas Aston. The mud walls of Nantwich were completed. Sir William had brought in two cannon in addition to his drakes. His cavalry were now increased to five troops. Ryder had plenty to keep him active. It was some days before he found Verity. As he stretched his legs at the close of a wearisome day he saw her trim figure coming, basket in hand, up the road from the Welsh Bridge. He walked, almost eagerly, to meet her.

"Let me carry your basket for you?" he proffered.

"Thank you, no. It is empty. I can manage. Indeed, Ryder, I have grown so accustomed to looking after myself that it would worry me to depend on others."

"So you no longer require a friend to help you?"

"I did not say that."

"Almost it appeared that you implied it. It may be my imagination, but I thought you were not pleased to see me. Verity, you seem different."

She resented the mere suggestion.

"What nonsense you talk! There will never be a time when I shall not be glad to see you. Nor shall I be too proud to accept your assistance should I be in need of it."

With that he had to be content. There was no reason to doubt her words or her sincerity. Sometimes he found himself consumed with curiosity. He wondered where she spent her time, the nature of the work she performed for Sir William. Verity appeared to leave the town or enter it as she chose.

"You look troubled, Ryder. Is anything amiss?"

"No. I know of nothing." Then he fell silent again. When Verity reached her lodging she entered. For the first time Ryder went into the room where she stayed. It was plainly furnished, neat as Verity. The woodwork shone with polishing. A bowl of flowers was on the table.

"I am not troubled," he repeated as he sat down. "There is nothing on my mind, and yet I am conscious of a feeling of depression as if I bore an invisible load."

"You may be overtired. You cannot yet have thrown off the effects of your long imprisonment."

"No, this weariness is a thing of the spirit. I am consumed with restlessness. I would be seeking something and yet I know not what I seek."

"I think it is the lot of the human heart to be restless. We are forever desiring, yearning, longing for something to satisfy a craving which refuses to be satisfied."

"You, surely, cannot experience it; you, who are so calm?"

"Indeed I do, Ryder. I think all human beings do at one time or another, in one form or another. Some seek to satisfy it with one thing; others with something different. Some desire peace, some pleasure."

Ryder sat staring at the ceiling, his thoughts far away. They were in Chester. He had forgotten Verity. His mind retained a vision of Rosea's dark eyes. Idly his gaze followed the carving on one of the beams. Letters quaintly fashioned by some long-dead hand assumed shape—and significance. The message cut in the wood was like a friendly voice from the past. This is what he read:

A BEWTIFUL FACE IS A DUMBE PRAIS
FAIRE WOMEN BE DAUNGEROUS MARKES FOR
*   YONG MENS EYES*
CHOOSE NOT THY WIFE BY HIR BEWTY BUT
*   BY HIR HONESTY.*[1]

Long he stared, thinking of Rosea, until he became aware of Verity's eyes fixed upon him. He coloured and smiled.

"I wonder how that came to be written." He tried to speak lightly.

"I have wondered that. Great is the power of the written word. Was he who carved those lines great-hearted—or embittered? We shall never know. But he, being dead, yet speaketh."

"When I was in Chester," said Ryder slowly, "I met a woman who was so beautiful that I had not thought it possible for such to be created."

"And you desired to have her for your wife?" Verity's eyes were averted.

"No!" Ryder spoke with a vehemence which surprised him. "She was of the King's party—and not for the likes of me."

"Then you had best not let your mind dwell upon her beauty," said Verity gently. "No good can come of desiring what you cannot have."

"Wise words!" quoth Ryder as he got to his feet. All the same he thought of Rosea as he walked to his billet. He tried to put her from his mind, but the harder he tried to forget, the

[1] From a beam preserved in Nantwich Public Library. Spelling slightly altered.

more he remembered. It was when he was active with his troop of horse that he ceased to recollect. Unless there was a night raid he usually called at Verity's lodgings when the day's work was over. If she was out he was conscious of a feeling of disappointment. He enjoyed his talks with Verity; they reminded him of the early days spent in Chester before the conflict had taken shape.

Yet she did not seem quite the same Verity he used to know. Ever since the Royalists had raided Dorfold Hall to punish the owner, Roger Wilbraham, for his leanings towards the Parliament, Verity had become less communicative. She would sit, hands folded in her lap, staring into space. Ryder could see she was preoccupied.

"Do you wonder how you can get back to Chester?" he asked one day.

Verity gave a start of surprise. "Why, yes. You might have read my thoughts."

"Is it necessary for you to go? There is grave risk now."

"It is necessary, Ryder," she said quietly.

"Surely Sir William could get another. It is no task for a woman."

"I have told you before, Ryder, that a woman is less liable to arouse suspicion than a man. Do not dissuade me. I intend to return."

"When?"

"I do not know. It requires careful devising. Neither side shows sign of weakening. This war may drag on . . . and on. . . ."

"You have no plan, then?"

"Plan? Oh, you mean about returning to Chester. No, no plan. I—I try to discern a plan in life, a pattern, but at present I am only aware that I see through a glass darkly. Instead of plan I see chaos."

"We must walk by faith," said Ryder piously.

"It is the same hard road we have to tread whether we walk by faith or not," said Verity almost impatiently. "If only life were not so confused! What is faith? A word. An expression. A straw to which a drowning person clings."

"Faith is one of the great truths of life. Remember, Paul placed it first—'faith, hope, love, these three'——"

"Go on!" Verity turned to him almost fiercely. "Finish what you were saying. 'And the greatest of these is love.' It was then, is now, and ever shall be."

"Verity!" Ryder was amazed. "This is not like you!"

"No, I am not myself today. Forgive me." She hurried from the room.

As Ryder walked more leisurely towards the door a gleam of steel caught his eye. It was the rapier which belonged to Royle Wilding. The sword was free from dust, bright from constant polishing.

Ryder went in search of Mark Trueman. He felt he needed a man's company. Not for the first time he decided he did not understand women. Hitherto he had liked Verity's company because she was so easy to understand. Now she had, without any reason that he could discover, become incomprehensible.

"I was about to send for you," observed Mark, looking up from the cuirass strap which he was buckling. "We go out again."

Ryder walked towards his harness. It had been like this for days. No rest—scouting parties, raids, sorties, responses to appeals for assistance.

It seemed incongruous to find the lovely halls and manors with which Cheshire's fair countryside was endowed turned into fortified posts. Already church walls were pitted with bullet-holes, or the stained-glass windows of ancestral halls shattered by firing. The stoutly built dwellings with their high garden walls and extensive outbuildings were well fitted to withstand an attack by small parties. Their walls offered ample protection from carbine or musket-fire. As for cannon, it was so difficult to secure these, and when secured so difficult to move them, that it was only when some operation of magnitude was contemplated they had to be contended with.

The troopers set out along the road to Whitchurch.

Mark Trueman was in a sombre mood. Sir Richard Wilbraham, arrested the previous September by order of the King, had died in prison at Shrewsbury. His body was to be brought for burial at Acton Church. Sir Richard was a power in the county and a pillar of the Parliamentary structure.

And now word came that Captain Massey's house was raided by Lord Capel's men from Whitchurch.

"They have driven off three score cattle and taken all his household goods," said Mark. The raiders had vanished when the Parliamentary party arrived. There was nothing for it but to return to Nantwich empty-handed. It became obvious that with the advent of Lord Capel the tide was turning in favour of the King's party. Sir William Brereton would have to strive harder if he meant to remain master of the field.

It marked the start of a new life in Nantwich. Citizens grew accustomed to the sound of the church bells being rung backwards—the recognized signal if an enemy force was seen approaching. The spacious gardens of the larger houses were turned into enclosures for horses and cattle. Here the animals were driven at the first sign of the approach of an enemy force. Old wells were reopened to ensure a plentiful supply of water. Barns were stocked with food and fodder. Trenches were dug within the town itself lest the walls should be carried. A deep trench encircled the Church of St. Mary's —Nantwich's last line of defence.

One evening as Ryder was about to mount the steps which led to the ramparts, he felt a touch on his arm. Verity was at his side.

"I was about to take over duty on the walls," he apologized.

"I will join you, if it be permitted. I cannot disguise from you, Ryder, that I am cast down in spirit. Do you remember that once you told me that you were restless and could not ascertain the cause?"

"I remember well. Has anything upset you?"

"No, and I am not given to melancholy. I feel Sir Richard Wilbraham's death. He was, I consider, a martyr to the cause as much as any soldier who gave his life on the field of battle. There is all the more cause why I should return to Chester."

"Is it safe there?"

"Is it safe anywhere, Ryder? I would sooner be up and doing than hide in a burrow like a frightened rabbit. Tell me, we are good friends, Ryder?"

"Good friends? Of course. I value your friendship more than mere words can tell. Why do you ask?"

"My mood, perhaps. I value your friendship too, Ryder. I do not make friends easily. Once I care I care for all time."

"I shall care for you always, Verity."

"Whatever happens?"

"Of course. A man cannot tell himself to stop caring, like giving orders to a trooper. You talk strangely tonight, Verity. Never have I known you in such a mood. What is it?"

"I scarce know. I am restless. A premonition perhaps. Thank you for tolerating me in this strange humour." She accorded him a sad smile as she turned away. "God keep you, Ryder. We shall be friends—always?"

"Always."

It was growing dark now. The stars were out. Some of them were reflected in a curve of the Weaver. Ryder, a solitary figure pacing the ramparts, was aware of a faint mist rising from the banks of the river. Often it was a little misty. It made distant objects hard to discern. He warned the sentinels to be vigilant. Then he examined the barricades which closed the roads leading into the town. These, he felt, were the danger-spots. At ten o'clock he was relieved. At midnight he returned to watch. There was a faint moon now, a new moon. The world was very still.

As he looked up at the church tower he could see a silvery gleam where a moonbeam struck the head-piece of a sentry. A swinging lantern showed where the night watch was passing along Pillory Street. Ryder paced the ramparts silently. Near the Hospital Street barricade he paused quickly as a slight sound struck his ear.

A dark figure was moving from the barricade away from the wall. He tiptoed forward and stared at the receding form. Mist and darkness combined to prevent his having a clear view. The unknown person walked quickly, keeping where the shadow lay thickest. Ryder descended from the ramparts, whispered to the sentry to let him pass through the barricade, and hurried in the wake of the intruder. On they went, past the old hospital, past the fine house which Mr. Church had built, past the Almshouses erected in Elizabeth's reign. They neared open country now.

Ryder redoubled his caution. The person ahead paused beneath a cottage wall. Moonlight flickered on the blade of a sword. Ryder slowly drew his weapon. A stealthy footstep rustled. A man was crossing a nearby field. Ryder crouched low so that he could catch the fellow in silhouette against the sky. There was no mistaking the garb. It was a Cavalier. A soft whistle sounded. The figure in the shade of the cottage stepped boldly forward.

"How good of you to come!" It was a woman's voice, low but distinct. "I have brought you your sword."

Ryder grew tense. He knew the voice. There was no mistaking the tone, though it possessed a new timbre. A drifting cloud crossed the moon, but not before the light had enabled him to see with stunning certainty the features of Mistress Verity Hill.

CHAPTER THIRTEEN

So long as Ryder was busy he was content. Once he had leisure to meditate he experienced all those agonies of mind a conscientious person can undergo when the emotions are stirred. The echo of a single sentence kept ringing in his brain. It was like a devil whispering in his ear.

"I have brought you your sword!"

Suspicion began to poison his mind with its detestable virus. What could be the true meaning of Verity's nocturnal tryst? Again and again he recalled the brief encounter he had witnessed. He had not seen much. A twinge of conscience, some sense of delicacy, caused him to beat a hasty retreat. He could not remain eavesdropping, yet he had heard enough.

During the night raid on Sir Vincent Corbett's quarters at Drayton Ryder fought furiously, striving to get away from the mocking demon in his mind. They slew and they captured. He saw Sir Vincent in his shirt leap into the saddle of a riderless horse and escape amid bullets and jeers. Then Brereton's men returned to Nantwich, each with as many muskets as he could carry, every foot soldier on a captured horse. But once the tumult was over Ryder's unrest returned. The whispering began again.

"*I have brought you your sword!*"

The surreptitious visitor could have been no other than Royle Wilding. Was Verity a traitor?

Or was Royle false to the King's cause? He could not imagine it any more than he could picture Verity disloyal. How came they to be friendly? Feverish questions fired themselves and to none was there a reply. His first act the following day was to go in search of Verity. He hated mystery. He liked straight dealing. Ryder lived as he fought, straightforward, downright, blow for blow. No dissembling. No subterfuge. No finesse. He would ask Verity for an explanation and put an end to these imaginings which mocked his peace.

Verity was not to be found. Later, Sir William, hearing that he sought her, called him into his presence and told Ryder that Verity was sent away on another secret mission. Ryder listened in stoical silence. It was his duty to have reported to his commander all that he had seen and heard. Some sense of loyalty held him dumb.

From Verity his thoughts turned to Royle Wilding. Ryder had deliberately refrained from going near the cottage at Acton Church, but he went there now. The old woman was reticent until Ryder, for the first time, put silver to ignoble use. He learned that the wounded man had been visited by a young woman who bandaged his head. They had talked long together. Since then the Cavalier had returned several times to the cottage by night and had left his horse in the shed while he walked towards Nantwich. She knew no more. She had not seen the young woman again.

Ryder went back to Nantwich more disturbed than ever. Instead of making matters easier to understand, he had made them worse. Thoughts tantalized and tortured until relief came unexpectedly. He recalled the night Verity visited him on the ramparts. He heard his own voice assuring her that he would be her friend whatever happened. Yet, he accused himself, he was faithless to her in his mind at the first testing. How could he doubt so innocent a face? How could he distrust a comrade who had never been anything but fair?

In his anguish he spoke aloud. "I *will* trust her. I cannot understand, but who am I to judge? Trust her I will, come what may."

For the first time for many hours tranquillity came like balm to his soul.

The patrolling of the roads went on. There were fresh skirmishes. Mark's troop lost its leader. Mark was promoted to captain-lieutenant and placed in charge. Ryder became a lieutenant. It was only a year since he joined the militia, but Sir William was lamentably short of officers. Ryder had attracted attention during the brief excursion against Chester undertaken the week after Easter. Though his troop advanced only as far as Boughton, where they killed one of the city guard, his enterprise had been noticed by Sir William. He had been in the assault on Cholmondeley House.

It was on the evening of the seventeenth of May that Lord Capel with fifteen hundred Cavaliers marched to attack Nantwich. Sir William Brereton and all the horses were at Stafford at the time, else the advance would have been detected earlier. When the scouts rushed in with the news the good folk of Nantwich were taken by surprise, but were at their posts by the time Lord Capel's forces had reached the end of Hospital Street.

Lord Capel had brought four pieces of ordnance with him, and planting these in Malpas Field he was preparing to open fire, when the town gunner dispersed them with wild-fire.

The fighting at the barriers was fierce enough. In the darkness the narrow street seemed jammed by a great multitude. It was said that it was easy to distinguish the Nantwich men, for, by reason of the shortness of notice given by the scouts, almost every man fought in his shirt. Ryder had never seen such confusion—the night was stabbed by fire from pistols and muskets. A burning thatch cast a lurid glow over the surging throng. At two o'clock in the morning Lord Capel withdrew his men *"with greate disgrace"*, laments the old Chronicler, *"haveinge performed nothinge nor soe much as hurte one man: onelie they killed a calfe of Mr. Thomas Maynwarings, which they lefte behind them"*.

The youths of the town made much of this victim. They slung the dead animal on a pole and marched the streets to the sound of beaten frying-pans. Some wag composed a doggerel in honour of the triumph, and by the time Sir William came hurrying back it was on everyone's lips.

> *"The Lord Capel with a thousand and a halfe,*
> *Came to Bartons Crosse & theire they kild a Calfe;*
> *And stayinge theire untill the brake of Daye,*
> *They tooke to theire heeles & fast they fled away."*

Sir William ordered a special service of thanksgiving to be held in the church. That was his way. There must always be a solemn occasion. If a triumph was vouchsafed to his arms it was the doing of the Lord of Hosts. If his forces met with reverse it was a sign of God's displeasure, and repentance and humiliation must follow. This pious duty performed, Sir William was ready for the battlefield again. Brereton was not the man to let a neighbour call without returning his visit. On the night of the twenty-ninth of May all the Nantwich horse and foot, save for a guard on the walls, marched for Whitchurch. It was three o'clock in the morning when Brereton's men attacked; it took them two hours to drive the Royalist gunners from their pieces. Mark Trueman and Ryder Yale led their troop down the main street, slashing through all opposition while the trumpets exulted. Whitchurch was captured!

"Are our losses heavy?" inquired Ryder as the victors assembled with their spoils.

"Two men slain and two mortally wounded," announced Mark.

"It amazes me where all the shots go!" said Ryder. "Well, we have four guns, twenty prisoners and much brave apparel."

"Including that of Lord Capel himself. Ah! Sir William is ready to move off."

The return to Nantwich savoured of a triumphal procession. "I wish," remarked Ryder a trifle wistfully as the mud walls appeared in sight, "that Verity was there to welcome us. Our homecoming is robbed of much of its glory."

"You grow fond of that lass," observed Mark shrewdly, as he glanced at Ryder, who had the grace to flush in the early-morning light.

"We are good comrades," he agreed with assumed indifference. "Tell me, Mark, has she returned to Chester for Sir William?"

"Sir William," replied Trueman drily, "has not yet honoured me with his confidence."

His horse shied at a flutter of paper at the roadside and he crashed against Ryder's leg before he could get the animal under control.

"Sorry, Ryder! Hurt?"

"Not a whit. You grow dangerous, Mark!" He laughed. "And I had best avoid dangerous marks!"

"Now, what on earth do you mean by that?"

"You cannot read my riddle? I do not wonder. In the house where Verity lodges is an old beam carved by some long-dead moralist. 'Fair women,' says he, 'be dangerous marks for young men's eyes'."

"True," said Mark sagely. "I thank God I have been spared such danger. But why does your mind run thus?"

"I hardly know, Mark, save that my words, uttered at random, struck some chord of memory and brought the rhyme to mind. Tell me, Mark, if—if a young woman went by stealth at night to meet a man, how would you interpret her conduct?"

"It is little I know of women, Ryder, for which I am thankful, but I would say that the wench was in love."

"Ay!" Ryder's brow was furrowed with thought. "But suppose the man she met were an enemy? What then?"

"There's no accounting for what a woman does," replied Mark profoundly.

Ryder was in no mood to refute this, so he fell silent and rode sombrely until the cheers of the populace brought his thoughts back to the world about him.

He missed Verity more than he would admit, though Sir William kept him so active that he had little chance to brood. On the fair day at Holt a raid resulted in four score and eighteen oxen being brought in to Nantwich. Then the horse went to Liverpool to escort heavy guns landed by a

London ship. Success may have made the Nantwich men care-
less. Lord Capel and his Welsh forces succeeded in ambush-
ing a party near Hanmer. It may have been this which
turned Sir William's thoughts again to Chester.

Mark Trueman brought the news. "Sir William means to
make another attempt on Chester." The words were spoken
casually, but to Ryder they carried tremendous significance.
It was as if a period of waiting had ended, and he was about
to make a new move along life's highway. The very name of
Chester brought to Ryder a medley of emotions.

Incontinently he forgot all about Verity. A vision of
Rosea appeared before him. The improbability of his ever
seeing her did not occur to him. Rosea was in Chester. His
imagination took fire. He pictured the capture of the city.
He saw himself rescuing her; receiving her grateful thanks.
Without restraint he gave himself over to day-dreams. Mark
Trueman, more practical and less romantic, busied himself
with his equipment. They might be absent a long time.
Almost defiantly Ryder allowed himself to recapture his
memories of Rosea. If Verity, as Mark Trueman surmised,
was in love with Royle Wilding; if Verity, on whose cool
judgment he set such store, could allow herself to cherish
fond thoughts of an enemy, surely he, Ryder, would be
justified in following a similar course? So he reasoned with
himself. So he endeavoured to justify his dreams.

"Fair women be dangerous marks for young men's eyes!"
The admirable axiom was already forgotten. Or ignored!
Something more virile than maxims was stirring in the young
soldier's veins: it was the wine of life. He was young. He was
ardent. He was blinded by the potency of his need. He had
tried to put Chester from his thoughts; he had tried sincerely
to put Rosea from his heart. It was futile. It was impressed
upon him that for better or for worse his future and that of
Chester were blended. The stay in Nantwich had been in the
nature of a sojourning. It was not his abiding-place. Now that
Chester was to the fore he became eager to be away.

His request to lead a scouting party ahead of the main
body was granted. He chose Corporal Garnett and a dozen
troopers, all well mounted, and went by way of Tarporley.
As they drew near to Chester Ryder forsook the road and

took advantage of each wood and hedgerow. Their cautious advance attracted no attention.

When the July day drew to a close Ryder made his men bivouac within the confines of a wood, and having seen the sentries posted he left Corporal Garnett in charge and ventured on foot towards Chester. The westering sun lit up the spires and turrets. It tinged the walls a deeper red. It revealed a line of outworks, more imposing and more extensive than those which encircled Nantwich. They commenced with a gun-mount on the river's bank close to the public gallows set up near Boughton Chapel. They crossed the turnpike and made their irregular way to Horn Lane. Here the pattern became confused to his eyes. He climbed a tree to see better.

There seemed to be inner and outer ramparts, one line taking a short cut towards the Phoenix Tower, the other running straight north to Flookersbrook Hall. He sketched the design.

Flookersbrook Hall! It must have been there where first he met Rosea. He could see the chimneys beyond the Warrington Road. A sudden desire to see Rosea took possession of him. He hated monotony and craved for adventure. Returning to the bivouac, he handed Garnett the sketch and said that he meant to spend the night reconnoitring.

As Ryder crept into the gathering dusk he told himself he meant what he said. He was reconnoitring. After all, he might not see Rosea. She might not be at the Hall. Yet he had a conviction that he would see her.

The mud wall was low and not completed. A few sentries were posted.

There was a guard, with lanterns, across the Warrington Road. As he wondered how he could escape their notice the sound of wheels caused him to turn. A string of captured waggons was being brought in. Several Cavaliers on jaded horses rode in front, a few foot soldiers trudged wearily beside the wains. Others, more footsore, sat dangling their legs from the waggons. A conviction that boldness paid caused Ryder to saunter towards a waggon and swing himself aboard. He lay back out of reach of lantern rays. He could hear the guards exhanging pleasantries. The waggons rumbled past the barricade with barely a pause. Once they were clear Ryder dropped to the roadway and stepped into a side lane.

It had been so easy he could hardly comprehend that he was inside the outer works. Beyond the road, lights glowed in Flookersbrook Hall. Crossing some fields, he scaled a wall, and found himself in a shrubbery; a shrubbery in which a dry branch cracked beneath his foot! A dog barked and he paused. The excursion was not going to be as straightforward as originally promised. The dog continued to bark. It was a small dog—a pet spaniel. He could see it plainly in a beam of light which showed as a door opened. A woman stood there.

"Who is there?" The voice was low, rich, unmistakable.

"Rosea!" Her name had crossed his lips before he was aware of it.

"Yes, it is I. But who is there? Royle, it is not you, surely?"

"It is Ryder Yale."

"Great heavens! Wait. Wait until I rid myself of this foolish dog." She carried the animal indoors. Ryder stood, apprehensive. Had she gone to summon help? What a fool he was to reveal his presence! The light went out. The door was opening again, softly this time.

"Ryder! It is really you?" She was coming towards him. He took his courage in both hands and stepped to meet her.

"I am here—alone. An enemy in your midst! Have me arrested if you are so inclined."

She came close to him without speaking and stood looking up into his face. Her eyes seemed more eloquent in the faint light of stars.

"I can hardly believe it. I feared you had gone out of my life. Why do you make this unexpected appearance?"

"An impulse. I wanted to see you again, if only for a moment."

"It is a perilous risk."

"I am aware of that. It is worth it to see you again."

He saw her smile. "That is how I would have you talk always, Master Puritan. Ryder, where have you been? Royle came back wounded last May with a strange tale of your befriending him. He told me that you lay for six months in captivity in Chester—taken the very night I aided your escape. Wounded and captured—was that so?"

"You did not know I was a prisoner?"

"Oh, Ryder!" There was reproach in her tone. "Would I have forsaken you? I did hear a shot or two in the distance as I walked back to my rooms, but I did not connect the firing with you. I so hoped you had made your escape. And now, with this war, I thought there was no chance of ever seeing you again."

"That was how I felt. You have been often in my thoughts. So—I took the risk and here I am."

"I am glad. Let us move further from the house in case we are observed. This way."

They moved quietly, side by side. Ryder was conscious of her nearness. "You have not forgotten me?" It seemed a foolish thing to say but he wanted to hear her answer.

"I shall never forget you, Ryder. Never. Nor your courage."

"Only that?" Ryder felt himself growing more daring.

"It would be unseemly to say more."

"Does my presence tell you anything?"

"It tells me you wish to see me."

"I do. More than anything in the world. Does it not tell you why?"

He took her in his arms. How soft and warm and slender she seemed!

But Rosea held back. "Ryder, please. I must tell you something. My dear . . . ."

A look of fear leapt into her eyes. Voices sounded. Loud, boisterous voices. There were steps on the gravel. Three Cavaliers came striding up the driveway. A bell clanged.

"I must fly. Hush!" She pressed her lips passionately against his. Before he recovered from his surprise she was hurrying away.

Ryder groped his way towards the wall. His brief excursion was ended.

*   *   *   *   *

Sir William was betrayed when he attempted to surprise Chester. Mindful of his success at Whitchurch, he marched by night. It was the evening of July the seventeenth that he set out, having with him all the Nantwich horse and foot except Captain Massie and the train-band of Nantwich Hundred. With them went men from Manchester and Stafford. It was Sir William's intention to have entered the outworks before the King's party knew of his presence, but a messenger gave notice of his coming two hours before he arrived. The forces of the city were ready. Forty guns in the Castle and other cannon from the gun-mounts opened fire with such vehemence that the Nantwich forces paused. They took cover and lay round about the city for several days on the land side. The frequent discharge of muskets was punctuated by occasional shots from several small cannon which Sir William brought with his force.

Ryder watched every shot anxiously. To his apprehensive eyes every bullet was directed at Rosea. Perhaps Verity was within the walls of Chester, too. It was in vain that he reminded himself how few men were slain during the attack on Whitchurch. He tortured himself by thinking that Rosea might always prove an exception. Finally he told himself that it was no use worrying. There were occasions in life when matters must be left to Providence—or chance. He found some consolation in this.

The Nantwich musketeers were busy. They had secured possession of several barns which stood near the outworks and from these they kept up a galling fire. There was much noise and smoke and commotion, but Ryder formed the impression that not much injury was sustained. Then word came through that Lord Capel was advancing with the Shropshire forces to the relief of the city. A vigorous assault was delivered the following day on the outworks at Cow Lane. It may have occasioned the defenders some anxiety, but those who stormed the walls knew that it was but a feint attack. Sir William had decided that Chester was too strong a place to be carried by assault. Its downfall would result only from a prolonged siege, and this he was not in a position to attempt.

So he raised the siege. His guns were limbered up and went

trundling down the road to Nantwich protected by his pikemen and firelocks. He carried off his guns in safety, having
lost during the four days' attack two common soldiers and
four others wounded. Dragoons in the barns kept up a
vigorous fire to deceive the defenders until the Parliamentary army were far enough on their way to be safe from
pursuit. Then the dragoons, too, mounted their nags and
rode away. Ryder was one of a small party of horse which
lingered to cover the withdrawal. He stayed long enough to
hear the jubilation of the church bells as it became apparent
to the besieged that their foe had retired.

The Governor of Chester had learnt a lesson during
those few days. No barns must be left standing to shelter
enemy marksmen. Ryder's scouts brought Sir William the
information that all barns outside the turnpikes at Boughton had been fired, that Spital Boughton chapel was pulled
down, trees were felled, and all houses in the vicinity of the
outworks razed to the ground.

So the summer dragged on.

Lord Capel still had his eyes on Nantwich. On the third
of August, while Sir William was at Stafford, he advanced on
the Parliamentarian stronghold at the head of three thousand
men. Advancing in thick mist, the Cavaliers were hard by the
walls before they were seen. Firing was kept up during the
hours of darkness, but with the rising of the sun the enemy
retired.

Nantwich was now so important that the mere word that
it was attacked was sufficient to set forces marching to its
relief. This time it was Sir Thomas Myddleton who came over
from the Welsh border.

"He has lost his Castle of Chirk," explained Mark as the
new arrivals made their way over Welsh Bridge. "Maybe
Sir Thomas thinks that if he helps Sir William, Sir William
in return will assist him."

"What matter so long as the cause prospers?" retorted
Ryder. "The seven large guns he brings are acceptable.
Well, we've beaten off five attacks by Lord Capel. I wonder
what the next move will be."

"Chester again, I expect. Sir William has set his heart
on capturing the city. He will give them no peace until

he has accomplished what he had resolved to perform. I predict Chester!"

But Mark Trueman was wrong.

CHAPTER FOURTEEN

Now there came about that daring thrust into North Wales which shook the Royalist confidence and drove those who adhered to the King's party to seek shelter in the castles which were scattered from the Dee to the Menai Straits. In Conway a veritable convocation of prelates crowded under the protective cope of Archbishop John Williams.

It was in November that Sir William Brereton elected to deliver this surprise; November, when all considerate commanders were seeking winter quarters. On November the seventh he set forth from Nantwich.

There was no forced marching. Two days were allowed for the infantry to cross the sixteen miles which separated Nantwich from Farndon and the famous Bridge of Holt, beyond which lay the land of Wales. They spent the first night at Woodhey and Ridley Green; the next at Barton-on-the-Hill and Stretton.

Ryder Yale rode alongside Mark Trueman well in advance of the marching men. A fine rain was falling and he was glad of his horseman's cloak. The two rode in silence with the drops dripping from their head-pieces as they glanced about them with the keen eyes of men who advance in front of an army. It was a land where they could look wide, a land of broad meadows, intersected by hedgerows, tufted by woods, and broken by an occasional low red farm or cottage.

Sir William had warned them to be on their guard, for the governor of Holt Castle, Colonel John Robinson, was active. Already he had given proof of that, for as the Parliament forces prepared to camp at Stretton an alarm sounded, and the King's horsemen were upon them. They had beaten them off, slaying several without loss. And now they were nearing Farndon, and Holt Castle. It behoved them to be vigilant.

"Watch for ambuscades," Sir William had warned them. "Young Robinson lacks not enterprise. See if the bridge is barricaded. If we cannot force a passage we must cross by boats. Be watchful, but bear in mind that men advancing from the north may be the party which Colonel Booth brings out of Lancashire to our aid."

So they rode, these two comrades, eager-eyed, until they came to the village of Farndon, and here they paused. The level land rises at this spot so that the houses stand conveniently high as though to make sure they suffer no inundation when the river drowns the meadows which fringe its banks.

Neither had been to Farndon before, though the name of Holt Bridge as one of the best crossings of the Dee was well known. To an artist's eye a river may be a thing of beauty; to a soldier it may represent a hazard which can only be overcome at the cost of lives. Ryder drew near to such a river. He could see clustering on either bank houses which indicated a passage in between. Then they saw the water.

The Dee had lost much of the dash and sparkle which characterized its upper reaches; it was a broad and moving stream which swirled between the edged pillars of the ten-arched bridge. The water was muddy and high from November rains. On the Farndon side the banks dropped abruptly, revealing sheer faces of red sandstone on which the strata showed where there was no covering of ivy or shrubs. The red sandstone bridge with its wedged bays held their attention. A tower with strong gates and a drawbridge had been built on the bridge. It was a substantial structure which carpenters were even then strengthening.

Troops lined the Welsh bank, musketeers with matches burning. Some horsemen were herding villagers from their homes which were being occupied by firelock men. Ryder could see the unfortunates, laden with household treasures, trudging up the gentle slope which led from the bridge to the village. The bridge, remarked Trueman grimly, was likely to prove a formidable barrier. It seemed apparent that the Royalists counted upon it to withstand any pressure. Hundreds of horsemen crowded the road at the approach to Holt.

Keeping under cover, Ryder and Mark moved upstream, to inspect the Castle which lifted its turrets from a red sandstone knoll. Though small in size it looked compact and formidable. The Dee meandered with several bends. Behind the Castle lay the village, separated from its protector by a deep fosse—a cutting which originally supplied the blocks of dressed stone which went to fashion the Castle walls. The battlements were alive with men. The royal flag, sodden with rain, drooped from a flagstaff.

"Never before have I seen a five-sided castle," commented Mark, as he stared with dubious eyes at the fortress. Four of the towers were round and each was crowned with a small turret. The fifth, which bordered the river, was square. The gateway faced the village. It was guarded by two round-towers. A drawbridge led to an outer tower which, in turn, gave access to a causeway. This crossed the fosse and terminated in a gatehouse flanked by stables and cow-houses. "It is fortunate for us that the Castle stands some hundred yards from the bridge, else of a surety we had never crossed that way."

"I think," observed Ryder seriously, "the game is already stalemate. The Castle cannot prevent our attack; we cannot carry the Castle."

"Do not say so until we have tried."

"Sir William will not try! We learnt our lesson at Chester. Small guns cannot breach massive walls. No, heed my words. If Colonel Robinson comes not out to fight us, we do not go in. Let us return to make our report."

They found Sir William at the joining of the ways where the roads merged at the village of Farndon. He sat his horse with Sir Thomas Myddleton at his side, talking to Colonel John Booth and Lieutenant-Colonel Peter Egerton, who had just reached the rendezvous with five companies of Lancashire foot, two troops of horse and two of dragooners.

Sir William rode to the crest of the incline and looked down upon the narrow, ancient bridge from which rose a strong wooden tower. A difficult, dangerous passage—very difficult if not altogether impossible. He left on record the thought which passed through his brain. The Commander curtly issued his orders. A feint was to be made on the bridge to keep the enemy occupied. Boats were to be launched to land the Parliamentary foot on the left bank of the Dee. It was one o'clock in the afternoon when the attack began. The bells of Holt Church were sounding their warning. Beacons passed their flaring message down to the coast of Wales.

As Brereton's marksmen ran for the cover of the bridge-end, pikemen, pushing a farm cart before them to serve as a shield, began to build a barricade. From the bridge tower came an irregular fire. The marching column which came down the Farndon hill scattered as hundreds of infantrymen broke away and hurried to the river bank. On the Welsh side a low shelf of river sward was backed by a sudden rise. This was crowned by scattered houses and hedged gardens. From this shelter a fierce fire was kept up by Royalist marksmen, so that it became impossible to launch the boats. There was firing, too, from the Castle ramparts, but this was for effect—the distance was too great for accuracy. One boat, out of control, swept down the river. Others, stuck on the high clay banks, were used as barriers by the foot, who crouched before the hail of bullets.

Sir William turned to Mark. "Request Colonel Egerton to lead the Lancashire horse and dragooners down the river bank as though he would essay a passage lower down. We must draw off their forces. I cannot see how we can attempt a passage in the face of such fire."

As Trueman rode off, Sir William turned to Ryder. "Find me an officer who will lead a forlorn hope against the bridge."

Ryder dismounted. "May I be permitted to undertake it, sir?"

"I would like you to, Ryder. God be with you and grant you good success."

"What instructions, Sir William?"

"None save that the bridge be forced. The manner of it is left to you."

An eager light showed in Ryder's eyes. Hurrying towards the waiting troop, he sent Corporal Garnett and a dozen men to a nearby farm in search of ladders. Then he called for volunteers.

Troopers and dragooners dismounted and waited with drawn swords. The men bearing ladders came up. Ryder stood motionless, his eyes fixed on the backs of the Lancashire horse which Colonel Egerton led downriver, watched from the Welsh bank by an irregular party of musketeers and cavalry. He waited until they were a mile away. Then he gave the signal for assault.

Broadsword in hand, Ryder ran ahead of his men. The musketeers behind the farm-cart barricade opened a covering fire. Several troopers dropped wounded as they crowded into the narrow approach to the bridge. Corporal Garnett clambered on to the coping. With the agility of a cat he ran towards the wooden tower. Ryder waited until the ladder-bearers were on the bridge, and then he too scaled the coping. Muskets and snaphances were spitting fire. A trooper, shot through the shoulder, splashed heavily into the muddy river. The spray wet Ryder's hot cheeks as he struggled towards the tower. A ladder was thrust back by the besieged. A longer ladder took its place. Ryder grasped the rungs and swung himself up. He could see Corporal Garnett swarming up the side of the tower. They reached its crest simultaneously.

There came a pause in the attack. A Cavalier with pistols was taking aim at Ryder who felt like a bird on a house-top. The double-works within the gates presented a formidable barrier. Several Parliamentarians ran forward and tossed grenades over the gatehouse. The explosions scattered the defenders. They spread consternation and gave the opportunity which the attackers needed.

"Cut the ropes!" yelled Ryder, struggling to get a fresh grip on his broadsword. A bullet chipped the tower close beside him and a splinter gashed his cheek. "Cut the drawbridge ropes, Garnett!" Two swords hacked viciously. The heavy wooden drawbridge shook, broke loose on one side and hung aslant. Ryder delivered a final slash and the rope parted. The drawbridge dropped with a crash which made the structure shake. Two luckless troopers were struck down by its fall. The heavy timbers rattled and jarred. Before they had settled into place a score of exultant Parliamentarians rushed across.

Axes and crowbars were thundering on the great gates.
The wood splintered. With a crash the doors gave way.
Pikes were thrusting. Trumpets were sounding. Amid
cheers and shots hundreds of Cheshire pikemen stormed
over the bridge, the foremost thrust forward by the sheer
weight of their excited comrades behind. They were through
the archway. The bridge tower was captured. Ryder,
breathless, seated astride the tower top, looked down upon a
swarm of triumphant Parliamentarians pouring like a
human river over the narrow bridge into the land of Wales.

They spread out fanwise, some downriver, some up the
hill towards the town; some, with greater caution, in the
direction of the Castle.

Colonel Ellis's regiment of foot and Major Trevor's
regiment of horse were in flight, a thousand horsemen and
seven hundred foot. Pikemen, weighted by their corselets,
broke into a heavy run as they set off in pursuit.

There came a shout which turned into cheers. There
sounded the trampling of many hoofs. Sir William Brereton
at the head of the Cheshire horse was crossing the captured
bridge, the bridge which was held to be impregnable, carried
without the death of a single Parliamentary soldier. They
were across. They were forming. The first troop was breasting
the hill at a round trot, eager to be on the heels of the
vanishing Cavaliers. Up the road they went, up to the
village green, where, on its plinth of eight stone steps, rose
the village cross.

The road to Wrexham stretched before them. The Parliamentary horse and dragoons turned that way. Soon they
would be in Wrexham—Wrexham, with its stately church;
Wrexham, with its town hall from which King Charles spoke
impassioned words a year before; Wrexham, some seven
miles away.

At six o'clock they entered Wrexham with the enemy
flying apace before them and removing what goods they
could to places of safety. Holt Castle still held out and a
large body of troops remained to besiege it. Prisoners,
captured when the Cavaliers' rearguard was overtaken, were
marched back to Nantwich. Sir William Brereton and Sir
Thomas Myddleton were well received when they entered

Wrexham. They were glad to quarter there for the night. The next day there was an early start. In the grey light of morning the horse and dragoons assembled and took the road to Hawarden. The lock of the Welsh gate was picked. From hilltops beacons flared fresh warnings. Where would the raid end? Would Hawarden Castle satisfy the invaders, or would Flint be assaulted?

Mark Trueman and Ryder Yale looked at each other as they awaited the next command. They, too, wondered what the day would bring forth.

CHAPTER FIFTEEN

THE loss of Holt Bridge was a blow to the Royalists; worse was to follow. Colonel Booth remained at Wrexham with nine hundred men. Sir William had with him six hundred. He appeared with these before Hawarden Castle. Mr. Ravenscroft, the Governor, instantly handed over the Castle at his summons.

Mark went in search of Ryder, who was trying to find shelter for his men. He was laughing. "A pretty trick Ravenscroft has played on the malignants," he remarked. "He applied to the Governor of Chester for a barrel of powder and a quantity of match, which were duly delivered to his representatives."

"I do not favour treachery or sharp practices no matter which side benefits," replied Ryder curtly. "Have you any word of what is expected of us, Mark?"

"They say that Sir Thomas Myddleton intends to return to Wrexham to draft a letter to Colonel Salusbury summoning him to surrender Denbigh Castle."

"From what I hear it is an impregnable place. It will require something stouter than paper and ink to get within its walls. But what of Hawarden?"

"Sir William stays here awhile. The Castle is unfurnished and requires a new drawbridge. It is barren of provisions, which may account for the readiness with which Mr. Ravenscroft responded to Sir William's summons to surrender."

"So we are to remain here? It is commodiously situated

for blocking the way to Chester. They will have to go without their Welsh coals."

"Ay. And their mutton and beef. But we are not to remain here. Only the foot are for Hawarden. The rest of us have to penetrate into Wales. We are to ride by way of Northop and are to attempt Flint and Holywell, and, I hear, Mostyn."

"Mostyn? It occurs to me that Sir William means to call at Mostyn Hall to return the visit which Colonel Mostyn's Welshmen paid to his house in Chester."

Trueman was correct in his surmise. It was not long before long lines of Parliamentary horse were splashing through the mud of the Flintshire roads. Through the drab November rain rode the horsemen, mired to the girths, hungry, weary, sustained by the adventure. They met with no opposition. Fighting-men from the country round about had flocked to Flint Castle, where young Colonel Mostyn had taken control after his escape from Hawarden. On they rode, these invaders of Wales, to Northop, where they stole a surplice. Then on to Holywell, where they found the inhabitants mostly Catholic, but pillaged nothing save the churches and the poor curate, being sadly in want of linen. Churches held for the men a fascination. They searched for anything which savoured of idolatry. A carved saint was found hacked to pieces, a face in a stained-glass window was knocked from its leaden frame, an altar dragged from the east wall and placed in the centre of the church, there to become nothing more menacing than a holy table. Altar rails, when pulled down, were very honestly reared against the wall. In Hawarden Church the Common Prayer Book was scattered about the chancel and the book of Genesis ripped from the great Bible.

Strange warfare. Indicative of the minds of the men who formed the train-bands of Cheshire.

Lieutenant Ryder Yale with a score of sodden troopers at his heels rode down the coast road which led to Flint. The rain had stopped, but the bare trees still dripped moisture. Beside them stretched the Sands of Dee with a grey sea flooding up the estuary.

The cry of the gulls sounded like a dirge. Before them lay

the town, encompassed by a double wall and a ditch. To the
north-east the Castle walls towered against the sky—the
King's Castle with its three round towers and its disconnected keep, joined to the town by an outwork and a fortified gate. Those grim walls had seen the doomed Richard of
Bordeaux pleading with the usurper Bolingbroke. It was a
low-lying castle built upon a sand-encircled rock, its eastern
towers washed by the tide. The town lay within a rectangle,
four roads crossing in the centre where stood the church.
It was a pleasant town with trees, and many of the houses
were set about with gardens. A few dwellings lay without the
walls—a homely, friendly sight, more pleasing to the eye
than the gallows which rose from a mound at the northern
shoulder of the town.

Ryder drew rein and stared at the Castle. A wet flag hung
from a flagstaff above the keep. The battlemented walls
were fringed with faces. Colonel Roger Mostyn—"Long
Roger" his friends called him—was resolved to hold Flint
Castle for the King. As Ryder Yale rested his horse under the
wayside trees and gazed across the strip of *morfa*[1] to the grim
bulk of the fortalice beside the sea, he wondered what kind
of spirit was contained within so stout a shell. Would the
resistance be stern?

In the light of the dying day the great walls seemed more
formidable than usual. They loomed through the gloom with
cuts of yellow light streaming from niches. There was no
sound but the lament of the herring-gulls and the thin eerie
note of oyster-catchers busy at the sand's edge. Ahead lay
the town of Flint, deserted, silent as the grave. Not a light
was to be seen. Had it not been for the curious faces peering
from between the Castle's merlons it might well have been a
place of the dead. Mark Trueman came splashing through
the mud and reined alongside.

"They appear to have forsaken the town," said Ryder
in a low voice.

"Withdrawn to the Castle for safety," agreed Mark.

Still they sat silent, watchful, scarce knowing what to do.
There was no movement save when a trooper's horse tossed
a restless head. Mark raised his right hand and pointed.

[1] Welsh for 'marsh'.

There was a sign of life. The slim form of a girl in a sad-coloured cloak broke the green of the *morfa*. Stick in hand, she drove a flock of white geese across the sward in the direction of the Castle.

"Shall I intercept her and secure the birds?" asked Ryder, gathering up his reins.

"No. We don't wage war on women."

"She takes the geese to the garrison."

"Bah! A mouthful among so many."

Ryder's mount moved impatiently. "Let me enter the town alone and explore."

"Let us all go."

"No, Mark. You had best return to Sir William with your intelligence. If we all go the garrison may make a sortie. Alone, I may be unobserved."

Mark rode beside his friend as far as the town ditch, reluctant to let him go. At the entrance to the town they paused. A tabby cat, stealthily crossing the empty roadway, turned to stare inquiringly at the mounted men.

"I don't like quitting you, Ryder, and that's a fact!" said Mark.

"Bah! It's safe enough. If they catch me you'll soon have me out again. The drawbridge is up and the town deserted. I'll search a few houses and see what I can discover."

Reluctantly Mark rejoined the troopers. Slowly Ryder walked his charger down the main street. The hoofs echoed in the silence. Every shop had its shutters up. Trees thrust their bare branches like claws against the darkening sky. A robin piped four notes and was still. As Ryder drew opposite an inn he heard a cough. It was a man's cough, a hacking cough. It made him think the man was old. He tethered his horse and, drawing one of his long holster-pistols, walked towards the inn. He tried the latch and found that the door opened. He bent his steel-pot and stepped inside. From a low doorway which connected with the back premises a man stood watching, a wrinkled man with wrinkled stockings. A sack was caped over his frail shoulders.

"Where is everybody?" Ryder spoke quietly.

"Gone." The man was laconic. He coughed and spat in the sawdust.

"A blind man could tell as much. Where? To the Castle?"

"Ay. They be fearful. The enemy overruns Flintshire. You be one of 'em? Is't true you toss new-born babes on pikes and roast 'em?"

"Not yet, though I'm hungry enough to eat almost anything. Our worst crime is to steal a poor curate's surplice to make shirts. Have you any food in this place?"

"Not a bacon-rind. They haven't left enough to feed a mouse."

Ryder dropped on a settle and began to tap the powder from his pistol. The old man watched with alarm."

"It's true what I sez. Wot are you going to do?"

"Not going to pistol you, you fool. I only wish to have a dry priming. Put some wood on the fire. If I have to stay hungry I may as well be comfortable. Have you anything to drink?"

"Water from the pump, master. Nothing more."

"It's lies he's telling!" A lilting voice sounded from the dimness. "There's good wine in a bin—hid from the soldiers."

"You dratted jade!" snarled the old man. A burst of coughing cut short his anger.

A girl darted into the room with a cobweb-covered bottle in her hand. Ryder stared into an elfin face about which rain-soaked hair clung closely.

"There's wine for you, *cariad*. Drink your fill. The best is for you always. Pay no heed to this miser."

"So it is you?" Ryder stared, amazed, uncomfortable.

"Ay. It's me. Your Myra. You know me now, yes? And I know you. I knew you when you sat your great horse under the trees, big and fine and spirited as you be. You did not treat me gentle when last we met, did you? *Duw*, it was well-nigh smothered I was before I got rid of that blanket. What a way to treat a girl who came to help you escape! You forgot, maybe, that if you went free you were to marry me."

"I agreed to no such folly. You are foolish."

"A woman in love is always foolish, *cariad*, but *diawl*, she does not fret about it. I am glad you escaped."

"I am sorry if I hurt you."

"Hurt me you did! I do not mind if you hurt me so long as you love me."

Ryder moved impatiently. "Is there food in this place?"

"There's loving you are! Just like a man. Belly before heart! Ha! The old devil has slipped away while we talk. Now, what is he up to? I'll warrant he had food hidden. Leave Myra to find what you want, *cariad*. Drink your fill while I'm gone."

He heard her singing in the kitchen . . . *"treat me so despitefully . . ."* The tune was 'Greensleeves' again. He moved uneasily, poured out some wine. The girl was back in the room with bread on a trencher.

"I have set an egg to boil. It is a goose-egg. You do not mind?"

"I could eat a dodo's egg if it be not addled, Were you the goose-girl who crossed the *morfa*?"

"I kept my head down so you should not know," she replied naively. She held up a warning finger. "Someone is in the street." She peered from the window.

"Damn! The old devil has been to the Castle to betray you. Soldiers are there. Quick, *cariad*, you must escape."

Ryder put down his wine and cocked a pistol.

"The back way!" cried the girl. "They will watch the front door."

"And the back, my dear." There was a Cavalier in the doorway. A blue silk arm encircled her waist. "And where is our crop-eared visitor, sweet?"

Ryder raised his pistol and stepped from behind the settle. "Closer than you imagine, sir."

A flame flickered, revealing the swarthy features of Royle Wilding.

"The devil!" exclaimed the Cavalier.

"Oh no. Ryder Yale, at your service."

Royle drew the girl closer to him. "A strange encounter," he observed over her head. "You are imprudent, Master Bull-Baiter. I am not alone."

"Neither am I. Several hundred visitors, little to your liking, are close at hand."

"Succour is even more close at hand for me. I have but to raise my voice——"

"And I should shoot you."

"Not you! You could not kill me in cold blood. Come, let

us bargain. I bear you no ill will. Put down your pistol and make your escape. I will not look which way you go.''

"It's wise you are!'' cried Myra. "Quick, *cariad*, before the fine gentleman changes his mind.''

She darted into the passage. As Ryder followed Royle threw him a smile. "I must remember to tell Rosea I have seen you.'' Royle blew a kiss to the girl as Myra looked back impatiently. It filled Ryder with disgust. He hesitated with his foot on the cobbles, but Myra ran back, seized his hand, and dragged him across the inn yard. "I know where you may hide, but it's quick you must be.'' She sped along an alley. Ryder was lost amid a maze of outhouses. She darted across a road, nimble, light of foot, almost feline in her movements. She crossed gardens until she came to a house which stood alone. It was empty. She unlatched the door and walked into a kitchen.

In the boarded floor was a trap-door. She slid back a bolt, inserted a finger in a metal ring, and raised the trap. "It is safe you will be here, my man,'' she said, pointing to a ladder.

Ryder looked into the darkness at his feet. "Have you no light? There is no occasion for me to hide. My comrades are coming down the road from Hawarden.''

"They are not here yet. And the King's men seek you. They have a French lord with them who has the Devil's own nose for mischief. It is timid you are. See, I will go first. There is nothing in the cellar but cheeses which the good men overlooked.''

She sat on the floor and swung her feet until they rested on the ladder. Into the dark descended the girl. Ryder felt ashamed. He followed and encountered her soft figure in the darkness. He drew back. Small though she was she possessed some magnetism which frightened him. She seemed to radiate primitive vitality. Ryder's eyes were growing accustomed to the gloom.

"Sit you down and be comfortable,'' said Myra, dragging a box forward. "I will fetch you a blanket. It is a good thing to keep you warm.'' She ascended the ladder. "A blanket is useful!'' She stepped on to the floor. "A blanket bound about the head can keep you quiet!''

The trap-door fell with a crash. Ryder was in Stygian darkness.

"Open the door!" he yelled. "What are you doing?"

"I am dragging a heavy press across the trap, *cariad*, lest the bolt should give way. You are so strong! It has been hard to catch you, my dear, but there you stay until you promise to marry me."

Sudden fury took hold of Ryder Yale. He dragged the holster-pistol from his belt and fired at the lilting voice. The crash made his ears tingle. He heard a scream. His nostrils were full of the pungent powder-smoke. As he listened he regretted his impulse. There was no sound in the room above.

From a round hole in the trap-door he could see a minute shaft of blessed light.

CHAPTER SIXTEEN

THE passage of time seemed to have lost significance. It was a period of waiting. The tiny hole in the floor above was the only indication Ryder had that it was day. His first reaction on realizing that he had been trapped was one of blank despair. Resentment followed. Then he calmed down and took mental stock of the situation.

He tested the trap-door. It resisted his powerful muscles. The girl had not merely bolted the trap but, as she had told him, placed some heavy weight upon it. Heave and strain as he might he could not move it. Ryder had to admit defeat. Descending the ladder, he began to grope his way about the cellar, which contained boxes and casks. Several times he ran his head against objects before he realized that they were cheeses suspended from the joists to be out of reach of the mice. At least, he mused, he would not starve.

He drew his sheath-knife and cut into a cheese. Water was his chief concern. Food was of little use if a man could not drink. It was his nose rather than his wits which attracted him to a source of supply. One of the kegs contained ale. Again he resorted to his knife—a heavy weapon fashioned to serve, if necessary, as a dagger. He cut into the head of the barrel. The wood was hard and the task proved laborious, but Ryder persevered. It occupied his energies so that the time did not appear interminable. The shaft of light grew less; then it faded altogether. The captive dragged boxes into position and made a seat. The cellar floor was damp and his couch, though hard, was at least dry.

Slumber was slow in coming and he had opportunity to muse. More than once, out of the stillness, came the rumble of distant gunfire. He hoped it meant that Sir William had opened his attack on Flint Castle. Perhaps Mark would find his horse and come in search of him. He thought of the chance encounter with Royle Wilding, and from him his thoughts strayed to Rosea and her incomparable beauty. From Rosea he turned to Verity. He wished he knew why Verity had met Wilding that night at Nantwich! Why was it, he wondered, that little groups of people were drawn together as though by invisible strings so that their lives impinged? A little over a year ago he had not known of the existence of Verity or Rosea or Wilding, yet now their actions, their emotions, their outlook, all had an effect on him.

His mind picked up a thought of Myra. She, too, had intruded on the pattern of his life—he knew not why. A strange little creature—half waif, half genius. He had met no one like her. Her music held him in thrall. Was it possible that music could be immoral? It contained the power to stir the emotions! Was this fragile girl possessed of some subtle gift whereby she could tap a source of inspiration of which he was ignorant? How marvellously her delicate fingers wove patterns on the harp-strings, embodying motion in melody. Then he recalled that she was the source of his dilemma and he forgot her musical powers as a wave of fierce resentment swept over him. Had he killed her with his pistol-shot?

Awakening from a cramped sleep he saw with satisfaction a faint light percolating through the bullet-hole above. Day was returning. He stretched his stiff muscles. A soft, suspicious rustling quickened his senses, stirred some primitive instinct within him. His hair began to bristle. Mice! He laughed aloud at his timidity. The fear of the unknown! Only mice foraging for crumbs of cheese. He breakfasted. A step sounded on the boards above—a hesitant, cautious step. Hope leaped.

"Mark!" he yelled. "Here! I am down here!"

But it was not Mark's voice which replied. The tone was lilting, it was a tone he had come to abhor.

"It is wide of the mark you are, my brave lad. Will you shoot at me again if I draw near?"

"No. I take shame that I fired. Thank God you are not slain. Myra, let me out of this pit of perdition and you shall have what you will."

"You know my terms. You must marry me."

"Anything but that. Name other terms."

"There are no other, my big man. Wed me or remain where you are."

"You are mad."

"Mad I am! It does not trouble me. I know what I want, if that is what you call being mad."

"My comrades are at hand. They will speedily have me out of this."

"They are too busy firing at Flint Castle to spare you a thought. We shall see. Colonel Mostyn cannot hold out long, for there are no provisions and the water in the well is brackish from the sea. Thirst will defeat them if Brereton's guns do not."

"Cease your talk and let me out."

"There's fierce-tempered you are, *cariad*. I like a man with spirit. It's quick-tempered I am myself at times. Good-bye, *cariad*; tomorrow I will call again. Maybe your temper will have cooled by then and you will be wanting a bride."

As he heard her steps recede he shouted until pride made him desist. Another dreary day dragged its tedious length. The point of light dimmed and vanished. Another night was at hand. The following day his captor was back with the same proposal. It met with the same refusal. The next day the girl failed to make an appearance.

Ryder waited, conscious of anxiety, conscious of disappointment. It was not that he desired her presence; it was because he craved for the sound of a human voice, any contact, however undesirable, that kept him in touch with the world of men. The strain was beginning to tell. Almost he welcomed the mice which scampered across his motionless feet when he rested, brooding in silence. The next day as Ryder lay staring at the peep of day he thought what a blessing light could be. Without light man would go mad. If only there could be more light. More light!

A thought struck him. What a fool he had been! He had his knife. He would cut the hole larger. Up the ladder he climbed, spurred by a fresh incentive. The wood was thick. The task was laborious. More than once the keen blade gashed his fingers. He hacked resolutely. By nightfall he had a hole in the trap-door big enough to take his hand. With the return of daylight he resumed his whittling. He slashed away sufficient wood to enable him to reach the bolt. He shot it back—all to no purpose. The weight above was still sufficient to resist the heave of his shoulders. Discouraged but still stubborn, Ryder began to slice the boards. He would cut away the entire floor if necessary.

By evening he was free. He crawled through the jagged hole and rose unsteadily to his feet. Light was beginning to fade. He listened but heard no sound, not even a distant report of a gun. He searched the deserted house. The larder was bare. From a well in the yard he obtained water; water to drink, water in which to wash the blood and dirt from his hands. It was only when he rinsed his face that he realized that he was again growing a beard.

He looked about him. There was no point in remaining in the house. A few lights showed amid the leafless trees. He walked stiffly towards them. He met a countryman and asked for news. The Castle had fallen. Colonel Mostyn had been allowed to march forth with all the honours of war. The Cavaliers went to Rhuddlan Castle, where they remained secure until Brereton, satisfied with taking a castle which he could not hold, withdrew his troops. But before he re-turned to Hawarden he went to Mostyn Hall, where he captured four guns. But this was something which Ryder Yale did not learn until later.

For the time being he was alone in a strange land. A shepherd to whom he spoke could not reply—he knew no English. Ryder walked on, a forlorn, ragged figure, yet ominous in the twilight. As he reached the top of the hill which overlooked the ocean he climbed a rock, the better to take stock of the landscape. His eyes were instantly arrested by the sight of ships, a dozen at least, anchored close inshore. He could trace their high poops and thrusting bows as they rode with brailed sails hanging from their yards. Other vessels, more distant, were endeavouring to reach the Wirral, almost becalmed in the faint evening breeze.

It could mean only one thing—the Marquis of Ormond's long-expected forces had evaded the Parliamentary frigates and crossed from Dublin. Help for the Royalists besieged in Chester was close at hand. Ryder's military training asserted itself. His Commander-in-Chief must learn of this menace without delay.

He forgot his own plight in his anxiety to carry word of the landing of the troops from Lord Ormond, yet even as he watched he became conscious of the murmur of voices and a shuffling sound: the steady tramping of many feet. Ryder leaped a roadside fence and took cover in a wood. Crouching behind the bole of an ivy-festooned ash, he waited, nor had he long to wait.

The roadway grew dark with marching men. In the van strode several officers—men of quality. Though their clothing was worn there was no mistaking its cut and fashion. Their plumed hats and swinging capes gave them an air of distinction. He heard one of the men addressed as "Sir Michael", and stared with pardonable curiosity. This, then, must be Sir Michael Ernely, who, with Major-General Gibson, led the English-Irish forces.

Then came the men. In his amazement Ryder forgot all about the officers. The men were gaunt and ragged, walking scarecrows. Most were without stockings. Some had cloths bound about their feet in place of shoes. Their jerkins were in shreds. They were lean, cadaverous, hungry, weary, unshaven and unkempt. Only their weapons were bright. Ryder took stock of them as they tramped the lonely road which led to Hawarden—dismounted horsemen bearing their saddles and bridles, pikemen and musketeers. They came steadily on—hundreds of them—until Ryder began to think the long column would never end. There must have been, he estimated, three thousand at least.

Ryder was not deceived by their tattered attire. These were formidable warriors who had known several years' wild campaigning in Ireland. Their presence would turn the scale in Cheshire. As the rear files rounded a bend Ryder turned away from Hawarden. It was no use following these troops. Unless he could get ahead of them his warning would prove valueless. His eyes were busy seeking signs of a farm. He found one and went in search of a horse. It was a small farm, impoverished, but a horse was in the stable. Ryder had the bridle on it quickly enough. There was no saddle, but a sack sufficed. As he climbed on to the animal's back in the farm-yard a man ran shouting from out of the house. Ryder paid no heed. Necessity knew no law, and though hitherto he had regarded horse-stealing as a most heinous crime, he beat the animal into a lumbering canter and rode out of sight, fol-lowed by imprecations and stones.

Through the night Ryder rode steadily onwards, coaxing some semblance of speed out of the decrepit creature he was astride, shaping his course by Orion, which hung encourag-ingly ahead. The challenge of a sentry in the darkness was as sweet music to his ears. He told his story to the officer of the guard and then hurried along the main road and turned towards the Castle. Sir William, roused from his slumbers, heard the news anxiously.

There was no more sleep for anyone. Drums shattered the stillness of the night. Trumpets sounded the assembly. Lanterns were flashing. Sir William's triumph was turned to tragedy. His six hundred could not withstand Sir Michael Ernely's three thousand! He must retreat. Retreat to Wrexham and carry the sad tidings to Sir Thomas Myddleton and Colonel Booth. Retreat to the Bridge of Holt and get back to Nantwich before all hope of retirement was cut off. Captain Elliot with a hundred and twenty men were left to hold the Castle. The Rev. Mr. Ince, with more valour than discretion, resolved to share with them the rigours of a siege. A few snow flurries added to the gloom of that dreary Novem-ber morning as the long line of Parliamentary foot trudged the tree-fringed road to Wrexham.

Ryder, who had exchanged his jaded horse for a charger, lingered with the rearguard. He had received no orders from

Sir William, who appeared to have forgotten his existence in his anxiety to escape from the trap. It was a severe blow to Brereton. Before the English-Irish landed he hoped that Chester could not have held out ten days longer.

Ryder drew aside as the troops passed on their way. A great curiosity assailed him. His taste of freedom was heady wine. When first he entered the service of the Parliament no soldier had been more amenable to discipline, more ready to obey orders. If an officer is dispatched for special service and taught to act on his own initiative it is hard to return to the established order of things. Ryder resolved that he would tarry to see the next development in the situation. As daylight crept over the scene it revealed the stone castle on its mound standing gaunt against the grey sky. The drawbridge was up. There was no sign of life save the head-pieces of the watchers on the top of the tower.

From behind the long screen of leafless trees something moved. Round a bend of the road came the leading files of the forces from Ireland. They broke into shouts and cheers. A dashing-looking officer ran forward and, standing boldly in the open within pistol-shot, shouted to the garrison to surrender.

"I presume you very well know my disposition! I am Thomas Sandford, captain of firelocks, no bread-and-cheese rogue, but ever a Royalist. I advise you to show yourselves faithful subjects to his Majesty and deliver the Castle for his Majesty's use. If you do so you will be received into mercy. If you put me to the least trouble or loss of blood to force you, expect no quarter. My hopes are not to starve you but to batter and storm you and then hang you all."

To this fiery demand Captain Elliot replied that the garrison feared the loss of their religion more than the loss of their dearest blood.

So the siege of Hawarden Castle began. Ryder saw a thousand of the new army taking up their position about the walls. Musketry fire broke out. Ordnance there was none. The remainder of the invading force went marching down the hill and along the flat road to Chester. News of their coming preceded them. A welcome awaited them from the Governor, Sir Abraham Shipman. The Mayor sent collectors through the city wards begging clothes for the ragged host. Wives brought out their knitting needles and began to knit stockings. Shirts, doublets, shoes, breeches, food and warmth—there seemed no end to the demands of the new-comers. Sir Michael Ernely and Major-General Gibson established themselves in the city, leaving the siege of Hawarden to Captain Sandford, who was joined by Welsh forces under Colonel Davies, and also Colonel Mostyn, who made speedy use of his freedom.

There was a brisk attack on the Castle on December the third. The next day Ryder saw the forsaken garrison at Hawarden hang out the white flag. He mounted his horse and rode towards Holt with the news.

Fresh hope dawned in Royalist hearts. Though the men from Ireland brought anxiety as well as good cheer to the good folk at Chester, their coming was a rare incentive to all who laboured for the Royalist cause. The King himself, when word reached him, sent orders for a special distribution of food and clothes and money. Mr. Orlando Bridgeman hurried back from Oxford to Chester to welcome the new-comers. And now that Sir Nicholas Byron, erstwhile Governor of Chester, had been captured by Colonel Mytton at Elles-mere, his nephew, Lord Byron, was sent by King Charles to take his place.

Once Hawarden had surrendered, Captain Sandford, that intrepid leader of firelocks, embarked on a more ambitious scheme. With Colonel Gamull and his firelocks he advanced on Beeston Castle. In the darkness of night they scaled the heights. When word came through that the Governor of Beeston had surrendered his charge to Captain Sandford, the blow to Sir William Brereton was staggering. Nantwich was girt about by foes. The swift triumph of the raid into Wales was a thing of the past. Sir William was now on the defensive. The eyes of England were on Cheshire. With the coming of the English-Irish army the war assumed a more deadly aspect.

CHAPTER SEVENTEEN

THERE was no lack of fuel in Nantwich, which was fortunate, for the weather had set in cold. Snow had fallen on more than one occasion. Sir Thomas Myddleton had hastened to London to recruit. Sir William Brereton remained in Cheshire. It was, for him, a time of testing. The loss of Hawarden Castle was a grievous blow; the loss of Beeston was a tragedy. Sir William frequently made his headquarters at the Lamb. It was convenient to the church, from the tall tower of which his sentinels kept vigilant watch over the surrounding countryside.

Sir William laid down his quill and listened to Ryder's report with an unmoved countenance. When the young man had finished the General sat deep in thought. He found in scriptural utterances the emotions which were in his heavy heart. *"Rejoice not against me, O mine enemy: when I fall I shall arise."* He looked up quickly. "The loss of Hawarden is serious, Yale. It has, for the time being, saved Chester. It is Beeston which troubles me. The enemy is on our very threshold now. He will be within our gates if we waver. The condition of these parts is less hopeful than when it pleased God to give us good success in Wales. I look to you not to relax your vigilance."

A cook and a barber were Ryder's first requirements after he left the Commander-in-Chief. When he reached his lodgings he found a message to say that Verity had heard of his return and was expecting to see him. He lost no time in making his way to her rooms. Verity was seated in an armchair beside a comfortable fire when he entered. She thrust a needle into her sewing and laid it aside as she rose to greet her friend.

Ryder stood in the doorway with the raindrops glistening on his lobster-tail helmet and dripping from his cloak to the floorboards.

"What a joy to see you again, Ryder!" exclaimed the girl. "Take off your wet things and sit by the fire. We have much to talk about. Mark told me that you vanished at Flint. He was concerned for your safety. What happened?"

"I was captured, but escaped in time to see the English-Irish army descend on Hawarden."

"And I was within the walls of Chester when those ragged warriors came trooping in. If they drink and steal, Ryder, I find it hard to condemn them, for they have been shamefully neglected. But how is it that you did not return with Sir William's forces?"

Ryder smiled grimly. "I remained behind to see what happened. I begin to discover new traits in myself, Verity—I stayed without orders to do so."

"I, too, find I am different from when the war started. It may be a good thing, Ryder."

"How so? To be truthful, I have felt concerned about the change in myself."

"For one thing, it shows that we are not stagnating. Great changes are shaping in this country; we must shape with them."

"I find I have different views."

"So has everybody—or should have."

"You console me when I feared you might condemn me."

"To condemn you would be to condemn myself. We grope for light—and so do our leaders."

"When war broke out I thought the issue was clear cut—who should rule—the King or the Parliament."

"You thought the issue was fixed?"

"Yes, Verity."

"That is where you were wrong. I have done much meditating during the last twelve months. I have had ample time for reflection. As a result of my thinking——"

"You see things more clearly. I envy you."

"No, Ryder. As a result of my thinking I am more confused than ever because the issue itself gets more confused. Cannot you see? When war broke out the issue was not decided; it has not yet begun to resolve itself. Before it is clearly defined years may pass. Years—or centuries."

Ryder looked troubled. "I imagined I fought to get an established government so that homes could be orderly and life secure."

"Nothing is stable, Ryder. Nothing can be. The only thing we can be certain will happen is change."

"I do not like it," he said, shaking his head. "And yet you are right. The war in these parts has changed already in character."

"And will do so now that Lord Byron is in command in Chester."

"You do not like him? Has his new peerage turned his head?"

"He is most active for the King. He is brave, but arrogant and oppressive. Have you heard of that sad affair in the church at Barthomley?"

"I am out of touch with everything."

"Twenty villagers took refuge in the tower. Pews were set on fire and they were smoked out and slain as they appeared. Byron boasted that he had them all put to the sword for mercy to such people was cruelty."

"I trust the day is not far distant when his pride may be humbled."

"I think the men from Ireland will prove doughty opponents," she remarked seriously. "Poor creatures, they are little better than beggars. The Mayor has set aside four hundred ounces of gilt plate to turn into coin for their payment. Their coming is a good thing for the King, but it is a bad business for us. Sir William has written to the Earl of Essex for two hundred more dragoons and fifty barrels of powder. And six hundred muskets."

"Does he anticipate a siege, then? I was just thinking, Verity, how good it was that you were safe out of Chester, yet it may be that you come to a place where there is even greater danger."

"What matter so that I am among friends?"

"You and I are friends?"

"Always. What makes you ask that?"

For a moment he did not answer. He sat staring at the carving on the beam—words to a young man on the choosing of a wife. "There is something I must say to you, Verity; something which has been on my mind for many weary weeks. I cannot bear a shadow to fall between us. You recall the night when we talked on the ramparts?"

"The night when I was restless, full of forebodings. I remember it well."

"I saw a woman leave the town by stealth. It was you?"

"Yes, Ryder."

"May I ask why?"

"Are you speaking now as the officer of the guard? If so, it is my duty to tell you."

"No. I speak now as—as a friend. There is no occasion for you to answer if you do not wish."

"Then although there is no occasion for me to answer you, I shall do so. I went to meet Captain Wilding."

"Why?"

"To return him his sword."

"You had no right to do so." Ryder sounded virtuous.

"No more right than you had to rescue him from the battle."

"That was different. I—I do not approve of your seeing him."

"Why, pray?"

"Because he is an enemy. You have no right to be friendly with a man of the King's party."

"Have you any right to be friendly with a beautiful girl who belongs to the King's party?"

The question disconcerted Ryder. "No," he muttered.

"Have *you* ever seen *her* by stealth?"

He turned in amazement. "Are you a witch? How did you know?"

"I did not know. Something suggested that it might be possible."

"I did see her—for a few moments. Only once."

"Then why do you object to my seeing Royle for a few moments and returning the sword which you said must be returned to him?"

"Oh, I don't know why!" he said miserably. "I can't explain. You—you are at liberty to do what you choose, of course. I have no right to say you nay. Only—only, Verity, I am concerned about your safety. These men have a strangely distorted conception of honour, or so it seems to me."

"I am capable of taking care of my own honour."

He hid his face in his hands. "The Devil is in me!" he groaned. He stood up, stretching himself to his full height. Verity glanced at him. Never had she seen him look so stern, never had he appeared so tall and strong. In his mud-splashed jack-boots and buff-coat he looked a typical fighting-man. He still wore a sword—his own sword, which had hacked its way through many an encounter.

"Was it only to return Wilding's sword that you went?"

"You have no right to ask me."

"As an officer I have a right to question you." He spoke almost savagely.

"You do not mean that?"

"Yes! No! I don't know. Verity, tell me, you are not in league with this fellow?"

"Ryder, look me in the eyes and repeat that. Tell me, you do not suspect me of anything dishonourable? You do not doubt me after all we have endured together?"

"No." He turned his head away, unable to meet her eyes.

"Say you do not distrust me."

"I do not distrust you. But, Verity, tell me plainly!"

"No, Ryder. Never! Not because I fear to, but because there can be no friendship without trust. You must trust me —implicitly. Tell me—for what are we fighting?"

"For freedom?"

"You take away my freedom when you demand of me an account of what I do."

"You are right, Verity. I apologize. I have no right to question you. But believe me, no one has your welfare more at heart. I say no more—except that I trust you."

He strode impetuously from the room.

No further reference was made to the incident when next they met. Indeed, there were other matters to think upon. The roads from Chester were alive with scouting parties. With Beeston Castle as their base the Royalists grew increasingly daring. By the fourth of January Lord Byron's men had assaulted Dodington Hall. Though well provisioned, and garrisoned by a hundred and twenty men, it surrendered. The defenders were allowed to march out to freedom. They went to Wem, not daring to face the indignation of Sir William Brereton. Nantwich was no place for the faint of heart.

Guards on the walls of Nantwich were doubled. It was cold work. Snow and sleet chilled their faces. The landscape grew white. But it was not in keeping with the spirit of Nantwich men to sit tamely behind mud walls. A party of horse, led by Lieutenant Yale, rode forth in search of a convoy which friendly villagers had reported. The country people were loyal to Sir William. Ryder found the convoy —seven carriages laden with goods. The heads of the oxen which drew them were turned to Welsh Bridge. Ryder came home in triumph.

But it cost Thomas Evanson his house and barn, which the irate Royalists burnt in revenge. Saboth Church, too, lost a lodge and many stacks of hay. The red glare lit the country-side. From the summit of St. Mary's Church dark clouds of smoke could be seen rising, and amid the haze, darkening the white roads, a long column of marching men. Horsemen hovered along the banks of the Weaver. Across the fields at Dorfold Hall oxen were drawing a heavy gun into position. A group of mounted officers watched the operation. Acton Church was alive with figures. The enemy were closing in on the town.

Where was Sir William Brereton while these preparations for a siege of his principal stronghold were being made? A week before he had met with a reverse at Middlewich when he ventured out to see if he could beat back Lord Byron's army which was advancing from Chester. But Byron was victorious. Brereton lost three hundred dead and two hundred captured—a total he could ill afford.

Sir William put Colonel George Booth in command at Nantwich and rode to collect the shattered fragments of his force and to get together reinforcements. Verity joined Ryder on the church tower. The women of Nantwich were resolved to play their part in the coming siege and many were to be found on the ramparts aiding the men. The church tower was a favourite vantage point of Ryder's when he was not on duty. It afforded a magnificent view of the country round about. He could look down on the woods which crept in places to the river's edge. The trees were bare now, a bristle of witches' brooms save where a holly grew darkly or ivy throttled a dying trunk. They could pick out some of the Royalists—men of the Red Regiment, men of the Green Regiment.

It was the big gun which had been planted on top of the slope near Dorfold Hall which held the attention of Ryder and Verity. Light was failing, but the cannon was visible, for a fire had been lighted not far away.

"To keep the gunners warm?" inquired Verity.

"Nothing so innocent," replied Ryder. "They are heating bullets. We shall have thatches ablaze before morning."

At eleven o'clock that night the gun began to fire. The red-hot shot fell in Welsh Row. Several cottages flared.

Ryder made his way to the barrier at Welsh Bridge. Here the greatest press of troops had assembled lest the Royalists should rush the barricade. Walls were manned on every side, for the King's forces completely surrounded the town. A great blaze lit up the sky. "It is Mr. Wilbraham's place: It is Townsend which is on fire!" said Corporal Garnett in explanation.

"And Master Roger lies ill of a fever," called out a woman.

Soldiers clamoured to be allowed to make a sally, but Captain Trueman, who had charge of the barricade, was adamant.

"Not a man must leave his post!" he ordered.

"If the men cannot go, the women can!" called out Verity, and ran across the bridge. A score of women followed, some pausing to seize buckets. They scooped up water or snow and formed a bucket chain as they endeavoured to check the flames. The gunners, seeing the crowd, concentrated their fire on the spot. The blaze was stopped after part of the building was lost. The women came home wearily and sadly, bearing the body of one of their number.

"It is Margery Davenport," explained Verity as she rejoined Ryder, "the daughter of John Davenport. She was slain by a cannon bullet—the first person to be struck in the town since the beginning of the siege."

House after house took fire. A sortie was at length made, and ten of the attackers were killed. The townsmen brought back two prisoners—two men prisoners, that is. They brought a woman captive, too. She was a more valuable prize than the men. They found she had twenty half-crown pieces in her pocket.

CHAPTER EIGHTEEN

THIS was the beginning of the great siege, a siege which was to place the name of Nantwich in the annals of heroism, a siege which delivered a telling blow to Lord Byron's pride.

The ill success which attended his lordship's impetuosity at Edgehill had taught him no lesson; his easy success over Sir William Brereton at Middlewich had made him confident of victory. It is true that Lord Capel had five times assaulted Nantwich without profit, but Lord Byron had greater confidence in his own prowess. Moreover, he had the English-Irish army to reinforce him. Not the least of the new-comers was Captain Sandford, a Cheshire man, he who had been so forthright at Hawarden and so intrepid at Beeston, a man whose bold words were matched by brave deeds.

Acton Church became a citadel. From its tower a constant look-out was kept by Royalist sentinels. Today, as the eye rests upon the sacred building standing in repose beside a country road, it seems hard to comprehend that Acton had the reputation of being the church which had seen more fighting than any in the country. Lord Capel made it his headquarters; so did Lord Byron. Until recent years the tower leads still bore the imprint of Cavalier boots, and the knife-point carvings with which sentries amused themselves when not gazing across at Nantwich's rival fane.

January was at its coldest. The weather was cruel. Besieged and besieger suffered equally. Through Brereton's foresight Nantwich was well provided with victuals and munitions. Within the mud walls, now frozen hard, dwelt men and women stubborn by nature. They drew confidence from the calm resolution of their commander. Grandson of Sir George Booth of Dunham Massey, Colonel Booth was a kinsman, through marriage, of Sir William and well worthy of the trust imposed in him.

The trees looked gaunt and bare against the white mottled landscape. The waters of the curving Weaver, not yet frozen, cut a deep furrow across the checkered scene. From the ramparts the townsmen could see Byron's pioneers examining the banks just out of musket range.

"They mean to throw a bridge across," observed Ryder to Verity, who, wrapped in a fur-lined cloak, joined him on watch.

"Does that mean they intend to assault the town from this side?"

"They will assault from any side or all sides; we are completely invested. Their leaguer holds us in a tight grip. It would seem they mean to entrench themselves in Snow Fields."

"Aptly named, at the moment, though there is no salt there."

Ryder was puzzled by Verity's behaviour. She was more reserved and at times seemed almost aloof, yet she was continually in his company. If, he asked himself, he had offended her, why did she still desire his friendship? Perhaps she did not know her own mind! Ryder was beginning to catch glimpses of the complexity of human nature.

His own life was not free from complications. He could stand contentedly talking to Verity and at the same time fall to dreaming of Rosea whenever a gaily clad Cavalier brought her to mind. On several occasions he had seen Royle Wilding. There was no mistaking that gallant figure. Even among the showy staff officers who followed close to Lord Byron, Wilding was conspicuous.

Ryder saw Royle saunter down to the men who tested the river's depth. He wore no cloak and his plum-coloured doublet made a patch of colour as he stood in the snow as though disdaining the cold.

"A friend of yours!" Ryder had made the remark before he realized what he said. Was the old belief true, that devils whispered in the ear? He was sorry he had said it. He saw a slight flush mantle Verity's smooth cheeks, but she showed no perturbation.

"Ah, yes. It is Captain Wilding. How quick of you to recognize him, Ryder!"

"It was not difficult. I have seen him on a number of occasions: in sunlight, in torchlight—and by the light of the moon."

"You also saw him lying unconscious in a field and befriended him. Why should you befriend a man who is our enemy?"

"We are told to love our enemies," replied Ryder, devoutly wishing he had not introduced the subject.

"Is that what you would have me do?"

"No!" he retorted hastily. "That is, charity is to be commended."

"That was why you helped him to escape?"

"Yes. He was kind to me when I was in Chester."

"He was kind, too, to me."

"That is a different matter."

"Of course. I was under a greater obligation. He came to my aid when the Nunnery was pillaged. You have doubtless forgotten."

"No, I have not forgotten. It is you who have forgotten. You forget that I, too, fought to save you from the mob. You remember his aid, you prefer to forget mine."

"Now you are being childish!" There was that in her tone which cut deep. Ryder flushed.

"You are right," he confessed.

A sudden feeling of unworthiness stole over him. Why should he question her thus? What right had he? What was his motive?

"I am jealous, I suppose," he muttered.

"That is very foolish of you."

"I am sorry. Forgive me. I have hurt you."

"No, you have not hurt me. It is yourself you have hurt. That is the price of jealousy. It has not a redeeming virtue. It harms everyone, harms most of all the person who experiences the jealousy. I pray you purge your heart of jealousy. It is a grievous sin. I cannot see why you should be jealous. You were my friend. You are still my friend. You will always be my friend. Why do you think that my knowing someone else affects my regard for you? Are you not strong enough and magnanimous enough to accept me as I am?"

"You make me feel unworthy. What you say is so true. I feel like a dog in the manger."

"But why, Ryder? What cause have you?"

He could not answer her. He could not tell her that he

loved her, for the image of Rosea was ever in his mind. If he fed on dreams of Rosea, what right had he to deny Verity her dreams?

"I feel humble, Verity. I was puffed up in my own conceit. Life is beginning to teach me many lessons. Let us talk no more of Royle Wilding."

"I will if you wish."

"No. I am glad he has his sword back—he will require it. Marry the fellow if you wish. We will still be friends."

"But why not? Do you not remember the talk we had on the ramparts? You promised then that you would be my friend whatever happened. You have forgotten so soon?"

"No, I have not forgotten. I will remain your friend come what may."

"You make me happy. Let us walk, Ryder. We have stood here so long that my feet are like ice."

The sound of a trumpet drew them to the Welsh Bridge. Along Welsh Row came a Cavalier trumpeter. Beside him walked a soldier with a white flag fastened to a half-pike. Behind them strode an officer, haughty of mien.

Lord Byron had sent to Colonel Booth his first summons to yield the town of Nantwich for his Majesty's use.

＊ ＊ ＊ ＊ ＊

The reply which Colonel Booth returned could have been little to his lordship's liking, for its receipt was a signal for a fresh bombardment of the town. Hitherto the firing had been sporadic. Now, every gun in possession of the Royalists opened fire. The demi-culverin set beside Dorfold Hall was the source of particular annoyance. The cannonade went on throughout the day, and though it abated at nightfall it did not wholly cease. Red-hot cannon-balls curved through the darkness. More than one roof was set ablaze. Two days later Lord Byron sent another summons to surrender. He accused the commandant of withholding from the inhabitants the contents of the first summons, and leading them to believe that every man, woman and child would be put to the sword.

"We never reported, or caused to be reported, that your lordship or the army intended any such cruelty," Colonel

Booth replied. "Your former summons was publicly read amongst the soldiers and townsmen, as your trumpeter can witness. For the delivery of this town we may not with our consciences and reputations betray the trust reposed in us. Though we be termed traitors and hypocrites, yet we hope and are confident God will evidence and make it known to the world our zeal for His glory, our unspotted loyalty to his Majesty and sincerity in all our professions."

The bombardment recommenced. Lord Byron was not allowed to remain uninterrupted. There was a sortie from Nantwich behind Mr. Thomas Mainwaring's house, where the Royalists had flung up earthworks for their protection. It was hot work while it lasted. Ryder found it so, for his sword was busy. The party returned bearing captured arms and ammunition, also clothing which the attackers had left behind in their eagerness to escape the onslaught. And this all for the loss of one man, one Hugh Blackshawe, a good soldier, who ventured too far.

The days had now crept on to January the seventeenth. It was a day to be remembered. The King's cannon were discharged four score and sixteen times, yet for all this the town suffered no harm.

And then, at break of day, came the great attack. There, in the grey light of dawn, dark masses of men hurried over the trampled snow. Townsmen, sleepy eyed, snatched weapons and stumbled out into the cold as the bells of St. Mary's clanged their warning. Women, too, hurried to the ramparts. With the clangour mingled the crash of cannon, the irregular discharge of musket and pistol, shouts, commands, cheers, groans. Down the road from Dorfold Hall marched a long column of Royalist musketeers. Their matches burning made them look like a fiery snake in the gloom. With every gust of wind a shower of sparks would rise in the air. Over near the demi-culverin on the slope stood a guard of firelocks. They were safer than musketeers, whose burning matches might ignite loose powder.

Those who led the assault against the mud walls bore scaling-ladders, or faggots to fill up the ditch. They were greeted with a fusillade—not merely from muskets and snaphances. Showers of bricks and stones were flung by the boys of the town. Ladders were hurled back, and as the scalers struggled on the ground they were deluged with boiling brine emptied on them by the women of Nantwich. Verity was among the defenders, who were led by an Amazon of the name of Brett. For the space of an hour the attack went on. At Welsh Bridge the assault was hottest.

It was Captain Sandford who led this attack. His dauntless courage inspired his men. Again and again he guided them to the foot of the wall. More than once Ryder caught a glimpse of Royle Wilding, sword in hand, urging forward the pikemen. Like Sandford, he seemed to be in the forefront while the fighting was hottest. A gentleman volunteer scaled the wall and leaped the coping, shouting, "The town is ours!" Ryder shot him with a pistol, and the man fell mortally wounded. Captain Sandford rushed for the ladder. A youth beside Ryder picked up a firelock which had fallen from the hands of a wounded man and aimed at the Royalist captain.

The kick of the piece nearly knocked the youth off his feet, but when the smoke cleared he saw that the valiant captain lay shot through the heart. It was one of the worst blows the Royalists sustained. The strife was too hot to last. By the time daylight was fully established the King's forces withdrew, leaving a hundred dead which they could not carry away, and many wounded.

Ryder paused from his exertions and looked down from the ramparts. It was a scene of desolation—the trampled snow on which the blood showed bright, smashed scaling-ladders, discarded bandoliers and hats, broken pikes, motionless forms of the dead; writhing forms of the wounded. The barricades were raised and the triumphant defenders streamed forth to collect weapons or booty.

They bore into the town the body of the gallant Captain Sandford and stripped it. In a pocket of his doublet was found a copy of the day's instructions from Major-General Gibson. The password was 'God and a good cause'. There was also an epistle addressed to the Nantwich garrison. Captain Sandford seemed as active with his pen as with his sword. "Your drum can inform you that Acton Church is no more a prison, but now free for honest men to do their devotion therein", and much more in a similar strain.

For all the brave words the attack had failed. Byron counted on the success of this sudden and violent assault delivered at five separate places simultaneously. In dead and wounded it cost him five hundred men. The townsmen were outside the barricades enumerating the slain. Many corpses were cast into the river.

At Wall Lane end Ryder found the dead body of Lieutenant-Colonel Boughton, one captain and many officers, together with the prime of the Red Regiment.

The spacious Church of St. Mary's presented an amazing spectacle. There were armed guards at every door. All captured Cavaliers, many of them wounded, were taken there and left to find what comfort they could. Verity, who had been foremost among the women who fought on the ramparts, was now conspicuous in a new role. She moved among the wounded, bathing and bandaging.

"More straw," she demanded of the Nantwich men about her. "You must fetch more straw. They must lie warm or the cold will get into their wounds. Why, you would give greater care to beasts in their stalls."

Some time elapsed before Ryder entered. He had military duties to perform. Lord Byron had received a severe check, a cruel lesson, but vigilance must never be relaxed. Colonel Booth saw to that.

"Oh, Ryder," exclaimed the girl as she saw him crossing the disordered nave, "I cannot understand myself. When the assault was in progress no one was more active than I in repelling the enemy. I flung down several ladders and exulted when they crashed. And now, here is one poor fellow with his leg all twisted. Doubtless he is one of the very men I injured. Instead of hating him I am filled with compassion."

Ryder went to examine the fellow in question and helped to set the fractured leg. Like many another soldier in those rough days, he had acquired a crude knowledge of bone-setting and treatment of wounds in the hard school of experience. Help was needed. The few surgeons in Nantwich were overworked.

"We must have more straw," insisted Verity.

"There is no more straw," Ryder informed her. "And we

cannot spare hay, for there is scarce enough to keep our mounts alive."

"Then the townspeople must give their blankets. Go, see what you can secure."

Ryder took his orders with rare docility. Hay and straw were at a premium, as well he knew, for in addition to the cavalry horses all cattle from the neighbourhood were within the walls for security. The town was beginning to experience scarcity. The attacks were resumed. Lord Byron was by no means beaten.

When next Ryder entered the church he could not set eyes on Verity. Finally he did see her. He noticed that she was seated behind one of the pillars soothing a wounded man who was stretched there. There was something about the look on her face, something about the poise of her shoulders, which told Ryder that this was no ordinary patient. He tiptoed towards her and found himself looking down upon the pale face of Royle Wilding.

"So we meet again, Master Bull-Baiter!" The voice was weak.

"I am glad to see that you are in good hands," said Ryder formally. Verity glanced at him. Her face, he thought, revealed anxiety. Ryder walked slowly away. He stood staring abstractedly at a window in which a coloured coat-of-arms caught the pale light of a wintry sun. Why did he keep coming across Royle Wilding? Was it pure chance or was it part of some subtle design that their ways should cross? He wished he knew. Life would be so much simpler if people knew what was expected of them. He could not analyse his feelings where Royle was concerned. Did he like or dislike him?

It must be one or the other. He could not be neutral. There could be no middle course where Royle Wilding was concerned. The man was too vital. Enemy though he was, Ryder could not help liking him. Yet—did he really like him, or was he merely drawn to him because of Rosea?

Here was a fresh complication. What was Royle to Rosea? Were they relatives, friends, or lovers? It was a relationship Ryder found beyond his comprehending. To Ryder it was a man's bounden duty to love one woman and

one only: to take her for life. Having done so it was a sin to
contemplate any other. Yet Royle was fond of Rosea; and
Rosea had offered her lips—Ryder shrugged his shoulders
in his perplexity. He turned impatiently away as though he
would escape from his thoughts.

The siege went on. By day and by night the heavy boom
of cannon shook the air. The crash of roundshot caused
townspeople to glance up apprehensively as they wondered
which chimney would totter next.

Now the snow began to thaw. Men on watch turned
anxious eyes to the Weaver. The meadows about the weir
were under water. A broad, muddy flood swept past the mill
and under Welsh Bridge. Some distance away was Beam
Bridge, a fine stone structure newly built. To save time in
crossing, the King's men had erected a bridge of boats, a
"platt" they termed it, nearer the town. This was threatened
by the rising river.

It would not withstand the water pressure much longer.
Watchers on the town walls could see the bustle as the
besiegers dragged cannon and ammunition-waggons to the
security of the left bank.

Horses, too, were taken across. Lord Byron had no
intention of having his forces divided if the bridge were
swept away. But his efforts were too late. The next day—it
was the twenty-fourth—the platt was wrecked. The men on
the right bank were cut off from their comrades. To rejoin
them meant a march of six or seven miles.

Ryder was quick to perceive their dilemma. He ran to
the nearest sallyport and, sword in hand, led a rush of
volunteers. They drove off a party of King's men who tried to
save the platt, making some of them prisoners. Men with
torches followed. Too long had Nantwich been endangered
because of buildings too close to its walls, buildings which
gave shelter to enemy firelocks. Every one must be destroyed.
Thatch after thatch went up in flames. Walls must come
down even though they were part of Mr. Geoffrey Myn-
shull's fair new house. Houses and barns and cottages were
razed. Lord Byron was now concentrating the main body of
his troops on Acton Church.

Up the open road came a messenger on a jaded horse.

Ryder walked to meet him. "Sir William is marching to the rescue! Hold on another day!" The courier rode into the town shouting the news. Even Colonel Booth walked into the street to greet the bearer of good tidings.

Sir William Brereton was on his way. There was yet hope.

CHAPTER NINETEEN

In those days Nantwich, important market town though it was, was little more than a village in size. Though dignified by a church which had the beauty of a cathedral, and by the spacious dwellings of several persons of quality, it was for the most part a humble place, a place where dwelt the beamers and wallers and other workers in salt, a place of buying and selling, as the swine market, the oat market and beasts' market testified. Yet it was the apple of Sir William Brereton's eye—perhaps by reason of the good hearts of the townspeople. Though Sir William was criticized for abandoning his little garrison in Hawarden Castle on the occasion of his hurried retreat from Wales, it was not his custom to leave friends to their fate. Men of Nantwich remembered how, when Lord Capel assailed the town, Sir William made a forced march from Stafford. During the tedious siege all felt that sooner or later Sir William would come to their relief. They knew that he would be pleading with the Parliament to send succour to loyal, hard-pressed Nantwich.

His plea to Parliament was such that they ordered one of their most brilliant young generals to go to Nantwich's aid—Lord Fairfax's son, Sir Thomas Fairfax, only thirty-two years of age, but linked with the older genius, Oliver Cromwell, as a man who would go far. And now, somewhere across the snowy land, Sir William Brereton and Sir Thomas Fairfax were marching doggedly from Manchester at the head of twenty-eight troops of horse and nearly three thousand foot. The men of Lancashire, raw levies for the most part, were learning to endure hardship. Despite his reverse at the assault on Nantwich, Lord Byron still had three thousand horse and two thousand foot under his command—

veterans most of them. He, too, learned of the approach of Sir William Brereton, and a party went forth skirmishing along the borders of Delamere Forest to contest his advance. It was here the first clash occurred. The King's men were driven back, leaving forty prisoners in Fairfax's keeping. The Parliamentarians found simple quarter at Tilston Heath that night, and the next day they began the five-mile march which was to carry them to Nantwich. Again a party from Lord Byron endeavoured to ambush them, without success.

They marched on until they came upon half of Lord Byron's army drawn up within cannon-shot of their works. Byron's guns opened fire, but did no damage. Brereton and Fairfax called a council of war to debate whether they should assault the entrenchments of the Royalists or march straight to relieve the town.

It was decided to enter Nantwich. Pioneers went ahead to level hedges and the army began to cross the fields. They had not gone far when word came through that the half of the Royalist army which had been beyond the Weaver had got across the Beam Bridge and were threatening the rear of the Parliamentary forces. The Cavaliers at Acton Church charged at the same time, so that Brereton's men were caught between two fires. The Parliamentary foot at first gave ground, but a charge of horse beat the Royalists out of the hedges.

Colonel Booth, watching from the tower of Nantwich Church, was able to interpret the movements beyond the river. He sent Ryder with a message to say that the Nantwich garrison would sally forth. Taking Corporal Garnett with him, Ryder made a detour to the southward, forded the river and so was able to get round the Royalists' flank. He recognized Sir William and spurred towards him. Brereton was sitting his horse near several light field guns which the relief force had just brought up. He turned at the sound of Ryder's approach. He looked pale from loss of sleep and exposure, but gave a slight smile as he recognized Yale.

"Ah, Ryder. It is cheering to see a friendly face. You have brought me good news, I trust?"

"Colonel Booth is collecting a force to unite with you, sir."

"He . . . will . . . be . . . welcome!" A tall, dark man with a hesitant voice came up. Ryder saluted, knowing that this must be Sir Thomas Fairfax himself. "Our . . . guns . . . are slow . . . in arriving."

There was no time for further talk. The Parliamentary cavalry were slashing down a hedgerow preparatory to a charge—bloodless work as yet, but soon their swords would be reddened. Fairfax's firelocks, taking advantage of wall and hedgerow, were pushing towards Acton Church. Lord Byron, who had brought the forces over Beam Bridge, began attacking the Parliamentary rear.

Sir William led his horsemen against the advancing Cavaliers, and though for a while he was in danger his men cut their way through. The Royalist foot were in retreat. The horse were wavering. A great cheer went up from the neighbourhood of Acton Church. Colonel Booth and the Nantwich men closed on the Royalists, who sought safety in the church. Sir William, encouraged by this onslaught, gathered his horsemen together, resolved to gain the day. Ryder was in the thick of the charge. Twice his head-piece saved him from injury, and though his ears rang and his head ached he was still unscathed. Sir William was most active of all. He had forgotten that he was Commander-in-Chief, and fought, a soldier among soldiers.

The enemy wavered. One more determined thrust! Tired horses trotted into the fray. Troopers whose sword-arms ached with weariness attempted yet a few more blows. Swords rose and fell. Lord Byron was drawing off his horse in good order. They were taking the road to Chester. Pikemen and musketeers were casting down their weapons. The Royalist horse trotted away. The Parliamentarians were too spent to pursue. The tumult and the confusion were at an end.

Sir William bared his head. "God hath given us the victory!" he cried. Then, in the fading light, he trotted across the battlefield towards Acton Church, where Sir Thomas Fairfax's men were in possession of the enemy's earthworks. There, amid the trampled snow, the two commanders shook hands. There they greeted Colonel Booth. The cheers rang

K

out long and lustily. Nantwich, after seven weeks' siege, had been saved for the Parliamentary cause.

The bullets were still rapping against the red sandstone walls of Acton Church, but resistance was at an end. A white flag was thrust from a window and a drummer walked out to ask for a' parley. The flag was but a surplice fixed to a pike-point, but it served its purpose. The surrender was accepted; no one desired further bloodshed. The Royalists were verily routed.

The roll of the prisoners was a long one—a heartening roll to Sir William Brereton, for many notable warriors from Ireland were there. At the head of the list were Major-General Gibson, Sir Michael Ernely, Sir Richard Fleetwood, Sir Francis Butler, and Colonel George Monck. Sir Thomas Fairfax and his brother Sir William Fairfax pored over the names by the light of a lanthorn. The record of officers was a lengthy one. Fifteen hundred common soldiers had surrendered. They had twenty-two colours, six guns and twenty carriages. Less official, but none the less warlike, were a hundred and twenty-two women who had followed the camp. Many of them had long knives, with which they had done mischief.

There was much coming and going in the dusk. Bonfires were lit, partly for jubilation, partly to dry and cheer the weary, sodden warriors. Ryder dismounted from his horse, which limped with weariness and from a pike-wound, and made his way across the churned fields. It seemed strange to be able to go outside the mud walls without apprehending a brush with the enemy. A line of captive soldiers under guard passed him on the way to St. Mary's Church, which was to be their prison. Oxen strained at the traces of one of the captured guns. Four men bearing a wounded captain in his broad sash slithered past. Then came a wain bristling with pikes and muskets picked up on the battlefield.

Ryder was glad of his jack-boots as he ploughed through the mud. Already townsmen were digging in a field near Acton Church, making graves for the slain—Ryder heard that two hundred had been killed. They lay in a white line along the edge of the field, stripped nude ready for tossing into the trench.

A group of young men came boisterously towards the river bearing the captured banners slanting across their shoulders. They shouted to Ryder that the enemy had lost all their colours save only the flags of Sir Robert Byron's regiment—Sir Robert, one of the Governor's brothers.

Ryder was reeling with weariness, but there was no time for rest. He followed the trail of the prisoners and baggage waggons into the town. The barricades were down at last. The streets were crowded with chattering, excited men and women, boys and girls. Nantwich was safe.

"If daylight had not faded few would have escaped," commented Sir William grimly as he thanked his officers for their support. He ordered Ryder to take a dozen of his best men and ride into the night to make sure that the vanquished enemy showed no signs of rallying.

The captured officers were taken into houses and inns. The common soldiers were lodged in the church, where they were fed by the town authorities. Wounded were an encumbrance. They were told to look after themselves.

It had been a notable triumph. Welcome indeed to the Parliamentary cause was the treasure taken, money and loot accumulated by the Cavaliers during the seven weeks' siege as they pillaged the country round about. This was brought to the town for the Parliamentary chest—though not before a few soldiers had managed to extract some of the valuables.

It was impossible to watch everything. Prisoners were numerous and must be guarded. The plight of some of the wounded was pitiable.

At the Welsh Bridge a throng of voluble women surged backwards and forwards in the light of torches. Ryder could hear the babble of their voices long before he reached the place. There were shrill imprecations, jeers, protests, and no little abuse. The virtuous housewives of the town were driving the hundred and twenty captured camp-followers from Nantwich's impeccable gates. With commendable thriftiness they first despoiled the Egyptians of the more presentable portions of their attire.

The horsemen had difficulty in forcing their way through

the throng. A covered waggon drawn by two horses came down the street and halted at the bridge behind the troopers. When the way was cleared Corporal Garnett led the troopers through the crowd, and Ryder, drawing on one side, beckoned to the driver of the waggon to follow. Already along the edges of Welsh Row a pitiful trail of wounded men could be seen hobbling, or resting against a friendly wall. He felt a surge of compassion for them. Some, of a surety, would not survive a night in the open. But what could he do?

The waggon creaked past. Ryder accorded it but a passing glance. When it was well up the roadway he urged his horse forward and followed. As he drew near he was conscious of a pair of eyes fixed steadfastly on his. In the darkness he did not recognize them. He was taken by surprise when a woman's voice spoke his name. He bent from the saddle and looked inside the waggon.

"Verity! What in the name of goodness are you doing here?"

"The wounded have been turned out of St. Mary's. The church is for prisoners of war only."

"So I have been given to understand."

"I cannot allow my patient to die, Ryder. He is not fit to be moved. So I have hired this waggon and I am taking him to some comfortable farm where he can be nursed back to health."

"Verity, you have a tender heart, but I see no occasion for so great a sacrifice."

"It is no sacrifice."

"I do not like to think of you leaving the security of the town at a time like this. The highways are full of masterless men, desperate characters. Turn back, I beg of you, before it is too late."

"No, Ryder. My duty is plain. I shall not turn back."

"I would accompany you as escort, but I am sent forward to reconnoitre. Cannot you rest at some house until the morning? The Star Inn, perhaps?"

She shook her head. Ryder toyed with his reins. The troopers were well ahead now and he ought to rejoin them, yet he could not tear himself away. A thought leaped to his mind.

"And who is this patient to whom you show such devotion? Not Royle Wilding?"

"It is, Ryder. He is faint from loss of blood."

"Then you shall not do this thing."

"Why do you speak like that? You are not addressing your men."

"I will not permit it." He spoke stubbornly.

"*You* will not? You have no right to dictate to me thus."

"I say it is not seemly."

"You are not my judge."

"The world will judge—and judge harshly."

"The world!" Her voice expressed contempt. "I care not. What does wound me is that you, whom I thought my friend, should already sit in judgment on me—condemning me for a Christian act."

They had passed the gates of Dorfold Hall and were nearing Acton Church. The soldiers still thronged the churchyard. A sentry, firelock in hand, stood on a flat gravestone beside the wall. He looked down curiously as the waggon turned into the road which led to Wales.

"Hi! Halt!" Ryder's peremptory shout caused the driver to rein up. He rode closer to Verity. "I cannot tarry longer. Remain at the Star Inn for the night. Tomorrow I will call and we can consider what step is best to take."

"No, Ryder. My decision is made." Verity dropped lightly from the waggon and crossed to Ryder's stirrup. She stood there, close beside his knee, gazing up into his face. There was a wistful look in her eyes. He noticed she was pale, but resolute.

"I cannot speak freely from the waggon, where what we say may be overheard. The ways divide here, Ryder."

"The roads do. Our ways do not. You are coming my way."

"No, Ryder. Your way is not my way. Here we part. Tell me—do we part friends?"

He would not answer her. "Why are you going with this man?"

"He is wounded. He requires me. Oh, Ryder, I watched three men die last night and I am sure they died of cold, there, on the trampled straw of the House of God. Royle has bled much. He is weak. If I do not tend him he will die.''

"What is he to you? I tell you this—he has a sweetheart in Chester.''

"The more reason why some woman should tend him, save his life.''

"You love him!'' He spoke accusingly as though she did some evil thing. The girl did not answer.

"I know it!'' he cried vehemently. "Something tells me. He is an enemy to our cause. A godless, swashbuckling fellow. No fit companion for you. Turn back, Verity, I implore you. You are taking the broad way which leadeth to destruction. I beg of you to turn back before it is too late. You cannot love an enemy.''

"We are told to love our enemies.''

"But not that way.''

"Which way, then?''

"Heaven help me, I do not know. I must go, Verity. My men are out of sight. Turn back. For the last time, I beseech you.''

"I shall not so much as look back. Remember Lot's wife. I go my way. Join me if you will, but I will not weaken. Do we part friends?''

Instead of replying he gave his rein a vicious jerk. His weary charger, taken by surprise, tossed its head and started so suddenly that Ryder's jack-boot brushed the girl before she could step back. She gave a slight cry, more of surprise than of pain. Ryder rode off, stiff of shoulder, head held high. Verity, a forlorn figure in the muddy road, gazed after him. How fine a soldier he seemed! But he never looked back. Verity lowered her head and walked sombrely across the rutted road to the waiting waggon.

＊ ＊ ＊ ＊ ＊

March came to Nantwich, but though the throstles sang and the cattle were turned out to the green pastures to graze, it was, to Ryder Yale, a lonely place. A place of memories.

CHAPTER TWENTY

EVENTS in Cheshire had taken so great a turn for the worse that Prince Rupert was asked by the King to visit Chester to restore the balance. It was a great day for Chester when the fighting prince rode into the loyal city. March the eleventh was the date, and flags and banners streamed in honour of the glad occasion. Bells rang a welcome as a courier galloped up the road from Shrewsbury with word that the royal cavalcade was in sight. The Mayor, Randle Holme, climbed stiffly into his coach, *"ill of a payne in his legg"* (so the old records affirm), and was driven to The Cross to meet his Highness. Soldiers lined the streets. The red robes of the justices and the sheriffs added colour to the scene.

The Prince himself eclipsed them all. There was something imperious about the long, saturnine face with dark and piercing eyes, the thick black brows which spoke of temper and arrogance. There was an air of dash and daring about this twenty-four-year-old general who rode his high-spirited black stallion with a cloak the colour of blood fluttering from his haughty shoulders. Two years before he was in Bavaria; now, by virtue of his Stuart mother, he was accepted as an Englishman and proud peers felt privileged to follow his whirlwind course.

Prince Rupert sat his steed as the Mayor poured out his loyal eulogy. As the Prince listened with simulated courtesy his eyes roved until they rested on the lovely face of Rosea, who had taken a place in the Rows to watch the stirring spectacle. Henceforth Rupert found the tedium of the address less exacting. It might have been on Rosea's account that his Highness responded so graciously to the mayoral welcome.

The populace shouted with delight when he extended his hand for the Mayor to kiss. Emboldened by this courtesy, his worship went so far as to beg the Prince to allow the citizens to be relieved of the burden of having soldiers billeted on them without payment. His Highness suggested that such mundane matters might be discussed on the morrow and rode on to the house of Mr. John Aldersey, where he refreshed himself. Lord Byron followed at the Prince's elbow. He tugged impatiently at his pointed beard. Now that his uncle was a captive he had full measure of authority as newly appointed Governor of Chester. It is possible he did not deplore his uncle's fate so deeply as a dutiful nephew ought, seeing that it opened so useful a door for his ambitious self.

Rupert, who usually mellowed after wine, was not in a gracious mood. He took more kindly to victory than defeat, and he told Lord Byron bluntly that the Nantwich rout was not to his liking. He did not approve of the loss of men. He did not like the Parliament's alliance with the Scots.

"That was a sorry setback at Nantwich, Byron," observed the Prince moodily. "You must learn to do better."

"Your Highness does not regret it more than I do. At first encounter we had the better of them and were possessed of many of their colours. I had them in a trap and would have inflicted a total defeat had not Sir Michael Ernely's men, notwithstanding the endeavours of their officers, retreated without fighting a stroke."

"What ailed them?"

"The rebels tamper with the men's loyalty. Many from Ireland say plainly that they enlisted to fight papists and not fellow Protestants. I wish they were, in truth, Irish rather than English, for the Irish would fight, whereas the English we have are already very mutinous and are so poisoned by the ill-affected persons hereabouts that they are cold in our service."

"We shall warm them, Byron. I wish my uncle would use the Irish. The rebels do not hesitate to call in the Scots."

"Since they do so, your Highness, I see no reason why the King should make any scruple about calling in the Irish or the Turks if they would serve him."

"I come north to teach these rogues a lesson."

"Your Highness cannot strike too soon."

"What is the latest word from Ormond in Dublin? Can he arrange a further transport of forces from Ireland?"

"The Marquis says numbers are decreasing. He writes promising a further four regiments of foot and a hundred and sixty horse under Sir William Vaughan. He asks that we provide for them."

"Which I trust you will do."

"I shall do what I can, as in the past. Chester is in no condition to offer hospitality, as your Highness can see for yourself. We have many wounded on our hands after the Nantwich fight. However, the Marquis says that his men are so used to want that any reasonable provision will satisfy them."

The Prince rose. "Order the horses," he said briskly. "I must inspect your defences. What I have seen does not satisfy me."

Followed by an escort the Prince and the Governor rode to the city limits.

The Prince had a quick eye. He gave his instructions rapidly. Lord Byron hung on his words. Old trenches were to be filled in. Fresh and more advantageous lines were to be adopted. Several new gun-mounts were marked near Cow Lane. A trench was to be cut in the rock beyond Northgate. "The escarpments," said Rupert, "must be deepened and widened. You must raise the parapets to provide complete cover for the defenders."

Lord Byron rode back in sombre mood. If matters were going so well for the Royal cause why was it that Rupert was anxious that Chester should be well prepared to withstand a siege? Was it due to the Prince's professional thoroughness, or had he in mind the possibility of making Chester a strong place to which the King could retreat in the event of a reverse? The King had said no more about making Chester his headquarters since the occasion of his visit. All the same, it was apparent that the loyal city had not been forgotten by those in high places.

Two days later Prince Rupert rode from Chester. He had his mind set on the relief of Newark. Within a week by a brilliant dash he had accomplished this and Chester bells recorded his triumph. The Prince left Chester's aldermen wrestling with fresh problems of defence and even greater problems of finance. The city gates were to be repaired. They were to have drawbridges and portcullises. The foul ditch near Eastgate must be cleansed. In the event of a siege health must be safeguarded. Arrangements were made for a stock of coals to be brought in from the Flintshire mines while the roads and river were open to traffic.

In three days Rupert's fiery, infectious, impetuous will had brought fresh zeal to discouraged Chester. It was not long before his Highness was back again. He had his eye on North Wales. It was a profitable recruiting centre. He rode across Dee Bridge and went to Ruthin. He wanted horse, more horse. It became known that he was planning to relieve York and that a big battle was imminent. Lord Byron, with the pick of the cavalry in Chester, went with the Prince, who appointed his bosom friend, Colonel Will Legge, as temporary Governor of the city. Byron was to command one of Rupert's brigades. Rupert's last imperious command was as ruthless as his passage across a hostile shire. Handbridge must be levelled to the ground and, until the war was over, no one must build any house there.

Word filtered through to Chester of the Prince's progress. He was marching through Whitchurch, Sandbach, Knutsford, recruiting as he went. He was always recruiting. On May the twenty-fifth he captured Stockport. Lord Derby joined him and together they stormed Bolton. Rupert with a princely gesture sent to Lady Derby twenty-two captured standards as a token that the men who had besieged her in Lathom House would harass her no more. Wigan was the Prince's next objective. He descended on Liverpool, furious that a vessel bearing arms for the Royalists at Chester should have been carried thither by her mutinous crew. The garrison of Parliamentary warriors sensed the approach of the storm and took ship to parts unknown, leaving Liverpool to its fate. Rupert was in a ruthless mood. Blood and fire and pillage marked his path. "Prince Robber", "the Prince of Plunderland", was living up to his reputation.

He found time to write to the Mayor and aldermen of Chester ordering them to raise a rate for the payment and maintenance of the soldiers in the city. Entertaining royal Rupert was not without its disadvantages. Now, in June, he was marching for Yorkshire and the good folk of Chester awaited the glad tidings which were to set the joy-bells ringing. Prince Rupert was to crush the Parliamentarians in the last great battle of the war. As good and pious citizens the people of Chester had held a special service of thanksgiving in St. Werburg's on the occasion of the capture of Bolton. Bells were rung and there was a bonfire in the streets before almost every door at his Highness's success.

But the news of Marston Moor set no joy-bells ringing. It was a sullen, savage Prince who led the shattered remnant of his defeated army back to Chester that August. There were few footmen—they could not keep up with his furious pace—but he was well attended by horse and dragoons. The Prince took up his headquarters in the Bishop's Palace, where great preparation was made for his housekeeping as though he meant to remain a long while.

He wanted men to replenish his infantry—Rupert's famous Regiment of Bluecoats—which had been cut to pieces at Marston Moor. He scoured North Wales—recognized as the nursery of the King's infantry. In Flintshire, in Denbighshire, in Caernarvonshire, the Commissioners of Array were combing the countryside for fresh men to carry pikes. In Chester Rupert was busying himself again in replanning the city's defences. His suggestions did not invariably meet with favour.

He wished to demolish Eastgate and Northgate Streets, Cow Lane and all the northern suburbs. There were grumblings at his extortions. The money he proposed to levy was twice the amount settled by the Parliament. Perhaps it was on account of the discontent rather than for military reasons that the Prince quartered five thousand horse and dragoons in North Wales, where the Dee kept them out of sight and, he trusted, out of mind. He stationed Colonel Marrow with six hundred horse at Tarvin lest Sir William Brereton came marching up the road from Nantwich.

Sir William, astute man, did no such thing. He remained quietly behind his mud walls trusting that Prince Rupert, by his lack of tact, his plundering and his exactions, would do more harm to the Royal cause than any conflict in the field could achieve. There was a great impressing of men for Rupert's army in Chester; there was almost as great a running away. Sir William smiled when a report came to him that a false rumour of his approach had broken up a muster on the Roodee.

Yet Sir William was not wholly inactive. Before August was out he joined forces with his former colleague, Sir Thomas Myddleton, and marched to Frodsham in the hope of meeting the enemy. They did not find them at Frodsham, but they did encounter the outpost under Colonel Marrow which Prince Rupert had thrown out in the hope of such a contact. What the Prince had not anticipated was the result. The Royalist forces were driven back with considerable loss and their brave commander mortally wounded. Colonel Marrow was borne back to Chester to die.

When the ill tidings were known, Prince Rupert lay at Ruthin. Colonel Legge, who was still Governor of Chester, dispatched a force to punish Brereton for his temerity. These warriors met with no better success. After losing three hundred men slain and a hundred captured, the shattered remnant hurried back to Chester's walls.

Despite the presence of Prince Rupert, Sir William Brereton remained master of the field.

CHAPTER TWENTY-ONE

RYDER, who accompanied Sir William Brereton to Marston Moor, came through the tumult unscathed save for bruises sustained when his horse was shot under him. When the vanquished Prince Rupert led the ragged remnant of his routed army across to Cheshire, Sir William was one to whom was entrusted the pursuit of the royal fugitive. Once the Prince departed from Chester Sir William, faithful to his trust, again took up his task. He followed Rupert into Wales, followed him into Shropshire, clashing more than once with the rear guard. Finally, Rupert, with five thousand men, got into Shrewsbury. The Parliamentarians drew a cordon round the place. Shrewsbury meant much to the Royalists. For one thing there was a mint established there, and they were getting notoriously short of coin.

Since Ryder had parted from Verity he had grown increasingly quiet. He performed his duties conscientiously, but his comrades found him reticent, almost surly. One hot August day Mark Trueman called him to account. They were off duty and lay on a high bank of the Severn idly watching the leisurely flow of the current.

"I am sorry, Mark," he admitted, pitching a stick into the stream. "I have something on my mind. My conscience gives me no peace."

"Conscience? Of all men I know you are the last I should have suspected of having an outraged conscience."

"Yet have I been a Pharisee, proud in my own conceit."

"Instead of heaping abuse on yourself, suppose you tell me what it is all about. Your mind is tortured. It will ease it to share the burden."

"You are right. You remember Verity?"

"Right well. A gracious little lady."

"I have hurt her, wounded her feelings. Would that I could undo all I said and did! When Sir William's city house was attacked a Cavalier defended her from the mob —I knew him slightly, a handsome rascal, Royle Wilding by name. He was among the wounded captured at Nantwich. Verity nursed him."

"And fell in love with him?"

"How did you guess?"

"Such things have happened before! And then?"

"When the wounded were turned out to fend for themselves she hired a waggon and was taking him to some farm where he could be cared for, when I came upon the waggon by chance. I implored her to turn back, but she would not abandon him." Ryder clasped his knees and stared moodily across the river. "I can hear her voice in my ears imploring me to part friends, but I would not harken to her. In my stubborn pride I hardened my heart. I brushed her aside and rode off without a word of farewell. Would to God I could take back that moment!"

"I understand," said Mark gravely.

"You cannot fully understand—not the misery I have gone through since. She has never shown me anything but kindness. If she loved him, what right have I to interfere? I, who should have wished her happiness, sat in judgment on her."

"You are in love with her yourself?" asked Mark shrewdly.

"I?" Ryder gave a hard laugh. "Perish the thought! We were but comrades. No more, I assure you."

"Then it will not be difficult to make amends."

"I do not know where she is or I should have humbled my pride and sought her forgiveness long since."

"Why not do so now?'

"I have left it too long. She would scorn me."

"Not if I know Mistress Verity. She holds no rancour in her bosom."

"Then she is better than I—I, who criticize her! Yet we have ridden many hundred miles since that day, as you know, and I do not know where to seek her."

"Make it your duty to find out. Go to Sir William. Tell him frankly all you have told me. Then ask his permission to go in search of the girl. Who knows, she may require your aid."

Ryder took Mark's advice. He found the Commander-in-Chief in a singularly benign mood. To Ryder's amazement Sir William acquiesced.

"You have my permission. Indeed, it would set my own mind at rest, for I have lost all trace of the girl. It has been in my mind for weeks to make inquiries, but Prince Plunderland has left me little leisure to attend to my own affairs: They say Rupert has left Shrewsbury and gone recruiting in Wales, but I doubt it. Bristol is more likely. We watch an empty nest, Yale. My informant seemed convinced that the bird has flown. We had best go where we are of greater use."

"Back to Nantwich, sir?"

"Possibly. I must confer with Sir Thomas. But you may have the release for which you ask. You merit a rest. Get into homespun, Ryder, and make inquiries. If your mission takes you to Chester, remember I need every new fact that you can glean."

Ryder had worn his buff-coat and jack-boots for so long a time that they seemed part of him. Their wrinkles and creases fitted his body like an extra skin. The leather about his shoulders was shiny from the chafing of his cuirass. One boot was patched where it had been ripped by a pike and there were stains on his shoulder from the close discharge of a pistol. His uniform had stood him in good stead in actions now growing too numerous to recollect in detail. It was with something like reluctance that he put it off. Shoes felt so light that he was tempted to hurry unnecessarily. He had no weapons but his sheath-knife and a pistol. Both were carried out of sight. After riding a hired horse to the border of Royalist territory he proceeded on foot. The search for Verity was not easy, neither was it safe. Ryder never knew what the next day would bring forth.

He made inquiries in villages which lay round about Chester. He called at cottages or farms. For the most part the people were well disposed once they were assured that he was not in search of a free billet. Soldiers had been billeted on them so often, particularly the half-starved wretches from Ireland, that tempers and resources were tried, enthusiasm for the Royal cause had waned, and the country-folk's desire was the end of hostilities, which would spare them the attentions of friends and foes alike. Again and again Ryder's inquiries met with no success, but he was of a stubborn nature and persevered. At length he heard that a Cavalier who answered Wilding's description was to be found at a farm. He had a lady with him. The man had been wounded, but was sufficiently recovered to be absent for days at a time, especially when Prince Rupert was in Chester. Ryder visited the farm.

With reluctance the farmer's wife admitted that Captain Wilding stayed there with a lady. Ryder experienced a peculiar reaction on being told of the presence of a lady. Why had Verity remained with her patient now that he was recovered? They were both out. Captain Wilding might not return for several days, but the lady said she would be back by nightfall.

"Please say to her that Lieutenant Ryder Yale will call to see her," he said, and was conscious of the effort called forth by the words. He walked quickly away, for he wished to be alone with his thoughts. Or rather he did not wish to be alone with them. He wished to escape from them, but there was no escape. They persisted.

In the silence of the woods he paced a mossy path. Then

he seated himself upon a fallen tree beside a brook, listening to the ceaseless gurgle of the water, which provided an obbligato to his sombre musings. One side of his nature was outraged. To think that she, brought up on Puritan principles, should act thus! What ought he to say to her? His other side (his better side?) told him that once you cared for a person you could not stop caring, no matter what they did. You could not dam emotions. They refused to be turned off like a tap. They resented such cavalier treatment. He must be charitable. Then he decided that emotion and sin were in some mysterious way interwoven. It must be the duty of a Christian to crush down emotion. He resolved to try.

The decision did not last long. Something within him shrieked aloud at the fallacy. Every spontaneous act of kindness was the product of the emotions! Ryder put his head in his hands and groaned aloud in his despair. The problem was too involved for his poor brain to solve. It was not so easy to determine what was right and what was wrong, as preachers had led him to suppose. This much he was resolved: right or wrong, he would utter no word of reproof to Verity. At least she had courage—courage to do what she considered right even if he considered it wrong. He must conceal his true feelings. He must act, only showing that he was an old friend who wished her well. It consoled and even encouraged him to feel that there was at last one tangible thought to which he could cling.

The light was failing when he rose, stiff and chilled, from his seat beside the stream. The shade under the trees deepened. The wood became an eerie place full of soft rustling sounds. These doubtless emanated from nothing more terrifying than small birds, but in the dim stillness they sounded weird. It was good to get to the open meadows and look up at the friendly stars. Two orange squares in the dusk showed where the farm reposed amid its barns and byres. Quietly he made his way up the front path. After a moment's hesitation he tapped on the closed door.

"Who is there?" It was a woman's voice, muffled by the thick walls. It set his heart beating faster. He nerved himself for the ordeal.

"It is Ryder Yale." He was conscious of the formality

of his tone. He would have to face Verity now. There must
be no turning back. His motive was good. He assured himself of this as if he were not quite sure. Almost without
realizing it he stood as rigid as a soldier on parade. The door
was flung open.

"Ryder!" The tone was eager.

He looked into the dark eyes of Rosea Cressage.

CHAPTER TWENTY-TWO

WHEN, after a lapse of time, Ryder was able to look back
on those moments dispassionately he was amazed to think
that Rosea had not commented upon the strangeness of his
conduct. He stood staring at her uncomprehendingly, having
lost, momentarily, not only the power of speech but the
power of motion. Rosea, never having known him to be
particularly articulate, saw nothing unusual. His rigidity
did not strike her as being anything out of the ordinary. Or
perhaps she herself was so excited that she did not observe
his reaction. She caught his hands.

"Ryder! This is wonderful! I could hardly believe my
ears when the woman told me you had been making inquiries. How monstrous friendly of you! Come inside, do.
Mind your head. What a height you are! These doors are
plaguy low. Royle is forever forgetting and bumping his head.
He vows he has no brains left, though the rogue is so good-
looking that brains would be superfluous."

She had one of Ryder's reluctant hands in her warm
grasp and was guiding, almost pulling, him into the small
parlour. It was obviously a room reserved for her. There
were flowers in a vase, a workbasket, a straw hat, some
ribbon, various touches of femininity. In contrast was a
broad felt hat with a red feather curling along the brim—a
touch of Royle Wilding which was unmistakable.

"Sit down here, Ryder," she exclaimed, dragging a high-
backed chair towards an empty grate in which fir cones were
piled for ornament. "Let me put the candles where I can get
a better look at you. How well you look! Lean, but well, and
as brown as a gipsy. Does campaigning suit you, dear friend?

L

But I need not ask. But why these clothes? Don't tell me you have fallen out with the mealy-mouthed rogues and are come to cast in your lot with the King's party?"

Ryder shook his head. He was at a loss for words. Not so Rosea.

"What an age since last I saw you! I suppose it is only a matter of months, really, but it seems years and years. You look older, too. I suppose you have been in all manner of battles and skirmishes? Tell me, were you at Marston Moor? I thought as much when we learnt that Brereton's horse were there. Royle was sufficiently recovered from his wound to ride with Lord Byron, but he had a terrible time of it. To think that you were one of those responsible for Rupert's downfall! I trust you feel ashamed! Isn't life strange, Ryder? You look so peaceful sitting in that chair, I cannot imagine you charging. Were you with that devil Cromwell when he broke the Prince's party? Of course our men were out-numbered two to one. I suppose you did not set eyes on Royle?"

Ryder shook his head. "There was great confusion," he said, finding words with difficulty.

"You were not wounded?"

"Only thrown when my horse was shot."

"Ah, I am glad you were not hurt. Royle has been wounded twice—but, of course, you know that. You were responsible for his escape. It was generous of you—chival-rous."

"Oh, I don't know." Ryder looked uncomfortable. "Let us call it repaying a debt. Once you tried to get me out of Chester."

"And failed. But I regarded that as repaying a debt. Oh dear! If we keep on repaying debts and incurring fresh ones, I wonder where it will end!"

"Ay, I wonder!" Ryder sounded grim.

"It is too one-sided, Ryder. I must do far, far more for you. Royle told me how, when the wounded were turned out of Nantwich, he would have died of exposure if you had not secured for him a waggon and escorted him to a place of safety. Why do you stare so strangely?"

"Did I?"

"You look shocked. Was it because it must not be known that you assisted an enemy? I must be more guarded about what I say. Royle tells me I chatter too much. If I do, you make amends, Ryder, for you have scarcely uttered a word."

"I grow less talkative. Campaigning leaves a man alone with his thoughts so often that he gets out of the habit of talking."

She seemed satisfied with this explanation and Ryder was thankful. He did not want Verity dragged in. So Royle had held back the true story of his escape from Nantwich! There was virtue in silence, thought Ryder, and grew more reticent than ever. Words could strike deeper than a two-edged sword.

"Brereton may have made a good soldier of you, Ryder, but he has not bestowed on you the gift of tongues. You have not said you are pleased to see me again. Are you?"

"Of course."

"How unresponsive you are! Could you not have said so? When Royle absents himself—and heaven knows that is often enough—he invariably greets me with, 'Ro, you look more radiant than ever.' It may be mere diplomacy, but I like it. You have not said so."

"There was no occasion to."

"Oh, come, Ryder! You improve. There is hope for you. That is the nearest approach to a compliment I have ever coaxed from your reluctant lips. My dear, do you not realize that a woman hungers to be told she looks beautiful? It is a phrase which never stales with time. How different you are, Ryder! I wonder what attracts me to you! It is, I think, a tremendous gratitude for your saving my life. It must be that, for you are so reserved and silent that I cannot comprehend how I could love you."

"You must not indulge in foolish talk, Rosea. You do not love me."

"Of course I love you, Ryder. I am overjoyed to see you."

"You cannot love me. You love Royle."

"Oh, naturally! I love Royle. I have loved him so long it has become a habit."

"You cannot love me and love Wilding. It is impossible to love two persons."

"I can and I do."

"This is sheer wantonness," said Ryder, rising to his feet. "I decline to listen to you."

"Oh, excellent! I have roused you at last. I don't mind if you are angry or indignant so long as you are human, so long as you are not a statue of flesh, devoid of feeling. I would sooner be called wanton and love, than be a cold, frigid Puritan who goes through life with sourness in his face and bitterness in his heart."

Her dark eyes were flashing; her cheeks had a deeper colour. Ryder, glancing down on the flushed face, thought he had never seen her so beautiful. Certainly animation became her.

"Great heavens!" exclaimed the girl. "I cannot understand people who are never happy unless they are miserable. As for me, I find there is enough sadness and suffering and disillusionment in life without adding to the score. It is not of my making. Sinful as I am, I would not have folks suffer if I could prevent it. But I refuse to pull a long face on that account and pretend that life is all good and merciful. Life can be cruel just as it can be kind. I for one will snatch what gladness I can while I can."

"Remember there will come a day when you must give an account of it all!"

"And what of it? I shall say, 'I have been happy and tried to make others happy.' What evil is there in that?"

"I will not listen to your temptations, Rosea."

"Temptations! What am I doing that tempts you?"

"You would have me forsake my principles. You would endanger my soul. I must resist you. I must go."

She strode to the door and flung it wide. "Go, then, Master Puritan," she cried. "Go to your psalm-singing traitors and be content with their perfidy. Take your principles with you, and much joy may they bring you." She paused. The flush of indignation passed from her face. She regarded Ryder wistfully. "You are nice, you know, for all your stupid ways. It is a pity so strong a man should be so dull. You might have kissed me tonight. I wanted you to. Once upon a time you did. Or does it trouble your conscience to recall that lapse, Master Puritan? I remember it with joy. I—I wonder what induced you to call on me?''

"Good-bye," he muttered, and strode into the night.

"Good-bye, Ryder," she called after him. "Hasten away and save your soul. And do tell me one day what you intend to do with your soul when you have saved it.''

CHAPTER TWENTY-THREE

OF all the Parliamentary commanders none was more indefatigable than Sir William Brereton. Hardly had he finished with the Tarvin affair—after which his valiant chaplain, Captain Sankey, chased the defeated horsemen to within pistol-shot of the walls of Chester—than Sir William was back at Nantwich getting ready for another move. If his horses were lean and his troopers saddle-sore it was not to be wondered at. He worked them as hard as he worked himself.

Ryder had been sent on scout seeking news of the Army of the North which Sir Marmaduke Langdale was bringing south to join the King, to whom, it was rumoured, Prince Rupert had also gone. On the Saturday after the Tarvin fight Ryder learned that Sir Marmaduke was encamped for the night near Whitchurch. Though the Nantwich horse were at Middlewich resting after their exertions at Tarvin, Sir William, that faithful and active patriot, wasted no time in summoning together what horse he could collect. He marched from Nantwich with seven companies of foot on the Sabbath day.

On Monday, the twenty-sixth of August, about the spring of day, he came upon the Royalist army encamped near Malpas. Forty colours floated in the air. Sir Marmaduke had several thousand men with him. Sir William's own troop charged several times. The brunt of the fighting fell on them, for by reason of the narrowness of the lanes the foot companies could not advance immediately. They beat back two parties of Royalists, killing and capturing many of their officers. Then, having driven the King's party back through the main street of Malpas, they resolved to wait in a lane until the foot came up to support them.

Sir Marmaduke had time to reform his army. He had them extended in six or seven divisions, in good order. While the Parliamentary infantry were recovering their breath, being spent with fast marching, the Royalists launched several vigorous charges against them. It was the boast of the weary pikemen that they yielded not a foot of ground. Ryder, at the head of a troop of horse, was fighting with the methodical coolness he had learned from long campaigning. It was businesslike. He conserved his strokes and his strength. At the sight of a Cavalier with a red feather his apathy left him. He recognized Royle Wilding, recognized his lovely light chestnut mount. At last he was to encounter Wilding as he had long desired to do—sword in hand. Regardless of military procedure, Ryder forsook his position with the troop and rode straight for Wilding. Royle saw his approach and accepted the challenge with a mocking smile.

"Welcome, my baiter of bulls!" he cried. Ryder was grim. He saw before him not a well-dressed gallant, but the man who had enticed Verity from her home and from her allegiance; the man who, likewise, held the affections of Rosea. He saw in Royle Wilding not merely an enemy of the Parliament, but a personal enemy, and an enemy of right-eousness. Ryder regarded himself as one who appeared in the role of an avenging angel. His broadsword cut with all the force he could muster. The smile left Royle's eyes. The rapier, which looked so slender when in Verity's fingers, turned the blow with consummate skill. Before Ryder could recover the rapier point had ripped his buff-coat and pierced his bridle arm.

The flow of blood served to stimulate his rage. He rose in his stirrups to deliver a down-cut which would have cloven asunder the head of a less adept swordsman. Again Wilding parried, though the blow cost him his plumed hat. The restive horses backed apart, and while the opponents manœuvred for position a rush of horsemen forced them asunder.

Cavaliers were fleeing from the field. Sir Marmaduke was wounded in the back. Almost every colonel was captured.

The officers fought desperately. Most were from the Earl of
Newcastle's army and, being papists, expected harsh treatment. Their loss unnerved the common soldiers, who broke
and scattered. The Parliamentary horsemen were too spent
to follow. Instead of going to Shrewsbury the King's party
fled to Chester, where they were refused admittance. Lord
Byron looked upon them scornfully for having been beaten
back by so inconsiderable a number.

The victory, Sir William assured his men, was a wonderful and extraordinary deliverance. Ryder Yale, bridle arm
in a sling, was glad to return to Nantwich for a rest. He had
meant to exterminate Royle Wilding, but he had found the
role of an avenging angel not as straightforward as he had
anticipated. He had lost some blood and was weary from
lack of sleep. A week's rest sufficed to restore him. Before
ten days he was in the saddle again, for Sir William, the indefatigable, was once more on the move.

This time he rode towards the borders of Wales. Word
had come through that the Castle at Montgomery, which
had been delivered up to the Parliament, was being threatened by Lord Byron. Sir William joined Sir Thomas Myddleton and Sir John Meldrum and planned to raise the siege.
Lord Byron had left Chester at the head of several thousand
men, many of them from North Wales, resolved to recover
Montgomery. It seemed, at the commencement of the battle,
that he might achieve his object. Brereton's men were out-
numbered, and when it came to push of pike the Royalists
were too many for the Parliamentarians. Brereton's horse,
victors in many a conflict, were at the start worsted. A fresh,
valiant charge of theirs turned the scale. The Royalists were
routed. Lord Byron escaped, but he left five hundred dead
and fifteen hundred prisoners behind:

Though the Parliamentarians numbered a thousand less
than their opponents they lost only forty killed. But among
these was Sir William Fairfax. Snatches of that forgotten
conflict fought under the walls of Montgomery Castle come
down in Sir Thomas Myddleton's report.

*"Sir William Brereton with the Cheshire foot did most
bravely behave themselves that day, and did beat the best foot*

in England, as they, the very enemy confess, being all Prince Rupert's foot, and the chosen foot of all the garrisons."

Ryder, who had come through many a skirmish without wound of consequence, received a pike-thrust in the right thigh. He set off for Nantwich, not in the saddle of his gelding but on the straw-covered bottom of a waggon. Even so he found the rough roads too harsh for his wound and he was left behind at the house of a well-disposed farmer. The days passed monotonously. The wound healed slowly. A stranger among strange people, his active body condemned to in-activity, Ryder had time to think. He had not realized until then how great a part a man's thoughts played in his life.

As he lay motionless, aware of his throbbing leg, he discovered that time and space had little significance in the realm of thought. He held imaginary conversations with Rosea, with Verity, with Royle Wilding. More than once he recalled that strange waif with the harp, Myra, with the angelic face and sensuous fingers. Sternly he dismissed her from his mind. Thoughts of her filled him with dread—the dread of the unknown. He would have none of her. He wondered why it was that some people made so much impression on one's life when others made no impression at all.

So he mused until one day the sound of hoofs aroused him. He listened, curious. A party of horsemen had stopped at the farm. In search of refreshment? Were they friends or enemies? Did they seek him? He raised himself on his elbow and listened more intently. A man's heavily booted stride sounded on the passage flags. Mark Trueman stood in the doorway and smiled with pleasure.

"I heard that you were wounded and came in search of you."

"That was kind of you."

"How do you feel?"

"The better for seeing you."

"Then you will make even better progress presently. I have brought you a nurse."

"A nurse?" Ryder's eyes changed their light.

"One whom, I trust, will be welcome—I have escorted Verity here."

"Verity!" It came as a shock. Ryder lay back with eyes closed. He was conscious of an increase in his heartbeat. Weakness perhaps!

"You will see her?" Mark's voice exhibited concern. "It was her wish that she should come to care for you. You will see her? You will be gracious to her?"

"Let me recover my composure first, Mark. This wound has left me weaker than I realized. Verity here! She appears to make a practice of nursing wounded men."

"A commendable one, surely?"

"Oh, undoubtedly. It would be unmannerly of me not to allow her to practise on me when she has ridden so far. Of course I will see her."

Mark hurried from the room. He did not return. Verity entered unaccompanied. The meeting was an ordeal to Ryder, who was tense with emotion. Somehow he expected to find Verity changed, but she appeared her old self as she stood in the doorway gazing at him. The same quiet, self-possessed Verity he had always known. His heart smote him.

"It is good of you to come to me." Ryder endeavoured to speak evenly.

She gave a shy smile and walked towards him. He took her hand when she stood beside his bed. "Before you speak," he said quickly—"before you utter a word, let me say my say. My mind has borne a load for weary weeks. Let me unburden it. When last I parted from you I treated you shamefully. God has humbled my pride. I went seeking you long ago to ask your forgiveness, but I could not find you. I was a boor. Nothing you ever did merited such behaviour on my part. I am filled with shame. Can you forgive me?"

"Would I be here now, Ryder, if I cherished resentment? You were upset, overwrought. I understood."

"You are an understanding person, Verity."

"Am I? Perhaps life has taught me to put myself in another's place. Is the wound healing?"

"The wound in my thigh—yes, slowly."

"Is there another wound?"

"There was. It was healed a moment since."

"Oh! I trust the other will heal as speedily! Ryder!"

"What is it, Verity?"

"Is there anything you wish to ask me? Anything you want me to explain? Anything which will set your mind at rest?"

"Nothing."

"You accept me without explanation? Just as I am?"

"Just as you are!"

Verity did not reply. She stared out of the window. Ryder, looking into her face, thought he detected the glint of unshed tears.

CHAPTER TWENTY-FOUR

THE cattle moved with irritating deliberation down a hedge-fringed lane despite the proddings of mounted spearsmen. The men on horseback were more conscious than their bovine captives of the exigencies of war. Ryder Yale was able to sit in his saddle despite a certain stiffness of the leg as he rode in the rear of the herd alternately cracking a whip and casting a watchful eye over his shoulder to make sure they were not followed.

The party was returning after raiding Royalist cattle, which they had snapped up almost under the walls of Chester. Ryder's mind went back to the previous winter when the beasts round about Nantwich had been driven off by Lord Capel's troopers. Now the tables were turned. Autumn was nearly over when Ryder returned to Nantwich, nursed back to health by Verity. He found the townspeople cheerful despite the execution of four soldiers condemned for running away from their colours during the battle at Montgomery. Markets were held again. There was plenty of food in the town. Danger from raids was remote.

General Brereton was intent upon recommencing attacks on Chester. Though the war had dragged its weary way through more than two years, Sir William, despite numerous activities, never allowed the capture of Chester to fade from his mind. And now that Byron had lost so many men at

Montgomery he was minded to start his operations against the loyal city afresh. Already he had placed a garrison in Tarvin, where Colonel Michael Jones was proving himself a zealous and enterprising commander.

His troopers thrust down Watling Street, encroaching on Chester's suburbs, intent on giving the garrison no respite. Ryder grew accustomed to the sight of the mud outworks of Chester rising from the broad meadows of Hoole Rake and Chester Field, and behind them the red sandstone walls, gables and spires, and, dominating all, the massive bulk of the cathedral. He could not look upon the city without calling Rosea to mind—Rosea, with her allurement which fascinated while it frightened. She was an enemy, he told himself. She was not the kind of woman he ought to think about, and yet his thoughts persisted in straying to her, try to control them as he might. He wondered where she was and what she did. On one of his raiding excursions he had passed by the little farm where he had seen her. He paused to make inquiries and was told that both she and Wilding had returned to the city when the district became unsafe.

Sir William removed his headquarters from Nantwich to Great Neston. He fortified Hooton House. The reason for this move was to be at hand in case his services should be required for the attack on Liverpool which Sir John Meldrum was pressing hotly. Liverpool surrendered to the Parliament in November and left Sir William free to devote his entire attention to the attack on Chester. Beeston was not forgotten. Its loss was a sore blow to the Parliamentary cause and to Sir William in particular. He must have that towering castle back if such a thing could be achieved. His troops invested the Castle Rock. Beeston, crowning the great crag which rose from Cheshire's undulating meadows, loomed like a spectre over all operations.

Ryder rode in to report the success of his raid.

"Five score head of cattle, sir. And when their horse and foot issued forth we beat them back with the loss of two of their cornets and several men slain. We took seven and captured twelve of their horses.".

"With what loss to us?"

"None, sir."

"I think my Lord Byron finds himself in a tight corner, Yale," observed Sir William, "and with God's aid we will make it tighter. I hear he has few troops left to assist him other than Colonel Mostyn's Flintshire men and a regiment under Colonel Hugh Wynn of Bodysgallen. It is unlikely that the Marquis of Ormond will spare him any more men from Dublin. Lord Byron has not been fortunate and has finished with the army Lord Ormond sent him almost to a man without their being the least service to the King."

That night the Parliamentary troops made an assault on the outworks of Chester, pressing home the attack with some stubbornness. They lost fourteen of their men before they were prevailed upon to withdraw to a distance. It was a slight affair in itself, but it was a foretaste of what was to follow.

In December Brereton began his leaguer in earnest. He posted garrisons at Upton, Trafford, Tarvin, Christleton and Aldford. In Wales he had posts at Dodleston and Lache and in the town of Hawarden, where Sir William Neale held the Castle for the King. At Christleton, a mile or so from the city, the Parliament forces erected mud walls. Sir William's own regiments of horse and foot were stationed there and were a thorn in the flesh to the besieged. Yet the Cavaliers in Chester did not submit tamely. They issued forth and many a fierce clash occurred. Twenty or thirty Parliamentarians were carried back as prisoners.

As Ryder was patrolling his lines one moonlit night in January he heard his name called softly from a hedgerow. It sounded so uncanny that he wondered for an instant whether it was the product of his imagination. Nevertheless he drew rein and listened.

"Ryder, I am here. Pull close to this hedge." It was a woman's voice.

Suspicious, he dropped a hand on the butt of one of his holster pistols. "Who is there?" he demanded, peering keenly.

"You should know my voice. It is Verity."

"What do you here?"

"I have been in the city, Ryder, seeking intelligence for Sir William. There is much I desire to say to you."

"'Walk to yonder gateway. I do not fancy talking through a quickset."

At the gate he dismounted. A slim figure came out of the shade of the hedge. In the moonlight he looked down upon Verity's calm features.

"How is the wound? Has it mended?"

"It pains if the weather is wet. Otherwise I am little the worse save for some stiffness. A tribute to your care, Verity."

"Do you know where Sir William is to be found? You must hasten to tell him that Lord Byron intends to break through his leaguer with fifteen hundred horse and relieve Beeston Castle."

"When?"

"Shortly. Byron has chosen the eighteenth of January, the anniversary of his assault on Nantwich."

"An unfortunate date for him."

"He is resolute to relieve Beeston garrison."

"Forewarned is forearmed. I trust with God's aid we will accord him such a welcome that the date will be impressed upon his mind for evermore. How comes it that you are in Chester again? I imagined you safe in Nantwich."

"It was too quiet. I asked Sir William to allow me to return."

"Had you no difficulty in gaining admittance?"

"None. Amos is still at the old house. There is still a coracle should any desire to cross the river. But now it is easy for me to enter. I have a pass."

"Wonderful! How was that achieved?"

"I don't give away secrets." She smiled. "But now I must return. I have awaited your passing so long that I am chilled."

"How did you know that I should come this way?"

"I watch your patrols from the walls with an optic glass. I know your figure so well, Ryder. How friendly it looks and familiar when seen from the enemy outworks!"

"I trust they will find it more familiar than friendly." He looked down upon her fondly, reluctant to let her depart— this little comrade who had been so loyal, so true, so consistent.

She seemed to read his thoughts. "I must go," she said firmly.

"I will escort you to the lane's end." He walked to his horse and tossed a stirrup across the saddle. "You had better ride."

He caught her under the armpits and swung her to the saddle. Verity gave a quiet laugh.

"You are as strong as ever, Ryder."

"Stronger, I trust. And you appear lighter. You do not get enough to eat!"

"Nonsense. I grow heavier. Tell me, does not this remind you of the day we met?"

"Yes. It occurred to me." She was smiling down at him in the moonlight. Suddenly he felt tender towards her. He raised her hand to his lips.

"My dear," he said.

A startled look crossed her face. "Please, Ryder, do not do that."

He smiled. "I have not been demonstrative before. I think it must be because I am glad, so very glad, to see you again. I have missed you, Verity. Tell me truly, is it necessary for you to go back to Chester?"

"Yes." Her voice was low, her head averted.

"You know that Sir William intends to press the siege. He is having heavy ordnance brought to bombard the town. There will be danger. There will be starvation. Please, please return to safety."

"I must go back to Chester, Ryder. I must!" Her voice was distressed.

"Verity, my dear, escape while you may. Come back to safety. I will care for you if you will let me."

"Oh, Ryder, my dear, dear friend, don't talk like that." She bent towards him. "You remember long ago we pledged our friendship. We would always care—whatever happened?"

"I remember. Once I broke that pledge. Never will I break it again."

"Never, Ryder? We will always be friends?"

"Always," he assured her again.

"I must test you, try you, hurt you, I fear. Ryder, dear friend, I am—wed."

She slid from the horse's back as he started as if she had

struck him. She held out her hands, but he brushed them aside.

"Dear God," he cried, lifting an agonized face to the sky, "why must these things be? Was it necessary that I should give my love now, when it is too late?"

But the silent heavens made no reply. It was Verity who spoke. "Oh, Ryder, dear Ryder. I do not desire to hurt you, my own dear friend. But I—I must return to the city, to my—husband."

He hardly heard her. He turned towards the camp and walked down the moonlit lane with head bent. She saw that his steps were unsteady. The faithful charger moved after him, pacing slowly after his master. Verity stood alone in the lane. There were tears in her eyes.

*   *   *   *   *

At two o'clock on the afternoon of January the eighteenth Lord Byron rode proudly from Chester's Eastgate. His lordship, arrogant as usual, had made his own plans and, as usual, had not made them wisely. His forlorn hope of horse were far in advance of the main body. They were into an ambush before he was aware of it.

Ryder Yale charged at the head of his half-troop with a fury that surprised all who witnessed the attack. The first intimation the Royalists had was the rush of hoofs and the clash of blades as the Parliamentary cavalry launched themselves resolutely from a lane. It was a fierce charge which completely routed the King's men. A few escaped and fled for the city. Lord Byron brought up the main body, but he was met with an equally terrible charge. Foremost among the attackers was Ryder. He fought like a man who held life cheap. His sword never spared. Into the thickest of the fight he drove, seeming to bear a charmed life. It was he who captured one of the colonels. It was he who carried off Captain Sankey from the mêlée when Sir William's fighting chaplain, caught unarmed, was sorely wounded. The Parliamentary foot, following up the success of their horse, drove the enemy back and back until fire from the city walls made them desist. Then they made an orderly retirement.

Sir William Brereton, usually phlegmatic, was overjoyed. He went in search of Ryder as he walked wearily from the field where his horse had been killed by a cannon-ball.

"Gallantly done, Ryder! My eyes have been on you. Surely the Lord was with you this day. You shall have a fresh horse from my own stable. I nominate you captain for today's brave work."

Ryder was conscious of Trueman clapping him on the shoulder; of colleagues pressing around him to shake him by the hand, but he stared at them with unseeing eyes.

Or rather with eyes which saw a slim girl in a moonlit lane. Verity was wed!

CHAPTER TWENTY-FIVE

"THE men grow mutinous," exclaimed Mark Trueman curtly as he entered the billet.

"Yes," replied Ryder, without looking up.

"The Derby horse have ridden away of their own accord."

"Yes."

"It is scarce safe for an officer to go out without his weapons. And this in our own lines!"

"Yes."

"What has come over you, Ryder? You sit moping like a broody hen. Pull yourself together, man. Anyone would think that Sir William had done you an ill service by appointing you captain. Does it not please you?"

"It neither pleases nor displeases me, Mark. I have no interest in the matter."

"Something's amiss. Out with it. What's on your mind?"

"It is Verity, old friend."

"What about her? She's not wounded—or slain?"

"She is married, Mark."

"Married? What, to this rake of a malignant you spoke of?"

"I do not know, but I believe he is her husband."

Mark unbuckled his belt and laid it on a table. "Well," he said deliberately, "if she is married she is married, and that's all there is to it. You did not love her. You told me as much."

"I did not love her then. I discovered that I loved her too late."

"But I thought you had lost your heart, or your wits, to some fair charmer you could not have as she was of the King's party."

"That is so, Mark."

"Then it seems to me that the affair is simple. You cannot have Verity, that's as plain as a pikestaff. That leaves you free to take the other."

"Ay! But you would think less of me if I took my life's partner from the ranks of our enemies."

"Maybe I would, but that is not likely to deter you. If Verity makes such a choice, there is nothing to stop you from following suit. So don't look so glum. Ryder, there have been times when I have felt lonely, but when I see what worry has been caused you by love I cannot help but be thankful that I am still heartwhole."

"Women have caused me misery, Mark," said Ryder, glancing up. "But, by my sword, they have brought me moments of happiness too! I still feel that I would endure the sadness for the sake of the gladness, and feel well repaid. It is easy for you to talk so sanely and sensibly, Mark, but you've never had your blood sent racing in your veins by a woman's touch. When you have, why, it's like strong drink! Once, for a brief moment, the loveliest woman I have ever seen pressed her lips against mine. It was, as I say, but for a moment, but I'll be an aged man before I forget the wonder of it."

"Then dwell upon that in your heart, and do not mourn because you have lost Verity. As I see it, you should rejoice in her happiness, the more so as it opens up a fresh opportunity for you. It is a sure thing you cannot have both of them, Ryder. You must make up your mind which you truly desire."

"Life has decided for me."

"Then accept the decision. You are fortunate. It saves you much tribulation. If you would learn wisdom, put women from your mind. Let the army be your bride."

M

Ryder sat silent listening to the sound of angry voices without.

"The proposed bride is something of a vixen, Mark!" he observed. "Ill-favoured, hard to please, dissatisfied with her bed."

There was something in what Ryder said. Discontent was spreading among the neglected, ill-paid soldiery. Instead of replying, Mark walked to the window and looked forth. "You will have to apply your own Self-denying Ordinance, Ryder," he said slowly.

"I should like it as little as Sir William does," retorted Ryder.

It was the time when the Self-denying Ordinance was on all men's lips—the drastic step whereby all officers who were members of either House were called upon to resign. Sir William Brereton, as Knight of the Shire, was one affected.

"Ay!" said Mark soberly. "It has hit Sir William shrewdly, though surely the Parliament will reappoint him. I cannot picture the war in Cheshire without him as leader."

"We shall probably be dispersed," said Ryder moodily. "The New-Model Army will require us. From what I can see there will be no more separate armies scattered about the land, but one big force to dominate all."

Mark moved suddenly and began to buckle on his sword. "Get your weapons, Ryder!" he said quickly in a changed tone. "Trouble is brewing."

Ryder's lethargy fell from him like a discarded cloak. He was on his feet in an instant, thrusting pistols into his belt. The two hurried out of doors. A babel of angry voices filled the air. Soldiers were swarming towards a roadway which was blocked by an excited throng. Ryder thrust his way rudely through the crowd of unkempt, haggard, ragged warriors to where Sir William, bare of head, was sitting his horse, motionless as a rock in an angry sea.

"I swear to you, men," shouted Brereton, "that I am doing all that I humanly can on your behalf!"

"Where are our arrears?" called out a cadaverous man with a shock of dark hair. "I have not seen a penny-piece for months. Is not the labourer worthy of his hire?''

"We weary of our taskmasters!'' yelled another. "Give us rags wherewith to cover up our nakedness!''

"Food! We need food!'' shouted a third.

Shoulder to shoulder Mark and Ryder forced their way to Sir William's side.

General Brereton rose in his stirrups. "My lads,'' he said, "I have applied to the House for your pay again and again. I will urge them once more. Money I cannot let you have, for there is none left; clothes are wanting, but food you *shall* have.''

"Where is it?'' The voices grew clamorous. "Show us the food!''

"You must win it if you would have it. I cannot show it you, but I can tell you where it is to be found. On the hills of Wales!''

"Into Wales!'' The hungry crowd broke up. Ryder and Mark forced an avenue through which Sir William could walk his horse. He thanked them with a grim nod. Sir William was still master, but he did not feel the security which once was his.

Ryder was sent into Wales at the head of a party of horse. It was necessary to search far afield for provisions. The country round about Chester was denuded for a depth of ten miles. There were sheep on the Berwyn Mountains. There were black cattle in the Clwyd Vale. Ryder's raiders came back with six thousand sheep and six hundred cattle. Hungry soldiers fed and grew contented—for a time. The foray had not proved bloodless. Near Holywell the soldiers were fired on from a gentleman's house. In retaliation they set the place alight. Between Northop and Caerwys a garrison was found in Widow Hanmer's house. It was attacked. Twelve soldiers were put to the sword, nine being roasted when the house was set alight. It was obvious to all that the war was growing more grim.

At the end of January Sir William again assaulted Chester. He reached the outworks at four o'clock in the morning. The stormers, by the light of their matches, found the walls strongly guarded. Once again Brereton had been betrayed.

Chester's plight did not pass unnoticed. Word came through that Prince Maurice himself was leading a force to the relief of the loyal city. The Parliament took alarm. Ferdinand, Lord Fairfax, was ordered to send five hundred horse to oppose the Prince's progress. But the Prince broke through. By the middle of February Chester was safe. Or so it seemed.

For several weeks Prince Maurice's army lay between Chester and Maelor in Flintshire, plundering and impoverishing the country. The Parliamentary scouts hung on their outskirts, watching. They saw a bridge erected across the Dee after a fashion they had never seen before. It was of canvas stretched tightly across between two boats, drawn so stiff that three men could walk abreast across it.

"An ingenious contrivance, Mark," observed Ryder. "It would be well to bear it in mind. We may find a use for it when we assault the city."

"*If* we assault the city!" replied Mark. "The chances grow less."

"Sir William will not give in; he is a stubborn man."

It was true. No sooner had Prince Maurice retired than Sir William began to close in on Chester again. He was encouraged by an unexpected success. Two of Lord Byron's brothers, Sir Robert and Sir Richard, had fallen into his hands, together with £500, when a convoy was captured. Chester's plight was such that the King himself set forth to effect its relief.

The siege of Hawarden Castle was pressed home. It was all in vain.

One morning Ryder drew up on the banks of the Dee and stared in amazement. It was low tide. A long line of Parliamentary soldiers were wading up the shallows, crossing the fords from Wales to Cheshire. It could mean only one thing. The siege of Hawarden was abandoned. The mere threat of the King's approach had proved sufficient. There was no need for his Majesty to come further. Though the lines about Chester on the Cheshire side remained intact the dissatisfaction among the troops spread.

Ryder, summoned to the presence of his Commander-in-Chief, found Brereton in a despondent mood. He had just executed two ringleaders of a mutiny and Sir William was not a man to take human life wantonly.

"I have no more heart to come amongst the men, Ryder," he said wearily. "Yet we must reform such destructive courses lest the judgment of God come upon the whole army. Ryder, you have been with me from the start. I have called you here to thank you for your loyal service. There is little I can do for you, my boy, but truly your fidelity is appreciated."

"I trust I may yet serve you faithfully, Sir William."

"That is as God wills," said Brereton sadly. "Today, at any rate, we part."

"Part, Sir William?"

"You and Mark Trueman are chosen to serve in the New-Model army."

"Orders, sir?" Ryder spoke quietly.

"Orders, Ryder! I am sorry. I know how you feel. You do not like to leave a task uncompleted. Neither do I. Yet a general, no less than a captain, is under orders. I have to report to London. The siege will be prosecuted under the charge of Colonel Jones." Sir William went on as though in soliloquy. "I have had desperate threats to the hazard of my life, yet have I not abated my efforts to prevent the spoil of the country." He rose and held out his hand. "God keep you, Ryder."

Thus is was that Ryder found himself amid the unfamiliar lanes of the Midlands. The turn of events in Cheshire made a fresh scene acceptable. He was glad to escape—escape from the vicinity of Chester, where Verity dwelt with her husband —escape from Nantwich, where his commander who had served the Parliament so loyally was now discredited.

Ryder sought Mark Trueman when they reached the great camp; the camp where Sir Thomas Fairfax, Lord General of the New-Model Army, was in supreme command. Never before had either of them seen so large a force as this, which was intended to crush the Royalist cause for all time. The men wore the red tunics which formed the first English uniform, all save the firelocks, who had a distinguishing yellow. The veteran Major-General Skippon was in charge of the foot. No one had charge of the horse. It was a post for

one man, for Lieutenant-General Oliver Cromwell, but under
the Self-denying Ordinance he was not eligible—unless the
House chose to re-elect him. It was said that he was to be
invited to assume the post, but would he, if he accepted, be
in time?

It was all strange to Ryder, strange and interesting and
bewildering. He seemed to lose his individuality in so great a
throng. It was good to see Mark's friendly face.

"Sir William has been scurvily treated," asserted Mark.
"No man could have pressed the siege of Chester more
closely considering the handicaps he was called upon to face."

"If our men were backward in attacking the outworks,"
added Ryder, "how comes it so many were wounded by
pistol-shots from the walls?"

"The folks talk as if Chester was the only place of danger.
There is as much to be apprehended from Beeston or Ruthin
or Holt."

"If our lads drove off sheep and cattle I would like to
know who set the example? What of Lord Capel's raiders at
Nantwich? Would the wiseacres in London have us starve
while they keep us in arrears of pay?"

"They accuse us of pillage, yet they know that all plate
and jewels are surrendered to the Public Treasurer for the
State's use."

"Bah! Those who know least criticize most!"

Both felt better for their grumbling. It was interrupted
by a shout. A mighty shout! Men were running across the
camp from all directions. At the eastern border a long line of
horsemen, grey with dust, were following a broad-shouldered
middle-aged man whose heavy face was grim. He rode alone,
bareheaded, on a powerful black horse.

A cheer went through the camp. "It's Old Ironsides! He's
here, lads! Brave Oliver is here!"

The two Cheshire captains of horse caught the contagion
of the shout. The days of uncertainty were ended. Cromwell
had received back his old command. He was at the head of
his Ironsides again. Let Rupert charge if he would! The
Army of the Parliament was ready to meet the Army of
King Charles.

The hamlet of Naseby lay not far away.

CHAPTER TWENTY-SIX

NASEBY had been fought. The New-Model Army had proved its worth. The King, disconsolate, was seeking relaxation at Raglan Castle. The siege of Chester was resumed. Ryder Yale and Mark Trueman were free to return to the familiar villages of Cheshire.

Ryder was in a disgruntled mood. He sat his horse in the shade of a wood and kept a vigilant eye on the outworks of Chester. The mud walls had been drawn in, for the garrison of the city had decreased. Now that so many of Colonel Mostyn's Welshmen had been sent home, and Prince Rupert had impressed so many to fill the gaps in his regiment of Bluecoats, there were not enough fighting men to defend the original earthworks. Prince Maurice, as a memento of his visit, had carried away fifteen hundred of the best soldiers from Ireland. Chester had to pay for entertaining royalty.

Conditions in Chester grew worse. The conduct of the besiegers grew bolder. Though Prince Rupert had relieved Beeston Castle he had not stayed to protect what he had gained, and the moment his royal back was turned the men of Cheshire returned to their trenches round about the Castle Rock. They meant to recover their lost fortress if it was humanly possible. Captain Valet inside the Castle was in no enviable position. He was short of food. He was even shorter of fuel, and the year was beginning to grow cold. They were stubborn men, those puritanical warriors of the County Palatine. Some watched Beeston. Some watched Chester. It was hard to say which place was in the greater peril.

Ryder could see activity outside the city gates. Cart after cart rolled out to deposit litter on the surrounding fields. Men with buckets and rakes and brushes and water were hard at work cleansing the city streets. After the occupation by so many troops the city was foul. Mayor Charles Walley, with the thought of possible pestilence should the siege be pressed —as there was every likelihood—was endeavouring to set his municipal house in order.

Although there was much to encourage the attackers

Ryder Yale remained in a sombre mood. Sir William Brereton was still in London. Ryder resented his commander's treatment by the Parliament. He, who had hitherto fought with a blind loyalty, began to feel resentful. Why should Sir William be called to account? No general had exhibited greater zeal. If there had been disorder and discontent among the troops the fault lay not with Sir William but with those in London, who had not seen that the wages were paid. Faithful soldiers merited their pay—so Ryder felt. He had not received his for many a day. He was in dire penury, having distributed what money he possessed amongst his needy troopers.

Ryder was a young man of simple tastes and high ideals uncomplicated by involved thinking. He did not understand politics. He could not understand why, when they were fighting despotism and Catholicism, there was occasion for Presbyterians and Independents to be at each other's throats. He could not understand why that mysterious process termed the Self-denying Ordinance was necessary Why should Sir William have to resign for no other reason than that he was a knight of the shire? It is true that, like Lieutenant-General Cromwell and Sir Thomas Myddleton, he had been reappointed, but Sir William as Commander-in-Chief was, in Ryder's estimation, a more useful man than Sir William as one of a committee of five! Nantwich had submitted a remonstrance to the Parliament pressing for assistance to enable them to accomplish the speedy reduction of Chester. The wealth of the county was well-nigh exhausted. The support of troops ought to fall upon the state and not upon a county.

Nothing came of the Nantwich remonstrance! It seemed to Ryder that while implicit obedience and loyalty were expected—nay, demanded—from the men who bore the hardships and the suffering and the danger, those in far-off London, who fenced with nothing more than edged words, evaded their obligations. He grew more bitter, more dissatisfied, more disillusioned.

Sir William's nomination of Ryder as captain had not been confirmed. His men called him captain, he did a captain's work, he accepted a captain's responsibility, but he drew a lieutenant's pay. Or rather he did not draw a lieutenant's pay. Was it two months or three since his last money was handed to him? He could understand why a penniless trooper was driven to loot. When one law was broken another followed, until only the oldest law in the world remained—the law of self-preservation.

Ryder asked himself what he really desired. Not wealth—he had enough to satisfy his modest needs. Not fame—life on his father's broad acres where he lived close to Nature was all he asked. No, not all! Most of all he wanted a place of his own—a home, small, humble, but all the same his own, a place where he was his own master. And he wanted someone to share it with him. Man was never meant to live alone. Surely that was not intended, else God had never created woman. He could have cursed himself for being so backward in recognizing Verity's worth. It was the gall of bitterness to feel that he had realized his love for Verity too late. Suddenly he felt resentful as though his tenderest feelings had been wantonly mocked. Why had he not appreciated her value sooner? Because his eyes were blinded by Rosea's beauty! Then his mind went back to the carving on the old beam in Nantwich. How did it run?

"*A beautiful face is a dumb praise. Fair women be dangerous marks for young men's eyes. Choose not thy wife by her beauty, but by her honesty.*"

The warning had been plainly set forth. He could blame no one but himself. Then his mind took another line of thought. Rosea had, he assumed, been betrothed to that rakehelly fellow Wilding. If it were Wilding who had married Verity, then Rosea would be free! It came to him that he was still bewitched by Rosea. The thought annoyed him. He moved impatiently; moved so suddenly that his dozing charger came to life and tossed its head and champed its bit.

"Steady, lad!" Ryder's soothing fingers patted the arched neck, not glossy, but rough from hard campaigning. The sun was westering and long shadows from the walls were flung across the grass. He could see meadowsweet in an adjoining ditch; a distant slope was yellow with ragwort. He turned his horse's head towards the billets. His day's work was ended. He met his relief, a Lancashire lieutenant, walking up the lane to meet him.

"All quiet," Ryder reported.

"It won't be quiet much longer, sir. I've heard rumours——"

"So much the better," said Ryder crisply, and rode on. He was in no mood to chat.

He discovered that there were more than rumours going about, there were definite orders. Troops detached from the leaguer at Beeston Castle were to be withdrawn for a night assault on Chester.

"Might I volunteer to join them, sir?" he inquired of Colonel Booth, who gave the information.

"There is no occasion."

Ryder walked away. Sir William would not have answered thus. At least, he did not think so. There might not be need, but he wished to go. He loathed inactivity. After he had supped he threw himself down to rest for an hour, bidding his man bring him a fresh mount when it was dark and to see that his pistols were primed. It was late August and the days were beginning to draw in. Ryder knew every road and lane in the neighbourhood. No one knew better than he where the troops from Beeston were likely to pass. When the stars came out he walked his horse quietly out of the camp, tethered it to a gate and sat silent on a roadside stile until his quick ears detected the soft thudding which told that horsemen were approaching, riding, for silence's sake, along the roadside grass.

"Friend!" he called softly and stepped into the roadway to be recognized. The captain in charge of the leading troop paused. He readily aquiesced when he heard Ryder's request.

Once in the saddle, Ryder felt happier. Nothing but action brought satisfaction to his restless disposition. As they neared the Chester outposts the troopers dismounted. It was still very dark. The attacking force stretched away into the darkness—no one could tell how far.

Ryder was told that it was a considerable force—five

hundred horse and two hundred dragooners. They were waiting now for the foot to come up—seven hundred of them. Surely, thought Ryder, the outworks would be carried that night!

The light paled in the eastern sky. It showed the river's bend. Ryder volunteered to lead an advance party of a score of dragoons along the river bank. Local men were selected, men who knew the district well. Leaving their more cumbersome equipment stacked by the roadside hedge, the men took swords and pistols and followed Ryder across the fields until they reached the water's edge. In the dim light they crept under the shadow of the bank and stole quietly forward. From the shelter of a clump of rushes Ryder surveyed the scene. He could see a gun-mount beside the Dee. Beyond it was the turnpike and on the inland side of the road another gun-mount. The one nearest the river was their objective. Once they had captured that they must open the barricade and allow their comrades to rush inside.

He could see a sentinel on the gun-mount sleepily leaning on his pike. Yard by yard the attackers crept forward. Stealth meant everything. Silence was of more value than speed. Wires stretched from the edge of the earthworks to posts embedded in the river. It might stop straying cattle but not night raiders from a hostile force. Ryder's powerful hands noiselessly pulled the wires apart until there was a gap sufficient to let him through. He helped the first dragoon and then crept forward. One by one the men came through, each drawing his sword once he was past the wire.

Half the forlorn hope were through. Glancing back along the bank, Ryder could see a long dark line of figures following where he led. He scaled the gun-mount and crouched for a spring. The somnolent sentry was caught from behind in a throttling grasp. His pike clattered to earth. Another sentry turned, shouted the alarm and fired a musket. There was a rush of feet. Excited dragoons were striking at every man who opposed them. They had the gun-mount. They were across the road, swarming up the sides of the next emplacement. The defenders, sleepy-eyed, came running forth with their points untied, to be cut down or pistolled before they could reach their weapons. They slew Lieutenant

Aldersey, the captain of the watch, and put the rest to flight.

Ryder led a party to open the turnpike gates. They worked feverishly, for they could hear shouts from the gatehouse at The Bars which indicated that reinforcements were issuing. A more encouraging sound was the rattle of hoofbeats on the Boughton Road, up which the Parliamentary cavalry were coming at a canter. Trumpets were sounding, muskets were cracking, bells were pealing. No longer was concealment necessary. Ryder had the gates wide open. The horsemen galloped in, horse and dragoons, a thousand of them. A thousand Parliamentary soldiers were within Chester's outer works.

Well might the bells of St. Werburg's sound a tocsin. The invaders swept past the Withen Trees, captured the Horn Lane gun-mount, took possession of Horn Lane. Another party skirted the river's edge and turned up Dee Lane. They attacked the great gate which defended The Bars from its inner side while comrades hammered at the outer. The guard was surprised and overpowered. There was a stiff fight with the guard in Mr. Egerton's House and Alderman Walley's house. The defence, valiant though it was, could not stem the flood of excited soldiery which flowed relentlessly onward engulfing lane and garden and dwelling.

The stormers were in Foregate Street now, firing into house windows, wrenching off shutters, bursting open doors. Ryder forced his way through the scurrying throng and made for the Mayor's house, anxious to protect the good man were he at home. There was no need. The Mayor was within the city walls. His house, however, yielded rich spoil. There were trophies there about which the victors could boast. A dragoon rushed into the street excitedly holding high the ancient civic sword. He was followed by a trooper bearing the city mace. The soldiers, gathering around these ensigns, passed down the street shouting "To the Town!"

A cannon-shot from the Eastgate cut down several roisterers and scattered the excited throng. It came as a shock to the good folk of Chester to find the enemy in possession of the suburbs; to see the foe at the very gates of Chester. People in Foregate Street who retired to rest in seeming security, well within the circle of the outworks, thrust anxious faces from upper casements and speculated upon their fate. House after house was entered.

Ryder, walking alone, sword in hand, along Foregate Street, paused at the top of Love Lane to look about him. As he stood taking stock of events he heard his name called. A door opened cautiously and a hand beckoned. "Ryder, come here. You must protect me."

What man could have failed to obey such a behest? Rosea was waiting for him, and her smile for once was troubled.

"You call *sans*-ceremony, Ryder! I regret we cannot give you a warmer welcome!" She laughed a little incredulously. "So you have truly captured the Foregate?"

"Yes. The outworks and the suburbs are ours."

"You cunning devils! I never thought you would achieve such success. And with such ease, such apparent ease. It is like awakening in the night to find a thief in one's bed-chamber. I was attiring myself when there was such a commotion of bells. I could hear distant firing and I knew that the outworks were attacked. Never did I dream of your carrying them. Then the shouting grew so near that I thought it time to seek the shelter of the inner walls and meant to hasten to Eastgate—but I was too late."

"You wish to go there?"

"Naturally, Ryder. I do not fancy remaining unprotected in the midst of licentious soldiery."

"Your honour would be safe. Our men differ from the rakehelly rogues who follow Byron and Gerard. A woman is safe—provided she be no Irish drab with a long knife concealed."

"I confess I feel more secure now that you are with me. Lord, how my heartbeats increased when I saw your familiar figure!" Rosea leaned back and smiled with greater composure. "And so, my dear Ryder, we meet again. Are you still seeking your soul? Faith, you've come to a queer place in search of it. In Chester courage and loyalty to his Majesty appear to be the only virtues which flourish."

Ryder attempted to look dignified, and failed. "Where is Royle Wilding?" he demanded. "How is it he is not here to care for you."

"Oh, Royle?" She shrugged her shoulders. "He rode to join the King. He was at the Naseby fiasco, you know. He is still with the King, for all I know."

"You do not sound greatly concerned."

"What would be the use? Long ago I discovered that one only hurts oneself by caring too much. Royle comes and goes —of late he goes more than he comes. I have no option but to make the best of it. When one is neglected the presence of a friend is welcome."

"You cannot regard me as a friend."

"I can and I do. Why need you be so formal, Ryder?"

"Your ways are not my ways."

"Possibly not, but why be disagreeable about it? I like you, Ryder. You are an enemy of my King. You associate with a crew of long-faced canting rogues I despise, but that does not prevent my liking you. It does not stop my heart from overflowing with gratitude because you saved my life."

"Oh, it was hardly a case of saving your life."

"Then let us say you saved my looks, which is more important. Cannot you see, my dear, that you set too great store on things of little consequence? Set first things first. Personal happiness comes first."

"Loyalty to the Parliament comes first."

"Pooh! They are naught but a set of place-seeking rogues. Tell me—what loyalty do they show you in return? Is your pay in arrears?" She saw him flush and laughed aloud to find her random shot had struck home so shrewdly.

"You are but a pawn in the game, Ryder. Take what you can. It will be little enough you get from them. You have qualities I admire, Ryder, but worldly wisdom is not one of them. I hate that psalm-singing hypocrite Brereton, but you can see how they have treated him. Give the Devil his due—no man could have been more loyal to his taskmasters. They are all corrupt, Ryder. All seeking their own ends. Power degrades whichever side has it. Look after yourself. You would be a fool if you allowed them to make a fool of you."

"What would you have me do? Desert?" There was irony in his tone.

"Lord, no! Never desert the winning side. The game is

nearly ended. Poor Charles. He's been at Raglan for weeks watching masques, seeking to forget his troubles, when he ought to have been making a desperate last bid. No, I'm not tempting you to desert or to do anything drastic. All I say is that there is no occasion for you to stand aloof. You always speak the truth. I remember that. It used to strike me as being amusing when first we met. I had become so used to countering Royle's blatant prevarications that the truth left me bewildered. So tell me, Master Truth-teller, am I not beautiful?''

He was conscious of her eyes upon him. Ryder tried to look away, but some hypnotic spell held him. What eyes they were—large, lustrous, dark, eloquent, expressive. Slightly mocking, too. Very alluring. He could read an invitation in them. Her lips were full. Never had he known such beauty in human guise. He shook his head stubbornly, but she persisted.

"You—who always speak the truth—am I not beautiful?''

A sudden passion swept through Ryder's veins so that the blood drummed in his forehead. His sight became blurred. There was something in what she said. The Parliament had not treated its servants well. Why should not a man seek his own interests? He wanted her, wanted her, but something within him held him in check.

"Am I not beautiful?'' The voice was soft, like a caress.

"Yes, damn you!'' he yelled, and ran from the room, out into the streets, where the shouting soldiers still surged by.

CHAPTER TWENTY-SEVEN

"THE King is at hand!''

The words, bellowed at the door of Ryder's billet, caused him to catch up head-piece and sword and rush out of doors. In the late September sunshine there was such bustle as he had never seen before. Pikemen and musketeers collided with each other as they scrambled for their companies. Troopers were flinging saddles on to their mounts, dragoons were loading carbines, trumpets were sounding, drums were beating. Ryder ran to the appointed place and found his troop assembling in a field. Chester was forgotten. The King was at hand. No one quite knew where. No one knew anything save that the word had come through, the amazing word which took every man by surprise.

Colonel Michael Jones caught sight of Ryder and beckoned to him.

"You have a good horse, Yale. Ride in the direction of Holt Bridge and see if you can learn the whereabouts of Sir Marmaduke Langdale. Bring me word of the number of his forces. Hurry."

"Is the King with him, sir?" Ryder's curiosity got the better of him.

"No, the King has advanced another way—through Chirk. I hear he got into the city from the Welsh side."

It was a situation sufficiently serious even for a captain of horse to appreciate. Ryder went off at a brisk canter. He evaded the swarming troops and made for the open meadows. The lanes were packed with men. The King was actually within the walls of Chester! It was fantastic. Three years before Charles was received with pomp and splendour! And now——?

The sudden turn of events seemed incredible. They thought the King still lingered in Mid-Wales, at Raglan, at Ludlow. And now, just when the Chester suburbs were captured, now when there was every prospect of the city being taken, his Majesty must put in a surprise appearance. Was it a whim of Fortune or was it a last desperate bid on the part of the King to wrest victory from the jaws of disaster? Ryder pondered as he rode.

His pace slowed as he reached a slight incline; he did not know what lay ahead and he had been trained to hold his horse well in hand lest an emergency should occur. At the top of the rise he paused to breathe his beast. As he looked about him Ryder thought that the flat Cheshire landscape looked as peaceful as if there was no war in the land. To his left stretched Rowton Moor with patches of heather; to his right was wooded country where trees glowed with the glory of autumnal russets and yellows and browns. He set off at a trot towards the Whitchurch Road. Before him lay Hatton

Heath. At every rise he pulled up, not merely to rest his mount but to stare, keen eyed, for the twinkle of sun on steel which would denote the advance of cavalry.

It was, he felt, no use heading direct for Holt Bridge. Sir Marmaduke was not a man to dally. Ryder pressed forward at a steady trot. His eyes were never idle. As he neared a cross-roads he halted. His listening ears caught a sound he knew only too well—the irregular clatter of hoofs, the tinkle of bit-rings. A large body of horse was approaching. He turned his steed about. Before he could move he noticed horsemen emerging from a field gate between him and Chester. His retreat was cut off.

A copse lay beside the cross-roads. Into this Ryder led his mount and stood with his hand over the animal's nose lest it should whinny. It was a necessary precaution. Along the Whitchurch Road came a great body of horsemen. Ryder kept his head low and watched the moving column through a screen of branches. The men moved slowly as though they had come a long way. It was not an enviable position for Ryder, yet he hoped that, by stealth, he might evade notice.

The hoofs clattered past without ceasing. He began to wish he had taken count. Two troops, at least, must have gone by. He parted the boughs and obtained a better view. He stared. Surely these were not Sir Marmaduke's? They had a familiar look. Those jack-boots and lobster-tail helmets were never worn by King's men! He recognized a lieutenant with whom he had breakfasted the morning before the Naseby fight. They were old comrades. This must be the force under Colonel-General Poyntz which had been deputed to watch the King's movements. Ryder leaped into the saddle and guided his horse towards the road. A few heads were turned in his direction. Little notice was taken. There were Parliamentary scouts on either flank. He rode alongside until he found a cornet, whom he asked where the General could be found. The man pointed towards the head of the column. Ryder spurred forward. The General turned at the sound of his rapid approach.

"Have you come from Chester with a message?"

"No, sir. I never expected to see you. I was sent to seek

N

Langdale's force, which crossed the Dee at Holt Bridge. The King is at Chester."

General Poyntz frowned. "I had hoped to prevent his reaching the city. There is yet time to meet Langdale if I could discover his whereabouts. I have come by a shorter route through Whitchurch, and trust that I am ahead of his force. Go to Colonel Jones. Say I approach by way of Rowton Heath and shall give battle if I come across the King's party. Let him sally forth to join me. The firing of two great guns shall be the signal of his coming. My horses are weary from forced marches."

Ryder wasted no time. He trotted past the forlorn hope which rode well ahead of the main body. Once free, he left the road and set off across country at a canter. He looked back and saw that General Poyntz had stopped his march and was forming his men on Hatton Heath. Ryder was puzzled until, beyond a lane, he caught sight of a body of cavalry facing Poyntz. They were on Milne Heath. Langdale was between the advancing Parliamentarians and the city. Faintly down the wind came the sound of trumpets and hoarse shouts. The ranks of Poyntz's horse bore down upon the enemy. Langdale's men met them bravely and hurled them back. As Ryder drew away he was conscious of the main body of Langdale's forces hurrying forward to support those who fought. Poyntz's men were thrust back.

Ryder spurred on. Straight for Colonel Jones's headquarters he rode. Outposts drew aside as he swept past in his headlong career. Only the utmost urgency could account for the furious pace. Colonel Jones himself came into the roadway as Ryder drew up his gasping horse.

"General Poyntz is on Hatton Heath and Langdale lies between him and the city! The General bade me ask you to go to his aid, for his horses are weary from the forced march. You are to discharge two great guns when you march."

"I will without delay," cried the colonel.

"The forlorn hopes of both parties had met as I rode hither, sir. So far as I could tell Langdale had the better of it"

Colonel Jones wasted not a moment. He issued orders, put himself at the head of the first troop to assemble. Men were hurrying into position on all sides, horsemen, footmen, from the villages round about Chester on which the leaguer was based. All were anxious to come to grips. The men who had captured the suburbs of Chester turned their faces to the new foe.

A messenger came through to say that Poyntz was beaten, that all was lost! Another horseman rode in on a foam-spattered mount to say that Poyntz had rallied and stood his ground.

Two shots from the great guns sounded. The horse moved ahead. The foot marched forth towards the moors. Behind Colonel Jones rode three hundred and fifty eager horsemen. Colonel John Booth marched in front of five hundred foot. Adjutant-General Louthian was left behind to hold the suburbs which had been captured.

Sir Marmaduke Langdale had mustered his forces, five thousand strong, on Rowton Moor. He had both wind and sun in his favour. It was five o'clock in the afternoon of September the twenty-fourth that the forces met. The battle opened with the firing of pistols at close range. Then the horsemen fell to with their swords, hacking and slashing, neither side gaining a foot of ground. The Parliamentary musketeers spread out on either flank and galled the Royalists with their accurate fire. Sir Marmaduke Langdale, having driven General Poyntz back, sent to the King for further orders. He chose Colonel Shakerley to carry the message. The Colonel hurried to the river, and getting a large washing-tub used for the slaughtering of swine, paddled it across the Dee, his horse being held by a manservant as it swam alongside. In a quarter of an hour he was thus able to carry the news to Chester.

Yet there was delay. The Eastgate had been blocked up and citizens were endeavouring to clear away the soil so that it would be possible to make a sally. It was the sight of Parliamentary soldiers marching from the suburbs that stirred General Gerard into action. He thought they were retreating and, accompanied by the Earl of Lichfield, he set off through the Northgate in pursuit.

King Charles climbed to the Phoenix Tower to watch their departure. Instead of victory he saw his Chester force suddenly attacked in the flank by a charge of Shropshire horse, while a hot fire from the Parliamentary marksmen in the houses smote the Royalists. The Earl of Lichfield was slain and Lord Gerard wounded. They never reached Rowton Moor.

There on the moor was an amazing spectacle. Sir Marmaduke was wounded. General Poyntz was attacking in front, Colonel Jones in the rear. The moor was a mass of wheeling, struggling horsemen. Buff-coated troopers, red-coated dragoons, brightly clad Cavaliers mixed in a kaleidoscopic medley. The Cavaliers showed great courage, but the musketeers from Chester shook the confidence of the Royalists' rearguard, which broke and fled. Poyntz's troopers took fresh heart at the sight and pressed home the charge. Langdale's forces scattered. Riderless horses galloped across the heath.

Men whose sword-arms were weary from slashing took up the chase of the broken enemy. Some they pursued to Holt Bridge. The greater part they chased to Chester. Across the heath the Cavaliers streamed, some four hundred of them, all that survived that fatal encounter. The narrow lanes and roads were blocked. Lord Gerard's men, who rode out too late to be of any assistance, were caught up in the general rout and swept back to the Northgate under the sad eyes of the despondent King. It was a blow more bitter than Naseby.

Carried away by the exhilaration of the charge, Ryder Yale cut his way through the Cavalier ranks. When they broke he was one of the exultant Cheshire horse who followed at their heels. A Cavalier turned and, steadying his pistol, sighted at Ryder, who let go his rein and reached for one of his holster-pistols. There was a moment's suspense as he watched the black muzzle pointing at him—pointing, so it seemed, at his heart. There was a spurt of flame and a pain stabbed through his bridle arm. His sword swung from its knot as he clutched his wounded arm and swayed in the saddle. His horse, unaware of its rider's agony, continued to gallop forward. Ryder, sick and faint, bent in his saddle. He heard a coarse laugh. Some instinct caused him to look up. A man in a purple doublet rode close beside him, sword upraised. "Here's a damned Crop-ear who's sorry he turned rebel!" he cried, and delivered a terrific down-cut. Ryder ducked his head.

His head-piece turned the blow, which ended on his cuirass. His armour saved his life, but the force of the impact nearly drove his steel pot into his skull. His ears rang. The hot blood trickled down his cheeks. Instinct made him wind the fingers of his right hand in his horse's mane before he sagged unconscious.

Thus he hung, bleeding and helpless, until his mount pulled up within the Northgate and Ryder slid slowly aside and crashed to the roadway.

Shaken into consciousness, he became dimly aware of a group of men looking down upon him, men who laughed, men who jeered in boisterous fashion.

"If you claim the horse, Jack, demme, I'll have his sword."

"I could do with his steel-pot, Milo. Damnation, it's a sight too large a fit. Here, Dick, you may have this. I'll try his jerkin."

The speaker commenced to pull the coat over Ryder's head. A groan burst from Ryder's lips. "Mind his arm, man, he's wounded!" said another voice.

"Hell! Why are you squeamish? He's only a damned rebel, and has got his due."

Someone dragged off the jack-boots. Ryder, divested of most of his clothing, turned on the cold earth and vomited. He was sick with pain.

"Why bother with half-measures," said the man called Dick. "Let me pistol the rogue and divide the rest of his clothing. What makes you stare, Milo?"

"Damn my sinful soul if I don't know the fellow."

"Queer company you keep, Milo!"

"I keep what company I choose. Do you raise objection?"

There was something familiar in the tone which made Ryder open his heavy eyes. He saw a roisterer in bedraggled finery standing arrogantly with a hand on his rapier hilt. It was his former gaoler.

"What need to be so damned touchy, Milo! Do you suggest we return our lawful spoils of war to this new friend of thine?"

"Take them to hell with you. Dick, catch hold of his legs. We must bear the luckless devil to my lodging. Demme if I thought I should ever be merciful to an accursed Puritan, but this fellow once showed me great civility and I'm not minded to let him die like a dog in the gutter. Up with him."

The jolting caused Ryder to swoon again. When he came to he lay on a small bed in a low-ceilinged room. His head was bandaged and his left arm in a sling. His head ached. His tongue was dry. He wondered how any human could feel so ill and yet live. He moved feebly.

In an instant a figure darted across the dim room and knelt beside the bed. A beaker of water was held to his lips. He sipped gratefully and lay back exhausted. He was conscious of the touch of a cool hand. A small, white, cool hand which stroked his cheek with a touch which was as soothing as it was caressing. It had an almost hypnotic effect on Ryder. His eyes closed. He felt he would like to lie in a trance and let that soothing touch go on for ever. It conjured up visions of the past. He was with Rosea again—Rosea, whom he had left so discourteously. Why did she not hate him? She ought to. Yet she was generous—magnan ... his brain was too weary to grope for the word.

He was weary of war, weary of suffering, weary of hardship, weary of disappointment. He had endured enough for one lifetime, endured patiently as a good soldier should. And now he was finished. He cared not who won—King or Parliament—so long as they left him alone to rest and rest and rest while that cool soothing hand smoothed his brow. He would never be unkind or uncivil to Rosea again. He would thank her for her forbearance, and serve her, and be kind to her. The touch of the little hand was wonderful.

"Ro," he whispered, "Ro, is it really you?"

"Ah, *cariad*," responded a lilting voice. "It is better you are. You are coming back to me, back from the grave. My love has given you new life."

CHAPTER TWENTY-EIGHT

RYDER slept fitfully and feverishly. In the morning he opened his eyes. A surgeon bent over him. He had a lancet in his hand. Myra, white of face, was holding a basin.

"Drink!" ordered Milo, and thrust the neck of a black bottle into his mouth. Ryder sipped. The fiery liquid burnt his throat and he pushed the bottle away. Milo was adamant. "Drink!" he ordered again. This time Ryder obeyed. He was soldier enough to know that it was kindly meant—Milo was fortifying him for the ordeal through which he had to pass. The surgeon began probing for the ball in the shattered arm. Ryder writhed in agony. Pride prevented him from groaning aloud.

Whenever he opened his eyes he saw Myra holding the basin. It was gory now. Her face was white and set but she never faltered. Ryder realized he had hold of her hand. His grasp must have paralysed her fingers but she never flinched. He saw when he let go that she had to prise her bloodless fingers apart. The bone was set and the arm bandaged. The scalp wound was superficial. The surgeon washed his hands, rinsed his instruments, slipped them into a leather case and hurried away. Ryder was only one of hundreds. He lay back with closed eyes, Milo produced the magic bottle again. It was crude surgery, yet, so far as they could tell, the arm was safe—provided gangrene did not set in. It throbbed abominably.

"I thank you," said the wounded man feebly.

"Get you to sleep, *cariad*, you will be better soon." Myra's soft fingers again caressed his face. No longer did Ryder resent their sensuous touch. He had gone past caring. He slept.

The sound which aroused him was a sound which no cavalryman could mistake—the irregular clatter of horses assembling. Ryder opened his eyes.

"What is it?" he muttered.

"Never you mind, boy *bach*. Noisy devils they are."

"Have—our troops—forced an entrance?"

"No, my dear. It is the King's men who gather. Hundreds of them. His Majesty, poor man, has to flee. He is escaping into Wales over the bridge into Flintshire, and five hundred horsemen are his escort."

"The King—flees?"

"Ay. He slept the night—if sleep he did, poor man—at Sir Francis Gamull's house in lower Bridge Street. Now he rides first to Hawarden, where Sir William Neale is Governor, and then to Denbigh. He will find a welcome from old *Hosanau Gleision*, Old Blue Stockings, as they term Colonel Will Salusbury. After that they say he goes to Chirk Castle, where Prince Maurice waits with a thousand men."

She rambled on, thinking to please him, but Ryder had lost interest. He had hoped that the city was captured, that he would be among his own people. But it was not to be. His fate was to lie wounded in the midst of enemies. Then a sudden rush of thankfulness swept over him as he recalled how Milo had saved him. And Myra, of course. How plucky she had been during the operation! He opened his eyes. "I want to thank you," he said slowly. Myra's drawn face suddenly became animated. "You would thank me, my man? It is proud I am to help you in your need. You will not lose your arm. You will get well. Myra will see to that."

He slept again. As the days passed his arm healed, though slowly. The surgeon visited him once. After that Ryder was left to fend for himself. It was Myra who changed the vile-smelling bandages, Myra who brought herbs to sweeten the room, Myra who gave him warm drinks and cared for him with a devotion which touched him.

Milo was rarely in the house. He seemed to divide his time between the taverns and the walls. On one of his rare visits Ryder thanked him. It occurred to him that he occupied Milo's bed. Milo waved aside his thanks grandiloquently. "I repay a debt," he said. "You returned me my sword. It was a noble act, sir, a generous act. I, too, know how to be generous."

"I could not keep your sword. I took it while you slept."

"I pride myself that it would not have been in your possession had I been awake. None the less its loss occasioned me rare distress. It is the sword of my ancestor. For its return I thank you."

On another occasion he revealed his gratitude in another way. Noticing the care Myra lavished on the ailing man, Milo said generously: "She fancies you, sir. If you fancy her, you may have her by all means."

"You crow like a bantam on a midden!" cried Myra,

suddenly vicious. Milo laughed and retreated before her fury.

"I shall play to you on my harp?" she remarked inquiringly. She spoke as one desirous to please.

"My head still aches."

"*Duw*, man, you talk as if my music would make it worse. It will soothe!"

It was evident that she had made up her mind to play, for her harp had been brought into the room. Carefully she tuned the strings. Once behind her harp she became a different creature. She turned spiritual. An angelic look of innocence transfigured her face. She became rapt. Her fingers touched the strings, touched them gently, touched them lightly. She played a lullaby. After the first verse she sang to her own accompaniment. There followed a Welsh air and then another lullaby.

Ryder watched fascinated as the tiny pointed fingers strayed with a touch like a caress across the strings. She seemed to weave patterns, patterns of sound. Myra was right. The harp did not make his head ache worse. Finally she played the air he had come to know so well—'Greensleeves'. He would always associate that tune with Rosea. How long ago it seemed since she had first sung it in his hearing! Was it only a matter of three years ago? He had been through so much since then that he felt like an elderly man looking back upon his youth. Ryder raised his right hand and stroked his cheeks. He had grown a beard. The last plaintive note died away. Myra crossed the room and looked down upon him.

"Myra?"

"What is it you want, *cariad*?"

"I want a razor. Could you shave me?"

The colour rushed to her pale cheeks. "Damn you!" she shouted angrily. "I play music which would charm the angels of heaven, music which will heal you quicker than that fool of a surgeon, and all you think of is your whiskers! Grow as hairy as a baboon for all I care. You are a fool. I waste time on you." She stamped from the room and slammed the door.

The ebullition was of short duration. When light was

fading the girl came tiptoeing into the room to light the candle. She peered down on the sick man with a wealth of anxiety in her eyes. "You must not mind me, *cariad*," she whispered, dropping to her knees. Her fingers caressed his forehead. "It is the devil of a temper I have. Pay no heed. It does not last. Nothing lasts but my love for you."

Ryder kept his eyes closed and spoke no word. The girl mystified him. All he knew was that his head still ached and her touch was soothing. The stroking was soporific. He slept.

Thus the days passed. His arm was nearly well. His strength slowly returned and with it a restlessness which would not be denied. One day he got up from bed and tried to stagger to the casement window. His legs played him false and he measured his length on the bedroom floor. Fortunately he did not fall on his wounded arm. Myra heard the crash and rushed upstairs. He was scolded. Ryder persevered and in a few days he was able to get dressed and sit in a chair. It was growing colder now. October had arrived. He reclined in the chair by the window, looking into the street, glad to watch the crowd. Sometimes he had in his lap the black-and-white cat Myra had adopted. She called him 'Sultan' and made observations about his wives which caused Ryder disquietude.

Now that Ryder sat by the window he became more conscious of the gunfire which went on day after day. It sounded closer. It was closer. He would hang out of the window trying to perceive what was going on. He could see the Eastgate packed with manure. Gates were not to be trusted.

"Shall I play to you on the harp, *cariad*?" asked Myra.

"No. Tell me the news. How goes the siege?"

Myra made a grimace. "I am not interested in your stupid war. The man who wants to hear guns when he could listen to a harp is a fool. Who cares which side wins? News! Let me think. Did you hear that when the battle of Rowton was fought the King climbed the Cathedral tower? Your cannoneers have a gun at St. John's Church. They fired at him, narrowly missing the King and killing the captain with him. Now his Majesty has got safely away into Wales. Lord

Byron had a screen erected across the bridge so as to conceal what went on.''

"What else?'' Ryder was hungry for news.

"Lord Byron's men caught a letter-carrier going to Tarvin and hanged him. The houses in Cow Lane, St. John's Lane and St. Thomas Street are all burnt. Now may I play my harp?''

There was an ingenuousness about her request which made Ryder smile his consent. He never ceased to marvel at the dexterity of her fingers. She played 'Greensleeves' again; that haunting melody. Something sweetly sad about the tune appealed to the girl. She paused to blow on her fingers. "I am cold. I cannot play today.''

"You should light a fire.''

"Wood is scarce. This will be a hard winter for fuel. We must husband our wood.''

"But Lord Byron cannot hold the city all winter, girl!''

"Milo says he means to try. The King asked him to hold out for eight days. Lord Byron says he will never surrender. I will not get you a razor, but I will trim your beard with my scissors.''

"Do not be ridiculous.''

"It is you who are ridiculous. With a beard, who will recognize you in the streets if you go out? If they know you for a Crop-ear they'll clap you into the Castle, or maybe the Dead Man's Room, thirty feet below street level.''

Ryder stared thoughtfully. There was truth in her statement. Thanks to Milo's magnanimity he had been allowed to recover unrecognized. Ryder had heard enough about Lord Byron to appreciate that he might get short shrift if he were known. Myra was right. A beard was a disguise. His wounded arm would exempt him from military duty. The streets held more and more bandaged men, the halt and the lame, sufferers from the Parliamentary broadswords. He would attract no attention.

As the days passed he found himself studying Myra Pughe. He marvelled afresh at the complexity of human nature. A year ago—a month ago—he would have classified her as a child of the Devil, yet she had given him life by her devotion. Never would he forget the heroism of her white, set face as she faced the ordeal of the bullet extraction. He could not help but be grateful to her. Why was life so complex? Ryder turned his head and groaned.

"Does your wound still hurt, my man?" There was concern in her face.

"Yes." Ryder's conscience smote him. "No. That is not true. My wound does not hurt. I think I need fresh air."

Myra gazed into the roadway. A man with a bandaged foot leant against an opposite wall. Another with a bandaged head walked by. No one paid heed.

"I think it will be safe for you to go out," she decided.

Ryder rose, but looked down at Myra ruefully.

"What can I wear? They have left me little beyond my shirt and breeches." It was true. She fetched him a pair of Milo's shoes. He could struggle into them but they pinched abominably. A coat of Milo's. It was far too narrow for Ryder's massive shoulders. Myra pointed out that, thanks to the wounded arm, one side could hang loosely. Feeling conspicuous, Ryder stepped cautiously, and painfully, into Eastgate Street.

The air was none too salubrious, for the kennels were choked, yet after being indoors for some weeks it was good to fill one's lungs, good to look straight up into the sky instead of seeing dark joists overhead. He walked a short distance: not far, for he felt weak, and Milo's shoes hurt excruciatingly. Except when some casual passer-by brushed against him he seemed to attract not the slightest attention. From the top of the Cathedral tower, not far distant, he heard musket-shots as the sentinels exchanged compliments with the Parliamentarians who held St. John's Church outside the walls. Occasionally a heavy crash would be followed by the sound of falling masonry and drifting mortar dust. To Ryder's practised ears it was apparent that the besiegers had brought up heavier pieces of ordnance. He meditated on the whims of circumstance. He, who had survived so many dangers, was likely to meet death at the hands of his own comrades. It did not worry him. There was a time when it might have done.

So he mused, standing against the wall in a patch of October sunlight. He would have worried at one time, but now something seemed to have gone out of life. It lacked purpose. He supposed he ought to be thankful he was still alive, that he still had two arms. That he was still free—or practically so.

There was muddle and confusion, not merely in his life but all about him. Already he sensed the atmosphere of a beleaguered city. There was something in the air. People were quiet, or if they were gay their gaiety was forced. They were apprehensive. Faces already looked haggard.

The eight days which the King had asked Lord Byron to observe were long since past, yet there was no sign of surrendering. Soldiers on the ramparts kept up a heavy fire on the attackers. Ryder got so used to the crackle of musketry that he ceased to notice it. It was as a background to his thoughts. A thud indicated that a roundshot had embedded itself in the filling with which the Eastgate was choked. Ryder shifted his position. He must start making his way back to Milo's lodging. He had been out long enough for an invalid. He must try to build up his strength—build up his strength to escape.

"Have you been badly wounded, my poor fellow?" A woman's voice, rich, compassionate, brought him out of his reverie. Standing close beside him was Rosea. She was dressed in the height of fashion and regarded him with eyes in which was no sign of recognition. Before his amazed tongue could reply she resumed: "I can see you have. In the Rowton Heath fight, of course. And you have been robbed of your clothing. I believe I have a cast-off suit which may fit you. If you care to call at my rooms I would be pleased to let you have it. Come to my place tomorrow—it is next to the Pied Bull Inn."

Rosea Cressage walked on, her velvet skirt daintily held free of the dirt as she crossed the roadway. Ryder, dazed, hobbled home. He accepted Myra's admonition without demur.

CHAPTER TWENTY-NINE

THE vicinity of the Pied Bull held no attraction for Ryder. He spent his time morosely walking the Cathedral close untroubled by the sporadic shots from firelock men on the roofs. He wondered whether Rosea had recognized him or whether her action was but a kindly gesture to a King's man who had fallen on evil times. If she had not recognized him —and with his beard he trusted that she had not—he did not intend that she should. If she had recognized him he would accept no assistance from her. A stubborn pride forbade.

He spent the evening exercising his left hand. The muscles were stiff and weak. The arm made him feel sick. The wound had healed, though there was a cicatrice which he would bear to his dying day. It was the bone which troubled him. The arm had been badly set, and Ryder realized that he would always carry a deformity to remind him of Rowton Moor. He was thankful that his arm had been saved. He must get it back into working order as soon as possible, even if he continued to wear it in a sling as an excuse for evading military duties. The following day, as he sat in the window idly teasing Sultan, a step sounded on the stairs. The cat darted beneath a curtain as a manservant walked in and placed a parcel on the floor. He left without speaking.

Ryder, curious, opened the package. It contained a suit, stockings, shoes and shirt. They were not new but were of a quality with which Ryder was unfamiliar. A note fluttered to the ground. It had obviously been written with effort. There was an ink-splash where the quill had spluttered.

Monney can not by Cloathes. Pleas axcept thes.

As Ryder regarded the clothing there was a pucker of annoyance on his brow. He held up the tunic. It would fit him, but his pride was stubborn. He removed the parcel to a corner table. As he did so the shoes fell out. He picked them up. They were his size. They looked comfortable. His cramped toes caused him mild torture. With sudden resolve he stooped, tore off Milo's offending shoes, and flung them with some of his pride into a dark corner. The new shoes fitted well; they were comfortable. Ryder stretched his toes—it was bliss. He lay back in his chair more content with the world. So frail is humanity that half an inch of shoeleather can alter life's perspective. Sultan came from under the curtain, sniffed the

package, and stalked with feline dignity down the stairs.
Ryder followed suit.

He was pleased with himself, and walked to the city
wall—farther than the previous day. He came upon a
battery and watched with interest the gunners from behind a
barricade, loading and firing, as they exchanged shots with
the Parliamentarians. A roundshot took off the corner of a
nearby house. Ryder brushed the fallen mortar from his
coat and walked to a safer distance. He made his way along
the Rows. Almost every shop had its shutters up. Only
taverns seemed open. As he passed the Pied Bull he glanced
at the adjoining windows curiously, but he did not pause.
When he reached his room he found Myra awaiting him. She
looked anxious.

"You are wicked! It's worried out of my wits I've been,
wondering what had become of you."

"I have been trying on some new shoes. I did not realize
how time was flying." He dropped thankfully into a chair
and rested his feet.

"It's lucky you are to come by them. Did you buy them
or find them on a corpse?"

"I have no money to buy shoes, Myra. You know that.
Get me something to eat, there's a good girl."

"Something to eat. Yes! That's all you men think about.
It's easier said than done, my man. However, we must get
your strength back if we can."

She bustled about getting a meal. Ryder noticed how
quick and light her movements were. She was paler, he
observed, and thinner—as flat-chested as a boy. A strange
little creature, hardly human. She reminded him of one of
the Greek wood-nymphs he had seen in an old book when he
was a boy—a book which his father had taken hastily from
him and reprimanded him for looking at; he could not tell
why. Myra's fingers were so expressive. Even when she picked
up a cup or a trencher there was grace and artistry in the
turn of her wrist. Her face, with the large, innocent eyes,
was the face of an angel. It was her mouth which fascinated
him. It was large and seemed to hunger. She seemed aware
of his scrutiny and wheeled.

"It's glad I am to have you safe back, my man," she said.

Crossing to his side, she ran her fingers through his hair—hair which now hung low, almost to his shoulders. He did not shudder as she touched him. If ever he were tempted he recollected the pale, set face of the girl who held the surgeon's gory basin.

Ryder had finished eating when Milo came in. They did not see much of him now, though he still regarded the place as his own. Often he spent the night on guard and would enter cold and heavy-eyed to sprawl fully clothed across the bed.

"Is food scarce?" demanded Ryder.

"Scarce? Ay, and so is wine, damn the luck. It'll be scarcer before bully Byron hauls down his flag. Eat while you may, my lad. You would not get half so much if that little fool didn't starve herself to feed you."

Myra turned on him in a blaze of anger. "Fool yourself! Get you gone with your silly lies. I eat all I want, so there." She abused Milo until he withdrew.

"You are welcome to the little wild-cat, Master Puritan. Tame her if you can. I've come across some jades in my time, but never a spitfire such as this. Though I mind me, I had a wench in Haarlem——"

"Out! Get out!" cried Myra, flinging a mug at his head. It crashed against the closing door and Ryder ruefully regarded the fragments.

"Mugs, like food, grow scarce," he reminded her gently.

"I shall smash every mug in the place on his thick head if he comes here with his stupid lies. Do not heed him, Ryder *bach*. His mouth is too big. You are upset, yes? I will play to you and make you content."

She crossed to her harp—her solace. Anger and passion had left her face. The rapt look returned as she played. 'Greensleeves' again! That sad, haunting air. She seemed oblivious of Ryder's presence. She was still dreamily playing a sad, plaintive melody, which she appeared to improvise, when he tiptoed from the room.

Ryder walked the city again next morning. The guns were never silent night or day. There were breaches in the wall, breaches filled with beds—anything which could be hastily flung there to hold back an assault. He found it interesting to notice what had transpired during the night, what chimneys were down, what roofs burnt. In a plot near the Cathedral was a great square opening, a communal grave into which the dead were thrown. He could tell if there had been a sortie or an assault during the night by the new mounds of fresh earth. When he returned Myra was gone out. She often went out—searching for food, he believed. He never asked. He was not really interested. His wound left him lethargic. He was resting in his chair when a light step caused him to open his eyes. Rosea stood in the doorway.

She looked lovelier than ever, or so he thought as she smiled.

"You did recognize me," he demanded, "despite my beard?"

"Of course, Ryder. You may grow a beard, but you can never alter your height or your square shoulders. I knew you from behind before ever I saw your face. The beard may disguise you from those who do not know you well. You cannot change the look of those honest eyes." She seated herself, leaning back with the calm assurance of one in her own home. "How come you here and why the disguise?"

"The disguise, as you term it, is unintentional. So, for that matter, is my presence. I was wounded at Rowton Moor and carried hither by my horse when my wits had forsaken me."

"And the beard?"

"Grown while I lay with a shattered arm, unable to shave. I merely left it."

"I think you are wise, though I like you better without it. Why have you not worn the clothes I sent you?"

He had the grace to flush. "My pride would not let me."

"Your pride does not extend to your feet."

"You have caught me there! I needed shoes—desperately."

"You perceive how ridiculous your pride can be? If you saw yourself you would realize that you needed clothes desperately, too. Don't be foolish, Ryder. Besides, as a Puritan, you ought to know that pride is one of the seven deadly sins. Have done with it! See! I have no pride. You would not come at my invitation, so I come seeking you. Do

o

you imagine it easy? Or do you think me so brazen that I have no self-respect?"

"Rosea, I could not possibly think ill of you."

"Oh yes, you can. And you do. You do not approve of the way I live, the way I act, the way I speak. I offer you friendship and you reject it with contumely. I do not know why I trouble my head about you. I think it is because I shall always be grateful to you for saving my life."

"You make too much of a trivial incident."

"I have faults, Ryder. Ingratitude is not one. I shall expect you to call on me tonight. Come before the wine is gone. We dined together one night—you remember? That was three years ago. And you have forgotten! You put your arms round me. You have forgotten that, too?"

"Have done!" he said hardly. "It is not a matter for trifling. If, for a moment, I cared too deeply, I have been punished."

"You! *You* cared too deeply? *You*, Ryder?"

He was not sure whether she mocked him, and he coloured.

"You will dine with me tonight?" she persisted.

"No!" He was emphatic.

"That was discourteous. You see, you can give no reason. I shall expect you."

She walked to the door and departed without a backward look. It was on his tongue to shout that he would not appear, but he paused. He sat thinking. Why should he not go? When Myra returned she found him in his borrowed suit.

"My, there's smart you look, *cariad*! You are a proper man and no mistake. If someone took pains with you, you would appear as handsome as any in the city."

He brushed her words aside. Ryder hated everything which savoured of flattery. He was proud of his strength and his integrity. His looks caused him no concern.

"And how came you by those fine clothes?"

"I had them from a man who did not want them."

"I hope he did not die of the plague. The stench grows worse, and they say the sickness is spreading. You will take care, *cariad*?"

"The man who owned these clothes has not died of any

disease." Ryder was able to speak the truth. He moved towards the door.

"You are not going out?" Myra's tone was anxious. "It grows late. You may take a chill."

"Yes, I am going out."

"But why? Where are you going?"

"I do not have to give an account of my movements to you." Ryder was haughty.

"You go to see a woman!"

Myra's voice was accusing. Her eyes were no longer angelic. They were hard, steely, penetrating.

"I decline to say where I go. You have no right to ask."

"No right? No right? And I saved you, nursed you back to life, fed you on my food, protected you when you might be in prison——"

"For all of which I am grateful."

"Then show your gratitude. Take off your fine coat. Is it love you want? I can give you love, *cariad*."

"Pray do not be ridiculous. I am merely going to call on —a friend."

"On a woman."

"Yes. A woman friend who has been kind enough to invite me——"

"She sent you those fine clothes!"

Ryder could have cursed her astuteness. "What if she did?"

"Then she loves you. No woman goes to such trouble without a reason."

"You do not know me!"

"Maybe not. But I know my own sex. She is in love with you, Ryder, and I shall not let you go, because you belong to me."

Her voice broke. There were tears in her eyes. Her head drooped. "Don't ever leave me, dearest man of mine. Stay with Myra, who loves you. I cannot let you go."

Almost he weakened. He hardened his heart. "I must go," he said gently.

"Go then, damn you!" She turned on him in a fury. "Go, stay with her. Only don't come back here again. The door is shut. I'm not fool enough to keep a man for another woman's pleasure. Get out. I will tell Milo, and he will run you through for your insults. Go! Go! Go!''

Ryder went.

CHAPTER THIRTY

IT was dusk as Ryder made his way through the streets. They were busy, for the night watch was going on duty and workers were hastening home for their evening meal. Candles or rushlights showed in many windows—rushlights mostly, for candles were scarce. Whenever a cannon was discharged a rosy glow hung for a space about the place and then melted into the darkness with the drifting smoke. Ryder stepped over a dead horse which lay with its back broken by a ball from a serpentine. Horses were getting scarce; he assumed the animal would be turned into meat.

The Pied Bull looked cosy as he passed by. The door of the house adjoining stood ajar. At the foot of the stairway he paused in the dark. As he stood hesitating it occurred to him that he, who would have lived a life of seclusion, was forced by the war to be in continual contact with women. There was Verity, whom he loved too late; Rosea, whom he loved too soon; Myra, whom he loved not at all, but to whom he owed his life and his freedom. In such a position how could a man choose? Indignation took possession of him. He felt he was a plaything of the Fates, and he resented it. He never wanted Myra to place him under an obligation. Why could he not have fallen in love with Verity instead of being infatuated with Rosea? If matters were managed thus how could one live a well-ordered existence? He grew weary of puzzling. He would accept life as it came.

With resolution he mounted the stairs and entered the room with more assurance than he had hitherto displayed. Candles were lit. Rosea was awaiting him. She had changed into an indoor gown cut low at the shoulders. She greeted him quietly.

"I am glad you were able to make your way here," she said. "Sit down, Ryder. I am sure you are weary. And draw your chair to the hearth—a fire is not to be ignored these days."

"It is the first I have sat by this autumn."

"Fuel is terribly scarce since the Roundheads captured the west bank of the river. Did you know your friend Brereton had returned from London to take charge? Captain Morgan told me. You knew that they have christened his gun-mount after him? I told him it would be his claim to fame—Morgan's Mount. He has duels every day with the demi-culverin posted at Brewers Hall battery across the Dee. When you are warmed, Ryder, draw your chair to the table. We must help ourselves. The servants are all gone."

Ryder watched Rosea critically. He had imagined her a spoilt child incapable of attempting anything practical, yet she presided at the meal with the ease of a society hostess.

"If the servants are gone, did you cook this?" he asked.

"All of it. Are you surprised? But it is not fair to embarrass you by asking when you always speak the truth."

"Yes, I am surprised. It is excellently cooked."

"Now, a little wine. I say 'little' advisedly. The stock grows low. It is the one thing which impresses Royle that the siege is a serious matter."

"So Wilding is in Chester?"

"Ever since the Rowton Moor fight. He rode out with Gerard. He sustained a slight cut and came back swearing like a fighting cat, but I think it was chagrin, not suffering, which provoked the outbursts. I see little of him these days. He is continuously on duty. Or so he says. I fancy he spends much time with the Lord St. Pol, who is General of the Horse. Oh, Ryder, I can hardly endure the monotony. He cares nothing for my weariness, my *ennui*, provided he has his excitement. It is cards or it is dice and then the French lord challenges him to some desperate deed against the rebels. They are forever devising fresh schemes. I do not mind the danger or the siege, Ryder, but *ennui* is more than I can bear. You will help me dissipate it, will you not, dear friend?"

Ryder eyed her dubiously. He thought she looked unhappy.

"Push back the table, Ryder, and draw up to the fire. We will not waste time clearing the things away—they can stay unwashed until tomorrow or the next day. Who the deuce cares! Why do you stare at me, Ryder, as if I were some designing creature who would tempt you from the path of probity?"

"You are a temptress, Rosea."

"But why? Why? What have I done? You are a friend. I invite you for a meal, and a cosy chat because I am lonely. Where lies the harm?"

"It is but the first step."

Rosea's eyes grew bright with suppressed laughter. "Ah! So you anticipate more to follow? Shame on you, Master Puritan. I should like to believe you were right, but I have ceased to delude myself. I might as well endeavour to rouse a gargoyle, so stony cold you are. See, I will sit at a respectable distance, and we will talk about all manner of solemn things. Souls . . . or matrimony. . . . Yes, matrimony. What is your conception of wedded bliss?"

"It is not a matter for jest!"

"I agree, O Solomon! Oh, how I agree!"

"An honourable man takes unto himself one woman and stays with her all his length of days, supporting her, cherishing her, having neither eyes nor thought for any other. It should be so with the woman until death them do part."

"Lud! How insufferably wearisome it sounds! I marvel any marry."

"It is solemn obligation and must be fulfilled."

"Obligation!" Rosea made a wry face. "What a term! Like an existence on bread and water with eyes averted from flowers and wine." She regarded him thoughtfully. "I wonder why it is you do not want to kiss me. Perhaps I am not attractive."

"You are lovely enough to tempt a saint."

"Delightful. That from you, who always speak the truth. I shall remember it."

"It is the truth."

"And it gratifies me more than all the fulsome compliments which Royle's smooth tongue devises. And yet you do not wish to kiss me."

"It is wrong."

"But why?"

"It arouses the emotions."

"They were given us to be roused, surely."

"It is a device of the Evil One."

"Well, I must say it is very civil of him. I trust he will accept my thanks. I like being kissed—by the right person. I care not who knows it."

"I presume you refer to Royle."

"Oh, Royle, yes. He is no laggard. But he wearied of me long ago, and I confess he grows stale. I am but one of many. But you, Ryder, are fresh and clean and strong and honest. And truthful! I covet your love."

"If you talk like this I shall leave."

"You always hold that threat over me when matters begin to grow interesting. Heigh-ho, I must guard this wayward tongue of mine. If I can! I want your love, Ryder, but if I can't have that, then let me have your friendship. I am not bad, my dear. Only human. You have such a strange conception of women. You think of all as being good or bad."

"A woman must be one or the other. There is no halfway."

"Whoever taught you such stupidity? Some parson, I'll be bound. Bad women have a lot of good in them, Ryder, and good women can be the very devil. It mystifies me how it will all get sorted out."

"Yet the Day of Judgment will come. The sheep will be sorted from the goats."

"My faith, I've no wish to be either. However, Ryder, I mean to tell you the real reason for asking you here. No, don't look scandalized. And don't say 'If you talk like that I shall leave.' I know you look upon me as a Scarlet Woman who has designs on your precious soul, though you are too courteous to voice your thoughts. Your resolute demeanour shows it. I can see you bracing yourself. You are thinking, 'Let this brazen hussy tempt me as she will, I will withstand her wiles!'"

"Please, Rosea!"

"Not a word. I am a sibyl. I read minds. Now harken. The reason, the real reason, is that we have arranged to get you away."

"Get me away?" He looked blank.

"Escape. No, not at once. We must wait until there is

no moon. Another week, perhaps. It is all arranged. Bowen, our one remaining manservant who is groom to Royle, will act as sentry. Royle will see that he is alone on the part of the wall which has just been breached by your batteries. Then you can slip out of the city—back to your friends."

"I do not understand."

"We are in for the devil of a time in Chester, my dear. Make no mistake about it. Brereton means to have the place. Byron vows he will not surrender. When Greek meets Greek! There's precious little fuel in the city, less food, but there are stout hearts and sharp blades. We're not surrendering the loyal city to mealy-mouthed rogues and hypocrites. May the Devil fly away with all rebels. So the sooner you get out of Chester the better, my friend. That is all I wished to tell you, Ryder."

He stood up. His face was so set and stern that she wondered what he was going to say. She prepared herself for an outburst. When Ryder did move it took her completely by surprise. With a quick stride he crossed to her, dropped on one knee on the hearthrug, and catching one of her hands, pressed it to his lips.

"Forgive me!" he muttered. "I despise myself. I have misjudged you, Rosea—Ro. My dear, you have a heart of gold. I—I distrusted you, and you are a saint."

"Never less, my dear. I am just a very human woman who cares for you and wishes you well. One who would make you happy if you would allow her. If you are grateful, Ryder, you can show it so easily."

"Tell me how!"

"By kissing me. Just once. Is it against your principles?"

"You know it is."

"But you did once."

"It was wrong. The most resolute can slip once. I shall never do so again."

"I should have thought you would have resolved that you might as well hang for a sheep as a lamb. It doesn't seem so terribly wicked to me! But if it really does disturb your peculiar conscience, Ryder——"

He was looking down at her. There was a light in his eyes she had never seen before.

"Yes," he repeated slowly, "it is against my convictions."
Then he bent and kissed her on the lips.

*　　　*　　　*　　　*　　　*

Ryder walked along a moonlit street with a medley of
emotions surging in his heart and a medley of thoughts
revolving in his brain. Rosea's generosity had achieved
what Rosea's beauty had failed to accomplish. His conscience smote him, not for kissing Rosea but for mis-
judging her. He felt despicable, ashamed to think that while
he attributed wrong motives, or judged her harshly by the
severe standard he had set himself, she, with spontaneous
kindness, was mindful only of his wellbeing.

Instinctively he turned his steps to the house in Eastgate. The door was closed and barred. He had quite forgotten
that he had fallen foul of Myra. He shrugged his shoulders
philosophically. Sultan, who dozed on the doorstep, stretched
his back and rubbed against Ryder's legs.

"It's the walls for both you and me tonight, Sultan," he
said as he stroked the cat. Ryder was too old a campaigner
to be disturbed. There was nothing in the house which
belonged to him save his shirt and breeches. He would
leave those as payment—as a memento! His idle steps carried
him to the ramparts. There were sentries posted at close
intervals along the walls. Since the gun-mounts on the
Boughton Road had been lost through carelessness, there was
extreme vigilance among the Royalists.

He leaned over the ramparts and stared into the night.
He saw the fresh gun-mounts which the Parliament troops
had erected within the earthworks. Coming down Cow Lane
he could see a fiery snake. A pretty sight in the blackness.
He knew what it meant. Matchlock men were on the march,
with their two-yard-long matches burning. Either they were
taking up their posts for the night or an attack was contemplated.

A pikeman touched him on the shoulder. "An unlucky
wight took a ball in his brain at this very spot not a week
since. They have some of their shot concealed in St. John's
Priory and have the distance well gauged by now. Best keep
under cover."

Ryder thanked him and walked away. He had not taken a pace when a musket flashed in the darkness and a ball whistled over his head. He descended to street level. Nor was he sorry he had done so.

The heavy ordnance of the Parliament opened fire with stolid deliberation. Guns in the city replied. More Parliamentary guns came to life. They were concentrating on a breach already opened near the Newgate. It was evident an attack of some magnitude was contemplated. Trumpets in the city were sounding. Companies of men were marching to man the walls. Others, aroused from slumber, came sleepily from their billets, girding on their armour and gazing about them to see from which quarter the attack was expected.

The bells began to toll. In the darkness their notes had an ominous sound. The tumult increased. Streets were alive with hurrying figures. In the light of torches and lanterns the steel of sword and pike glittered like silver. One of the Parliamentary guns was firing red-hot shot. A house in Eastgate was ablaze. Its glare lit up the scene. Men laboured to fill the breach with beds, woolpacks, barrels and carts— anything which would close the gap and check the rush. Coarse wool cloth, taken from the glovers, was made into sacks and filled with earth. Behind the breach were rows of pikemen with their eighteen-foot pikes advanced—a formidable *chevaux de frise.*

Ryder became aware of Royle Wilding moving along the front of the pikemen. He was dressed in the height of fashion and coolly looked about him as though disdaining excitement. Towards him walked a tall, swarthy stranger, even more elaborately dressed. No Englishman would have worn such wide-topped boots, such a profusion of lace.

"It is the French lord," muttered a musketeer near Ryder. "He dresses like a dandy but he fights like a demon."

Ryder nodded. He had picked up a discarded half-pike from the ground. It would be well to make a pretence of fighting at a critical hour like this.

And then the storm burst. With a terrific cheer and a loud shout of "God be for us!" the Parliamentary infantry charged the breach. By the light of flames from the burning house Ryder could see their red tunics through gaps in the

fortification—men of the New-Model Army, resolved to
carry the breach if human valour could accomplish it. From
the wall above firelocks were sending down volley after
volley. Officers on the ground coolly discharged their pistols
at each head which appeared and then, throwing aside their
empty weapons, drew their swords. Musketeers, having
fired their cumbersome pieces, tossed them aside and used
their short swords or else clubbed their weapons. It was
fierce, primitive fighting in which strength and daring
counted more than skill and cunning.

Amid all the hacking and thrusting Royle Wilding moved
with the grace of a dancer. He and the French lord, M. de
St. Pol, had taken up their places in the forefront. No sooner
was a Parliament soldier within reach than one or the other
would transfix him. Ryder thought he had never seen a
rapier so long as the one which the Count St. Pol used. Both
he and Royle rivalled each other in nonchalance.

"Another bird for your spit, my lord," Royle would
remark with a bow.

"Another rebel the less, M'sieur Royle. These knaves
seem desirous of our company."

A pile of bodies at their feet testified to their dexterity.
It troubled Ryder sorely thus to stand idle while his comrades-
in-arms were slaughtered before his eyes. The game did not
remain one-sided. A dragoon levelled a snaphance at Wilding
and blew the plumed hat from his head. Royle shook his
long hair and laughed.

"I never lose my head, my lord," he cried, and resumed
his rapier.

More and more men swarmed into the breach; more and
more Royalists flung themselves forward with pike and
sword to beat back the attackers. Amid the clash of steel and
the firing Ryder could hear the shouts of encouragement. At
one moment a wild desire came over him to leap from the
wall top and join in the fray.

And then, above the fusillade, came the blare of Parliamentary trumpets sounding the recall. Reluctantly the
attackers fell back, bearing with them such of their wounded
as they could carry. The loyal city still held out for the King.

Cheers and jeers resounded. Musketeers on the walls sent

volley after volley at the retiring foe. More beds, more woolpacks, more barrels were flung into the breach. Wounded were picked up, fallen arms gathered—those belonging to the enemy being carried to The Cross to be displayed as trophies of yet another success.

The attack was over. Ryder, jammed in the moving throng, was borne back into Pepper Street. There was chattering, there was jostling, there was jubilation. He wondered how long Chester could hold out. Sooner or later, surely, these attacks must bear fruit. Yet there appeared no sign of weakening or wavering in the men round about him. It seemed obvious that Royle Wilding stood high in favour. He must be a colonel at least. Well, he was brave enough and cool enough. Ryder admired his nonchalance.

Ryder felt a touch upon his arm. He turned quickly, imagining that Royle Wilding must have recognized him. But it was not Wilding, it was an elderly man with a wrinkled, weather-worn face which was vaguely familiar.

"You remember me, sir?" The voice, too, struck a chord of memory.

. "Do you know me?" countered Ryder. He was never quite sure how much his beard had altered his appearance.

"I think so, sir, though you had no beard when you stayed with a young lady at a big house in the city."

"Ah!" Light came to Ryder. "You are Amos—Amos something."

"Amos Bowman. Correct, sir."

"And what of your young mistress? Do you ever see her?"

The man glanced cautiously over his shoulder. The crowd was thinning. Tired men were anxious to get back to their beds.

"My mistress, sir, is in a bad way. That is why I was so bold as to speak to you. She sore needs a friend."

"What! Is she in the city? May I see her?"

"She is in the old cottage in Nuns Walk; the one you know."

"May I see her?" Ryder was conscious of the eagerness in his voice.

"Of a truth, yes. It will be better for her than medicine.

She has been through the Valley of the Shadow, sir. You shall have word with her in the morning. Follow me."

It seemed that Ryder, after all, was to have a lodging for the night.

CHAPTER THIRTY-ONE

It was with a feeling of unreality that Ryder followed the old retainer. The side streets were dark and deserted now. The citizens were divided into two classes—roisterers who filled the taverns and caroused without restraint; sober burgesses who felt the pinch of penury, realized the seriousness of the siege, and foresaw even grimmer days ahead. The latter hastened home to sleep and to prepare for the morrow.

Amos motioned to Ryder to make no noise. He entered the cottage and lit a rushlight. By its pale glimmer Ryder watched the old soldier make a rough bed of rugs and blankets in a corner of the room. He endeavoured to fan the embers into a blaze, but failed. "You may sleep here, sir," he said softly. "She is asleep upstairs and must not be aroused till morning."

"Is she ill?"

"Ay, and weak. But not so much ill as crushed—crushed and bewildered, poor lamb, and knows not which way to turn."

"I will stand by her."

"I know it, sir. I know it. I thanked God when my eyes lit on you. But we must not talk now. It may disturb her slumbers."

Ryder kicked off his shoes, loosened his belt and got between his blankets. He lay for a while listening to a mouse gnawing at a floorboard. Once he heard a slight creak as though someone turned restlessly in the room overhead. It seemed strange, unreal, to be so close to Verity again, after so long a time. He thought tenderly about her until he fell asleep.

Day had dawned when Amos cautiously entered the room. He unlatched the door without speaking and stepped out into the misty morn. He returned with a handful of

sticks, moist with dew. Taking some dry sticks from a
secret hoard, he started to prepare his tinder-box. Ryder
watched him drowsily from the warmth of his blankets,
thinking how scraggy his wrinkled neck looked and how
much thinner he had gone. Once the fire was alight Amos
picked up a pail and disappeared. It was time for Ryder to
get up and go in search of a pump for his morning wash.

Guns were still firing, this time from the Welsh bank.
There were isolated shots, random shots, as though the
gunners were reluctant to cease fire. Amos was boiling milk
when Ryder came into the room. The old man cut bread
into cubes and bore a basin of milk upstairs. When he came
down he explained that it was still possible to get milk, as a
few cows grazed on the Roodee. He did not know how much
longer this would be possible. A tapping on the floor above
caused him to point to the narrow stairs. "She's ready to
see you!" he said.

Ryder climbed the staircase, little wider than a ladder,
ducking his head as he went higher. He was conscious of
mingled feelings, curiosity mingled with dread.

Morning sunlight streamed through a small window in
the bedchamber as Ryder, after a timid knock, entered.
Verity was sitting up in bed with a shawl drawn about her—
a wan, pale Verity. She gave Ryder a brave smile which
wrung his heart.

"My very dear friend," she said softly. "When Amos told
me of his discovery I could scarce believe my good fortune.
To think you should have been in this house while I, unconscious of the fact, slept soundly! I suppose I ought to have
dreamt about you, or had some premonition, but truth
compels me to say that nothing even hinted that you were in
Chester until Amos arrived with my breakfast and the great
news. How strange you appear with a beard, Ryder, and in
Cavalier clothes! You look as if you, too, had suffered."

"You have been ill?" he asked.

"Oh yes, but let's not talk about me. Tell me about yourself. Your arm looks as if you had been wounded."

"In the charge at Rowton Heath. My horse carried me
into the Northgate, while I clung unconscious to his mane."
He told her of the manner in which Milo had repaid his debt,

he spoke of Myra—her devotion and her temper. But he never mentioned Rosea.

"That wild Welsh girl is in love with you, Ryder."

"I suppose so." He shrugged his shoulders. "It does not interest me. The affair is none of my seeking. She was kind to me. None the less the door was shut in my face. So far as I am concerned it shall remain shut."

"There is another door open here, Ryder, as long as you wish it. Humble though this cottage is, it is yours to use as you will. But if I read the girl aright she will be all contrition when next you see her."

"I have told you about myself. Now let me hear what has happened to you. Have things gone amiss?"

She stared out of the window. "When things go amiss," she said slowly, "it is not fair to burden others with the fruits of folly."

"My shoulders are big enough to bear your burden, Verity."

"That is sweet of you, but I think not. Not just yet, anyhow." Verity lay back and closed her eyes. Ryder watched her anxiously, fearing he had tired her. She opened her eyes quickly and read his thoughts. "I was only thinking," she explained. "We must get you out of the city. I think it can be done with Amos's help. There will be more risk now. Much more risk, but then, you do not fear risk."

Ryder permitted himself to smile. It was not often he smiled, but when he did it gave him a curiously boyish appearance. So Verity thought as she watched."

"It savours of the grotesque," he said. "Here am I, a fighting man, strong save for a deformed arm, and I must be smuggled out of a beleaguered city for safety's sake while frail women remain. Doubtless, my dear Verity, you consider yourself better fitted to withstand the rigours of a siege, more adapted to endure hardships, than I."

"I must remain in Chester," she said quietly. "It is your duty to escape and rejoin your army."

"As I see it I ought to remain to care for you. You have been ill?"

"Not ill, exactly, Ryder. Did you not guess?" She drew

back her shawl. In the curve of her arm lay a baby a few weeks old. She saw amazement in his eyes.

"You did not suspect, Ryder?"

"I never gave the possibility a thought. Verity—I cannot picture you a mother."

"You will have to do so now."

"I—I wish you happiness."

"So you see, Ryder, why it is manifestly impossible for me to leave the city."

He sat bewildered. There were questions he wished to ask, but he did not like to ask them. He assumed she had married Royle Wilding. If so, why was Wilding lording it with the Governor while his wife—and child—faced death in squalor? A sense of delicacy intimated that these were questions which must be left unspoken unless Verity chose to mention them. Perhaps a suggestion might persuade her to talk.

"It would be difficult for you to leave in the circumstances. Of course your husband is with the garrison?"

"Of course." Verity spoke quietly.

"It is all wrong that such things should happen," burst out Ryder impetuously. "Surely, surely a flag of truce could be arranged so that you could leave the city."

"I think not. It may not be long before our forces capture Chester." She gave a forced laugh. "You notice I say *our* forces?"

He could see that he was tiring her, so he made an excuse to leave, moving softly down the narrow stairs.

The streets of Chester were busy when he went forth. The approach of November had sent persons searching for fuel. Men of the Welsh regiment under Colonel Mostyn were clamouring for better food. There were rumours that the Archbishop of York at Conway had promised to get a ship-load of food through the blockade if Captain Stephen Rich in the watch-ship *Rebecca* could be enticed away. It was said that a relief force was assembling at Conway and Denbigh to break the leaguer.

The gossip interested Ryder. Hoping to hear more, he entered the Blue Posts Tavern and was sitting quietly on a settle when a drawer approached to ask what he would drink. Ryder thrust a hand into an empty pocket and realized he had not a coin in his possession.

"I was robbed while I lay wounded," he explained awkwardly. The man turned away. Ryder's voice had attracted attention. Captain Milo swaggered across.

"You shall drink with me, my bully," he cried heartily. Ryder shook his head, but Milo was adamant. "Drink while you can, you fool. The ale won't last for ever. Demme, we begin to feel the pinch. I came across two poor devils dead of starvation as I went the rounds last night. Does your arm mend?"

"It gets stronger every day," said Ryder, working his fingers.

"You could hold a rein? Then you shall ride with us, my merry lad. The Lord St. Pol is getting horsemen together to round up some cattle. It may be the last time we shall taste beef, so let us make the most of it."

Ryder felt trapped. To refuse would be to proclaim his party. "I have no sword," he said lamely.

"I am awake so you cannot borrow mine!" Milo laughed at his joke somewhat boisterously. "You shall have a sword, bully. Come to my rooms and I will find you one."

"I have no wish to see Myra again."

"Ah ha! She is a very hell-cat when roused. Her temper is like a furze bush ablaze; fierce while it lasts but it soon dies down. She asked me this morning if I had seen you."

It was with reluctance Ryder followed Milo down East-gate Street. The captain had exerted no pressure and yet Ryder was conscious of an implied threat. Probably it appealed to Milo's humour that he should persuade a rebel to fight against his own kin. A sword was put into his hands— a broadsword which had been picked up at the breach. Milo left him with a parting instruction.

"We muster at The Cross at noon. The General of Horse leads us in person. He is a lad of mettle and likes late-comers no better than those who hang back." Milo strode away. A mine had been exploded under the wall during the night and he wished to see the extent of the damage. Ryder sat morosely, turning the blade in his hands. It was thus Myra found him.

P

"You come back to me, *cariad*," she cried, and flung her arms about him. Ryder thrust her away roughly. She misinterpreted his gesture. "Ah! Did I hurt your arm? It's sorry I am. I forgot your wound."

"I do not want you to touch me. I have not forgotten your parting words."

"The sooner you do, the better. What has Milo been up to? Are you to ride with him on the raid? Do not go, *cariad*. You might be killed by your own men."

"A fitting ending to a farce!" Ryder was bitter. He rose to his feet, slipped a leather baldrick over his whole shoulder and settled it comfortably so that his bridle arm was free. "I could manage a quiet animal," he said, moving his fingers.

He made his way to The Crossing. He was in a mood which welcomed any deviation and found himself almost looking forward to the raid. He was troubled about Verity, troubled about Rosea, troubled about Myra. He wished profoundly he could be left alone to go through life without these complications. They were not of his seeking. He felt resentful. He did not wish Myra to place him under an obligation; nor did he want Rosea to plan his escape. He could make his own plans without interference. As for Verity, if she chose to have a child it was a matter which her husband must see to!

He clambered somewhat clumsily into the saddle of a horse which Milo led towards him. There was no danger of the animal being restive. Every rib showed. Ryder felt it would be a miracle if he coaxed a canter out of the starving beast. The Northgate, like the Eastgate, was now blocked with earth, so the cavalcade went by way of the Watergate and walked, four abreast, across the Roodee. They had not ridden far before a cloud of smoke spat from the black muzzle of the demi-culverin which the Parliamentarians had mounted near Brewers Hall. A roundshot ploughed its way through the ranks, upsetting half a dozen mounts and killing several troopers. It put the Lord St. Pol in a fighting mood. He urged his horse into a canter, the troopers following as best they could. They strung out, each man's position governed by the stamina of his mount.

For one wild moment Ryder wondered whether the irate

Frenchman intended to take them across the Dee to attempt
an attack on the gun-mount, but he had other ideas in mind.
Across the sward he led them north until they were level with
the flank of the Parliamentarian trenches which hemmed
in the Northgate. Then they charged. The movement took
the Parliamentarians by surprise, for their entire attention
had been concentrated on the walls. They had not contemplated an attack on the flank. Ryder could see pikemen
hastily assembling to form a defence. The Lord St. Pol was
amongst them, plying his long rapier. Other Cavaliers were
hard on his horse's heels. A few musketeers opened fire and
some horses fell.

With several empty saddles the ragged charge swept on.
Royle Wilding was among the foremost. He rode with
haughty ease, as fastidiously dressed as if he attended a
levee. The horsemen wheeled and circled to get back to the
Roodee. Troopers were straggling. Ryder put his horse to a
low fence. The spent animal blundered and crashed, flinging
Ryder heavily. Experience had taught him how to fall and
he rolled clear of the threshing hoofs. The horse struggled
to its feet and stood with hanging reins, glad of a chance to
recover its breath. Several other horsemen took the hedge
and galloped after their leader. Not so Ryder. He was shaken
by the fall, but his wits were sufficiently alert to send him
crawling quickly towards the hedge, where he lay, concealed
by the long grass.

Escape had come more easily than he anticipated. Once
again Captain Milo—this time unwittingly—had stood his
friend.

CHAPTER THIRTY-TWO

WHEN Ryder Yale made his way through the Parliamentary
lines until he reached his former billet the thing which
impressed him most was the casual nature of his reception. His
escape was, to him, a matter of paramount importance. It
was almost like a return from the grave. To his amazement
he found that he had not been missed. The siege was being
pressed with the utmost resolution. Men were wounded.

Men were killed. Men were sent to fresh stations—the Welsh bank, perhaps, or the siege of Beeston. Anything might have happened to him. The overworked soldiers with discomforts and worries of their own had other matters to think about. His name was entered on the list of missing and there the matter ended. Only Mark Trueman seemed delighted to see him, and even Mark was almost too busy to talk. He was preparing for an advance into North Wales.

"You are just in time, Ryder," he exclaimed. "You'll find your buff-coat and head-piece in my quarters. I have clung to them hoping you might make an appearance some day. Tell me your adventures once we are on the march. There's not a moment to spare now. Sir William Vaughan has a rendezvous at Denbigh and means to break the leaguer if we do not scatter his forces first. Brereton hopes to catch Vaughan unprepared. We are to unite with Colonel Mytton's forces at Ruthin. Hasten, Ryder. I will arrange that you have a horse."

Ryder, nothing loth, went in search of his buff-coat. He found it hung somewhat loosely from his frame. He had not fared sumptuously at Chester!

And now he was riding, lighter of heart, through the pleasant land of Denbigh. There were hills in the distance, and valleys and groves and rushing streams. A pleasant contrast to the broad meadows of Cheshire. Even if October were at an end the landscape was good to look upon. The trees clung to their russet leaves, the hedgerows were bright with hips and haws, the fields were sometimes furrowed brown where a farmer had attempted ploughing. Hilltops took on blue hues which reflected drifting clouds, though some slopes were still rusty with bracken. Men of the Parliamentary army looked about them with curious eyes as they tramped onward. It was another invasion of North Wales. Sir William Brereton had returned from his four months in London resolved to make his presence felt.

North Wales was still hot for King Charles. Every castle held out for the King, solidly built castles which would defy any guns but the heaviest siege trains, and all the great ordnance of the Parliament was in England. Chester, 'the masterpiece of the kingdom', was the object of all eyes.

Every loyal heart in North Wales concentrated on its relief.
Captain Bartlett in his daring pinnace the *Swan* continued
to run the gauntlet with supplies—and messages of hope.
At Conway Archbishop John Williams, far from his see of
York, devised schemes for sending supplies to Chester.
Colonel Mostyn had escaped from the city and crossed to
Dublin, there to endeavour to raise a fresh regiment.

At Beaumaris, at Rhuddlan, all along the coast, there was
but one topic of conversation—Chester must be relieved.
Some Irish forces had been landed at Beaumaris and these
were marched to Denbigh by way of Llanrwst Bridge.
Denbigh was the rendezvous: Denbigh, so finely situated,
with its massive castle rising high above the plain: Denbigh,
where King Charles had stayed for three nights after his
escape from Chester. Sir William Vaughan had abandoned
his governorship of Shrawardine Castle to take the field. He
hoped that the forces got together in North Wales would be
able to unite with Lord Astley and so make an attack
simultaneously on the Parliamentary lines round about
Chester. Sir William Vaughan was as full of optimism as he
was of loyalty. Companies of men kept arriving to swell the
ranks of his footmen. He billeted them in the houses flanking
the long road which climbed steeply through the town of
Denbigh up to its castle.

From Conway there marched a company under Captain
Robert Pugh of Penrhyn with drum and colours. Sir William
Vaughan had marched through Montgomeryshire bringing
with him troopers from Ludlow, and soldiers from other
garrisons along the marches of Wales. Unknown to him,
Lieutenant-Colonel Michael Jones with fourteen hundred
horse and Adjutant-General Louthian with a thousand foot
were coming from Chester over the bridge at Holt.

It was an imposing force, for Sir William Brereton had sent
the cream of all those parts. For the most part they were men
of Cheshire, victors of many a hard-fought field. On Thursday
night they were at Mold, on Friday at Ruthin, where Colonel
Mytton had gathered with his forces from Shropshire.
Ruthin Castle held out stubbornly, but the Parliamentary
troops made use of the town. And so they came down the
winding road from Ruthin to Denbigh. It was on the first

day of November that they came in sight of the old town of
Denbigh. Forty men from each regiment were selected to
form a forlorn hope, and these, advancing well ahead of the
main body, found the hedges lined with troops which Sir
William Vaughan had hastily advanced to meet them when
news of their approach came through.

Sounds of the firing came down the still air to where
Ryder Yale was stationed. To his chagrin he found that his
arm was not sufficiently healed to permit him to take his
place with the troop. It was in vain that he pleaded that his
sword arm was unimpaired; the surgeon was adamant.
So the troop which he had just rejoined with such elation
was handed to another and he was given charge of carriages
in the convoy, where his experience would be of value. His
charger was commandeered—good horses were scarce—
and he had to content himself with a dragooner's nag
which ambled with due docility alongside the creaking
waggons.

They had passed through the picturesque hamlet of
Llanrhaiadr which dozed beside its twin-roofed thatched
church and now had the broad plain before them. Ryder
could see the tall tower of Whitchurch on his right. The
white church looked strangely isolated at the foot of Denbigh's hill, as though it had been rejected by neighbours who
had risen to greater heights.

The Royalist horse and dragoons flanked the road and
charged the Parliamentary forlorn hope fiercely as they
approached. Though outnumbered they fought stoutly until
the foot came up. It was found that the passage of the road
was too difficult, so the reserve forces were formed in the
open fields.

More and more men were arriving down the road from
Ruthin. On the advice of some who knew the district the
main body was drawn to Denbigh Green so that they might
have open country across which to fight. The pikemen drove
the Royalists out of the lane which they had held so stoutly,
routing both horse and foot so that they hurried for shelter
under the Castle. They had handsomely disputed the hedges
for an hour, but the pressure was too great. The Royalists
rallied upon reaching the houses. Sir William Vaughan sent

forward his horse to challenge Colonel Mytton's troops as
they formed on Denbigh Green. They could not stand up to
the Parliamentary charge. A body of Arcal horse and part of
Prince Maurice's life-guard charged the pursuers, but it was
in vain. The Royalists scattered. Many of the horse galloped
for Llanrwst through Llangerniew; others made for Conway
along the St. Asaph Road, being chased for eight miles.

Ryder could not remain with the waggons. When the
tumult was at its height he drew his sword and urged his
mount into the press to take his share of cut and thrust. He
was weary when the exultant cheers told him that the day
was won. Trumpets were sounding. Royalist foot were
hurrying up the hill to take shelter in the Castle. Hundreds
of prisoners were taken. A hundred lay dead on the field. An
amazing spectacle it must have been for Colonel Salusbury,
the Governor, as he looked down from the high walls of
Denbigh Castle and saw the day go ill for the King. He could
do no more than open his gates to the vanquished foot. His
was the responsibility of the Castle and he meant to hold it
until his King gave him permission to surrender.

It was a staggering blow to the Royalists in Chester.
Their hopes of relief were shattered. Ryder, who had
recently been within the hard-pressed walls, could imagine
their feelings. He watched the counting of the prisoners;
watched parties of weary horsemen ride in to boast that no
group of enemy horse exceeded seven score in number, so
faithfully had they scattered them; watched Colonel Mytton
establish himself in the suburbs of Denbigh even as he had
done in Ruthin.

Ryder was one who marched back to the bridge at Holt.
He was in no enviable frame of mind. It was obvious that his
bridle arm was still weak. Nor had he recovered his full
strength. He had changed in mind as much as he had changed
in body. He contrasted himself with the ardent young
idealist who enlisted in Sir William's troop. He believed
then in the righteousness of his cause. He felt he could be
steadfast, clinging to what was right and abhorring what was
wrong. He obeyed orders without question, implicitly. Now
he found himself dissatisfied with many things, inclined to
question, beset by doubts, and growing increasingly restless

under restraint. He had been guilty of dereliction in leaving the convoy at the Denbigh fight, but in the confusion no one had noticed his conduct.

When Colonel Jones's force returned to the lines before Chester, Ryder sought his billet, settled himself before a fire, and rested. The siege was being pressed more closely than ever. He could hear the periodic explosions of heavy guns.

He drew comfort from the hearth. As he watched the flicker of the flame he wondered whether those he knew in the beleaguered city had any firing. His thoughts were divided but they lingered most with Verity. There was something about her frailty which stirred him deeply; she who had been so virile and independent was now weak and dependent. She had Amos to care for her, but Amos might be killed. And then? What had the man meant when he said that she was crushed and bewildered? Had her husband deserted her in her hour of need? If such had been the conduct of Royle Wilding, Ryder felt that he had one more score to settle. What would happen to Verity and her tiny child? It seemed all wrong that women and children should be called upon to suffer.

His thoughts turned to Rosea. She would fare better. Rosea was able to care for herself—she had strength and a home and money. Yet even she must suffer. Ryder had a conviction that secretly she suffered more than she would reveal. And that strange waif Myra! He could never rightly assess her. At times she frightened him, or even repulsed him, yet he could not help but recall her devotion. Human nature was very complex.

He held his left hand to the blaze. The cold was making the wound ache. Some muscle or nerve or tendon seemed to have been torn away. The strength would not come back. He of the mighty muscles had not now the grip of a child in his left hand. Still, he could hold the reins of a quiet horse—but what a makeshift soldier he had become! The arm had been carelessly set and it curved. That hurt his pride. What hurt his pride even more was that he should have been taken from his troop and sent to the commissariat.

He, who had been a fighting man from the moment the first angry shot was fired! Impatiently he rose to his feet and put on his barred helmet. He slung a cloak about his shoulders, for November had come in damp and chill. Then he went in search of the Commander-in-Chief. He was glad Sir William was back. Colonel Michael Jones was an admirable officer, so was Colonel Dukinfield, but he had known Sir William since boyhood and he would always regard him as his leader. A sentry halted him as he approached the headquarters. His name soon secured him admittance.

Sir William looked older. He sat behind a table strewn with papers. As Ryder stood before him he studied his face carefully by the light of a cluster of candles.

"It is a long time since I saw you, Yale. You have been wounded I hear, and captured."

"In the Rowton Moor fight, sir."

"Would that I had been here for it. The news caused a rare stir in London. For the King it is the beginning of the end. The King's party are vanquished, Ryder, but they are stubborn. There is no hope for Chester, especially after our good success at Denbigh, yet Byron will not listen to reason. When you were a prisoner in the city how were matters with them?"

"They were short of food and fuel but there was no talk of surrender. A score or two of cattle remain, and some horses. All are underfed."

"Their courage is more to be commended than their wisdom. Why is it you wish to speak to me?"

"I wish to return to my troop, sir. I am told that my wound disqualifies me."

"Show me your arm."

Ryder stripped off his coat.

"A bad wound, Ryder, and the bone was ill set. You could never manage a restive horse. I am glad the arm was saved. You must obtain a post where there are less demands on your strength."

"Sir, if I cannot fight with my troop I had as soon resign."

"Ryder Yale! You, who have been with me from the start?"

"Have I not earned my release, sir?"

"And Chester on the point of falling! Ask me again after

we have marched in triumph through the streets of the city."

Sir William sat staring into the young man's face. His eyes were shrewd. "There is more in this than meets the eye. Put on your coat. I know you, Ryder. I know you well. You are not faint-hearted. Be frank with me. What is in your mind?"

"I saw Verity in Chester, sir."

"Ah! I have lost all track of her. How is she?"

"Ill and in sore distress, sir. She is married and has a child a few weeks old. I desire permission to return to the city so that I can stand by her in her need."

"Whom has she married?"

"She has not told me his name."

"One of the malignants?"

"So I assume, sir. I have not seen him."

"Probably some rake who has betrayed her. Why do these young women act as they do? I thought better of Verity. I am sorry. She served me well. But she has made her own bed and I fear she must lie on it. In any case you could not get through the leaguer."

"I believe I could, sir. Amos Bowman is with her and he has shown me a way. I know their habits. They are alert on the east and the north. A mouse could not get through. They are less vigilant on the river side. The Welshmen are posted there. They are discontented and mutinous on account of the lack of food and are more neglectful in their look-out as a consequence."

"All the same I cannot let you go, Ryder. You are too valuable an officer. Though you cannot ride with the horse we can make good use of you in other ways. I grieve for Verity, but I cannot release you at such a time on so flimsy a pretext."

Ryder flushed, saluted, and withdrew without speaking. He was in a rebellious mood. Sir William was undoubtedly right, and yet ...! It was impressed on Ryder how remorseless war could be. He wanted to be loyal. His whole nature was loyal. Suddenly there came to mind a talk he had once had about loyalty. It seemed to him that all life was an issue of rival loyalties. It was not whether one was loyal or disloyal, but which loyalty had the greater claim. And that was an issue each man must resolve for himself.

As he sat staring into the embers a step caused him to glance up quickly. There was a cautious knock. He wheeled. A bent figure crept cautiously inside. Ryder reached for a pistol. The man straightened his back. It was Amos.

"What is the matter? How did you get through our lines?" Ryder spoke sharply.

"I had to seek you, sir. It is Mistress Verity."

"Is she killed? Wounded?" He shot out the words.

"No, sir. Her child has died and she is fair breaking her heart."

To Ryder the way of life no longer seemed befogged. There came to him a great and shining light. He walked to the next room. With methodical carefulness he doffed his buff-coat, folded it and laid it upon a table. By this he placed his head-piece and his sword. He stood his jack-boots beside them. Then he put on the clothes in which he had escaped from Chester. He picked up a knapsack and filled it with what provisions he could lay hands on. He slipped a pistol in his belt and saw that his sheath-knife was in position. Amos watched without uttering a word.

Ryder put out the light. "I will come with you, Amos," he said quietly. Together they went out into the night.

CHAPTER THIRTY-THREE

CROUCHED among bushes which crested the Welsh bank of the Dee, Ryder Yale and Mark Trueman conferred in low tones. The night was cold and damp. Periodically the great gun on Brewers Hall Mount belched forth orange flame. The battery on Morgan's Mount replied. Otherwise the night was dark. Mark Trueman had never been more perplexed. He, too, was experiencing the pull of rival loyalties.

"You are resolved to carry out your purpose, Ryder?"

"Yes. Nothing will make me deviate a hand's breadth."

"If caught you will be shot for deserting the colours."

"I am aware of that. I am also aware that Verity lies broken-hearted, deserted, and in danger in Chester. I asked

Sir William's permission to go to her aid. She has served him faithfully. It would have been a little matter for him to have granted my request. I am loyal to those I serve. I consider there is equal obligation from those who are served."

"You are unreasonable, Ryder. A Commander-in-Chief could not have countenanced such conduct. You know it."

"Then I save his conscience by acting unofficially. There was a time when she went away from Nantwich with the man she loved and I, like the Pharisee I was, turned from her when she implored me to remain her friend. Now I make amends. I shall stay by her in her hour of need."

"It is not in my heart to condemn you, Ryder, though I am greatly troubled. I admire your singleness of purpose. You face starvation."

"I know conditions in the city better than you." Ryder was grim.

"Here is my snapsack full of provisions. And here is a good Cheshire cheese—if you can get so much in the coracle. When should Amos return?"

"I do not know how long it will take him to get into the city now. He may have difficulty in getting past the sentries. Tell me, Mark, you will not fail to watch for the signal should you be needed?"

"I will watch day and night. If you can get safely to the water's edge there will be no difficulty in landing this side. I shall tell all sentries that friends of ours are expected to escape."

A dark object moved across the river. Both men descended to the water's edge. Amos stepped ashore. Ryder and Mark gripped hands without speaking. The food was placed in the fragile craft. Ryder crossed first, and Amos hauled the coracle back with a line. Then he led the way across the dark Roodee. Where an old, low archway had been blocked up Amos had removed loose stones sufficient to permit their crawling under the walls. The two entered unmolested.

"It keeps me young," muttered the old soldier as they entered Nuns Lane. "It reminds me of times in the Low Countries when first I went soldiering. Days when I, too, had a lass."

"Mistress Verity owes much to your fidelity. Does she know you came to summon me?"

"No. You must break the news as best you may." Amos peeped through a chink in the shutter. "She sits beside the fire—such as it is—dreaming. Go to her."

The scene was one which Ryder never forgot: the pale girl crouching over the tiny blaze, the helpless, hopeless look in her eyes. She turned anxiously on hearing Ryder's step. The suspicion of a smile animated her features when she recognized her visitor.

"Ryder, how good to see you! You have been so long absent I feared you had been killed. Such terrible things happen these days."

"I was pressed into service—under the Lord St. Pol," he said. "I could not send you word of what had happened."

With an impulsive gesture she reached up and stroked his face. "You look nicer without your beard, Ryder; more like the Ryder I used to know."

Mentally he resolved that he would not grow a beard again. All he said was: "I am still the same Ryder. I have not changed save that my left arm is robbed of its strength."

"How strong you used to be!"

"And still am; strong enough to guard you." He was fencing for time, wondering how he could introduce the dread subject. With characteristic directness he took the difficult fence.

"Your baby died! I came to tell you that I grieve for you more than I can say."

"Yes," she said quietly. "A beleaguered city is no place for a baby. Perhaps he is happier away. We buried him in the garden opposite."

"The garden of Sir William's house?"

Verity nodded. "Amos found some snowdrop bulbs and planted them; they will look pleasing when they break through the brown earth. It seems strange that a woman must go through such suffering to bring a child into the world and then have it taken from her. If the child were not wanted, why should it be born? Tell me that."

"I cannot."

"What troubles me is whether one so young has a soul. Shall I see him again in the future life? Shall I recognize him?"

"You must ask a minister, not a soldier, Verity."

"I did ask a minister and his replies were evasive. I do not think he knew. They talk with great assurance until we come to something vital, something which affects one's whole life, and then they look profound and say, 'The ways of God are beyond man's comprehension.' I want to *know* if I shall see my baby boy again."

"All things are possible to those who believe," said Ryder, not knowing what to say.

"Believe! And what does 'believe' mean? How can you *make* yourself believe something? Either you do or you don't. I want assurance. I want something definite. Can a heartbroken mother find solace in something as vague as belief?"

Ryder was distressed. This was a Verity he had not hitherto encountered. Life had changed her even as he had been changed. "My dear," he said tenderly, "my heart aches for you in your distress, but I do not know how to answer your question."

"Of course you don't, Ryder. Nobody does. It is foolish of me to talk like this, but it is such a blessed relief to unburden my heart, to give utterance to the tortuous thoughts which rack my brain. Oh, Ryder, it is good to have you back again. I have only had Amos. He is so dear and devoted, but I could not talk to him. Oh, the blessed relief of speech! See, pull up that stool and sit as near to the fire as possible. Wood gets so scarce that we have to husband every stick."

Ryder was glad of the warmth. The night vigil beside the river had chilled him. He noticed that he was more susceptible to cold since the wound at Rowton Moor. He held his left hand towards the blaze. Perhaps the comfort of the heat gave him confidence.

"May I ask you a question, as an old friend, Verity?"

"Of course. I think I know what it is you wish to ask. I— I have been wanting to tell you, yet I could not bring myself to do so."

"About your husband?"

"Yes."

"I have no right to ask, but something tells me that things are not as they should be."

She sat staring into the fire. "One of life's tragedies is that we can look back and see we have made a mistake; see so plainly that we made a mistake—when it is too late to remedy it, when nothing remains but to abide by the result of one's error. Why doesn't some angelic voice whisper, 'You are about to do something which you will rue all your days; do so at your peril'? No angel with a flaming sword bars the way as in the days of Baalam. Ryder, I am an orphan and I have yearned for a home of my own. I longed to be a good wife and mother. I soon found that a good wife was not needed. And now—now I am denied motherhood."

He had no words. All he could do was to stretch forth his strong right hand and lay it tenderly on hers.

"It was Royle Wilding you married?" he demanded.

"Of course."

"Has he deserted you?"

She would not answer. Yet her silence gave the reply he required.

"Does he know about the child, Verity?"

She shook her head. Ryder rose to his feet and his hand instinctively groped for the sword-hilt which was not to be found. He dropped his hand with a gesture of despair. He had left his sword behind at his billet: left it because he was honest and would not take what was not his own.

"What is it, Ryder? You are angry! Your eyes frighten me."

"That man is not fit to live."

"Sit down, Ryder. It is not for us to judge him."

"He merits judgment."

"We all get judged, Ryder, sooner or later, though I think we must judge ourselves. The hour may come when Royle will be made to perceive that he has not chosen aright. Remember this, Ryder. His standards are not our standards. He holds lightly things which are sacred to us. I believe he loved me when he married me. I am sure he did. The trouble is he ought never to have married. Some men were never intended to be married—they are too restless, too change-able. Are we to blame a man for the nature which he has in-herited? His military duties have carried him away from me. It was when Prince Rupert cast a spell over him that I felt myself losing him. I could see him going from me and nothing I could do would hold him. He was too wild a bird to encase in a matrimonial cage.''

"At least he should have provided for you.'' There was indignation in Ryder's tone.

"But he does not know where I am, Ryder, and I am too proud to let him know.''

"It is evident to me that he has been at no pains to find out. I shall make it my duty to acquaint him of the true facts.''

"Ryder, you are not to do anything of the kind. I do not want dissension. Please respect my wishes. There is trouble enough in this unhappy city. I came here of my own accord because I still care for him, because I still love him and want to be near him lest he should be wounded again.''

"You still love him? After the way he has treated you, you still love him?'' Ryder was incredulous.

"Yes, Ryder. Love does not cease because of neglect or ill-treatment. He may hurt me, but I shall always love him.''

Ryder stared at her, a little awed. Never before had he encountered such revelation of the human heart. He felt strangely moved towards her and also, in juxtaposition, furious with the light-hearted Royle Wilding. It might be well for a man to be debonair—but not at the expense of human suffering.

Not knowing what else to say, he suddenly became practical. He went outside and returned with the provisions over his shoulder, a Cheshire cheese under his arm, and a small ham in his hand.

"Ryder! You are a magician!'' The housewife was in-stantly in the ascendant. "Oh, let us have a meal! I am sure we shall all feel in better spirits. The last meat I tasted was a sparrow pie which cost Amos a deal of time and no little birdlime. And some of the sparrows were starlings. What is in the bag, Ryder? Not bread! And biscuits! It is unheard of!''

She paused and regarded him suspiciously. "Ryder, where have you been?"

He had to laugh. He felt so much like a small boy caught in the larder.

"Yes," he confessed, "I managed to get across to the other side. That is how I am shaved. Mark is the good angel who procured these delicacies for you. He came to the river bank with me. He will be there to greet you when you get across."

Verity laid down a knife with which she was preparing to carve the ham. "But I am not going across, Ryder. I stay here—near my husband."

He could have reproved her for her folly, but something told him that this was not an occasion to dispute with her. He made no comment. Instead, he walked to the door and looked into the roadway. Part of the wall opposite was down. The rubble had been cleared sufficiently to allow a cart to pass. There was a dark stain on the road as though a horse had bled to death.

"I think I will go for a walk and see what goes on," he said.

"Be careful you are not recognized." Verity looked up from the cooking-pot she had placed on the fire. "You had better grow your beard again."

"I shall have to: I have no razor." Ryder laughed and ventured forth. He still wore the suit which Rosea had given him. It was probably Royle's most sober apparel, but it was more stylish than anything he had ever worn before. His presence attracted little attention. A man might wear velvet or rags; his fellows had other things to think about. Many soldiers were in the streets, glad of their off-duty freedom. Workmen were mending a breach in the sandstone wall, strengthening it by barrow-loads of earth heaped on the inside. There were musketeers on the ramparts. In the more exposed places the parapet had been heightened by baulks of timber. The demi-culverin at Brewers Hall Mount was causing annoyance.

At The Cross he saw displayed Parliamentary colours captured in the raid on Eccleston. Lord Byron had not yet lost the power to strike back.

Q

From the Bowling Alley two of Brereton's cannon were methodically shooting at the Water Tower and at the Dee Mills. Ryder found it ironical to be within the walls and assess the results of his companions' aim. From where he stood he could see part of the bridge of boats which the Parliamentarians had thrown across the river near Dee Lane. A party of men armed with mattocks and spades made their way down the street. Annoyance was caused by a small gun which the Parliamentarians had hoisted to the tower of St. John's Church, where they erected it on a platform.

An arrow slapped into a beam and stood quivering. Several men rushed towards it and tore off the paper which was wrapped round it. In its place they tied some tow dipped in tar. A man with a bow mounted the walls. Another brought flint and steel and set the tow blazing. The flaming arrow was fired back to the suburbs.

"A summons to surrender!" commented a man who read the paper over his companions' shoulders. He saw curiosity in Ryder's eyes. "It is not the first they have sent us. We return their arrow with wild-fire attached. They are slow to learn their lesson."

Ryder stepped into the shadow of the Rows as a party of Cavaliers came down the roadway.

Lord Byron walked in front. He wore a cuirass. Ryder instantly recognized the Governor. Those dark eyes, the pointed beard, gave him a hard and intolerant appearance. Beside him swaggered the French nobleman, Count St Pol, he of the long rapier, and with him was Royle Wilding, dressed with fastidious care. Several other gallants in velvet cloaks completed the party. They walked to the Bishop's Palace, doubtless for a conference. Ryder was about to pass on his way when he felt a tug at his sleeve.

Rosea was beside him. "Where on earth have you been all this time?" she demanded. "I have been concerned about you." And then, before he could reply, she added: "Come to my rooms. I cannot be seen talking to you here. Follow me."

Ryder followed with a docility which surprised him. Perhaps, after all, he was not sorry to see Rosea again. The room, he noticed, was as smartly furnished as before, but no fire burned in the grate. Rosea noted his gaze and nodded her head. "I save firing for the evening," she said. "You have removed your beard. I like you better thus, but was it wise?"

"It will soon grow again."

"Sit down, Ryder, and tell me what you have been doing. I saw you ride forth for a raid, but you never came back. Were you captured? Did you ride of your own accord, resolved to fight for your King in his need?"

"I was given no choice. It so happened that Milo Preen accosted me. I had to go or reveal my identity. My horse stumbled at a hedge and flung me. So I returned to our lines."

"Commendably wise." She smiled her approval. "What I cannot understand is that you should return to Chester. It is a city which possesses charm, but at present there are disadvantages which detract. A scarcity of fuel. Little food. A wine-cellar which is now as dry as a sermon. I should have imagined you would have been glad to absent yourself when you had the chance."

"Shall I tell you the true situation, Rosea?"

"Whatever you tell me will be true, Ryder. One of your worst handicaps in life is your inability not to speak the truth."

"A young woman in the city was in dire distress."

"You care for her?"

"Yes. She is a very dear friend."

"And you came to her rescue! How romantic! No wonder I have failed to entice you. I have endeavoured to rouse a spark of romance in you for years without success, and now this woman succeeds where I fail. How ravishingly beautiful she must be!"

"She is not."

"Ungallant, Ryder. Most ungallant. There must be some powerful lure."

"There is none. She is already married."

"My dear. You improve. Really, you begin to intrigue me. Our Puritan takes an interest in a married woman! I vow you develop qualities I never suspected. And do you console her during her husband's absence?"

"Her husband has deserted her." It cost Ryder self-control to withstand the bantering.

Rosea's eyes were dancing with mischief.

"I sense romance, Ryder, for all your Puritan ways! Pray tell me the name of her husband. It would be *so* amusing if I knew him!"

"You do! It is Royle Wilding!"

CHAPTER THIRTY-FOUR

RYDER admitted to himself later that he felt vicious when he drove home the unexpected thrust, sharp as the stab of a poniard. No sooner had he allowed himself to be goaded by Rosea's teasing than he repented. Every trace of colour ebbed from her cheeks and her eyes grew wide. He thought she might faint. With perfect composure she walked to a chair and seated herself with deliberation. She appeared dazed, and sat staring with an intent look Ryder had never seen before.

"Shut the door, Ryder," she observed in a carefully modulated tone. "If you will look in the corner-cupboard you will find half a bottle of wine. Would it trouble you to pour me a glass?"

She sipped it slowly. The intent look was still in her eyes. She seemed to be looking into the future.

"Thank you, Ryder. I have never had a knock-out blow before. To think that it should come from you—you whom I teased!"

"Forgive me, Ro. I was thoughtless, inconsiderate. I was brutal."

"Oh no, Ryder. You answered my question. Being you, you spoke the truth. Being you, you went direct to the point. I see wisdom in your methods. If a hurt has to be inflicted, let it be short and sharp. No dallying. No prolonging the torture. Get it over quick. Well, you have done it. You have done what no other man has succeeded in doing— taken me off my guard. If you use your sword as well as you do your tongue, Ryder, you must be a fearsome man in a charge. So—Royle is married!"

"Yes, Rosea."

"I knew, of course, that he had a swarm of fascinated

females fluttering round him. Moths about a candle. But I never, never thought of marriage. You have me there, Ryder. As shrewd a blow as ever was struck. I congratulate you. What sort of a creature is it who has trapped him?''

"The creature is my dearest friend, and one of the rarest, choicest women who ever breathed.''

"Ryder, I am sorry. I apologize. I was bitter. Can you blame me? I have no right to speak like that. If she is a friend of yours she must, of necessity, be beyond reproach. You think much of her—so much that you return voluntarily to share the dangers of the siege.''

"I think it must have been her great goodness which attracted him.''

"Possibly. Royle was always fascinated by novelty. He had probably never met a good woman before.'' Rosea held out her glass. "Just half full, Ryder. What the deuce! We have to measure wine by the drops these days. Still, this is an occasion. Even you will admit that. Lud, I'm inhospitable! Damnably selfish. Won't you help yourself?''

He shook his head. "If you have any doubts about the character of——''

"Oh, none whatever. I spoke wildly. Forget my foolish and unjust words. As I say, you must think much of her when you return——''

"I had to. She was so frail after the birth of her baby ——!''

Rosea caught her breath. "Go on, Ryder! Don't spare me! So she has a baby! Royle's child. I have never done you justice, Ryder. When you strike, you strike mercilessly. Not content to stab me to the heart, you turn the blade in the wound. So Royle has a child!''

"And when the serving-man came through the leaguer to tell me the child was dead——''

"Dead! Her baby dead! *His* baby dead! Ryder—I think I am going to laugh. You see . . . it isn't real! You are just making it all up. It could not possibly be real. If I do laugh, Ryder, deal firmly with me. I must not get hysterical. I never have. All that now remains is for you to say that the child was a son——''

"It was.''

"You see? I knew it. Notice how calmly I took that blow. He had always wanted a son to carry on the family name. I do not appear the least disturbed, do I?"

"Your calmness amazes me."

"That is how it should be. It does not do to parade one's emotions. Never show when you are hurt, Ryder. Lord, no! When you get hurt, you just laugh. Ryder, I shall have to act tonight, when . . . I see Royle. It will be a theatre piece. Would you care to stay to watch?"

Ryder shook his head. He felt awed. Rosea jumped impulsively to her feet. "My cloak, Ryder, please. And my hat—it is over there."

"Where are you going?"

"Where? To see his wife, of course!" She laughed. "How quaint that sounds! I have not become accustomed to it. To see Royle's wife. To see the mother of his child."

She caught him by the coat. "Ryder!" She was so tense that she might have been play-acting, only something told him she was in earnest, in deadly earnest. "Ryder, you have thought me fast, bold, shameless. No, don't shake your head. I can read your thoughts. I am not really bad. Only I have had to act, Ryder. To—act. Ryder, I do like you, like you greatly. You know why? Because you are so wholesome. Because you are strong—not merely strong of body, but strong of mind. You speak the truth—brutally, if need be, but, by heaven, it is the truth.

"I have grown up in an atmosphere of courtly lies. Men pleased me, but I would not trust them. And you are steadfast. No fair-weather friend. You come back to a starving city to be with a friend in trouble—knowing she is another man's wife. That is friendship. That is loyalty. Would you be a friend like that to me, Ryder? Only a friend? I am in as great distress as ever your other friend was."

"Yes," he said slowly, "I will stand by you." Suddenly, moved by an impulse hitherto strange to his nature, he pulled her lovely head against his shoulder. His fingers stroked the lustrous hair.

"Oh, Ro!" he said brokenly. For a second he felt her shoulders shake in a suppressed sob. She wrenched herself free and ran to the casement. "Damn!" she exclaimed savagely. "Don't pity me. I shall start sobbing if you do. Let's go, Ryder. Out of doors. Walk! And laugh!"

She caught up her gloves. At the door she turned. "Ryder——?" She paused.

"What is it?"

"I want to tell you something. No, I cannot do it! What is this woman's name?"

"Verity."

"A lovely name. Do you think I shall like her?"

"I am sure of it."

"Hum! The question is—will she like me?"

"She could not help it."

"She could—quite easily. Ryder, we must get her out of the city without delay. Can it be arranged?"

"It has been arranged. My colleague watches from the other side of the river. We have but to give the signal. The difficulty is——"

"Well?"

"Verity herself. She vows she will not leave Chester so long as her husband is here. She thinks he may be wounded and need her."

"Ah!" Rosea became thoughtful. "We must get her out of the city. We must."

They paused at the cottage door and looked at one another. Rosea pushed Ryder gently aside, opened the latch and walked in first. Verity looked up with surprise on her face. For a second she did not see Ryder, only the fashionably dressed woman standing regarding her keenly. Suddenly Rosea smiled and walked quickly across the humble floor.

"You are Verity," she said. "Ryder has told me about you. I am Rosea and we are going to be friends." She held out her hand.

"I cannot shake your hand," said Verity with calm dignity. "Mine are all over soot."

"I do not mind," said Rosea impulsively. "Ryder has told me about your losing your baby and I came to say how sorry I was. Very, very sorry. Ryder, leave us alone, will you? We have so much to talk about."

*   *   *   *

Ryder walked out into the streets. He lost track of time as he paced the roadways. His brain seemed a fiery wheel. The rushlights were glowing when he returned to the cottage.

Rosea welcomed him. She seemed to have taken possession of the place. "It is all arranged," said she with a smile. "I have made Verity see how wrong it is of her to stay in Chester while her husband is lying wounded at Eccleston——"

"Wounded at Eccleston! But I saw——"

"You saw him ride out on the raid. I remember your telling me. He is sure to be worried about Verity. She is very stubborn. She is willing to go tonight, but only on the understanding that you will follow."

Verity walked across and looked pleadingly into Ryder's face. "You came to protect me, dear friend. Now I am leaving you, and your sacrifice seems vain. You will follow? Promise me?"

Ryder looked down into the troubled face. He must get her out of the doomed city. He must get her away from that rake of a husband whom he meant to call to account. He must get her among friends where she would be nourished and nursed back to health, where she would be cared for if he should fall. So Ryder, the truth-teller, lied.

"Yes," he said. "I will follow."

Verity seemed well content.

When darkness fell he and Amos helped Verity through the gap in the ruined arch. Ryder and Rosea waited in the darkness; waited until a lantern flashed thrice. It was the prearranged signal. Ryder knew that Mark had Verity in his safe keeping. A wave of thankfulness engulfed him. He felt almost weak as if he had been carrying a burden too heavy for him; a burden from which he was now released. He was conscious of Rosea's hand upon his arm.

"You acted like a gallant gentlemen, Ryder."

"God forgive me the lie," he said, and his voice was troubled.

"Why do you require forgiveness? What lie have you told?"

"I do not intend to follow. I intend to stay here."

"Why, Ryder?"

"You are still in danger. I cannot desert my friends. I must remain and care for you."

"That is dear of you, Ryder. But there is no need." She sighed. "I am cared for."

"Not as you ought to be. I feel I shall be needed."

Rosea was silent. He glanced down at her. She seemed fatigued. Then it occurred to him that Rosea, too, had been subjected to strain.

"When did Royle marry Verity?" asked Rosea in a subdued voice.

"Shortly after the siege of Nantwich."

Quite unexpectedly Rosea laughed. It was a strange laugh. A hard laugh.

"Our dear Royle is *so* forgetful!" she said. "It was only twelve months before that he married me."

CHAPTER THIRTY-FIVE

THE fighting grew grimmer. The siege of Chester had become the greatest issue in the Kingdom. Beeston Castle had surrendered. Its small but valiant garrison was allowed to march with the honours of war to Denbigh Castle. Hawarden Castle was ready to fall. Soon Chester would be alone, bereft of her last friends. The Parliament was spending thousands of pounds in their endeavours to reduce the obstinate city. Sir William Brereton wrote that the leaguer had already cost £2000 in ammunition before the additional supplies were sent from London. The blockading force was now increased to seven thousand five hundred men. Of these seventeen hundred horse and eleven hundred foot were on the Welsh side of the Dee.

Nor was this all. To check attempts to run the blockade with supplies from Rhuddlan or Conway, Sir William fitted out several small vessels, armed them with serpentines, and placed them under the command of Captain Stephen Rich, off the mouth of the Dee. It was now impossible to get supplies of bacon and corn through from Wales while these

barks lay in Chester Water and bodies of horse patrolled the
Flintshire roads. Staffordshire and Shropshire men were
added to the guards at St. John's Church.

If Lord Byron had his trials, Sir William Brereton was by
no means exempt. He complained that there was not enough
money for troopers to shoe their horses. The regiment of
Reformadoes were begging money as they had not clothes
to cover their nakedness. The weather set in bitterly cold.
There was ice on the Dee. The Lancashire contingent became
insubordinate. Colonel John Booth's regiment, under Major
Brookes, marched home of their own accord. Men fell ill.
Officers were forced to drink water. The army grew more
impatient of their hard duty and want of pay. So Sir William
informed the Speaker of the House.

If conditions in the lines of the besiegers were bad, only
those within the walls knew the extent of suffering which
went on in Chester. Many died of starvation. Poor people
tramped the streets crying for bread. Many of the Welsh
soldiers under Colonel Wynn and Colonel Mostyn, unable to
explain their needs, became mutinous.

After his dramatic parting with Rosea, Ryder made his
way back to the cottage in Nuns Lane. He watched for the
return of the old soldier, but Amos failed to appear. For
several days Ryder kept to himself. He was waiting for his
beard to grow. He need not have been sensitive. The streets
were full of unshaven, bedraggled men. With the exception
of a few exquisites, friends of Royle Wilding, men had ceased
to give thought to appearance. What they demanded was
food. They shouted and clamoured for bread.

The Lord St. Pol at the head of a few troopers rode the
streets to preserve order. The populace cared nothing for
this display of force. They had ceased to respect the General
of Horse. "Thou French rogue!" came the shouts. "Would you
starve us?" The taunts brought a sardonic smile to the face
of Count St. Pol. The Parliamentarians still fired on the Dee
Mills. The miller lost a leg and died of his wound. Before the
ice formed thick the attackers launched a tub containing a
huge granado[1] to which four burning matches were attached.
It failed to wreck the mills, but the explosion fired Royle

[1] An early form of grenade.

Wilding's imagination. He stood on the walls and stared at the Parliamentary bridge of boats.

Fire arrows were in frequent use by both sides. Every inflammable building was a mark. There were no thatches left. The smell of burning wood hung on the air. It partly stifled the smells from the streets, for no form of sanitation was possible. The very frost which chilled the bones of the starving garrison was, perhaps, their salvation. It quenched the stench of the bodies in the half-filled grave between the cathedral and the wall.

The mortar pieces of the attackers did great execution, breaking and wrecking houses and slaying some of the citizens. Night-time was the worst. When their bombardment commenced at two o'clock in the morning women and children betook themselves to the cellars.

Some of the citizens were for surrendering, but these were overawed by the stubborn attitude of the Mayor, and by Sir Francis Gamull and Sir Richard Grosvenor. Beef was still obtainable in small quantities. It sold for fourpence a pound in the market. Bread was scarce. Not more than twenty cattle remained in the city . . . little enough for the three thousand fighting men still in Chester. About fifty horses survived. The Water Tower was tottering. December the tenth was another awful night. Both Northgate and Eastgate were attacked. The Talbot was set on fire and women and children buried in the ruins. Despite the incessant explosions of granadoes the city authorities still held the council meetings regularly. They had much business to transact.

At times a man would penetrate the leaguer and come over the wall with news. It was reported that Sir William Vaughan had recovered from his defeat at Denbigh and was preparing another relief force with the assistance of Lord Gerard. Another rumour was that ten thousand men under the Earl of Glamorgan were marching to the relief of Chester. The Earl of Northampton with fifteen hundred horse was expected to break through. But the days dragged on and no help came. Another of the Royalists' cannon was demolished by a thirty-pound shot.

That night enemy artillery fire presaged another

hideous storm. There was a breach in the North Wall.
Ryder was swept along in the rush of men who strove to
thrust the attackers back. The night was alive with noise
and fire and the clash of combatants.

"*Two hours lasted this conflict*" [runs the old account],
"*where My Lord St. Paule (almost as naked as his sword) ran
rageing in his shirt up to the North Breach, where the enemy
prest extreamely for an entrance, but were by him so bravely
back'd that sudden death denies them tyme to call for quarter.*"

So once again was the city saved. The assault cost the
defenders Sir William Mainwaring and Captain Adlington
with six or eight common soldiers. The consolation was that
the suburbs were filled with the carcasses of the attackers—
a hundred to one, so the Royalists claimed.

By this time the women of Chester were on fire with
enthusiasm, and strove with gallant emulation to outdo the
men in holding the walls against all attacks. Seven were
shot and three of them slain, yet they scorned to leave their
undertaking and continued to man the defences for ten days
—"*like so many exemplary goddesses*"

The Lord St. Pol made a sally at the head of horse and
foot, dashed across the bridge and raided the Welsh shore
until, outmanned, he was compelled to retreat. The reserve
of foot consisted of Colonel Roger Mostyn and his Welshmen,
whose blood proclaimed them gallant.

Lieutenant Morgell was slain on guard near Newgate.
Sheriff Richardson shot dead and buried the next day with
lamentation.

. The horses of the cavalry grew less and less. By this time
every horse was known by name. When a sortie was contemplated a rider was specially chosen. A steed so precious
was not to be wasted on a novice. Most of the animals came
from the stables of the nobility—the lords of Derby, of
Cholmondeley, Rivers—horses of proved mettle which, with
the spirit of thoroughbreds, stood the strain while poorer
animals drooped and died.

Among those chosen to ride was Milo. Despite his boasting he was as useful with his rapier as with his tongue. As

he came back from one of these raids, swaggering down the street, boasting that they had raided the Parliamentary horse lines and brought back a dozen animals, his eyes picked out Ryder in the throng. He greeted him boisterously and dragged him indoors. Ryder was not wholly averse. Several days of isolation in the cottage had filled him with a yearning for human company. The course events had taken saddened and bewildered him. He would, he knew well, have to visit Rosea again, but before he did so he wished to clarify his thinking. He wanted his emotions to subside so that he could look on life with a clear mind. It was a time not merely of suffering, but of surprises and shocks.

To desert the army he had served so faithfully had not been easy! It had been a strain to see Verity suffer so, and now, just when he felt that Rosea might be for him, he found that she, too, was married, and married to the man he had grown to hate. It was too much to cope with at once. He would put it from his mind for a while. Try to forget! Already he had discovered that a man could not try to forget—the more he tried the more he remembered. The best way was to occupy the mind with something else, and that was not easy when one dwelt alone. Company was the solution, or a possible solution. He almost welcomed Milo's vainglorious verbosity. Associating with Milo caused him to think of Myra.

The girl walked into his thoughts. "Ah, *cariad bach*!" she cried, as she paused in the doorway. Her face expressed delight. It was a different expression from the last encounter. She ran to him, eager as a child. "You have come back to me. You have come back! It is foolish you are, Ryder, to return when you might be in safety, but I am glad you are foolish. Is your arm recovered?"

She caught his left hand gently in hers.

"It is as well as it ever will be. I am grateful to you for saving it for me."

"Myra is right, you are a fool to return," said Milo. "I saw you come a cropper at the hedge, and when you did not return I thought you had used your wits to escape. In the name of all the devils why come to this accursed place when there is no need?"

"Because there was a woman in Chester who needed my help."

Myra glanced quickly into his face, reading a meaning he had never intended. He had not the heart to tell her that she was not the woman. There was an almost childish ingenuousness about the girl. She began to hum happily to herself and went in search of her harp. "I will play something to celebrate your return." The tune which her happy fingers plucked was more joyous than Ryder had ever heard her play. He said so.

"That is because I am glad," she explained. "I make it up as I play. You like it?"

Before he could answer she thrust her harp aside. "My hands are too cold to play. This frost! *Diawl*, it spoils my strings. Milo, why cannot you get wood for a fire?"

"I do nothing else in my hard-earned leisure," he grumbled. "That and search for food. A fine occupation for a fighting man. We carried off a few of the rebels' cows today."

"That will mean milk for Sultan." She stooped to caress the scraggy cat which dozed on the mat. "He's the devil for milk, is Sully. When he can get it."

Milo returned with some charred wood and laid the broken sticks in the fireplace. "Every man in the place seems to be searching for firewood," he grumbled. "There is not a tree left standing. Damn this cold! We have enough to put up with!" He wiped his sooty fingers on the hearthrug. "Not a drop of water!" he growled.

"The pipe from the river was cut by a mortar shell."

Ryder spent less time in the deserted cottage and more time with Milo and Myra. A strange couple, he mused, but war had brought many people unusual companions. Amos had not returned. Ryder took the cheese away when next he visited the cottage. Myra welcomed it with an expression of delight. Ryder noticed that she was thinner and paler and more ethereal-looking. He wondered how she could possibly survive the siege. Women ought to be allowed to leave!

But women continued to play their part. Rosea, he noticed, was now taking her share in the defence of the city. Hitherto she had held aloof; now she went to the other extreme and assumed her place in the firing-line as regularly

wooden frame which exercises their in-
pons can be discharged rapidly by a single
d changed. "Why do you wish to meet him,

ll him. He is not fit to live." Ryder was

horrified. "My dear, he is far more likely
ier play is perfect. Promise me you will not

s head. "He has wronged the two women I
must give an account of it."

ish you to fight him. My dear Ryder, I am
is life. It is your safety I am concerned
wife though I am for confessing it."
d to meet him. It is kind of you to care for
hall remember it. I will not give you my
I do not wish to break my word."

his side and looked down at him as he
ange world, this, is it not, Ryder? The
en get bound to each other and find their
Yet the parsons assure us that marriages
"

e loved Royle or you would not have

, Ryder, heaven knows. But deliberate
slights, brazen infidelity and frequent
tion no matter how hard a woman may
nd loyal. Do you think me bold, Ryder,
o proud to let the world see that Royle
y heart? I would never let the gossips
of knowing that, damn them. I'd rather
as a hussy."

'I salute you," he said. Then he took her
s what lies ahead," he said earnestly,
by you in your hour of need, count on
am, I have condemned your conduct.
ame. You have taught me much about
eatest of all virtues. You have courage,

ou think so, Ryder. It means that I am

as any musketeer. Many a man glanced at her graceful form
as she loaded her carbine and sighted as coolly as a veteran
soldier would have done. She paid little heed to cover, and
Ryder trembled for her safety.

She noticed him one day and turned with a smile to wave.
He responded, but did not go to her side. Yet he knew that
sooner or later he must face the ordeal of speaking to her.
Perhaps it would not be such an ordeal as he anticipated—
he knew that he wanted to speak to her, only he did not
know what to say. She was Royle Wilding's wife! There was
no escaping from that. And Verity was, too! Or she believe
she was, which made matters even harder. And he had to go
through the days holding these secrets in his breast; having
this knowledge of problems for which there appeared no
solution. Perhaps a granado might provide the answer. He
started. Was that why Rosea exposed herself so recklessly on
the ramparts?

Three days later he encountered Rosea as she came down
the steps from the Eastgate. She had her carbine with her
and walked with just the suspicion of bravado!

"Ah, Ryder! How good to see you again! I have just
hurried two pious rebels to the delectable paradise they long
to reach! I trust their souls are in proper condition." She
laughed at the disconcerted look on Ryder's face, but continued to tease him. "Is there a close season for Crop-ears?
I have had some excellent shooting this week, though I am
unable to boast of my bag. I have shot so many foul birds
that I think I am entitled to term my carbine a fouling-
piece, don't you? I must try that joke on Royle—he will
appreciate it! You look as cheerless as a Christmas repast in
Chester."

"You ought not to run such risk!" said Ryder
gravely.

"Don t tell me I might get shot! How terrible! Risk, my
dear Ryder, adds a little spice to the somewhat stale food of
life. As for risk —there seems little more danger on the ramparts than in the city now that Brereton is sending these
huge stones from his mortars, and it is vastly more entertaining there. Ryder, please accompany me home."

He hesitated and she smiled. "Still decorous, Ryder?

My husband is aware that you have seen me. I made a point of acquainting him. He is, I think, relieved that someone helps me to pass the tedious hours; it allows him his freedom with an easier conscience—not that Royle's conscience troubles him unduly. If ever a man's conscience atrophies it will be his. I often tell him so."

She strode into her room, tossed her hat on a table and leaned her carbine in a corner. "Sit down, Ryder." She dropped into a chair and sat regarding him thoughtfully. "You have been avoiding me!"

He flushed.

"Do you not wish to see me, Ryder? Do you wish our friendship to end? Is it because I am married? Why, in heaven's name, should friendship be sacrificed just because a woman is foolish enough to marry? I do not want our friendship to end. I value it. I cherish it. You may stay away from me as much as you choose, but that will not prevent me from thinking of you warmly and kindly; recalling with gratitude that you saved my life. When it became so obvious that you did not wish to speak to me again—well, I confess it —it wounded me not a little. Is it because you have learnt that I am married?"

"It is hardly that, Rosea. I have been bewildered by the strange course of events. I want to do what is right. I wished to think clearly before I saw you again."

"You have taken plenty of time. Have you succeeded?"

"No, Rosea. Truth compels me to admit that I have not. I am as bewildered as ever. I cannot bring myself to talk about your husband yet. I am fond of Verity, and his conduct rankles."

"We must never let her know, Ryder," said Rosea hastily. "I say that kindly. During the short while I was with her I grew to like her greatly. She is a sweet girl, sincere, generous. If she knew that she had been betrayed it would break her trusting heart. She is not like me, Ryder, hardened. She still holds ideals. Let us conspire to preserve them for her. We do not want to have her feelings lacerated, her pride outraged. And—there is always the hope that I might be slain. It would provide the solution with such delightful ease."

no longer utterly alone. The thought will give me fresh strength to carry on the struggle.''

As Ryder walked back to his room he felt in a chastened mood. He was gaining knowledge of many things not listed in the manual of war. He had hitherto judged people by their acts—as a tree was known by its fruits. Now it seemed that life was not quite so simple. One had to know also the motive behind conduct. It might alter things, modify them, qualify them.

The streets grew more unsightly—debris and glass and filth littered them so that a man had to walk with care. He found Myra serving a hot meal when he entered. She was unusually reserved and did not speak. Milo was seated at the table with a basin of stew before him.

"Well timed, brother Royalist!" he cried, with a nod to Ryder, and dipped his horn spoon in the stew. "I am reminded of the time in Rotterdam——"

"Will you keep quiet!" shouted Myra, and rushed from the room.

Milo winked. "A little touchy today, brother Cavalier," he quoth. "Fall to. Such delicacies are not forthcoming every day."

Ryder ate hungrily until he had emptied his bowl. Nothing remained but a few bones.

"Sultan will experience difficulty in getting fat on what we have left," said he.

"Ay," observed Milo sententiously. "It would puzzle Sultan to make a meal of this. Good Brother Royalist, it is apparent that you have not appreciated the sacrifice our gallant Sultan has made to provide you with your meal."

Then it was that Ryder realized why Myra was not at the table. "You mean," he said, gazing at the bones, "that this is——?"

"I mean that Sultan, like a good warrior, has sacrificed himself for the cause. You'll fare worse before the siege is over. I remember at Breda we were reduced to eating rats and mice. . . ."

But Ryder had lost interest in food for the time being. Milo lit his pipe and strolled nonchalantly from the room. He seemed less perturbed than Ryder over the fate of the cat.

Ryder tactfully refrained from any allusion when Myra cleared the table. She looked unhappy. To cheer her he asked her to play to him.

"You really wish it, Ryder? My harp is not all it might be—like me, eh, *cariad*? This weather plays the devil with it. I have lost four strings. I will try. What would you like?"

Ryder spoke without thought. "'Greensleeves'," he asked.

Her fingers ran over the chords. Ryder never ceased to marvel at the grace of those slender fingers. She plucked as if she coaxed harmony from the instrument. She sang softly, and her eyes were on his as she sang.

> *"If you intend thus to disdain,*
> *It does the more enrapture me . . ."*

So suddenly did it happen that Ryder was not conscious of any warning. There was a crash, a rending, a shattering! A great stone ball from a mortar swept through the roof, smashing a corner of the casement. Amid a flurry of broken glass he raised his hands to his face and bowed his head instinctively to ward off falling timbers. The music stopped abruptly. He cleared the blood from his face. His eyes were closed by mortar dust. He blinked and opened them painfully. In place of singing there came a soft moaning. Myra lay stretched on the floor. A great rafter was across her chest, and about it were entangled the broken strings of her harp.

CHAPTER THIRTY-SIX

IT was Royle's fertile imagination which suggested that it would be a seemly expression of goodwill to set fire to the bridge of boats on Christmas Eve. The ease with which the Parliamentarians passed from the Welsh bank to the Cheshire bank was very prejudicial to the Royalist designs, as they could transfer reinforcements from one side of the Dee to the other with ease.

The Lord St. Pol and Colonel Egerton with several troops rode out to ensure that no interference with the as any musketeer. Many a man glanced at her graceful form as she loaded her carbine and sighted as coolly as a veteran soldier would have done. She paid little heed to cover, and Ryder trembled for her safety.

She noticed him one day and turned with a smile to wave. He responded, but did not go to her side. Yet he knew that sooner or later he must face the ordeal of speaking to her. Perhaps it would not be such an ordeal as he anticipated— he knew that he wanted to speak to her, only he did not know what to say. She was Royle Wilding's wife! There was no escaping from that. And Verity was, too! Or she believed she was, which made matters even harder. And he had to go through the days holding these secrets in his breast; having this knowledge of problems for which there appeared no solution. Perhaps a granado might provide the answer. He started. Was that why Rosea exposed herself so recklessly on the ramparts?

Three days later he encountered Rosea as she came down the steps from the Eastgate. She had her carbine with her and walked with just the suspicion of bravado!

"Ah, Ryder! How good to see you again! I have just hurried two pious rebels to the delectable paradise they long to reach! I trust their souls are in proper condition." She laughed at the disconcerted look on Ryder's face, but continued to tease him. "Is there a close season for Crop-ears? I have had some excellent shooting this week, though I am unable to boast of my bag. I have shot so many foul birds that I think I am entitled to term my carbine a fouling-piece, don't you? I must try that joke on Royle—*he* will appreciate it! You look as cheerless as a Christmas repast in Chester."

"You ought not to run such risk!" said Ryder gravely.

"Don't tell me I might get shot! How terrible! Risk, my dear Ryder, adds a little spice to the somewhat stale food of life. As for risk—there seems little more danger on the ramparts than in the city now that Brereton is sending these huge stones from his mortars, and it is vastly more entertaining there. Ryder, please accompany me home."

He hesitated and she smiled. "Still decorous, Ryder?

My husband is aware that you have seen me. I made a point of acquainting him. He is, I think, relieved that someone helps me to pass the tedious hours; it allows him his freedom with an easier conscience—not that Royle's conscience troubles him unduly. If ever a man's conscience atrophies it will be his. I often tell him so."

She strode into her room, tossed her hat on a table and leaned her carbine in a corner. "Sit down, Ryder." She dropped into a chair and sat regarding him thoughtfully. "You have been avoiding me!"

He flushed.

"Do you not wish to see me, Ryder? Do you wish our friendship to end? Is it because I am married? Why, in heaven's name, should friendship be sacrificed just because a woman is foolish enough to marry? I do not want our friendship to end. I value it. I cherish it. You may stay away from me as much as you choose, but that will not prevent me from thinking of you warmly and kindly; recalling with gratitude that you saved my life. When it became so obvious that you did not wish to speak to me again—well, I confess it —it wounded me not a little. Is it because you have learnt that I am married?"

"It is hardly that, Rosea. I have been bewildered by the strange course of events. I want to do what is right. I wished to think clearly before I saw you again."

"You have taken plenty of time. Have you succeeded?"

"No, Rosea. Truth compels me to admit that I have not. I am as bewildered as ever. I cannot bring myself to talk about your husband yet. I am fond of Verity, and his conduct rankles."

"We must never let her know, Ryder," said Rosea hastily. "I say that kindly. During the short while I was with her I grew to like her greatly. She is a sweet girl, sincere, generous. If she knew that she had been betrayed it would break her trusting heart. She is not like me, Ryder, hardened. She still holds ideals. Let us conspire to preserve them for her. We do not want to have her feelings lacerated, her pride outraged. And—there is always the hope that I might be slain. It would provide the solution with such delightful ease."

She spoke lightly, casually. Her face was calm—unnaturally calm. Ryder gazed at her pensively. He felt that she posed.

"Rosea, is that the reason you are so reckless on the ramparts? You are not to seek death. It would be wrong. Merely another way of taking your own life."

"My dear Ryder, whatever could have put that absurd idea into your head?"

"I believe that is the motive at the back of your conduct. Rosea, please don't. I implore you."

"Pooh! My life is of no more worth than that of any soldier who serves his King. Probably it is of less value. As I look back I seem to have lived an entirely worthless and selfish existence—which I do not regret in the slightest. If I get a bullet in my silly head there will be one less mouth to feed. I should not be missed. I do not wish to do Royle an injustice, but I cannot imagine my demise causing him prolonged grief. And I am sure he would persuade some wench to console him. No, Ryder, my death is a matter of extreme unimportance."

"It would mean much to me." His voice was low and troubled.

Rosea raised her brows. "You surprise me, Ryder. You have been at pains to avoid seeing me. Don't tell me that you are going to set your principles on one side sufficiently to comfort me, to care for me."

"I care for you too much to allow you to throw away your precious life needlessly."

"Your altruism is misplaced, I assure you. My life is not precious. I am just a plaything—and a discarded plaything at that. Look in the corner-cupboard again, will you, Ryder? No, it is futile. I recollect. Royle entertained some of his cronies last night."

"Where is he now? Sooner or later I must encounter him. I think the sooner it is seen to the happier it will be for all concerned."

"Where is Royle? With Lord St. Pol, I suppose. The mad devil appeals to Royle. He has an itching mind. They vie with each other devising schemes whereby to harass and plague the rebels. At present it is a number of muskets clamped on to a wooden frame which exercises their in-genuity. The weapons can be discharged rapidly by a single soldier." Her mood changed. "Why do you wish to meet him, Ryder?"

"I mean to kill him. He is not fit to live." Ryder was direct as usual.

Rosea was not horrified. "My dear, he is far more likely to kill you. His rapier play is perfect. Promise me you will not fight him."

Ryder shook his head. "He has wronged the two women I care for most. He must give an account of it."

"But I do not wish you to fight him. My dear Ryder, I am not pleading for his life. It is your safety I am concerned about—undutiful wife though I am for confessing it." .

"I am not afraid to meet him. It is kind of you to care for my safety, and I shall remember it. I will not give you my assurance, though. I do not wish to break my word.".

She crossed to his side and looked down at him as he sat at ease. "A strange world, this, is it not, Ryder? The wrong people so often get bound to each other and find their mistakes too late. Yet the parsons assure us that marriages are made in heaven."

"You must have loved Royle or you would not have married him."

"I did love him, Ryder, heaven knows. But deliberate neglect, persistent slights, brazen infidelity and frequent rebuffs can kill affection no matter how hard a woman may strive to be dutiful and loyal. Do you think me bold, Ryder, just because I am too proud to let the world see that Royle has nearly broken my heart? I would never let the gossips have the satisfaction of knowing that, damn them. I'd rather they condemned me as a hussy."

Ryder stood up. "I salute you," he said. Then he took her hand. "No one knows what lies ahead," he said earnestly, "but if I can stand by you in your hour of need, count on me. Pharisee that I am, I have condemned your conduct. I hang my head in shame. You have taught me much about life. Courage is the greatest of all virtues. You have courage, Ro."

"I am glad that you think so, Ryder. It means that I am

no longer utterly alone. The thought will give me fresh strength to carry on the struggle."

As Ryder walked back to his room he felt in a chastened mood. He was gaining knowledge of many things not listed in the manual of war. He had hitherto judged people by their acts—as a tree was known by its fruits. Now it seemed that life was not quite so simple. One had to know also the motive behind conduct. It might alter things, modify them, qualify them.

The streets grew more unsightly—debris and glass and filth littered them so that a man had to walk with care. He found Myra serving a hot meal when he entered. She was unusually reserved and did not speak. Milo was seated at the table with a basin of stew before him.

"Well timed, brother Royalist!" he cried, with a nod to Ryder, and dipped his horn spoon in the stew. "I am reminded of the time in Rotterdam——"

"Will you keep quiet!" shouted Myra, and rushed from the room.

Milo winked. "A little touchy today, brother Cavalier," he quoth. "Fall to. Such delicacies are not forthcoming every day."

Ryder ate hungrily until he had emptied his bowl. Nothing remained but a few bones.

"Sultan will experience difficulty in getting fat on what we have left," said he.

"Ay," observed Milo sententiously. "It would puzzle Sultan to make a meal of this. Good Brother Royalist, it is apparent that you have not appreciated the sacrifice our gallant Sultan has made to provide you with your meal."

Then it was that Ryder realized why Myra was not at the table. "You mean," he said, gazing at the bones, "that this is——?"

"I mean that Sultan, like a good warrior, has sacrificed himself for the cause. You'll fare worse before the siege is over. I remember at Breda we were reduced to eating rats and mice. . . ."

But Ryder had lost interest in food for the time being. Milo lit his pipe and strolled nonchalantly from the room. He seemed less perturbed than Ryder over the fate of the cat.

Ryder tactfully refrained from any allusion when Myra cleared the table. She looked unhappy. To cheer her he asked her to play to him.

"You really wish it, Ryder? My harp is not all it might be—like me, eh, *cariad*? This weather plays the devil with it. I have lost four strings. I will try. What would you like?"

Ryder spoke without thought. " 'Greensleeves'," he asked.

Her fingers ran over the chords. Ryder never ceased to marvel at the grace of those slender fingers. She plucked as if she coaxed harmony from the instrument. She sang softly, and her eyes were on his as she sang.

> *"If you intend thus to disdain,*
> *It does the more enrapture me . . ."*

So suddenly did it happen that Ryder was not conscious of any warning. There was a crash, a rending, a shattering! A great stone ball from a mortar swept through the roof, smashing a corner of the casement. Amid a flurry of broken glass he raised his hands to his face and bowed his head instinctively to ward off falling timbers. The music stopped abruptly. He cleared the blood from his face. His eyes were closed by mortar dust. He blinked and opened them painfully. In place of singing there came a soft moaning. Myra lay stretched on the floor. A great rafter was across her chest, and about it were entangled the broken strings of her harp.

CHAPTER THIRTY-SIX

It was Royle's fertile imagination which suggested that it would be a seemly expression of goodwill to set fire to the bridge of boats on Christmas Eve. The ease with which the Parliamentarians passed from the Welsh bank to the Cheshire bank was very prejudicial to the Royalist designs, as they could transfer reinforcements from one side of the Dee to the other with ease.

The Lord St. Pol and Colonel Egerton with several troops rode out to ensure that no interference with the

cherished plan should deprive the Parliamentary forces of
the Christmas present which Royle was preparing. Two
boats were laden with combustibles. They waited the
coming of the spring tide, and as the flood advanced upriver
slow fuses were ignited and the floating mines launched on the
dark waters.

Rosea entered into the spirit of the venture and was at
her husband's side as the two boats were swept away by the
swirling current.

"I hope," observed Royle coolly, as he watched the faint
glow of the burning matches trace the boats' course upriver, "that we shall prohibit the rebels' excursions." Rosea
glanced up at his handsome face. He seemed unaware of her
presence. For once he was serious, intent on the success of
his experiment. "There are several containers charged with
small shot on board," he explained. "They should annoy the
rebels if they approach. Damnation!"

"What is it, Royle?"

"The tide is slower than I anticipated. It is too far spent.
The boats tire by the way. They will not reach the accursed
bridge. Ro, you had best seek shelter. The explosion will
come any moment now."

"Thank you, Royle. I will remain here. A fragment of
metal in my head might relieve you of embarrassment."

He did not appear to have heard her. "There they go!" A
dazzling flash of orange flame burst from one of the boats.
There were a series of disconnected explosions. The second
boat blew up. The air was full of the sound of firing. Somewhere on the bank the Lord St. Pol was attacking the
besiegers' trenches at the bridge head.

"They say the Devil looks after his own!" observed
Royle, shrugging his shoulders. "A disappointing result, my
dear. I had hoped to have blown dozens of those sour-visaged
rogues to perdition. It was worth the attempt. I must have
just missed the tide. True to life, Ro, is it not?"

He sauntered nonchalantly back to the city defences.
His face was expressionless. Only Rosea, who knew him,
realized the disappointment he felt at the failure of his
carefully conceived scheme.

So Christmas Day dawned. It was a day of travesty. No

celebration marked the birth of the Prince of Peace. A woman was shot in Eastgate and died where she fell. The Lord St. Pol had lost two men killed in his sortie, and about six were shot, whereof two died the following day.

In the Parliamentary headquarters a Council of War was held. It was resolved that the Cheshire and Derbyshire foot should advance into Wales to strengthen the leaguer on that side of the Dee. A hundred of the Nantwich firelocks were to go with them.

There was even less observance of Christmas within the city. One entry of that sad day comes down to posterity in faded ink.

> *"Because it is a festivall, instead of stones*
> *they send us in a token four granadoes, one of*
> *which burst among themselves."*

Ryder paid little heed to what went on in the city. All night long he sat beside the bed of a moaning girl. Myra, with several ribs crushed and a fractured wrist, lay with blood on her lips. She had recovered consciousness only once. When she spoke it was not for herself that she mourned but for her harp.

Her harp was shattered. Her fingers were shattered. Her hope was shattered. Milo fetched a surgeon, but he could do little beyond strapping the fractures and giving the agonized girl an opiate.

When morning came Ryder went forth into the streets, leaving Milo to watch beside the bed. He felt limp and jaded, less from lack of sleep than from compassion. The crisp air refreshed him. He was walking abstractedly when Rosea accosted him.

"You look as if you had been on duty all night. Come inside and rest. Have you helped at a barricade?"

"No. I watched beside the bed of a badly injured girl."

Rosea mocked him. "My dear Ryder, for one of your puritanical leanings you do manage to acquire numerous friends of the forbidden sex."

"Stop, Rosea! It is no matter for jest. One of those accursed stones carried away a portion of the roof and the beams fell across the girl, crushing her ribs. That is not the worst. She has lost her harp, which means more to her than life. Truly, if a human can be inspired from a divine source I think she must have been, for I have never heard music to equal hers. The beam which crushed her smashed her harp. It is beyond redemption. She seems to have lost the desire to live.''

Mockery faded from Rosea's brown eyes. ''Poor child!'' she exclaimed impulsively. ''Take me to her, Ryder. Wait, there is still a bottle of wine left. Royle hoarded it for Christmas. He wished to drink a toast to peace and goodwill. It appealed to his distorted sense of humour. Let us put it to more charitable use.''

As they walked along the littered streets Ryder explained his meeting with Milo. The tattered captain was dozing beside the patient when the sound of their approach aroused him. One look at Rosea's beauty was sufficient to jerk him to his feet and set him bowing obsequiously. He dusted a chair and placed it for the guest. Rosea thanked him with a smile which must have set his heart racing, but her eyes were quickly on the patient. The ragged coverlet was stained with blood. Myra's eyes were closed. Her sunken face was ashen white. It was a pathetic, frail figure which gasped painfully for breath. Heaped against the end of the bed was the harp, an equally forlorn object. Its bent wires trailed and writhed as though in agony.

''Remove that,'' said Rosea. ''The sight will cause her pain.''

''Mistress, we would have done so but she would not part with it.'' Milo replied before Ryder could utter a word. The man had pulled himself together and was bent on making a good impression. His voice disturbed Myra, who opened her eyes. She gazed about her with the heavy, somnolent look of one who rouses from a drugged sleep. Her face brightened when she saw Ryder.

''Ah, *cariad*,'' she whispered, and stretched out her whole hand. Ryder knelt beside the bed and took the frail fingers in his. ''It is good of you to come to me before I go on the journey.''

''You are not leaving us, you are going to get better,'' Rosea assured her, with simulated brightness.

"I do not know you." Myra closed her eyes. "I do not wish to live. My harp is no more."

"I will get you a new harp," Rosea assured her. "Better than that."

It was an unfortunate expression. Myra's eyes opened with a flash of the old fire. "There is no better harp than mine. No! Not in the whole of Wales! It is the best; and I, Telenores Elwy, am the best harpist."

The animation weakened her and started her coughing. Rosea poured a little of the wine into a glass and held it to her mouth.

"Do not waste good wine on me," said Myra. "Give it to Milo; he likes wine, does Milo. Keep good wine for those who live."

"You are going to live."

"*Diawl!* And why should I? See my hand!" She endeavoured to move the injured wrist. "My hand is gone, gone. I can play no more. Without music what is there to live for?"

"There are many other wonderful things for which to live," Ryder assured her.

"Ah, *cariad*, there was a time when I would have wished to live for you. My man, so strong and so brave. I would have lived to wed with you, but now it cannot be. And you do not desire it."

"Oh yes, he does," said Rosea calmly.

Ryder opened his lips to protest, but a glance from Rosea silenced him. "He will wed you, my dear. Take my word for it." She laid her hand gently on the girl's forehead.

There was wonderment in Myra's eyes. They seemed unnaturally bright. Ryder stared dumbly. He felt stunned. He could not dispute with Rosea at such a time, and Rosea seemed to be arranging matters with an imperious manner which became her like a new robe.

"Who are you?" demanded Myra, turning to Rosea. "My man came back to Chester to help a lady who had need of him. You are beautiful. Yes, it is lovely that you are. Are you the fine lady he loves?"

"Great heavens, no! I have a husband, girl."

Myra closed her eyes. She seemed content. She dozed a

while as they watched in silence. Ryder touched the frail hand which lay on the crumpled coverlet.

Myra smiled faintly. "My man!" she whispered. "A dream has come true. I shall sleep content if you are at my side."

Her eyes closed. She seemed to slumber peacefully. Ryder glanced at Rosea. "She will recover?" he whispered, but Rosea shook her head sadly.

"There is no hope," she said softly. "You will not repent having made her happy."

Myra never roused from that sleep. Two days later they buried her in a quiet corner of the Cathedral grounds as far away from the communal grave as they could get. Few noticed the ceremony. Those who noticed paid little heed. There were deaths every day. Familiarity bred contempt, or at any rate indifference. There were deaths from wounds, from disease, from hunger. The siege went on.

December dragged to a forlorn conclusion. There were few horses left. Marksmen in the suburbs were using house-roofs now and it was unsafe to pass down any main street by light of day, so watchful were they. Women of the town dwelt in the cellars. More granadoes were flung into the town. Sentries were doubled and made to stand behind one another lest an enemy should get through the cordon. There was a fresh disappointment for the besieged. Friends in Denbigh-sire had attempted to drive a hundred cattle towards Chester. They reached Holywell, but Colonel Carter with some of Brereton's horse intercepted them, and scattered the relief force throughout the mountains. A few venture-some horsemen under Lord St. Pol made a brief sally and cut down a few Parliamentarians. They came back with a few prisoners. It was a gesture of defiance. Lord Byron was beginning to despair. Where was the relief force they had been promised?

In an attempt to cheer the spirits of the attacked Royle Wilding devised a movable fort. He had a great waggon covered with sheets of iron and in it placed several musket-eers with apertures to fire through. Rosea watched with curiosity as several emaciated horses dragged this towards the Parliamentary lines, where a brisk fire was opened into the nearest trench. It caused momentary consternation, but it was not long before the firelocks recovered from their surprise, shot down the horses, and captured the musketeers behind the iron plates. Royle led a furious charge and rescued his men, while others laboriously hauled and pushed his fort back to safety. Royle walked towards Rosea laughing grimly.

"A pleasant deviation, Ro! The idea is sound. I must tell St. Pol. But the horses must push the fort next time, not pull it."

Lord Byron interfered. Horses were too valuable to be flung away with such abandon. There was a sortie that night and the dead beasts dragged back with ropes. Horseflesh was a delicacy which was not to be lost.

The cannon mounted on Anchorite's Hill near St. John's Church was becoming troublesome. Royle led a sortie, captured the mount, spiked the guns and returned with the loss of two men. The episode occasioned him concern. He had torn the sleeve of his doublet.

Throughout the siege he had never failed to maintain his immaculate appearance. Though he went hungry he must have his linen washed, his lace pressed, and his leather as glossy as much polishing could make it. Ryder made a point of avoiding a meeting. This was not difficult, as Royle was rarely at home. Ryder, now that Myra was dead, called more frequently at the house beside the Pied Bull.

He was waiting for Rosea in the front room when he heard steps on the stairs.

"Ro, where are you, lass? I've ripped my doublet. Go, seek your needle, my angel. St. Pol rides for Wales and wishes me to accompany him. There's a muster at Conway, where Mostyn is getting together enough men from Ireland to break this damned leaguer——" He paused abruptly. "And who the devil might you be in my rooms?" His stare was haughty until a light of recognition dawned in his eyes. "Lord, it's our acquaintance the Bull-Baiter! I had forgotten your existence. With a beard, too. And damn my eyes if he isn't wearing my cast-off suit!"

Ryder flushed at the satirical tone but held his peace.

"I presume it was given you by my wife?" drawled Royle.

"Which wife?" The words were out of Ryder's mouth before he realized what he said.

He saw Wilding go white. His eyes dilated. The Cavalier picked up a pair of gloves from the table.

"Those two words," he said, "will prove the most costly you have ever spoken." He flicked Ryder in the face.

"I am grateful to you for relieving me of an intolerable situation," said Ryder. "I have, for weeks, desired to punish you, but out of consideration for Rosea I have held my hand."

"Your consideration has undoubtedly prolonged your life."

Before Ryder could reply a door opened. Both men paused.

"There is no reason for her to know," whispered Ryder quickly.

"I agree, Master Bull-Baiter. These women are spoil-sports. The Nunnery Gardens at four."

Rosea entered with a smile. "Lud, Royle, I imagined I caught your dulcet tones. You are before time today. Do you rise early or return late? You remember Captain Yale?"

"Quite well. We have already exchanged compliments. In last night's sally a damned rebel had the bad taste to thrust his pike so that it ripped my sleeve. If you would be so kind——"

Ryder made his excuses and walked from the room. He was conscious of a feeling of relief. The issue was no longer his. The man who had brought such misery into the life of Verity could now receive his punishment.

The day seemed interminably long. He went in search of Milo, to whom he explained the situation. He asked Milo if he would act for him. It was a task after Milo's own heart. The captain insisted upon Ryder borrowing his cherished rapier. He also found a case of pistols, which he cleaned and loaded with fastidious care.

The afternoon was chill and Ryder was glad to walk briskly to the place of meeting. Royle was already there, and with him the French lord whose rapier seemed to Ryder to be longer than ever. The two seconds drew aside to confer. Ryder walked impulsively to Wilding.

"A word in private before we begin——"

"This is deuced irregular," protested Royle. "Anything you wish to say must come through the seconds."

"Very well—if you wish them to know details of your matrimonial adventures."

Royle hesitated and then walked to confer with the seconds. The Frenchman expostulated and shrugged his shoulders. Royle sauntered back.

"They consent. Only be brief."

"I cannot kill you," said Ryder.

"You are late in discovering that!" Royle's smile was sardonic. "We will try pistols then. At least they will give you a sporting chance."

"You misunderstand me. The reason why I cannot take your life is out of respect for Rosea. Take mine if you will. Long ago I ceased to take much interest in an existence where rogues flourish and an honest man is deprived of what he desires. Before you die—or I die—let me say this. To wed a pure and saintly girl like Verity, knowing you were already married, was the act of an unprincipled rogue."

"I had intended to spare you, Yale, but I am afraid that you will have to die for that insult."

"Your insult almost cost Verity her life. When her child died——"

"Her child?" The cynicism left Royle's face. "I did not know there was a child!" He seemed bewildered.

"Yes. Her child . . . your son! He died of starvation while you were lording it with the Governor of Chester."

"Son!" Wilding stepped back apace. His face was white. "What you say is the truth?" he demanded.

"I always speak the truth."

"Where—is—Verity? I lost all track of her. I did not know she was in the city. On my honour, I did not know."

"She has left. She is in a place of safety. More I will not tell you. She has suffered enough at your hands."

Wilding stood like a man dazed. Count St. Pol strode angrily towards them. "Enough! Is this a meeting or a parley? Take your places. An affair of honour is not arranged thus."

They selected their pistols and took their positions. It was agreed that Lord St. Pol should drop a handkerchief. Milo had no handkerchief to drop. It was to be the signal for both to fire. Soldiers on the walls paused and watched with fascinated eyes. All stood motionless.

The handkerchief fluttered to the grass. Both men raised their weapons. Ryder was a shade the quicker and fired first. He had resolved that he would not kill Wilding. Royle's weapon fell to the grass. He clutched his right arm, from which blood dripped. Ryder could see him biting his lips. Painfully Royle bent and picked up his undischarged pistol in his left hand. Ryder clicked his heels together and stood erect, facing the slowly moving barrel. He might have been on parade. The muzzle pointed to his waist. His eyes followed its upward course. It covered his heart, his throat, his forehead.

Royle Wilding deliberately pointed the pistol high in the air and fired, flung the discharged weapon on the ground, and walked away, his fingers clutching his bleeding arm. Ryder noticed that his steps were unsteady.

There was a renewal of the bombardment that night. Gun by gun the Parliamentary batteries rained great shot against the walls. The storm lasted two hours.

The following morning the Lord St. Pol at the head of a troop of horse crossed the old bridge, broke through the lines of the besiegers and swept impetuously towards the security of Flint Castle. Royle Wilding did not ride with them.

A beacon fired on top of Hawarden Castle gave notice to the people of Chester of Lord St. Pol's safe arrival. And after that—silence.

CHAPTER THIRTY-SEVEN

AFTER Lord St. Pol, General of the Horse in Chester, had moved out to hasten the relief the leaguer was drawn more close. Special care was expended on the sands between Flint and Hawarden, for it was by that route succour for Chester was expected. A prisoner who escaped from Chester

brought word to Brereton that the soldiers in the city
threatened to mutiny and break out through the leaguer and
escape. No forage for the horses was left. Sir Francis Gamull
was reported to have wounded with his own hands several
men who spoke of yielding. The taunts which the besiegers
flung at the men on Chester's walls aroused their fighting
spirit and made them conduct the defence more obstinately
than ever. There was yet hope of relief.

Lord Byron's brother, Colonel Gilbert Byron, Governor
of Rhuddlan Castle, commanded some six hundred men
raised in Caernarvonshire. Colonel Mostyn was at Beaumaris, just back from Ireland with a piece of a regiment. He
had been able to secure only a hundred and sixty men. He
hoped to raise two hundred more in Flintshire. Lord St.
Pol put himself at the head of this mixed force and marched
by way of Denbigh and Ruthin to unite with the forces Sir
William Vaughan had assembled at High Ercol. But he was
destined not to reach the rendezvous. Colonel Mytton issued
from Ruthin as he had done before, and scattered the forces
so that they fled to Conway. Byron's last hope of relief had
gone.

Chester was doomed. Grimly the authorities toured the
houses, taking stock of the scanty remnant of food. Out of
a hundred and sixty families in Eastgate Ward, one hundred
had no corn. St. Bridget's Ward was as badly off. The cold
grew more intense. Ice on the river formed so thickly that
the Parliamentarians were forced to remove their bridge of
boats for safety. Nature had achieved what fire-boats had
failed to do. Word came through that three vessels lay at
Rhuddlan with cargoes of wheat and bacon, but Captain
Rich in the *Rebecca*, with several other armed ships, hovered
off the mouth of the Dee and there was no opportunity for
them to break the blockade.

The Mayor's house was ablaze—no one knew for certain
whether by accident or design. What they did know was that
a great part of the house was burnt and a considerable
store of provisions discovered.

On January the seventh Brereton sent a trumpeter to the
Eastgate with a flag of truce and a summons to surrender.
Lord Byron rejected the summons and the trumpeter was

fired at from the walls. It was a brave display of defiance.
Inside the city many citizens were troubled that Lord Byron
had rejected it. Soldiers mutinied that morning for lack of
provisions. A number of Welsh soldiers were found dead of
hunger. One of the Welsh captains was killed by a shot fired
from St. John's Church steeple. Copies of Sir William
Brereton's summons to surrender were flung into Chester.
Lord Byron's reply was sent back—in his lordship's own
handwriting.

*"Keep your foolish, senseless paper to yourselves and know
there are none in this city such knaves or fools to be deluded
thereby."*

By January the twelfth Lord Byron was in a less arrogant
mood. To Sir William's next summons he wrote:

*"If, within twelve days, we be not assured of our relief,
we shall then be content to enter upon a treaty for the delivery
of the city, castle and fort, upon honourable and soldierly
conditions."*

Meanwhile, by day and night, the fighting went on.
Great stones were flung into the city by mortars; granadoes
exploded; the cannoneers trained their guns on the breaches
until the wall crumbled; sharpshooters on the roofs of the
suburbs maintained a ceaseless fusillade.

Chester still resisted. Lord Byron promised the King he
would hold out for eight days—he had held out four months.
Men and women manned the walls. There was not a person
who was not gaunt with hunger.

Rosea was paler than Ryder had ever seen her when he
called at her house. Her carbine lay across the table, still
warm from recent use. She sat down wearily.

"How much longer can this go on, Ryder?"

"Until Byron gives in."

"He is a wilful man. Can this assist the King, Ryder? I
fear he is past our aid."

"I see no useful purpose in refusing to surrender. Nothing
demands it but Byron's pride. There is no prospect of relief

now Mytton has scattered St. Pol's force. I see no reason why the fighting should go on.''

"The only reason is because men like to fight. They make much of their silly pride. Royle has been wounded in the arm —did you know? It heals slowly, yet he will not absent himself if there is an assault. He must be in the forefront with his rapier in his left hand. He loves slaying for slaying's sake. He seems insatiable.''

She sat staring wearily out of the window. "Ryder, I hate like the devil to admit it, but I believe you are right. Chester is doomed. What folly to throw lives away needlessly! Pay heed, Ryder—you have heard of Captain Tom Bartlett?''

Ryder nodded. "Who hasn't heard of Tom Bartlett of the *Swan*? He bears a charmed life.''

"Ever since war broke out the rebel watch-ships have tried to catch him, but he has sailed from Dublin whenever he chose. Captain Bartlett is through their blockade. He is in Chester Water now. I have been in communication with him. He will, for a price, carry across to Ireland any who wish to escape. I would go if I could pay my passage. I can assure you, Ryder, I have no desire to grace Brereton's chariot wheels.''

"I would help you to escape, Rosea, but I have no money.''

"Life will be intolerable in this country henceforth. Our estates are sequestrated. We shall be downtrodden by beggars on horseback. Sorry, Ryder, but I simply refuse to connect you with these smug Crop-ears. Do you know what some of us are scheming to do? Depart forever from this land we love—cross the Atlantic and start life anew in Virginia. Ryder, dear, will you take me there?''

She came close to him. Never before had her eyes seemed so eloquent, so appealing, so beautiful. "Ryder darling, I would be faithful to you. I would endure any hardship with you at my side. You have seen me fight: I am no coward. I have never cared for any man like I care for you.''

"But your husband?''

"Oh, damn Royle! I am weary of him. I have given him every chance but he does not respond. He would be glad to have me go. Let him seek his other wife . . . his other *wives* for all I know! And, Ryder, you must escape, dear. Your life is at stake. It's a firing party for you if Brereton catches you once the city falls."

"I know full well, Rosea. It is the price I must pay. I shall not flinch. I shall face their muskets as calmly as——"

"As you faced Royle's pistol! You did not know that I knew. I find out many things. I was told you fired only at his arm because you would spare his life for my sake. It is true . . . Royle told me himself. He reveals sporting qualities at times. Ryder, you struck him a shrewd blow when you spoke of the death of his son. His son! He always wanted a son! He held it against me that I had not provided him with one. Do you know what makes him court death so persistently? It is chagrin. To think that he had a son and lost him! It is more than courage which urges him on in the forefront of every fight. It is remorse. It is gall and bitterness."

Rosea paused. "He vows that if he survives the siege and can no longer serve his King, he will take his own life."

Ryder stared thoughtfully at the lovely woman who pleaded with him. All that his heart desired was there for the taking, and yet he hesitated. Before he was aware of what was contemplated two warm arms were about his neck. "Ryder, dear one, have done with your stupid ideals. Let us escape while we can. Let us start life afresh in a world of our own choosing. Let us be happy while we can—we have earned it."

He flushed. "You tempt me!"

"I *shall* tempt you, Ryder. Tempt you and tempt you! I intend to be shameless. I know my way is the right way. I *can* make you happy, dear heart. I *will* make you happy."

He tightened his arms about her and kissed her tenderly. "You know that I want you," he said brokenly. "Want you more than I have ever wanted anything in my life."

"I know. And you have me, Ryder. I am so yours!"

He shook his head sadly. "Dreams! You have aroused in me a wild desire to cross the Atlantic: to have done with all this folly and suffering. But even if we would, we cannot go. We have not the means to pay our passage."

She drew back, serious, discouraged. "You are right. I have but a few coins left—and nothing on which money could be raised. All our plate went to the King years ago, and my jewels."

Ryder gripped her shoulders in a way which startled her. "What is it? Why do you stare so wildly? Ryder, you are hurting me."

"Jewels! Fool that I am!"

"I have no jewels, Ryder."

"But I have! Or I know where there are some. Enough to pay a score of passages. Is there a carved powder-horn here?"

"Yes! Yes! On the wall of Royle's room. He would not part with it. It is one of his treasures."

"Fetch it instantly." Ryder issued orders. Rosea ran from the room and returned with the trophy held in hands which trembled with eagerness. Ryder whipped out his knife and explored the depths with the point.

"It is there!" His voice was awed. "It has not been found." The leather bag came forth. Ryder spilled a tiny cascade of gems on the dark oak table.

"Oh, how lovely!" It was typical of Rosea that she saw their beauty before she saw their worth. Ryder, with an abandonment foreign to his nature, caught her in his arms and swung her off her feet.

"Darling, how strong you are! But let me down. Those jewels! They make all things possible. Tell me, did Royle know of their existence?"

"Of course not."

"Ah! The subtle humour of it! He, who was always bewailing his penury, had a fortune at hand!"

"He did not know the value of a jewel!"

Rosea coloured. "Ryder, that's the prettiest thing you have ever said. You must warn me! I am not accustomed to compliments from you. And now, sweet heart, there is nothing to prevent our escaping—this very night. We issue from the sally-gate, get by stealth down the river and row out to the *Swan*. Then Ireland, freedom, and Westward ho!"

Ryder's eyes glistened. "You have counted the cost?"

"I have burnt my boats. I will face any hardship in Virginia with you."

"Dear one—as bravely as you faced dangers on the ramparts of Chester's walls. What you say is true. Once

Brereton enters the city I am doomed. I defied him, for he forbade me leave the army."

"Then go we must."

"And go we shall. You are prepared to abandon Royle for ever?"

"For all time, dear heart."

Ryder gazed long and earnestly into the lovely face upturned to his. He kissed her fondly again and again. As they stood thus, heart to heart, a step sounded on the stairs. They drew apart, turned, stood listening, curious, puzzled. It was not Royle's boisterous stride. It was a feeble, shuffling gait. The step of one who was aged, infirm.

As they watched, the fingers of a hand came round the door. A hand which hovered white against the dark oak. A hand which groped.

Ryder was conscious of a sickening sensation. It was like the hand of death. There was something eerie about this groping hand. Then came a velvet-clad arm. A man moved into the doorway: a man who wore Royle Wilding's clothing but had not Royle Wilding's face. In place of features was a raw red mark with sightless eyes.

"Royle!" Rosea's cry was almost a scream. She ran towards him. "Royle, what has happened? You are not blind!"

"Ah, Ro!" His arm groped for her and he pulled her towards him as though desiring warmth from her form. "I apologize for this unseemly appearance. I fear I must look a disgusting object. Those Crop-ears have scored again. They've put my lights out, my dear. One of their damned granadoes! I counted on getting wounded or killed, but never on this. Can you guide me to a chair? I am sorry to put you to the trouble. Never was a night so black."

As Rosea helped him, Ryder stepped forward and caught the injured man's arm in a strong, sympathetic grasp.

Royle collapsed in a chair. "Who is this?" he inquired, turning his sightless eyes. Rosea, with a calmness which astounded Ryder, was wiping the blood and the powder-stains from Royle's face with her handkerchief.

"It is I, Ryder Yale."

"Ah! My bold baiter of bulls. Well, I little thought at the start that you would be on the winning side, but demme, in this game it looks as if a knave was higher than a king."

"Are you in much pain, dear?" inquired Rosea tenderly. Ryder hurried away in search of water. Together they bathed and bandaged the shattered face.

"Let me apologize again for giving you this trouble. A demmed unpleasant task I've set you, I'm sure. I shall try not to be a burden to you, Ro."

"You will not be a burden, Royle," Rosea assured him.

"I'm glad you are here, Yale. Rosea, I've been thinking lately. You thought me incapable of it, did you not? But I have made an effort. Now St. Pol has gone I've had more leisure. I've been a damnably rotten husband to you, Ro. You have borne with me most sportingly. I am glad Yale here is able to take care of you. He is an infinitely better man than the one you have been bound to. Lord, I feel positively benign making my confession and giving my blessing. You two must love one another. Yale, you'll find a pistol in that drawer. If you'll just place it near my hand and take Rosea from the room I'll attend to matters which will remove a lawful impediment—isn't that how they word it?—from the path of your happiness."

The voice of the blind man trailed away.

Ryder was conscious of Rosea's eyes; eyes which mutely entreated him to understand her dilemma. He nodded his acquiescence.

"There *is* no other way?" Rosea's whisper was pleading.

"There is no other way," agreed Ryder gravely. "God bless you."

"Royle dear," she said, bending over her husband, "you shall do no such thing. You are wanted. You shall not walk alone in the darkness. I shall be at your side, always; I shall stay by you always."

"My dear Ro, you are far too beautiful to be fettered to this useless hulk."

"It is my wish. It is *our* wish, isn't it, Ryder?"

"It is our wish," repeated Ryder calmly.

Royle sighed. "Heigh-ho. This is what the parsons call

coals of fire with a vengeance. But I shall not dwell in
this land once the city has fallen. It will not be worth living
in."

"There is no need, Wilding," said Ryder quietly. "There
is a ship—Bartlett's *Swan*—waiting to carry you to Ireland.
The passage is arranged. Rosea will take you there."

Royle sank back exhausted. He put a hand to his brow as
if the effort to think was too much for him.

Suddenly on the February air there sounded the clear
call of a trumpet. The bells of St. Werburg began to toll.

Rosea said calmly, "Byron has surrendered!"

CHAPTER THIRTY-EIGHT

THE day of departure was at hand. The formalities of
surrender were completed. It had been a slow task, made
arduous because Lord Byron quibbled. His commissioners
visited Sir William Brereton repeatedly. His lordship was
punctilious and drew up a list of thirty-six stipulations.

"I should not have expected proposition of so high demands as those you have sent," wrote Sir William. "I will
not trouble myself with answering the particulars of your
unparalleled demands."

Again Lord Byron protested, and again, quoting the
concessions granted by Commanders 'far greater than
yourself' for places beleaguered either by the Spaniards or
the Hollanders. Sir William grew exasperated.

"You may, therefore," he replied, "in pity to all those
innocents under your command, tender their preservation
and the preservation of the city; for which end I have sent
you fair and honourable conditions; which being rejected,
you may expect worse."

The Mayor next attempted, with no better success. Word
came through that Lord Astley and Sir William Vaughan
had retired to Worcester. There was no hope. Byron
surrendered.

The victors were agreed that they had not met a more
gallant enemy in any part whatsoever. The siege of Chester

had made its garrison renowned throughout the Kingdom
for their fidelity, valour and patience.

Included in the eighteen articles of surrender over
which the commissioners conferred several days was the
concession that Lord Byron with his horse and arms should
have ten men to attend him, and that his lady should
travel with her servants in two coaches each drawn by four
horses. Eighty of the said lord's books with his writings
were to be carried away, but not above forty pounds in
money and twenty pounds in plate. All classes were dealt
with—the noblemen with their servants, knights and
colonels, the captain, graduate, preaching minister, gentlemen of quality, down to the inferior officers, each of whom
was to retain his sword and not above twenty shillings in
money. All troopers, soldiers, gunpowder-makers and
cannoneers were to march without arms. None was to be
plundered, searched or molested.

Two hundred Parliamentary horse were set aside to
accompany the vanquished host and to see that these
stipulations were not abused. So they prepared to set forth on
their long, sad march to Conway.

Byron's army was assembling in Chester's streets now,
watched by the starving citizens. The ragged soldiers endeavoured to make what appearance they could. They still
had their pride. The cavalrymen took their place in the van—
a small enough body, for most of the chargers were eaten—
and endeavoured to assume a brave appearance. Milo was
among them, his rapier freshly burnished. The horses stood
patiently with drooping heads, held together, so it seemed,
by their harness. They were to march to Conway. Man looked
at man and wondered how many would have strength to
carry them that far.

Rosea made her way through the crowded street, guiding
the blind Royle Wilding to one of the waiting coaches. As
soon as Ryder saw them he thrust his way forward to assist.
Royle subsided in a corner of the seat. "You are a good
fellow, Yale," he said quietly. "How the devil you got mixed
up with those canting rogues passeth my comprehension."

Wilding drew a hand from his pocket and opened it.

Ryder saw that ivory dice lay on his palm. The Cavalier rattled them fondly. "What have I thrown?" he inquired, spreading his fingers.

"A six and a five," answered Ryder primly.

"Damned good throw for a blind man! Yale, I shall have to devise a way of getting the spots raised so that I can tell them by touch."

"You could pass your time to greater profit."

"Impossible. These shall be my companions. They afford me comfort by their touch. And these!" Again he fumbled and drew out a pack of cards. "Lud, I shall miss cards like the devil. I wonder if I could mark them in some way so that I might still play. But no! Some astute devil would be sure to memorize my system. Already I can tell the queen of hearts. She is slightly bent. What card is this, Yale?"

"The four of clubs!"

Wilding sighed.

"Ah, the jade, she has betrayed me! I have not mastered it yet, but I shall have leisure in which to practise. Yale!"

"Yes?"

"Has it occurred to you? Life's like a pack of cards."

"It had not struck me."

"But it is! The thought has just come to me. It's damned clever. You see, no two people get dealt the same hand. And some hands are good and some bad to start with. You don't know who'll win till you play."

"Yes," agreed Ryder, "some of us have a handicap and others are well favoured."

"But listen, Yale. I become positively inspired! There's more in it. A man with a good hand may lose by faulty play. A man with a devilish shabby lot may, by skill and tenacity, bring off the hazard. Byron has played with a damned poor pack, but you'll admit he's made a good showing. Ay! but if the cards fall badly you are nearly always doomed. Give good cards to a man and let him play them well and there's no withstanding him. Yale, I've had damned good cards dealt me but I've played 'em badly. No one to blame but myself. And now life's shuffled the cards and dealt a fresh hand. Let's see what I make of it."

He fell to fondling the pack. Ryder noticed how tapering were Royle's fingers. "I shall miss the cards," said Royle slowly. "They are a great consolation, are they not?"

"I have never played."

"No? What a lot you have missed, Yale! No dice or wine or wenching. How the deuce have you passed your time away?"

"Chasing the armies of Charles Stuart from the field!"

"Ah! You got under my guard there. Perhaps if I had taken my soldiering a little more seriously I might have been of greater service to his Majesty!"

As Ryder looked at the sightless eyes a vision came to him of a figure, brave and debonair, in the forefront of the fighting.

"You made a gallant effort," he said. "I salute you."

"Oh, it proved pleasant sport. Lud, I shall miss St. Pol. He was a gay dog if ever there was one. You heard about him and the minister's wife? But that must keep. Where is Rosea?"

"I can see her."

"Go to her, Yale. She'll need comforting. And sink your Puritan principles for once and kiss her adieu. It will please her, and demme, I shan't mind. . . . Well, Yale, you have won. It is all over now save the cheers and the gloating. This is the end of our good King, too. I'm glad my eyes are spared the sight. Yale—a last favour."

"What is it?"

"See that my collar is straight. When we pass these rascals we must not let them see that their behaviour has incommoded us!"

Ryder could see Rosea leaning against the wall of the Rows as though for support. The day might be an occasion for triumph but Ryder felt unconscionably sad. They had fought so stoutly, these Englishmen, these Welshmen, these Irishmen. Where would it all end? He walked towards Rosea, and when she saw him she forced a smile of animation into her weary eyes.

"So it is destined that you and I shall not go hunting barbarians in Virginia, Ryder, after all! The prospect looked wondrous fair to me. Heigh-ho, perhaps it is as well. I might

.have become enamoured of some befeathered chieftain. And that Puritan conscience of yours might have kept niggling. Ryder!"

"Yes, Ro?"

"You do not blame me for remaining with Royle? It is you I love! I would have shared your life so willingly, but when I saw those sightless eyes . . . and he did not complain . . ."

"You could not have done otherwise, Ro. You are a noble woman. I—I feel a better man for having known you."

"Lud, and I imagined I was enticing you along the broad way which leads to destruction." She spoke lightly. "You know, Ryder, I cannot help feeling that you are unduly troubled about the flames of hell."

"There must be a Day of Judgment, Ro."

"Of course. It is here now. We punish ourselves. Has not Royle made his own hell? Is he not reaping what he has sown?"

"Ay. His blindness is a terrible affliction."

"It goes deeper than that, Ryder. He sits silent for hours. It is not like Royle to refrain from jesting. When he does appear gay, his mirth is forced. He is brooding, Ryder. More than once he put out his hand and caught hold of mine. At first I thought he wanted something to cling to in his blindness. Now I feel he is seeking a forgiveness for which he is too proud to ask. He is suffering—Ryder, suffering. The deepest wound is not his blindness. You struck him a mortal blow when you told him his child, his son, his heir, had died."

"If Verity meant so much to him, why——"

"Why did he not seek her? I do not know. He has not told me and I shall not ask him. The heart has its own secrets. I know this—he craved for a son. I think much of his recklessness was because I had given him no son to plan a future for. He desired above all else that the proud line of the Wildings should continue. Ryder, much as I love you, much as I shall always love you, much as I long to be with you, I could not desert him in his hour of need."

"I understand." Ryder spoke quietly.

"He will be easier to live with now. He is contrite. More gentle. I shall have no difficulty in keeping him under my eye. Royle's roving days are ended." She spoke with assumed lightness. "I shall never forget you, Ryder, never. Last night I stood by my window alone, lonely, when the world was still, to gather strength for the morrow. Often I shall stand thus. I shall lift my eyes to the stars—and remember. See, it is time we moved. The horsemen are mounting. Let's hope the poor brutes do not fall to pieces. I want to ask you a favour. Once you told a lie at my request. Will you tell another?"

He regarded her dubiously.

"Oh, come, Master Puritan, why hesitate when a lady pleads? It is in a right noble cause. Ryder, you must seek out Verity without delay. She will need all the consolation you can give her. You must tell her that her husband has been killed. It will set her mind at rest. It may make her sad but it will not wound as the truth would wound. Never let her know that Royle was already married. Promise me?"

"I will act for the best, Ro."

Rosea laughed. "You do not alter, Ryder. Can a leopard change his spots, or a Puritan his ways? To think that is the most I can coax from you. Oh, Ryder!"

The brazen notes of a trumpet rang down the street. The weary, waiting men straightened in their ranks.

"They are moving. Good-bye, my dear. Good-bye, Ryder darling. I shall never forget you. I could have taught you a lot about love if you had let me. Now it is too late."

Ryder was conscious of a last glimpse of her dark eyes as the coach rolled clumsily past—eyes which smiled bravely through a mist of tears. A hand waved. Rosea went out of his sight. Rosea went out of his life. For ever.

Ryder stood staring at a column of weaponless pikemen. He did not see them. He was trying to pierce the veil of the future, trying to visualize what life would be without Rosea. He had planned and schemed, but it had come to naught. Was there an influence at work shaping destiny, an influence too powerful for man to combat?

A hand dropped on his shoulder and brought him out of his reverie. Mark Trueman was beside him.

"Get out of sight, man. Our vanguard will be here almost

any moment. I came in search of you. You must not let
Brereton see you or you are doomed."

"It does not matter."

"It matters very much," protested Mark, dragging him
into a side street.

"Life has ceased to hold any attraction, Mark. I have
sacrificed too much of late. A bullet would put an end to my
tortured thoughts. Indeed, I should welcome it."

"Stuff and nonsense, Ryder! There are brave days ahead.
Days of liberty."

"But not days of love."

"Why not? Verity is close at hand. She came with me in
search of you. You used to love her; of that I am persuaded.
If she is a widow, there is nothing to prevent your marrying
her. It is an honourable estate. And the girl needs a protector
after all she has endured."

"How did you know she was a widow, Mark? Did she
tell you?"

"Not in so many words. It was what I concluded. Don't
tell me that she is not!"

"There is great confusion at present," said Ryder
vaguely.

"Well, Ryder, you had best ask her yourself. She is
awaiting you at the cottage in Nuns Lane."

Mark Trueman left his friend at the door. "I must return
to my troop for the triumphal entry," he explained.

Verity was waiting for Ryder, waiting with an eager if
anxious look in her eyes. Ryder thought that she looked
better and told her so.

"I am better already for the sight of you," she assured
him. "It is good to know that you have come through this
fiery ordeal alive."

Ryder felt ill at ease. Perhaps it was the recent parting
from Rosea which stirred him. It was not easy to readjust
one's life with such speed. He was glad to see Verity, yet the
contrast was great. He checked himself. He must not start
contrasting and comparing.

There was something soothing and comforting about
Verity's calm, a steadying influence of which he stood in sore
need. What disturbed him most was Rosea's message. Ought

he to tell Verity all that had transpired, or leave her in happy ignorance? When anything troubled Ryder he had to deal with it quickly. With him it was always a direct frontal attack, no manœuvring.

"Verity, why did not your husband come to you in your distress?"

"He did not know that I was in the city. When he rode south to rejoin the Prince he left me in the country."

"He returned to Chester. I saw him. You knew that he was here?"

"Yes, I knew that. But he stood in high favour with the Governor. He had his circle of noble friends. I did not wish my presence to embarrass him."

"I cannot understand women!" Ryder's confession caused Verity to smile. He sat pondering. How could he break the news? Verity helped him.

"Can you tell me what has happened to Royle?" she asked calmly.

"A few days ago a granado burst close by him."

"And he was killed?"

Rosea's face was before his eyes. He must lie now, lie as he had never lied before. In his agitation he rose to his feet. "God help me!" he exclaimed aloud. "I cannot do it. No, he was not killed. He was blinded."

"Blinded! Oh, Ryder! Poor Royle! And he set such store on his appearance. What will happen to him?"

"He is being cared for. Verity, I must tell you something which will wound you terribly."

"Do, Ryder. I can bear anything except not knowing."

"Royle was already wed when he married you."

Verity lowered her eyes. He was amazed at her calm. "Yes, Ryder," she said quietly. "I know."

"You *know* he is married?"

"I heard some weeks ago. I have recovered from the shock."

"He has been taken away by his wife. They go abroad. He will never trouble your life again. Try to forget him, Verity. Start life afresh."

"That is what I am resolved to do. I do not mind the hurt. It is—it is the feeling of being sinful which cuts so deep.

I have given birth to a child and I was not married. No man will ever look at me again. No man would ever marry me."

"I would!"

The words were out without hesitation. It was unlike the Ryder of old. Rosea's influence, perhaps!

Verity gazed at him in amazement. Such spontaneous generosity bore no likeness to the man she used to know: stern, resolute, calculating. Then the eagerness passed from his face. "I trust the knowledge will give you satisfaction. It is, I fear, all I can give you. I will wed you to bring you peace of mind, my dear, but you will be marrying a dead man."

"Ryder, you are not ill?"

"No. But I have deserted my colours. There is a firing party to be faced as soon as I have been before a Council of War."

Verity leaped to her feet. Her face was animated. "They shall not take you, Ryder! I—I cared deeply for you until Royle's fascination made me lose my head. Now, all my first love for you comes surging back, deeper, more intense than ever. They shall not take you. I have sacrificed enough. Let us escape. I will make you a good wife, Ryder. I swear it. Hasten, Ryder, let us get away while we may. Let us go to another part of the country and start life anew. Oh, Ryder darling, I have endured so much. I could not bear to lose you now that you have come back to me."

"Yes," he said quickly, "let us go. We will escape amid the confusion. The guards are relaxed. Everyone is in a good humour."

He caught her in his arms and she kissed him with a warmth and passion that were a revelation to them both. They were happy: happy and well content. Ryder felt like a mariner whose bark had come into haven after braving tempestuous seas. Then his mind drifted away. Verity glanced up. With the eyes of love she noted the change.

"What troubles you, my darling?"

"I cannot do it."

"What! You cannot marry me?"

"No. I will marry you. But I cannot run away. I should feel a coward. I have myself to live with. If they want to try me and condemn me, let them do so. I will not evade them. I will go straight to Sir William and have it out with him."

"Oh, Ryder!" She drew back a pace and her face was troubled. Then the calm resolve he knew so well returned to her face. "You are right, dear—so right. You could not act otherwise. Go, my dear one, and my prayers shall go with you. And remember, whatever happens, my love will be yours, now and through eternity. And with my love, my gratitude."

It was not difficult to find Sir William Brereton. The guards outside the Bishop's Palace testified that he had taken residence in the premises so lately vacated by the Royalist Governor. The bells of St. Werburg's were pealing joyously. The banners of victory ruffled in the morning breeze.

A captain of horse came out to say that the Commander-in-Chief would see Ryder. The officer regarded Ryder curiously. He was from the Derby horse and did not know Ryder as a Cheshire man would have done. What could this unkempt fellow have to say to the victorious general?

Colonel Dukinfield and Colonel Jones were seated with Sir William when Ryder entered.

"So, Ryder," said Sir William casually, "you come to congratulate me."

"No, sir. I come to surrender myself."

"Surrender! I do not understand."

"I disobeyed your orders, sir, and entered Chester."

"Ah! I recollect your visit when the siege was at its height. We discussed your plea after you had gone." He turned to his brother officers. "Did we not?"

"And decided," remarked Colonel Dukinfield, "that because you were weakened by your wound, and because you had served the Parliament faithfully for so long, you had earned your release."

"I sent word to that effect, but apparently it did not reach you," added Sir William. "So you see, Ryder, where you happened to go subsequently was a matter for yourself alone."

The long strain was ended. Ryder felt himself swaying.

He was conscious of Colonel Jones's hand gripping his arm. The room ceased to swirl.

"I thank you, sir. I—I fear we have been somewhat short of food of late, and your great kindness has affected me." He moved towards the door as in a daze.

"Sir William," he said, turning.

"What is it, Ryder?" The tone was kindly.

"Verity is safe."

"I am aware of it. I rejoice. Rejoin her, my boy. She needs you."

* * * * *

Ryder paused at the cottage threshold. It marked, for him, the threshold of a new life.

Rapidly he reviewed the recent years; he did so deliberately as though this were the last opportunity he would have of thinking of them without disloyalty. Thus he stood staring seriously at the starry heavens. The same stars looked down upon Rosea—Rosea, who had gone out of his life as suddenly as she had entered it.

He experienced a pang of anguish so great at the thought that he would never see her again that for a moment he wondered whether it would have been better if he had never set eyes on her. Fiercely he vowed that he did not regret their meeting. Just knowing Ro had lifted him out of the rut of commonplace things. He had tasted exultation. He might never know it again. Ah, the beauty of her! The glory of her eyes! And to think that she cared for him! It was worth the anguish and the suffering, though, verily, fair women were dangerous marks for a young man's eyes.

Now he must put Rosea from his mind and heart; or endeavour to!

He had desired Verity; he had grieved when he lost her. Now he had recovered her. Verity was his. Almost it seemed unreal. She was, after all, a fitting partner. He found, to his amazement, that he cared for her more deeply now that she had tasted life. How young and innocent they were when first they encountered! Now they were both experienced, wiser, mature. They had drunk of the bitter and the sweet.

They had climbed the heights and descended to the depths. They had lived. Life had tested them; proved their worth. Ryder smiled at the silent stars. The smile was for Rosea. Then he lifted the latch.

He found Verity beside the hearth in the deserted cottage—the very position in which he discovered her on the night when Amos Bowman brought him to her aid. She looked up on hearing his step.

At first her gaze was troubled, but she read the answer to all her unspoken queries in his eyes. She was in his arms, and for a while his lips were too busy for words.

"Darling, I am free! Free to be with you, free to wed you, free to serve you all the length of days."

"I will make you very happy, Ryder. I am glad you went, dear heart. You did what you thought best. Oh, Ryder, I am so convinced that if we do the right thing from right motives good must come of it, even if we cannot see it at the time."

"Good has come of it, sweet heart. Sir William was kind. He was magnanimous."

"He could afford to be, Ryder. He is still master of the field."

THE END